CONVICTS AND EXILES

A Blaine McFadden Adventures Collection

GAIL Z. MARTIN

SOL

eBook ISBN: 978-1-939704-91-7
Print ISBN: 978-1-939704-92-4
Convicts and Exiles: Copyright © 2019 by Gail Z. Martin.
Ice Forged © 2013 by Gail Z. Martin | Orbit Books
King's Convicts © 2016 by Gail Z. Martin
No Reprieve © 2015 by Gail Z. Martin | Orbit Books
King's Exiles © 2019 by Gail Z. Martin
Reconciling Memory © 2018 by Gail Z. Martin

Cover art by Lou Harper
SOL Publishing is an imprint of DreamSpinner Communications, LLC.

CONTENTS

KING'S CONVICTS

INTRODUCTION

King's Convicts and *King's Exiles* fill in the "missing" history of Blaine "Mick" McFadden during the six years that get skipped over at the beginning of *Ice Forged* in my Ascendant Kingdoms Saga. These novellas pick up immediately after the events in the first chapter of *Ice Forged* and focus on Blaine when he is a prisoner in Velant, and then on Blaine and his convict friends adjusting to the relative freedom of becoming colonists once they receive their Ticket of Leave.

Most importantly, these stories shed light on how Blaine, Kestel, Verran, Piran, and Dawe forged a found family and built a friendship strong enough to endure hardship and then return to win back their shattered kingdom. Some events that are mentioned in passing in Ice Forged are filled in here, shedding light on the circumstances which further shaped Blaine and his friends.

In an attempt to reconstruct the timeline, this collection begins with an excerpt from *Ice Forged* which sets the stage for Blaine's exile. The short story *No Reprieve* has been slotted into the timeline where it fits, in between events included in *King's*

Convicts. *King's Exiles* follows chronologically after Convicts. The bonus story at the end, *Reconciling Memory*, takes place years beforehand, and is Kestel Falke's origin story.

The *King's Exiles* novella ends several months before the story resumes in *Ice Forged*.

CONVICTS & EXILES

GAIL Z. MARTIN

PROLOGUE

Excerpt from Ice Forged

"THIS HAS TO END." BLAINE MCFADDEN LOOKED AT HIS SISTER Mari huddled in the bed, covers drawn up to her chin. She was sobbing hard enough that it nearly robbed her of breath, and leaning against Aunt Judith, who murmured consolations. Just sixteen, Mari looked small and lost. A vivid bruise marked one cheek. She struggled to hold her nightgown together where it had been ripped down the front.

"You're upsetting her more." Judith cast a reproving glance his way.

"I'm upsetting her? Father's the one to blame for this. That drunken sonofabitch…" Blaine's right hand opened and closed, itching for the pommel of his sword.

"Blaine…" Judith's voice warned him off.

"After what he did…you stand up for him?"

Judith McFadden Ainsworth raised her head to meet his gaze. She was a thin, handsome woman in her middle years; and when she dressed for court, it was still possible to see a glimpse of the beauty she had been in her youth. Tonight, she looked worn. "Of course not."

"I'm sick of his rages. Sick of being beaten when he's on one of his binges..."

Judith's lips quirked. "You've been too tall for him to beat for years now."

At twenty years old and a few inches over six feet tall, Blaine stood a hand's breadth taller than Lord McFadden. While he had his mother's dark chestnut hair, his blue eyes were a match in color and determination to his father's. Blaine had always been secretly pleased that while he resembled his father enough to avoid questions of paternity, in build and features, he took after his mother's side of the family. Where his father was short and round, Blaine was tall and rangy. Ian McFadden's features had the smashed look of a brawler; Blaine's were more regular, and if not quite handsome, better than passable. He was honest enough to know that though he might not be the first man in a room to catch a lady's eye, he was pleasant enough in face and manner to attract the attention of at least one female by the end of the evening. The work he did around the manor and its lands had filled out his chest and arms. He was no longer the small, thin boy his father caned for the slightest infraction.

"He killed our mother when she got between him and me. He took his temper out on my hide until I was tall enough to fight back. He started beating Carr when I got too big to thrash. I had to put his horse down after he'd beaten it and broken its legs. Now this...it has to stop!"

"Blaine, please." Judith turned, and Blaine could see tears in her eyes. "Anything you do will only make it worse. I know my brother's tempers better than anyone." Absently, she stroked Mari's hair.

"By the gods...did he..." But the shamed look on Judith's face as she turned away answered Blaine's question.

"I'll kill that son of a bitch," Blaine muttered, turning away and sprinting down the hall.

"Blaine, don't. Blaine—"

He took the stairs at a run. Above the fireplace in the parlor hung two broadswords, weapons that had once belonged to his grandfather. Blaine snatched down the lowest broadsword. Its grip felt heavy and familiar in his hand.

"Master Blaine…" Edward followed him into the room. The elderly man was alarmed as his gaze fell from Blaine's face to the weapon in his hand. Edward had been Glenreith's seneschal for longer than Blaine had been alive. Edward: the expert manager, the budget master, and the family's secret keeper.

"Where is he?"

"Who, m'lord?"

Blaine caught Edward by the arm and Edward shrank back from his gaze. "My whore-spawned father, that's who. Where is he?"

"Master Blaine, I beg you…"

"Where is he?"

"He headed for the gardens. He had his pipe with him."

Blaine headed for the manor's front entrance at a dead run. Judith was half-way down the stairs. "Blaine, think about this. Blaine—"

He flung open the door so hard that it crashed against the wall. Blaine ran down the manor's sweeping stone steps. A full moon lit the sloping lawn well enough for Blaine to make out the figure of a man in the distance, strolling down the carriage lane. The smell of his father's pipe smoke wafted back to him, as hated as the odor of camphor that always clung to Lord McFadden's clothing.

The older man turned at the sound of Blaine's running footsteps. "You bastard! You bloody bastard!" Blaine shouted.

Lord Ian McFadden's eyes narrowed as he saw the sword in Blaine's hand. Dropping his pipe, the man grabbed a rake that leaned against the stone fence edging the carriageway. He held its thick oak handle across his body like a staff. Lord McFadden might be well into his fifth decade, but in his youth, he had been an officer in the king's army, where he had earned King Merrill's notice and his gratitude. "Go back inside boy. Don't make me hurt you."

Blaine did not slow down or lower his sword. "Why? Why Mari? There's no shortage of court whores. Why Mari?"

Lord McFadden's face reddened. "Because I can. Now drop that sword if you know what's good for you."

Blaine's blood thundered in his ears. In the distance, he could hear Judith screaming his name.

"I guess this cur needs to be taught a lesson." Lord McFadden swung at Blaine with enough force to have shattered his skull if Blaine had not ducked the heavy rake. McFadden gave a roar and swung again, but Blaine lurched forward, taking the blow on his shoulder to get inside McFadden's guard. The broadsword sank hilt-deep into the man's chest, slicing through his waistcoat.

Lord McFadden's body shuddered, and he dropped the rake. He met Blaine's gaze, his eyes, wide with surprise. "Didn't think you had it in you," he gasped.

Behind him, Blaine could hear footsteps pounding on the cobblestones; he heard panicked shouts and Judith's scream. Nothing mattered to him, nothing at all except for the ashen face of his father. Blood soaked Lord McFadden's clothing and gobbets of it splashed Blaine's hand and shirt. He gasped for breath, his mouth working like a hooked fish out of water. Blaine let him slide from the sword, watched numbly as his father fell backward onto the carriageway in a spreading pool of blood.

"Master Blaine, what have you done?" Selden, the groundskeeper, was the first to reach the scene. He gazed in horror at Lord McFadden who lay twitching on the ground, breathing in labored, slow gasps.

Blaine's grip tightened on the sword in his hand. "Something someone should have done years ago."

A crowd of servants was gathering; Blaine could hear their whispers and the sound of their steps on the cobblestones. "Blaine! Blaine!" He barely recognized Judith's voice. Raw from screaming, choked with tears, his aunt must have gathered her skirts like a milkmaid to run from the house this quickly. "Let me through!"

Heaving for breath, Judith pushed past Selden and grabbed Blaine's left arm to steady herself. "Oh, by the gods Blaine, what will become of us now?"

Lord McFadden wheezed painfully and went still.

Shock replaced numbness as the rage drained from Blaine's body. *It's actually over. He's finally dead.*

"Blaine, can you hear me?" Judith was shaking his left arm. Her tone had regained control, alarmed but no longer panicked.

"He swung first," Blaine replied distantly. "I don't think he realized, until the end, that I actually meant to do it."

"When the king hears—"

Blaine snapped back to himself and turned toward Judith. "Say nothing about Mari to anyone," he growled in a voice low enough that only she could hear. "I'll pay the consequences. But it's for naught if she's shamed. I've thrown my life away for nothing if she's dishonored." He dropped the bloody sword, gripping Judith by the forearm. "Swear to it."

Judith's eyes were wide, but Blaine could see she was calm. "I swear."

Selden and several of the other servants moved around them, giving Blaine a wary glance as they bent to carry Lord McFarlane's body back to the manor.

"The king will find out. He'll take your title...Oh Blaine, you'll hang for this."

Blaine swallowed hard. A knot of fear tightened in his

stomach as he stared at the blood on his hand, and the darkening stain on the cobblestones. *Better to die avenged than crouch like a beaten dog.* He met Judith's eyes and a wave of cold resignation washed over him.

"He won't hurt Mari or Carr again. Ever. Carr will inherit when he's old enough. Odds are the king will name you guardian until then. Nothing will change—"

"Except that you'll hang for murder," Judith said miserably.

"Yes," Blaine replied, folding his aunt against his chest as she sobbed. "Except for that."

———

"You have been charged with murder. Murder of a lord, and murder of your own father." King Merrill's voice thundered through the judgment hall. "How do you plead?" A muted buzz of whispered conversation hummed from the packed audience in the galleries. Blaine McFadden knelt where the guards had forced him down, shackled at the wrists and ankles. Unshaven and filthy from more than a week in the king's dungeon, Blaine's long brown hair hung loose around his face. He lifted his head to look at the king defiantly.

"Guilty as charged, Your Majesty. He was a murdering son of a bitch—"

"Silence!"

The guard at Blaine's right shoulder cuffed him hard. Blaine straightened and lifted his head once more. *I'm not sorry, and I'll be damned if I'll apologize, even to the king. Let's get this over with.* He avoided the curious stares of the courtiers and nobles in the gallery, those for whom death and punishment were nothing more than gossip and entertainment.

Only two faces caught his eye. Judith sat stiffly, her face unreadable although her eyes glinted angrily. Beside her sat

Carensa, daughter of the Earl of Rhystorp. He and Carensa had been betrothed to wed later that spring. Carensa was dressed in mourning clothes; her face was ashen, and her eyes were red-rimmed. Blaine could not meet her gaze. Of all that his actions cost him, title, lands, fortune, and life, losing Carensa was the only loss that mattered.

The king turned his attention back to Blaine. "The penalty for common murder is hanging. For killing a noble—not to mention your own father—the penalty is beheading."

A gasp went up from the crowd. Carensa swayed in her seat as if she might faint, and Judith reached out to steady her.

"Lord Ian McFadden was a loyal member of my Council. I valued his presence beside me whether we rode to war or in the hunt." The king's voice dropped, and Blaine doubted that few aside from the guards could hear his next words. "Yet I was not blind to his faults."

"For that reason," the king said, raising his voice once more, "I will show mercy."

It seemed as if the entire crowd held its breath. Blaine steeled himself, willing his expression to show nothing of his fear.

"Blaine McFadden, I strip from you the title of Lord of Glenreith, and give that title in trust to your brother, Carr, when he reaches his majority. Your lands and your holdings are likewise no longer your own. For your crime, I sentence you to transportation to the penal colony on Velant, where you will live out the rest of your days. So be it."

The king rose and swept from the room in a blur of crimson and ermine, followed by a brace of guards. A stunned silence hung over the crowd, broken only by Carensa's sobbing. As the guards wrestled Blaine to his feet, he dared to look back. Judith's face was drawn, and her eyes held a hopelessness that made Blaine wince. Carensa's face was buried in her hands, and although Judith placed an arm around her, Carensa would not be comforted.

The soldiers shoved him hard enough that he stumbled, and the gallery crowd woke from its momentary silence. Jeers and catcalls followed him until the huge mahogany doors of the judgment chamber slammed shut.

———

Blaine sat on the floor of his cell, head back and eyes closed. Not too far away, he heard the squeal of a rat. His cell had a small barred window too high for him to peer out, barely enough to allow for a dim shaft of light to enter. The floor was covered with filthy straw. The far corner of the room had a small drain for him to relieve himself. Like the rest of the dungeon, it stank. Near the iron-bound door was a bucket of brackish water and an empty tin tray that had held a heel of stale bread and a chunk of spoiled cheese.

For lesser crimes, noble-born prisoners were accorded the dignity of confinement in one of the rooms in the tower, away from the filth of the dungeon and its common criminals. Blaine guessed that his crime had caused scandal enough that Merrill felt the need to make an example, after the leniency of Blaine's sentencing.

I'd much prefer death to banishment. If the executioner's blade is sharp, it would be over in a moment. I've heard tales of Velant. A frozen wasteland at the top of the world. Guards that are the dregs of His Majesty's service, sent to Velant because no one else will have them. Forced labor in the mines, or the chance to drown on board one of the fishing boats. How long will it take to die there? Will I freeze in my sleep or starve, or will one of my fellow inmates do me a real mercy and slip a shiv between my ribs?

The clatter of the key in the heavy iron lock made Blaine open his eyes, though he did not stir from where he sat. *Are the guards come early to take me to the ship? I didn't think we sailed until tomorrow.* Another, darker possibility occurred to him. *Perhaps Merrill's "mercy" was for show. If the guards were to take me to the wharves by night, who would ever know if I didn't make it onto the ship? Merrill would be blameless, and no one would be the wiser.* Blaine let out a long breath. *Let it come. I did what I had to do.*

The door squealed on its hinges to frame a guard whose broad shoulders barely fit between the doorposts. To Blaine's astonishment, the guard did not move to come into the room. "I can only give you a few minutes. Even for another coin, I don't dare do more. Say what you must and leave."

The guard stood back, and a hooded figure in a gray cloak rushed into the room. Edward, Glenreith's seneschal, entered behind the figure, but stayed just inside the doorway, shaking his head to prevent Blaine from saying anything. The hooded visitor slipped across the small cell to kneel beside Blaine. The hood fell back, revealing Carensa's face.

"How did you get in," Blaine whispered. "You shouldn't have come. Bad enough that I've shamed you—"

Carensa grasped him by the shoulders and kissed him hard on the lips. He could taste the salt of her tears. She let go, moving away just far enough that he got a good look at her face. Her eyes were red and puffy, with dark circles. Though barely twenty summers old, she looked careworn and haggard. She was a shadow of the vibrant, glowing girl who had led all the young men at court on a merry chase before accepting Blaine's proposal, as everyone knew she had intended all along.

"Oh Blaine," she whispered. "Your father deserved what he got. I don't know what he did to push you this far." Her voice caught.

"Carensa," Blaine said softly, savoring the sound of her name, knowing it was the last time they would be together. "It'll be worse for you if someone finds you here."

Carensa straightened her shoulders and swallowed back her tears. "I bribed the guards. But I had to come."

Blaine shifted, trying to minimize the noise as his heavy wrist shackles clinked with the movement. He took her hand in both of his. "Forget me. I release you. No one ever comes back from Velant. Give me the comfort of knowing that you'll find someone else who'll take good care of you."

"And will you forget me?" She lifted her chin, and her blue eyes sparked in challenge.

Blaine looked down. "No. But I'm a dead man. If the voyage doesn't kill me, the winter will. Say a prayer to the gods for me and light a candle for my soul. Please, Carensa, just because I'm going to die doesn't mean that you can't live."

Carensa's long red hair veiled her face as she looked down, trying to collect herself. "I can't promise that, Blaine. Please, don't make me. Not now. Maybe not ever." She looked up again. "I'll be there at the wharf, when your ship leaves. You may not see me, but I'll be there."

Blaine reached up to stroke her cheek. "Save your reputation. Renounce me. I won't mind."

Carensa's eyes took on a determined glint. "As if no one knew we were betrothed? As if the whole court didn't guess that we were lovers? No, the only thing I'm sorry about is that we didn't make a handfasting before the guards took you. I don't regret a single thing, Blaine McFadden. I love you and I always will."

Blaine squeezed his eyes shut, willing himself to maintain control. He pulled her gently to him for another kiss, long and lingering, in lieu of everything he could not find the words to say.

The footsteps of the guard in the doorway made Carensa draw back and pull up her hood. She gave his hand one last squeeze and then walked to the door. She looked back, just for a moment, but neither one of them spoke. She followed the guard out the door.

Edward paused and sadly shook his head. "Gods be with you, Master Blaine. I'll pray that your ship sails safely."

"Pray it sinks, Edward. If you ever cared at all for me, pray it sinks."

Edward nodded. "As you wish, Master Blaine." He turned and followed Carensa, leaving the guard to pull the door shut behind them.

———

"Get on your feet. Time to go."

The guard's voice woke Blaine from uneasy sleep. He staggered to his feet, hobbled by the ankle chains, and managed to make it to the door without falling. Outside, it was barely dawn. Several hundred men and a few dozen women, all shackled at the wrists and ankles, stood nervously as the guards rounded up the group for the walk to the wharves where the transport ship waited.

Early as it was, jeers greeted them as they stumbled down the narrow lanes. Blaine was glad to be in the center of the group. More than once, women in the upper floors of the hard-used buildings that crowded the twisting streets laughed as they poured out their chamber pots on the prisoners below. Young boys pelted them from the alleyways with rotting produce. Once in a while, the boys' aim went astray, hitting a guard, who gave chase for a block or two, shouting curses.

Blaine knew that the distance from the castle to the wharves was less than a mile, but the walk seemed to take forever. He kept his head down, intent on trying to walk without stumbling as the manacles bit into his ankles and the short chain hobbled his stride. They walked five abreast with guards every few rows, shoulder to shoulder.

"There it is—your new home for the next forty days," one of the guards announced as they reached the end of the street at the waterfront. A large carrack sat in the harbor with sails furled. In groups of ten, the prisoners queued up to be loaded into flat-bottomed row boats and taken out to the waiting ship.

"Rather a dead man in Donderath's ocean than a slave on Velant's ice!" One of the prisoners in the front wrested free from the guard who was attempting to load him onto the boat. He twisted, needing only a few inches to gain his freedom, falling from the dock into the water where his heavy chains dragged him under.

"It's all the same to me whether you drown or get aboard the boat," shouted the captain of the guards, breaking the silence as the prisoners stared into the water where the man had disappeared. "If you're of a mind to do it, there'll be more food for the rest."

"Bloody bastard!" A big man threw his weight against the nearest guard, shoving him out of the way, and hurtled toward the captain. "Let's see how well you swim!" He bent over and butted the captain in the gut, and the momentum took them both over the side. The captain flailed, trying to keep his head above water while the prisoner's manacled hands closed around his neck, forcing him under. Two soldiers aboard the rowboat beat with their oars at the spot where the burly man had gone down. Four soldiers, cursing under their breath, jumped in after the captain.

After considerable splashing, the captain was hauled onto the deck, sputtering water and coughing. Two of the other soldiers had a grip on the big man by the shoulders, keeping his head above the water. One of the soldiers held a knife under the man's chin. The captain dragged himself to his feet and stood on the dock for a moment, looking down at them.

"What do we do with him, sir?"

The captain's expression hardened. "Give him gills, lad, to help him on his way."

The soldier's knife made a swift slash, cutting the big man's throat from ear to ear. Blood tinged the water crimson as the soldiers let go of the man's body, and it sank beneath the waves. When the soldiers had been dragged onto the deck, the captain glared at the prisoners.

"Any further disturbances and I'll see to it that you're all put on half rations for the duration." His smile was unpleasant. "And I assure you, full rations are little enough." He turned to his second in command. "Load the boats, and be quick about it."

The group fell silent as the guards prodded them into boats. From the other wharf, Blaine could hear women's voices and the muffled sobbing of children. He looked to the edge of the wharf crowded with women. Most had the look of scullery maids, with tattered dresses, and shawls pulled tight around their shoulders. A few wore the garish colors and low-cut gowns of seaport whores. They shouted a babble of names, calling to the men who crawled into the boats.

One figure stood apart from the others, near the end of the wharf. A gray cloak fluttered in the wind, and as Blaine watched, the hood fell back, freeing long red hair to tangle on the cold breeze. Carensa did not shout to him. She did not move at all, but he felt her gaze, as if she could pick him out of the crowded mass of prisoners. Not a word, not a gesture, just a mute witness to his banishment. Blaine never took his eyes off her as he stumbled into the boat, earning a cuff on the ear for his clumsiness from the guard. He twisted as far as he dared in his seat to keep her in sight as the boat rowed toward the transport ship.

When they reached the side of the *Cutlass*, rope ladders hung from its deck.

"Climb," ordered the soldier behind Blaine, giving him a poke in the ribs for good measure. A few of the prisoners lost their footing, screaming as they fell into the black water of the bay. The guards glanced at each other and shrugged. Blaine began to climb, and only the knowledge that Carensa would be witness to his suicide kept him from letting himself fall backward into the waves.

Shoved and prodded by the guards' batons, Blaine and the other prisoners shambled down the narrow steps into the hold of the ship. It stank of cabbage and bilge water. Hammocks were strung side by side, three high, nearly floor to ceiling. A row of portholes, too small for a man to crawl through, provided the only light, save for the wooden ceiling grates that opened to the deck above. Some of the prisoners collapsed onto hammocks or sank to the floor in despair. Blaine shouldered his way to a porthole on the side facing the wharves. In the distance, he could see figures crowded there, though it was too far away to know whether Carensa was among them.

"How long you figure they'll stay?" a thin man asked as Blaine stood on tiptoe to see out. The man had dirty blond hair that stuck out at angles like straw on a scarecrow.

"Until we set sail, I guess," Blaine answered.

"One of them yours?"

"Used to be," Blaine replied.

"I told my sister not to come, told her it wouldn't make it any easier on her," the thin man said. "Didn't want her to see me, chained like this." He sighed. "She came anyhow." He looked Blaine over from head to toe. "What'd they send you away for?"

Blaine turned so that the seeping new brand of an "M" on his forearm showed. "Murder. You?"

The thin man shrugged. "I could say it was for singing off-key, or for the coins I pinched from the last inn where I played for my supper. But the truth is I slept with the wrong man's wife, and he accused me of stealing his silver." He gave a wan smile, exposing gapped teeth. "Verran Danning's my name. Petty thief and wandering minstrel. How 'bout you?"

Blaine looked back at the distant figures on the wharf. Stripped of his title, lands and position, lost to Carensa, he felt as dead inside as if the executioner had done his work. *Blaine McFadden is dead*, he thought. "Mick," he replied. "Just call me Mick."

"I'll make you a deal, Mick. You watch my back, and I'll watch yours," Verran said with a sly grin. "I'll make sure you get more than your share of food, and as much of the grog as I can pinch. In return," he said, dropping his voice, "I'd like to count on some protection, to spare my so-called virtue, in case any of our bunkmates get too friendly." He held out a hand, manacles clinking. "Deal?"

With a sigh, Blaine forced himself to turn away from the porthole. He shook Verran's outstretched hand. "Deal."

KING'S CONVICTS

A Blaine McFadden Collection

ARCTIC PRISON

1

EDGELAND

"GET BACK ON YOUR SIDE, OR BY THE GODS, I'LL PUT YOU BACK where you belong." Blaine "Mick" McFadden growled. He stood at the forefront of a line of men, shoulder to shoulder inside the dark, stinking hold of the *Cutlass*, a convict ship bound for Velant Prison.

"He's already killed one man," Verran Danning added, standing slightly behind Blaine. "He's got nothing to lose."

Coan Atwell glowered at the men who had formed a cordon to separate him from his intended victim. Large, thick-set, and hot-tempered, no one had to guess what won Atwell his sentence to the notorious prison colony at the northern edge of the world. "We've got the rest of our lives on that godsforsaken block of ice," Coan snarled. "I'll get you, sooner or later."

"Not if we see you coming, mate," Dunbar Colling taunted from beside Blaine. "Best keep one eye open for a shiv in the ribs."

Forty long days and nights had passed at sea aboard what might as well be a floating coffin. The *Cutlass* bore its human cargo to Edgeland, in the arctic north, where years of hard labor in a notorious prison awaited them. Exile was King Merrill's idea of "mercy," sparing them a hanging—or worse.

"Watch your mouth, Dunbar," Coan replied. "You won't always have someone to hide behind."

"You think you can take me?" Dunbar stepped forward. Blaine brought a heavy hand down on his shoulder.

"Not now. Not here," Blaine murmured. "There will be plenty of time—and better opportunities—in Velant. We're almost to Edgeland. Let's make it off the boat alive."

Reluctantly, Coan and his bully boys stood down, returning to their side of the fetid hold muttering threats. Blaine and his mates held their line until they were certain Coan was not going to reverse course and rush them, and then warily headed back to the part of the hold they had claimed as their "territory."

"Would have served him right if we'd have mashed him to a pulp," Dunbar muttered. He bleated in surprise when Blaine grabbed him by the neck and hoisted him off his feet.

"We don't need more trouble," Blaine said in a low voice that brooked no argument. "Unless you want to leave this ship in chains." He gave Dunbar a shake for good measure and set him back down.

"Yeah, sure Mick," Dunbar muttered. Sulking, he retreated to his group of friends but did not try to make trouble.

"Nicely done," Verran said as Blaine found a seat where he could keep an eye on Coan and his crew.

Blaine raised an eyebrow. "Do you have to play the "murderer" angle quite so often?"

Verran grinned. "I say, stick with what works." And with that, he pulled a small pennywhistle from his pocket and began to play. Blaine was certain that no small part of Verran's desire for an impromptu concert came from his knowledge of how much Coan had grown to hate the tunes during their long sea voyage.

How in the name of Charrot did I end up here? Blaine wondered. But the answer was no mystery. Blaine and his siblings had endured a lifetime of blows and cruelty at the hand of his father, Lord Ian McFadden, violence that had killed their mother and a number of unfortunate retainers. But when Lord McFadden took indecent liberties with Mari, Blaine's sister, it was the breaking point. Blaine killed his father in cold blood and had no remorse. King Merrill himself had ruled on the case. It would have been well within the king's purview to hang Blaine for his crime, but Merrill knew just what sort of man Ian McFadden had been. And so the king granted "clemency" in the form of exile instead of execution.

One week aboard the *Cutlass* had convinced Blaine that hanging would have been more merciful, and they had not yet reached the arctic wasteland where they were to live out the rest of their miserable lives. Now, nearly forty days had passed, and they were nearing the end of their journey.

"I heard that we're only a few days out from Skalgerston Bay," Rinne said. "Maybe tempers will cool once we're not packed on top each other like herring in a barrel."

Verran paused his playing. "You think it's going to get better? Forget that. These are the good days. Haven't you heard about Velant? Only two convicts in ten lives long enough to earn a Ticket of Leave. That's what I've heard." He went back to his playing.

"Verran's a bit dramatic," Blaine said with a glare in his direction which was promptly ignored. "But I suspect grudges and revenge are all that keep people alive in Velant."

Velant Prison was notorious for sadistic guards and brutal conditions. Commander Prokief, the prison warden, was as much an inmate as his charges. A war hero known for his utter remorselessness in battle, Prokief and his soldiers earned their assignment to Velant because civilized society could not tolerate their bloodthirstiness.

Yet hope remained. Prisoners hardy—or lucky—enough to survive three years in Velant could earn a Ticket of Leave, which allowed them to leave the prison and become a colonist of Edgeland. In reality, they were just as much exiles as before, but as a colonist, they gained some distance from the prison and its guards, and a chance to make some kind of life for themselves far from Donderath and the homes they would never see again.

"Thanks," Dunbar said awkwardly. "I mean, for keeping him from taking me apart," he added with a nod toward Coan, who glowered from across the hold.

"Just keep your damn mouth shut until we're in port and I don't have to be around if someone spatters your brains all over the hold," Blaine grumbled.

It was a long way from his family's manor at Glenreith to the vomit-crusted, shit-covered hold of a convict ship. A very long way to fall. But Blaine had managed to trade his life as the son of a down-at-the-heels nobleman for that of a convict and exile. The price of freedom from his father was dear.

Four-hundred tortured souls languished in the hold of the *Cutlass*, just one of the ships that would bear their wretched human cargo to Edgeland before the year was done. Blaine counted himself lucky that on their ship, the decks were spaced far enough apart to allow the unwilling passengers to stand up, and that they were not shackled for the duration.

Mercies were few. The sea was rough this time of year, and those who were seasick frequently either learned to keep their dinner down or grew weak from throwing up their meager rations. Fever took more than its share among the convicts, so much so that the hold that had been tightly packed when they left Castle Reach harbor now only had a third as many occupants.

The dead were consigned to the sea, and Blaine wondered more than once whether they were the lucky ones.

"Don't look so gloomy," Verran prodded, elbowing Blaine. "While there's life, there's hope." At that, he struck up a tune that had been popular at dances, and despite everything, Blaine could not help a wan smile.

He had met Verran Danning—sometime thief and occasional minstrel—as the *Cutlass* sailed out of Castle Reach. Verran was mouthy, short, and wiry and had immediately struck a bargain for Blaine's protection in return for Verran's share of grog. It was an unlikely friendship, but over the weeks Blaine had grown to like his light-fingered companion. Verran was full of entertaining tales that helped to pass the long hours in the dark, stinking hold. Whether or not the stories were true mattered little.

The tunes he played reminded Blaine of better days, and of Carensa, the red-haired lass he left behind on the docks of Castle Reach. They had been betrothed to wed come spring. She had insisted on coming to the waterfront to watch the *Cutlass* sail for the horizon, silent and brave in her gray cloak. Though Blaine had begged her to forget him, he had kept his eyes on her until the ship left the shoreline behind.

Maybe it's for the best, he thought with a sigh. *At least I don't have to protect her—or anyone else—from Father anymore.*

He looked around the hold. In the dim light, he could make out the desperate faces of strangers who had become, if not exactly neighbors, then equally imperiled sojourners. The brand on Blaine's forearm marked him as a murderer, the worst of the lot. But many of those aboard the *Cutlass* had committed far less serious crimes. A disgraced lord might cheat the hangman with exile, but for those from the ginnels and closes, stealing a loaf of bread or a few coppers was enough to rip them from their homes and families and send them to the frozen reaches of the world.

"Might as well enjoy the comforts here," Verran said. "Velant won't be as homey."

"Aren't you just cheery," Blaine replied.

"Whole new pecking order. Plus bigger guards," Verran said with a shrug, returning to his music as if the comment had no bearing on their future.

Blaine had never intended to emerge as a champion in the cramped, miserable conditions aboard the *Cutlass*. But over the course of more than a month, it had become clear that Blaine's wretched father was not the only one who delighted in taking advantage of those who were weaker. There was little left to lose, and Blaine gave vent to his temper, discovering that he could be a fearsome fighter when circumstances demanded. It helped that he stood a head taller than many of the other men, was strong from working on Glenreith's lands to escape his father's reach, and quick from a lifetime's practice dodging blows. He had gathered a group of like-minded prisoners who had sufficient nerve and muscle to stand up to the worst of the bullies and ruffians in the *Cutlass's* hold.

That led to an uneasy truce in the dark, cramped space. On one side were the convicts who sought protection, at least until they reached Edgeland's frozen shores. And on the other side of the hold were their rivals, the ruffians and their hangers-on. Once they reached Velant, they would all be strangers in a strange land, far from home, and at the mercies of a harsh and unforgiving wasteland and its remorseless masters.

I'm nobody's hero, Blaine thought. *But I'll be damned after all I've been through if I'll be anybody's whipping boy, ever again.*

"Think it'll smell any better, once we get to Edgeland?" Dunbar asked. Now that the prospective entertainment of a fight had been eliminated, the *Cutlass's* passengers went back to playing cards or dice, talking quietly amongst themselves or more likely, staring straight ahead, looking at nothing, lost in private thoughts.

"Maybe," Blaine allowed. "But it'll be a damn sight colder, too."

Dunbar nodded. "Aye. Not a bad thing, perhaps. I've heard freezing to death isn't the worst way to go."

"If that's your plan, you might as well pitch yourself overboard and there'll be more food for the rest of us." Garrick's gaze slid to appraise Dunbar as if he were measuring him for a coffin. Garrick was stout and hairy, with a full, long beard and unruly light-brown hair. From what little Blaine had gathered about his shipmate during the voyage, Garrick had gotten into one too many bar fights and been exiled so that the Castle Reach constables did not have to deal with him anymore. Dunbar was tall and thin like a stork, with a short temper and a talent for theft. Blaine wasn't sure which had gotten him passage to Velant.

Dunbar glared, but to Blaine's relief, did not seem inclined to cause trouble. "You think you're going to be one of the ones who makes it to colonist?" he sneered.

Garrick shrugged. "Yep. Don't see why not. Won pretty near every fight I've been in, and the ones I didn't no one else can claim to have won, either. Ain't no stranger to cold or bein' hungry, and I can work hard if I have to."

"It's not Edgeland you have to worry about," Verran said. "It's Velant."

"I hear that if you make it three years in the prison without causing too many problems, you get some money and a bit of land to call your own," Garrick went on as if he had not heard Verran. "Pshaw. That's a better deal than the likes of me would ever get back in Donderath."

"I heard that's just a lie they tell you to keep you in line." Fultz looked up from where he played dice with Jern. "The guards down at the Rooster and Pig would tell stories when they were good and drunk. They said that the prisoners mine rubies and fish herring to send back to the kingdom, so why would anyone let such good slave labor go?"

Garrick gave him an irritated look. "Because it's not letting them go far, you dumbass. We don't ever get to come home. Being a colonist still means you're on Edgeland until you die, just not in the prison." His features took on a crafty expression.

"See, I figure that it's actually to their advantage to let the strongest prisoners go be colonists. After all," reckoned Garrick, "they've got to feed prisoners. Colonists have to fend for themselves, and someone's got to grow food and tend the livestock. There ain't but three or four ships to Edgeland in a year, and they're mostly stuffed with convicts. So the prison and the colony aren't gettin' most of their food and things they need from back home."

That was something Blaine had never considered. He had not thought beyond the prospect of Velant Prison and its brutal reputation. "Garrick's got a point," Blaine said. "There's always plenty of herring in the market at Castle Reach. It's not caught that far south, so it's got to come from Edgeland. And I've heard sailors at the Rooster and Pig talking about making the Edgeland run, coming back with a hold filled with barrels of fish."

"Three years is a long time, mates," Verran said, taking a break from his music. "Might want to hold off making plans."

The hold fell quiet, except for the creaking of the hull. The days had grown steadily shorter as the ship sailed north, until the sun seemed to almost disappear completely. That left the prisoners in near-darkness for much of the day. If the seas were not too rough and the weather was reasonably clear, they might get up on deck once a day, long enough to breathe the cold, fresh air, and glimpse the sun low on the horizon.

Blaine could barely make out the faces of his unwilling companions in the gloom. Most of the convicts were men, but about two dozen women had been unlucky enough to be sentenced to exile, perhaps to ensure the eventual survival of the colony. The women looked hard-worn and ill-used, most likely sent away for theft, or prostitution. One or two looked capable of having killed men who treated them roughly. They grudgingly watched over the other female prisoners, keeping the men at bay as best they could in the tight confines of the hold.

As for the others, it looked to Blaine as if someone had cast a dragnet along Castle Reach's waterfront and hauled in its ruffians. Most looked as if they had started at the bottom of the city's residents and managed to fall even farther. Blaine was grateful that no one knew his story and had resolved to keep it that way. *The old Blaine McFadden is dead. We'll see who the new man becomes—and how long he lasts.*

Still, it had not dawned on Blaine until they were hustled aboard the ship that he might be one of the few convicts who could read and write, though he was unsure what good it would do him. And while many of the prisoners seemed to accept the sailors' derision and their own reduced status as their lot in life, Blaine still struggled to reconcile himself with the idea that he would never again be a free man.

If I'd intended to die and get it over with, I could have jumped overboard in Castle Reach harbor, Blaine told himself sternly. *This is my inheritance now. And if I'm to have any future at all, it will have to be what I make of it, what I fight to get and keep.*

One good thing about the cold; it would probably kill the lice. The warm, crowded hold had been a breeding ground. Blaine had learned to tolerate the itching like he had grown accustomed to the smell of unwashed bodies and spilled latrine buckets.

"You think they'll live long enough to see Edgeland?" Verran asked later that night, after the soldiers had brought down the wormy biscuits and brackish water. He inclined his head toward the far side of the hold. Now that the ship had quieted down for the night, the fevered moans of the sick carried in the stillness.

"Only if the gods are cruel," Blaine replied. "And we already know the answer to that."

Illness had taken its toll throughout the voyage. Some of the prisoners were sick when they boarded, infected in the wretched public jail or the miserable boarding houses. Packed into the stifling hold with its lack of fresh air, abysmal sanitation, and poor food, it was amazing to Blaine that they had not all come down with fever and died.

"They say sharks followed the ship, because of the bodies thrown overboard, 'til the water got too cold," Verran added.

"I saw them," Blaine confirmed. "Damn things seemed to know when someone died. Worse than vultures." He wondered if the other prisoners had felt a twinge of envy for the dead, escaping their uncertain fate in Velant. On the darkest days during the voyage, he had certainly coveted their final rest.

"Maybe they figure the voyage is a winnowing," Verran remarked. "I mean, only the strongest survive, right? So the ones who probably couldn't handle the cold and the work don't even make it off the ship. Less for the prison guards to bury."

The same cynical reasoning had occurred to Blaine, though he assumed the real reason was that no one cared whether any of them lived or died. He had overheard the sailors say that they were paid to deliver their cargo by the shipload, as if the miserable men and women stuffed into the *Cutlass's* hold were no more than crates of tools or barrels of fish. Velant's guards surely did not want more charges, unless they might be pressed to work the mines or the herring fleet in the absence of enough strong backs. And Blaine very much doubted the colonists wanted more mouths to feed. The sharks were the only ones glad to see them.

By daybreak, two of the sick passengers were dead. Their

bodies had been stripped in the night of anything of value—shoes, belts, and extra clothing. The dead men's companions were more afraid of the relentless arctic cold than they were of contagion, or perhaps they reasoned that if they were fated to fall ill, they would have already done so.

Two sailors tossed the naked bodies overboard, into the cold gray sea. Blaine and the others stood back from the rail, but he could not tell whether they feared that they too might be pitched into the water by their dodgy companions or whether they all fought the same small voice that murmured *jump*.

"Land!" The prisoners crowded toward the other side of the ship, hungry for a glimpse of Edgeland.

"That's Estendall, the volcano," one of the sailors said, pointing toward a bleak gray mountain off the coast of the distant shore. "Blows up now and again. Blots out the sun when it does, not that you can see much now anyhow."

The sun barely peeked above the horizon this far north. The "Long Dark," as the sailors called it, would last until spring when the sun would not set for six months, stretching into the "White Nights." Blaine and the others strained to see the wasteland that was to be their new home.

Frigid air stung Blaine's skin and whipped his chestnut-brown hair into his eyes. He shivered. The prisoners wore what they were wearing when they boarded the *Cutlass* in Castle Reach, with the addition of one threadbare blanket apiece. Only those who had stolen or "inherited" clothing from the other passengers or the dead had more than a single layer of cloth between them and the arctic wind.

Velant had better make some provision, or we'll all be dead in a few days at this rate, Blaine thought. Still, he was as curious about Edgeland as the others and pushed forward for a better look.

Edgeland was more shadow than substance at this distance.

Blaine could make out the coastline and mountains in the distance. Faint lights shone near the waterfront in Skalgerston Bay, the harbor town and only large settlement beside the prison. And to the left of the harbor, high on a rocky bluff, sat the menacing silhouette of Velant Prison. Even at a distance, the fortified prison looked ominous.

"Not exactly welcoming, is it?" Verran quipped, but Blaine could hear the nervousness in his tone. "Wonder if it looks better in daylight?"

"We won't know that for six months—if we live that long," Dunbar added.

Blaine stared at the unforgiving landscape, wondering which of the rumors he and the others had heard were true. Throughout the voyage, the prisoners had traded information of dubious veracity, things overheard and half-remembered about their destination.

"I heard the wind can freeze a man dead in minutes," Garrick observed.

"They say there are bears twice as tall as a man out on the ice that can smell your blood from miles away and can rip through rock walls to get to you if they're hungry," another man said.

"What difference does it make if the monsters get you first?" one of the female prisoners asked, her voice quivering with the cold. "I heard there are all kinds of strange things prowling around in the dark. And they don't just eat the living. I heard they dig the dead out of the ice and gnaw on their bones."

"Wild dogs'll do that," Dunbar replied, unimpressed. "So will rats and other critters, if you don't dig the grave deep enough. Don't need monsters for that."

"The dead should rest in peace," the woman reproved.

Dunbar gave a coarse laugh. "Like the ones that got tossed to the sharks? Bloody little rest they'll get, I wager."

"See those lights?" one of the sailors said, pointing toward the line of lanterns that marked the harbor. "Got some mighty fine whorehouses in Skalgerston Bay, sure enough. 'Course, the likes of you won't get to visit, seein' as how you're prison-bound, but the lasses of Bay-town can warm up a man, that's certain."

"And the whiskey and ale at the Crooked House aren't half bad, though a sane man wouldn't sail halfway 'round the world to drink it," another sailor added, and his companions guffawed.

"That's what's in Bay-town?" Blaine asked, genuinely curious. He and the others were unlikely to get more than a glimpse of the harbor city until they earned their Tickets of Leave—if they were fortunate enough to survive that long.

The first sailor waved vaguely toward the dark shoreline. "Oh, there are a few shops for the colonists—like tools and candles and cloth. The ships always bring provisions for the colony as well as the prison—things they can't grow or make for themselves. We bring back barrels of their damned fish—salted, pickled, and dried. But we spend most of our coin with the ladies and in the tavern, so they get the best of us, I wager."

"Get below, all of you!" The first-mate strode toward them, carrying the short whip he was known to use on prisoners who were slow to obey his orders. This time, there was little resistance since the convicts were shivering with cold. The bitter wind seemed to cut right through Blaine's clothing, making the cramped warmth of the hold feel inviting.

"We'll be in port in the morning," Verran remarked as they lined up to go below. "That's when it'll really get interesting."

Blaine turned to get one last look at the Edgeland shoreline before he descended into the hold. The kingdom of Donderath and his life there was completely lost to him now. All that remained was an uncertain future, bleak as the gray sea, unyielding as the ice.

2

WELCOME TO VELANT

BLAINE SLEPT FITFULLY. NOW THAT THE *CUTLASS* WAS CLOSE TO Edgeland, the reality of his situation sank in. He woke before dawn and had gathered what few possessions he had other than his clothing. Just a blanket and a tin cup, and a small, sharp knife he had looted from a dead man's pocket.

"So that's Edgeland, huh?" Verran said, straining to see out the wooden grating that covered one of the few portholes in the hold.

Blaine nodded. He had been watching at the porthole for the last candlemark, though in the arctic twilight, there was little difference between noon and midnight. Like Verran, he strained to make out details in the gloom. As the *Cutlass* sailed into the harbor, the details of Skalgerston Bay remained maddeningly hidden in the shadows.

"Not much to look at," Blaine replied.

"Wonder if I'll run into some of my old mates," Verran mused. "Could be a good thing—or maybe not."

"Did you owe them money?"

Verran flashed an insolent grin. "What do you think?"

Perhaps that was one small consolation. Blaine was unlikely to encounter anyone he knew—or anyone who knew him. Members of the nobility were rarely convicted of crimes, and when judgment was passed, it usually resulted in banishment from court or house arrest. High crimes, such as treason, warranted beheading. That made King Merrill's dubious "mercy" all the more unusual, and Blaine knew that for many among the nobility, the thought of being stripped of title, lands, and noble standing, let alone condemned to live among commoners, would be considered worse than death.

"Now that I recollect, I can think of at least a dozen of my old acquaintances who might be up here," Verran went on, paying no mind to Blaine's lapse into silence. "About half of them I wouldn't mind seeing again, and the other half I'd just as like pretend we'd never met, if you know what I mean."

"Any who might be happy to see you?" Blaine asked. It had never occurred to him that his passengers might be rejoining friends, family, or co-conspirators who had been sent into exile. *Depending on whether they've got friends or foes waiting for them, that could make the difference in surviving—or not lasting through the first week.*

"Well now, that depends," Verran said. "Jakey used to run a pawn shop down on the waterfront. Good deals to his friends, bad cess to his enemies. We did a lot of business together."

"You mean, he was your fence."

Verran slid him a sly look. "I'm not confirming, and I'm not denying. I'm just saying—we did good business, and he cheated at cards less than most people I knew."

"Anyone else?"

Verran thought for a moment. "Hmm. Elsie was a fine girl and kept me company many a night down at the Rooster and Pig. I heard they caught her for lifting a bit of coin to feed her children, and sent her up here. Been a year or two. She might even be a colonist now, if she made it." He looked wistful.

"Nat Candle got nabbed for running a crooked betting game winter before last," Verran added. "I told him he was skimming too much off the winnings, but no one ever listens to me. 'Twasn't the bets themselves what upset the guards, and if he'd stayed mostly honest, he'd be a free man today."

Seems like the friends Verran is likely to have here are a colorful crew, Blaine thought. Then again, Verran and his pals knew all about getting by on their wits and surviving on little else than nerve, a skill Blaine would need to learn quickly if he intended to earn his Ticket of Leave.

"You think most folks here have friends up here?" Blaine asked, growing more aware every day just how sheltered he had been.

"Friends—or enemies," Verran laughed. "Sure. You don't?"

Blaine shrugged. "Don't know. Didn't keep track."

"Uh-oh," Garrick observed, coming up behind them. "For better or worse boys, Looks like we've arrived."

———

"Line up, single file!" the ship's first mate shouted as sailors slid back the bolt that secured the hatch to the hold. "Take what you've got with you, you're not coming back. You'll stop on deck to get your manacles, and then down the gangplank and good riddance."

Fear. Resignation. Desperation. Anger. Blaine saw a variety of emotions in the eyes of his fellow prisoners. He wondered what they saw when they looked at him. After more than a month in the hold of the *Cutlass* they were rank and filthy. The wind whipped at their thin blankets and lashed their hair. He counted it as a small mercy that it was not raining.

Blaine had feared this far north that even in the summer there would be snow. He assumed that was true for the mountain peaks, but the temperature as they shuffled down the gangplank, wrists chained, felt more like a late-autumn evening back in Donderath. The worst was yet to come, and Blaine doubted spring came early on Edgeland.

"Move," the sailors shouted, shoving one or two of the prisoners for good measure.

The sun was barely visible above the horizon, giving Blaine to guess that it was daytime. He strained for a better look at the Skalgerston Bay harbor front, but it was still too dark to make out much more than the outline of the buildings. Garrick was in front of him, and Dunbar, as the convicts shambled onto the dock. Verran was behind him, then Jern, and Fultz. A few more of the prisoners who had kept to Blaine's side of the hold brought up the rear. Coan and his buddies had been first in line. Blaine had signaled for his allies to hang back. There were some situations where being in front was a good thing. This, he suspected, might not be one of them.

Guards were waiting for them on the docks, along with heavily built farm wagons drawn by massive plow horses. Blaine tried not to shiver as the wind gusted. The guards, he noted, wore woolen uniforms, solid boots, and hooded, heavy capes.

"Pick up the pace," the lead guard snapped, grabbing Coan by the chain that bound his wrists and hauling him toward the wagon.

Coan growled and tried to take a swing at the guard. The other soldiers were ready, and four of them set on Coan with short, stout staves, beating him mercilessly until Coan was a bloody heap on the dockside road. In the half-light, Blaine could not see whether or not the big man was still breathing.

"Anyone else have an opinion about getting in the wagon?" the lead guard challenged, holding his bloodied staff at the ready.

No one was stupid enough to reply, though there was no mistaking the malice in the prisoners' eyes as they stepped around Coan's broken form. One by one, Blaine and the others hauled themselves up into the wagons. Groups that had clustered together in the hold tried to stay with each other, though the guards directed some to one wagon and some to another with no discernible reason.

They probably know we've formed alliances on the ship, Blaine thought. *They'll want to isolate us, make us more vulnerable without anyone to watch our backs.*

When all of the other prisoners had been loaded into wagons, two of the guards lifted Coan and tossed him like a sack of turnips into the back of the last cart. The big man groaned but did not move.

Most of Blaine's companions managed to stay together. Verran's expression was unreadable, but his eyes were haunted. The horses headed away from Skalgerston Bay and its rough village, toward the imposing shadow on the cliffs, Velant Prison. The iron manacles, connected by heavy links of chain, bit into Blaine's wrists. He guessed he should be grateful that they were not shackled at the ankles.

A few of the prisoners traded whispers, one eye on the guards to avoid a beating. Now and again, Blaine caught a snatch of prayer to Charrot or the High God's consorts, Torven and Esthrane, but he suspected that most had given up on beseeching the gods long before they reached Edgeland's shores.

During the long sea voyage, Blaine had searched his memories for any remembered mention of Velant Prison or the colony on Edgeland. He had spent little time at court, so he had not been privy to any of that gossip, though he doubted that courtiers would have deigned to mention such a vile place. Hangings were common in Castle Reach, and how the magistrates determined who should hang and who should go to exile was a mystery to

Blaine, since his own sentence had been handed down by King Merrill himself.

Perhaps it's true, he thought. *Maybe the magistrates did choose who lived and who died based on which prisoners might make good labor for Velant and Edgeland, and settled for hanging those unlikely to survive the journey.* If so, Donderath's "justice" was even more cynical than he suspected. His father had enjoyed timing his trips to Castle Reach to witness the monthly public hangings. Blaine found no sport in watching people die, some of whom were only a year or two older—if that —than his younger brother, Carr.

Carr's only twelve. He won't remember much about me. Maybe that's for the best. Or maybe Mari and Aunt Judith will tell him stories, let him know that I wasn't always the criminal who destroyed what was left of the family's fortunes.

Saving Mari and the others from Lord McFadden's rages came at a price beyond Blaine's exile. Even if his aunt was able to keep Mari's shame from public knowledge, Blaine's crime and trial had been sensational news at court. He remembered bitterly how crowded the galleries had been when the king passed sentence, people who might have barely recognized him on his rare visits to Quillarth Castle jamming in for the spectacle of seeing a nobleman condemned for the murder of his father.

Judith and Blaine's fiancé Carensa had insisted on attending the sentencing, though Blaine had tried to warn them away, for their sake as well as because he did not want them to see him, chained like a beast and forced to kneel before the king. Thanks to Blaine's father's temper, the family had been on the fringes of court society. With a criminal—a convict—in the family, Blaine knew his family would be unwelcome at court, shunned by the nobility and the townspeople, reviled and outcast.

Carensa and Mari might never find suitors willing to over-look the stain on their reputations cast by their connection to

Blaine. Carr would inherit a title and an impoverished manor. Judith would have all she could manage to keep the manor and lands functioning when Blaine's infamy tainted the willingness of tradesmen and merchants to trade with them. In saving them, Blaine had ruined their lives and his own along with it.

And if I had the choice to make over again, I would do the same thing. Father was a monster. Someone needed to put him down. I'm only sorry that the backlash affected anyone else. I knew I would pay a price when I drew my sword. Then again, he had expected a few weeks in the king's dungeons, a humiliating walk to the gallows, and then death by the hangman's noose. *Did Merrill really mean exile as a 'mercy' or was it his way of extending the punishment—and sending a signal to any other noble son who considered murder as an option?*

Blaine would never know the answer to his questions, though they came repeatedly to him in the candlemarks after midnight when the world was quiet, and he had no way to drown out his thoughts. *Judith will find a way to take care of Mari and Carr— and Glenreith,* he assured himself. *She's the strongest woman I've ever met. Carensa will surely rise above the scandal. I never wanted to hurt any of them.*

"We're here." Verran nudged Blaine in the ribs with an elbow, with a look that acknowledged Blaine had been lost in thought for the dark ride up the cliff side.

The massive gates of Velant Prison loomed dark and forbidding against the twilight sky. An eerie green ribbon of light glimmered high in the sky, against stars that had never seemed so clear and bright. The wind had picked up since the wagons left the port, and it was colder now, too. Blaine held his blanket close around him, turning his back to the wind. At least in the wagon, packed tightly against each other, they had the warmth of shared body heat, but once inside the prison, they would lose even that small comfort.

"Get out. Here's where you end." The guard likely intended his comment to sound just as ominous as it did. Blaine hoped his eyes held the flat, cold look that so many of his fellow prisoners affected, eyes that had already seen the worst life had to offer. A lifetime of dealing with his father had taught him how to hide his fear, conceal his emotions. And in self-defense, he had learned something of fighting.

Who am I kidding? I was still a noble. My worst days were much better than the best days most of these folks ever had. I wonder how many of them would have endured father's beatings for the chance to have a place to live, food to eat, and clothes to wear. Everything I think I know means nothing as soon as I walk through those gates, Blaine thought. *And my real education begins.*

The huge gates opened, and the wagons rumbled into the prison's inner courtyard. Torches in iron sconces cast a red glow, illuminating the open space nearest the gate. Velant was larger than Blaine had supposed, with at least a dozen large, boxy wooden buildings, likely barracks, dormitories, or work buildings. A single squat, ugly building of hewn stone hunkered on one side of the courtyard. Rows of soldiers stood not far beyond where the wagons came to a halt.

The prisoners stumbled out of the wagons, heads down, doing their best to attract as little attention as possible. They were all hungry, since there had been no food since early that morning. A few of the convicts looked as if they might collapse, and Blaine wondered if the guards would leave them where they lay, a warning to the others.

Even Verran had the sense to remain quiet as the soldiers who drove the wagons lined the new convicts up for inspection. Now that his eyes had adjusted to the torchlight, Blaine could make out more details—a set of stocks, a whipping post, and a large, prominent gallows. The guards marched them to stand in front of a hole dug in the ice that looked an awful lot like an open grave.

While Blaine had been lucky enough to know little of Velant before his sentencing, his fellow prisoners had heard plenty of rumors from the sailors who frequented the bars in Castle Reach, and from the family and friends of other unlucky convicts. On board, they had traded tales, and even if the stories had grown with the telling, Velant was a place of horrors.

Standing in the cold night air beneath the flickering torches, under the merciless gaze of the guards, Blaine could believe it. Though the prison guards, like the convicts, would never return to Donderath, sailors gained plenty of news from the colonists in Bay-town. Aboard the *Cutlass*, Blaine heard the whispered rumors of oubliettes, of prisoners left to die in of exposure or staked out for wild animals to savage, of convicts worked until they dropped in the ruby mines or hard-scrabble farm fields or tossed overboard from the herring ships when their usefulness was over. Velant was likely all those horrors and more.

"Attention!" The guards snapped to rigid formation as two men strode from the stone building toward the new prisoners. "Prepare for review by Commander Prokief and Warden-Mage Ejnar."

Prokief was a bear of a man with the manner of a brawler, tall and broad shouldered with a cloud of unruly dark hair and a full dark beard. He wore a full dress uniform here at the end of the world, where Blaine would have thought such formalities were likely to have given way to practicality. Prokief's chest glittered with a row of medals, a medallion hung from a wide ribbon around his neck, and a gold ring with a huge ruby glistened on his right hand. His cape was draped over one shoulder as if to show that Prokief defied even the weather. On first glance, Blaine might have been inclined to dismiss Prokief as a puffed-up martinet, but a glance at the commander's cold, pitiless eyes revealed that would be a mistake.

Prokief was known for his brutality on the battlefield as much as for his effectiveness. Blaine had heard whispers about Prokief, a man some still called the "Butcher of Breseshwa" for a battle he had won by sheer brutality and unmatched cruelty. Prokief had been awarded a medal for his service, then 'promoted' to his position at Velant Prison when King Merrill no longer had need of the monster Prokief had become.

Ejnar was taller than Prokief but thinner and wore long gray robes beneath a smoke-colored cape. The guards seemed to regard him with even more fear than they felt for Prokief. Where Prokief's hair and beard were trimmed to military regulation, Ejnar had long dark hair and a shaggy, unkempt beard. He had the look of a fanatic in his eyes, and a hard set to his mouth.

Prokief stopped halfway down the line of assembled prisoners. He regarded them disdainfully, eyes narrowed, as if already deciding who to winnow.

"Today, you are dead men." Prokief's voice boomed over the quiet courtyard. "There is no escape from Velant and no return from Edgeland. Your lives are in my hands. There is no higher authority than me, here in Velant Prison. I decide whether you live or how you die, whether you eat or starve."

Two of the guards strode forward when Prokief snapped his fingers. One man lifted a horn and blew the mournful notes of a song Blaine recognized with a shudder, a hymn to the god Torven, lord of the Sea of Souls, a petition for the dead. The second soldier sang the chant, a litany familiar to most Donderans, the last words said over a corpse before it was lowered into the ground.

Prokief snatched a cloth away that covered something at the head of the icy grave. A body lay shrouded on a pallet, and in the dim light, it took Blaine a moment to realize it was an effigy and not a corpse.

"You are the dead," Prokief shouted above the cold wind. "This is your grave, your body, your ritual of passing. No one returns from Velant, as no one returns from the Sea of Souls or the Unseen Realm. Here, you are the ghosts, and I am the left hand of Torven, empowered by the king and gods to mete out your punishment. So shall it be."

The singer and the horn finished the notes of the funeral dirge as soldiers lowered the effigy into the grave and shoveled the ice in on top of the "body." Blaine knew that it was all sadistic theater, part of Prokief's way of breaking their spirits, but he could not suppress the shiver that chilled his soul.

Prokief raked the prisoners with his gaze, but no one was bold or foolhardy enough to challenge him. Blaine noted the bullwhip coiled at Prokief's belt. It did not look as if it were for show. But his attention returned to the tall, silent man who stood just behind Prokief and whose presence raised the hackles on the back of Blaine's neck.

Ejnar is a mage? Blaine wondered. *It would make sense for Prokief to have an unfair advantage. After all, there must be more prisoners here than guards, and even an army can't hold off a rebellion when they're outnumbered without reinforcements.*

"Tonight," Prokief said, "you will be assigned to barracks, given clothing adequate to the environment, and put into the work groups you will form in the morning. Life here in the arctic is very simple. Obey my rules, obey the guards, do what is required of you, and you may live to collect your Ticket of Leave, if the gods smile on you." The hard line of Prokief's mouth gave Blaine a suggestion of just how unlikely the commander considered the odds of that working out well to be.

"Disobey, cause problems, and you will be punished.

Repeated infractions will not be tolerated." Prokief eyed the line of new prisoners. "You cannot hide from the warden-mages. Step out of line, and I will know. Death in Velant, to those who cannot or will not comply, is not quick or painless." A cold smile came to his lips. "I assure you, there are much, much worse things than death, and those who break the rules discover that."

Prokief and Ejnar stood back, and a man in a captain's uniform stepped forward. "I am Captain Jumon. Let me introduce you to your new home," he said. "Over there is the gallows. How often there's a hanging depends on you. We don't have the food or the patience for shirkers or troublemakers. Just realize that the more prisoners we hang, the more work there is for the rest of you to do." His implication was clear. Prokief intended to rely on the self-interest of frightened prisoners to keep the would-be rebels in line.

"Hanged men are the lucky ones," the captain continued. "That pole in the yard gets used for whippings. Sometimes, once discipline has been administered, the prisoner is left hanging there until the body freezes solid, as an example to the others." There was no inflection in the captain's voice, no acknowledgment that the prisoners were human beings. Any humanity the captain possessed had disappeared long ago.

"And then there are the Holes," Jumon said. "Deep in the ice, dark and cold. Toss the strongest man in one of those Holes after a thorough whipping and let him freeze for a few days in the darkness, and what's left of him that doesn't freeze off comes out crying like a baby." A glint of satisfaction in the captain's eyes told Blaine the man enjoyed seeing prisoners put in their place. "Got gibbets too—they get plenty cold in the winter wind. Best you keep that in mind."

"Magic is forbidden," the captain continued. "The warden-mages will know if you've got magic and they'll know if you use magic. Any use of magic against the guards or the warden-mages will be dealt with swiftly, painfully, and permanently."

Interesting, Blaine thought. Most people in Donderath had some kind of small magic talent, whether it was being able to call a flame without a spark, keep milk from souring, or heal a wound gone bad. *Can they actually keep people from doing magic or just intimidate them out of trying? And if magic works here, I can't believe prisoners don't use it—they just don't dare get caught.*

"Female prisoners will work in the kitchens and laundry," Captain Jumon shouted above the wind. "You'll tend the sheep, shear them, and spin the wool, run the looms and sew the clothing." He paused and looked up and down the line.

"Male prisoners are not to be in those areas unless delivering materials; any disobedience will result in flogging. Try it a second time, and you'll lose your balls." His smirk made it clear that he would not object to meting out punishment.

"The rest of you will work where you're needed. That means the ruby mines, the farm fields, and on occasion, the herring fleet. There are chores to be done—blacksmithing, cartwright, tanner, joiner, and gravedigger," he added. "We're on our own up here, so there are crops to sow and harvest, livestock to tend and butcher, nets to weave, hides to tan. How much food is available depends on how hard you work. You don't work, you don't eat."

Prokief and his bully boys seem to figure that if they set us against each other, they'll have less trouble keeping us in line, Blaine thought. *I wonder how it really works, out of sight of the guards.*

"In case you thought about trying to get out over the walls, forget it," the captain added. "Our warden-mages can track you, if the bears and the wolves don't get you first. The colonists won't hide you. They owe their freedom to Commander Prokief's good will. We patrol the town. Try to escape, try to hide in the mines or run from the farm fields, and we will draw and quarter you and feed you to the crows."

Maybe a saner man would have despaired at the overwhelming odds. Blaine found his anger rising, felt his jaw set against the challenge the captain and the guards set. *I didn't get rid of my father to knuckle under to Prokief,* Blaine thought. *I'm going to survive to get my Ticket, just for spite. I'm just going to have to be smart about it.*

Prokief and Ejnar headed back to the squat stone building that Blaine assumed was the commander's headquarters. The guards plunged into the ranks of prisoners, separating them into barracks groups, though Blaine could see no method to their choices. Verran, Dunbar, and Garrick ended up in Blaine's group, as did Coan and two of his buddies. Fultz and Jern were taken for another group. Blaine wondered how often the different barracks saw each other, and whether the work details kept them separated or moved men around.

Prokief may be ruthless, but he doesn't look stupid. I wonder how they test for skill and ability. Not everyone's suited for every job, and you can beat a man senseless for having no talent, or match the man to the task. As he and his new bunkmates trudged toward the processing building where they were to receive clothing and rations, he tried to figure out what useful skills he might parlay into an advantage.

As far as Prokief's concerned, reading and writing are probably a liability, and he'll be harder on me if he suspects I'm noble-born, Blaine thought. *I've helped the hired men put crops in the field and handle the harvest, but beyond that, I'm good for nothing except general labor. Goddess help me! That means the mines or the fields—or the boats—for certain.*

Blaine and a group of forty other men followed five guards toward one of the large wooden dormitories. *We outnumber them eight to one,* he thought. *Even unarmed, we could over-*

power them. But then what? Ships came from Donderath every few months with supplies and additional soldiers. Blaine suspected that Prokief made some kind of report back to the king, carried on those ships. *Even if the whole camp rose up and killed the guards, killed Prokief and his warden-mages, word would get back to the king. More soldiers would come, and there would be reprisals—against the prisoners and the colony.*

He pushed the thought of vengeance to the back of his mind. It had been a long time since any of the prisoners had last eaten or had water to drink, perhaps another intentional humiliation to weaken them and make it clear just how dependent they were on Prokief's goodwill.

When they neared the barracks, Blaine caught the scent of food. "Smells like roasted meat and cabbage," Verran murmured.

"I'm hungry enough to eat the salt pork and biscuits from the ship," Blaine returned. A glare from one of the soldiers silenced them, but Verran managed to shoot Blaine an insolent grin.

They were herded into a large room with bare wooden tables. Tin plates and cups were stacked on a pile near where two men stood beside a large cauldron and a basket of bread. Blaine guessed that the cooks were also prisoners. They regarded the newcomers with bored looks.

"Line up," the lead guard shouted. "Take a cup and a plate. You get one pass through the line, and you get what the cook gives you—no more. Better eat it when you get it, because there's nothing 'till morning. Just after dawn, you'll hear the morning bell ring. Best you be among the first in here—food doesn't always last, and the slow ones go hungry."

Blaine and the others waited for the guards to unlock their manacles. He shook his hands to get the circulation back, and warm them from the touch of the ice-cold metal. His fingers were numb, and he was chilled to the bone. The large open room was warmed only by a small brazier beneath the cauldron, but it was better than the rapidly dropping temperatures outside.

The closer Blaine got to the food, the less appetizing it smelled. Then again, after more than a month of sea rations, he was ready to eat almost anything. He accepted a scoop of the questionable stew and a piece of bread hard enough to break teeth. The water in his drinking cup smelled fresh and lacked the greenish cast the barrels of drinking water had gained onboard the *Cutlass*. Blaine and Verran moved along quickly, eating their portions before they even got to the tables. Blaine had a nagging sense that something was going to go wrong, and when it did, he did not want to miss out on his meal.

"Hey! That's not food," a burly prisoner shouted as he got close enough to see into the cauldron. "Looks like someone cleaned out the shit house, and it smells like it, too."

The man next in line slapped the complaining prisoner across the back of the head. "Shut up," he hissed. "You'll get us all in trouble."

Too late. The guards were already heading for the stocky man and the prisoner who hit him. They grabbed the two men out of line, though the second convict protested that he was just trying to keep the big man from causing a problem. Three large guards went after the two prisoners with fists, boots, and bludgeons, and when they were finished, the two troublemakers lay in a still, bloody heap.

"You there," one of the guards said, pointing to Blaine and Verran, still breathing hard from the exertion of beating the two men. "Haul their worthless asses out to the courtyard and leave them by the pole."

Blaine and Verran exchanged a glance but moved quickly to comply. Blaine was glad he had downed his dinner and did his level best not to have it come back up on him as he and Verran hefted the two unconscious prisoners. They were slick with blood, and at least one of the men had been beaten badly enough to soil himself. Someone had retched, and Blaine had to close his eyes and swallow back his own dinner, reminding himself that there would be nothing more until daybreak if he lost the contents of his stomach.

"We don't like problems," one of the guards lectured the others as Blaine and Verran dragged their charges toward the door. "That's what happens to people who cause trouble. Anyone want to wager their grog ration on whether or not they'll last the night outside?"

Verran was half as big as the man he was trying to drag. Blaine gave the limp body a shove, as Verran ducked to get his shoulder under the unconscious man's arm, while Blaine had taken the larger of the two men and staggered under the weight.

"You think he means it, about wagering?" Blaine asked as he and Verran trudged into the courtyard with their burdens.

"I'm sure he does, mate," Verran replied. "That's prison guards for you—always up for a wager, and willing to turn a blind eye some of the time if you let them win more often than not." It was apparent from his tone that this was a truth widely known to all but Blaine.

Why not? Blaine thought. *After all, the guards are prisoners here themselves, and probably eating the same food. If they can be bribed, then there might be a way to survive this place.*

"Mine's not going to mind the cold, that's for sure," Verran said as he dropped the man he carried near the blood-stained whipping post. "He's dead. They broke his damn neck." Verran was covered in the dead man's blood, and Blaine suspected that he did not look any better himself.

"This one's still breathing," Blaine replied, letting the big man tumble from across his shoulders and fall beside the corpse.

"Ah well," Verran said, managing a wan smile and wiping the worst of the blood onto his pants. "At least it's not us this time, eh? And we got our food down before the shoving started, so all in all, it could be worse."

Blaine nodded. "We'd better get back in there, or they'll be dumping us out here next."

"Just a minute," Verran said. He bent down and searched the men's pockets with the efficiency of someone who knew what he was looking for. "Here," he said after a moment, palming a few coins and a couple of other small items for himself. He passed a dirk to Blaine, along with a bit of thin rope. "Never know when it'll come in handy, and they've got no use for it now, poor blighters."

He and Verran hurried to return, arriving just as the cooks ran out of stew before the last dozen prisoners went through the line. The looks the hungry prisoners gave to the cooks were murderous, but after the guards' demonstration, the disgruntled men grabbed for what remained of the bread and went sullenly to their places.

———

Overhead, it sounded as if a fight was going on. Blaine expected that the guards would charge up the stairs, but they made no move to do so, not even when a body came tumbling down with a knife deep in its chest.

"We don't police the barracks," the lead guard said. "Just remember—kill off your bunkmates, and your quotas remain the same, so you all work harder." He gave a nasty grin. "Let's go meet the fellows you're going to have to trust won't knife you in your sleep."

3

INSIDE THE WALLS

BLAINE AND THE NEW PRISONERS RECEIVED THEIR PRISON clothing as they reached the bottom of the stairs to the barracks. Solid boots that appeared to all be one size. A heavy jacket, knit cap, sheepskin mittens with the wool on the inside, a knit scarf, and a heavy woolen cape.

"Lose them or damage them, and you'll have to get a replacement off the dead—and fight for it, I wager," the lead guard warned them. "Now up the ladder with you. Mind you make your mark this first night—you'll want your place in the order of things." He gave a nasty leer as they filed past.

Blaine arranged to be in the middle of the line of men who made their way up the ladder. Verran was behind him. When he emerged into the second-floor room, he found rows of bunks stacked four high, floor to ceiling, with barely enough room for a man to roll onto his straw ticking mattress.

Twenty men watched them climb up the ladder. Some stood with arms crossed, clearly unhappy to have new arrivals. Others regarded them with wary, cold gazes. The men wore the same style prison garb that Blaine and the others had just received, and from their stained shirts and frayed hems, it was clear that replacements were not easily available.

None of the men appeared starved, but they had the gaunt, lean look of wolves in winter, and their gaze tracked the newcomers like prey—or adversaries.

"Welcome to your new home." The speaker was a short, powerfully-build bald man. "Your bunks are in the back. Might want to get rid of the straw. The last men back there died of fever."

The newcomers had cleared the ladder. Below them, the guards removed the ladder and bolted the trap door shut. *Where do they think we're going to go?* Blaine wondered. He eyed the lanterns. Fire was a constant worry, especially in wooden build-ings. *If the barracks goes up, I guess we go with it. Maybe that's what they want us to keep in mind.*

A door slammed on the floor below, as if the guards wanted the prisoners to know that they were on their own.

Verran and Garrick had been looking around in the dim light. "Stefan!" Verran said. "And Pioter!"

"Verran Danning! You thieving little shit!" The man Verran hailed as Stefan elbowed his way through the group.

Blaine and Garrick stepped up to block his way.

"Let me through!" Stefan yelled. "I've got business with that son of a dog!"

"Not here and not now," Blaine said levelly.

Ten of the convicts advanced on the newcomers. "Just give us Danning, and we'll cause the rest of you no problem," Stefan said. "He stole my girl, and she stole my money. Got me sent here, the bastard did, because I couldn't pay my debts."

Blaine glanced at Verran, who managed a weak smile and shrugged. "I had debts, too, mate. And she was over you. But if it makes you feel better, she ran out on me with the last of my coin when I got arrested, and wouldn't come to pay off the guard."

Blaine, Garrick, Verran, and Dunbar stood back to back facing the ten advancing convicts. The other men stood against the wall, unwilling to make this their fight.

"Just give me Danning's scrawny ass. He can be my bitch since he took mine." Stefan's fellows sniggered.

Then Stefan's hair caught on fire.

Stefan leaped around like a madman, slapping at his burning hair with his hands, desperate to keep the fire from spreading to his beard. Blaine saw the bald man who had greeted the newcomers surreptitiously set aside a newly-snuffed candle and throw a blanket over the man's burning hair.

"Stay still! I'll put it out!" he said, and proceeded to beat the big man about the head and shoulders with his open hand until the others laughed. Finally, the bald prisoner pulled away the blanket, revealing a burned and angry Stefan.

More of the convicts got into the fight. Verran kneed one of the men hard in the balls, while Blaine landed a roundhouse punch that decked the man who came for him. Garrick hefted his attacker by the neck, making it clear that if he twitched, the smaller man's spine would break. Dunbar ducked and punched, rolling his assailant over one shoulder to hit the ground with a thud and then dropping knee-first onto the downed man's chest.

The fight was over in less than a minute.

"Leave the newcomers alone tonight, and I'll make sure a healer takes the sting out of those blisters on your head," the bald man said, barely concealing his own laughter. Stefan glowered but turned away, trudging to his bunk where he glowered at the newcomers.

Blaine gave the bald man a curt nod of thanks and headed warily toward the bunks in the back. Verran sported a newly blackened eye but otherwise looked entirely too pleased with himself. He claimed a bunk, eyed the straw and decided the extra warmth and questionable comfort was worth the possibility of contagion and sat down with his back to the wall.

He and his shipmates were exhausted, but no one wanted to risk going to sleep while so many of the others were awake. Not after the rough welcome they had received. *We'll be catching shit for weeks since we're new here,* Blaine thought resignedly. *As if it isn't going to be hard enough.*

Stefan and his gang of supporters were on the far side of the barracks. Blaine doubted they had seen the last of him and suspected that Stefan's loss would just make revenge a higher priority. Verran appeared unconcerned. He sank down cross-legged and began to play quietly on his pennywhistle.

Garrick and Dunbar and several of the other men from the *Cutlass* began a game of dice. Toward the front of the barracks, another group went back to the card game the newcomers' arrival had interrupted. Blaine found his attention wandering too much to suit betting, so he leaned against the bunk and observed their new companions.

Twenty of the men from the *Cutlass* had been assigned to the second floor of the barracks, and Blaine presumed that the other twenty were on another floor. This floor had room for forty men. That meant there were equal numbers of new men and old-timers, which boded in Blaine's groups' favor.

Stefan, Verran's enemy, and his knot of supporters sat together playing cards. The bald man who had intervened in the fight was trading off-color jokes with two of the other prisoners. A few of the men in the front of the room lay on their bunks, not asleep but taking no part in what went on around them.

Blaine looked up as a tall man headed toward them. The man had dark hair, a hawk-like nose, and piercing blue eyes. He kept his hands open and out to the side, showing that he intended no harm.

"Garrick!" the tall man said. "Didn't know if you recognized me, back there before the scuffle."

Garrick stared at the man for a minute before recognition dawned. To Blaine's relief, Garrick grinned. "Dawe Killick! As I live and breathe! I knew you disappeared, but how in Torven's name did you end up here?"

Dawe glanced around at the others, realizing he was on their side of the room. "Mind if I sit down?"

Verran gestured magnanimously as if the question was directed at him. "Sure, mate. Have a seat. Unless you're a music hater," he added, with a glare.

Dawe eyed the pennywhistle askance. "Fine with me. Just keep it down, or you might get more attention than you bargained for."

Verran sniffed. "No one appreciates musicians," he muttered and went back to his jaunty tavern ditty.

"So Garrick," Dawe said. "What got you sent up here?"

Garrick grimaced. "We had a wet spring, and the crops didn't come in well. Couldn't make enough money to pay my debts. My whore-spawned neighbor took everything—my land, my cows, and my house. My wife and daughter went to live with her folks, but the neighbor wanted his coin as well as what he stole from me, so he took me to court." He shrugged. "And here I am. You?"

Dawe sighed and then pulled at his sleeve, revealed an "M" branded on his forearm, just like the one that marked Blaine as a murderer.

Garrick's eyes widened. "Truly? Who'd you kill?"

Dawe gave him a look. "No one. I was set up. My wife— may her soul rot in Raka—was having an affair with the other silversmith in Castle Reach. I'd had a pretty public row with a client who didn't pay his bill. Then all of a sudden, that client turns up dead, and my wife and my rival supply enough 'evi-

dence' to hang me." He shrugged. "I guess they needed smiths in
Velant, so they exiled me instead—although it's a big difference
making horseshoes compared to teapots!"

Garrick clapped him on the shoulder. "Ah well, look at the
bright side," the red-haired man said. "At least you don't have to
run into your wife up here on another man's arm!" He guffawed
at his own joke. "Here—meet a few of my shipmates," he said.
"That's Mick, and Dunbar, and Verran's the one with the
whistle."

"So I figured when Stefan went after his hide," Dawe
observed drily. He dropped his voice. "Stefan's a little tetched.
Don't poke at him," he warned Verran.

"You don't need to tell me he's tetched," Verran replied.
"He's still sore over losing coins that wouldn't even pay for a
couple of tankards of ale!"

Dawe looked as if he doubted that was the total of what
Verran had "stolen" from Stefan, but said nothing. "Stefan's got
his followers, but the rest of the group is all right, most of the
time."

"Who's the bald one?" Blaine asked. "He's got an unusual
sense of humor." He glanced over to where the man was telling
bawdy jokes that grew more obscene—and implausible—with
each new example.

"That's Piran Rowse," Dawe replied. "Court-martialed. Must
have been bad, because he won't say why. But he's great at
knocking heads together, and he doesn't suffer fools gladly. He
tends to keep the others in line, if they don't relish a slap to the
side of the head." He gave Blaine and the others a warning
glance. "Just don't play him at cards."

"What about the rest of them?" Garrick asked.

Dawe shrugged. "Thieves and roustabouts, drunkards and
deserters, along with some brawlers and smugglers. Donderath

didn't want us, but even King Merrill has a limit to how many of us he can kill."

"What about the work details?" Blaine asked. "What's going to happen tomorrow?"

"If you look like you can take it, they'll put you in the mines," Dawe said. "Unless you've got some kind of skill—like blacksmithing, woodworking, or doctoring animals. The women get sent to the kitchens and the laundries—the only men allowed for that are the hunters' trail cooks and the tailors who keep the army in uniforms. Without a skill, you're just a beast of burden." He rolled his eyes. "On the other hand, they can't kill us off too fast, or Prokief won't make his quota of goods to send back, and the king will take notice."

"So Prokief's accountable to King Merrill?" Blaine pressed.

Dawe gave him an odd look as if the question wasn't the sort he expected from a convict. "In a way," he said carefully. "Merrill doesn't care whether we live or die—as long as too many of us don't die all at once," he added. "Velant's got to earn its keep. Donderath pays the soldiers to keep them from revolting, or deserting, and they pay the ships to bring prisoners up and take cargo back. And it's the cargo—rubies and herring—that Merrill cares about. So in a way, Prokief needs us if he doesn't want trouble from the king." He gave a jaded smile. "He just doesn't need any individual one of us much at all, so long as there are enough bodies to do the work."

"If we're sent to the mines, do we stay there?" Dunbar asked.

Dawe shook his head. "No. Work shifts rotate. Right now, it's coming into winter with the Long Dark. Fishing is better in the summer. If the herring are plentiful, they'll run the ships in two shifts and need the colonists plus the prisoners to man the boats and process the catch." He wrinkled his nose. "Nothing smells as bad as the herring boats. Not even the latrines."

"And the farms?" Garrick asked.

"Not much to do in the winter except tend the livestock," Dawe replied. "And they're choosy about who gets to do that. There have been...problems...on occasion. Some people here are sick bastards. And it's hard enough not losing the lambs, calves, kids, and foals given how cold it is in the spring. That's one place where they'll let a little magic slide, if you can doctor the animals."

"And people?"

Dawe's expression hardened. "Not so much. Prokief's got his warden-mages. They keep a tight rein on the magic. Most of the time if you get hurt, you're on your own."

Most of the time, Blaine thought. *There's more he's not telling until he knows he can trust us. Interesting.*

Garrick and Dawe got talking about the old days. From what Blaine gathered, Garrick had been a regular at the Rooster and Pig, a favorite bar down near the Castle Reach waterfront known for its excellent bitterbeer. Before his exile, Garrick had been one of the harbor city's more successful peddlers, with a donkey cart from which he sold everything from tin pots to fabric, tools to trinkets. He traded with the sailors for the exotic wares they brought from distant shores and turned a tidy profit reselling those items to the residents of the city, until his temper got the best of him one too many times.

"I don't blame Engraham," Garrick said, naming the Rooster and Pig's owner. "It wasn't the first time I busted up the place. And it might have been the guards who happened to be on duty that day. But the next thing I knew, I was in front of a tribunal and then on a ship to the end of the world."

"You're not the only one with a story like that," Dawe said. "And I wouldn't be surprised to find out that Prokief offers a bounty on certain types of prisoners, ones who can do the work or have skills we're short of up here." He grimaced. "And women. If you hadn't noticed, they're in short supply, but the colony needs them to survive."

Blaine leaned forward. "You think Prokief is paying the guards for prisoners?"

Dawe looked over his shoulder, as if aware that the conversation had entered a dangerous turn. "I can't prove it. But I've heard bits and pieces, and from what I've seen in the time I've been here, I think it's possible. Not just for prisoners—for prisoners with certain talents or skills, people who can keep this place functioning."

Blaine took a deep breath as the implications sank in. *The ships come from Donderath every few months. It wouldn't be hard for Prokief to send instructions for the sailors to pass along to the guards in port, and some of those guards are bound to be friends of the guards at the prison. Prokief's probably got supporters back home—he was a military hero—and likely a friend or two among the judges. Wouldn't be hard to trump up charges against someone, and who's going to go against the guard's word?*

His attention came back as Garrick was filling Dawe in on the men who had come from the *Cutlass*. "Not a bad bunch in our group, considering," Garrick said. He looked behind him to make sure Coan and his cronies were out of earshot. "That big guy," he said with a nod of his head to indicate who he meant. "Coan. He and his buddies are trouble."

"I figured," Dawe replied, "since he looks like someone busted his nose recently."

"Yesterday," Garrick said with a pointed look in Blaine's direction. "For good reason."

"Undoubtedly," Dawe said, with an appraising look at Blaine.

"I don't know everyone who got assigned to this barracks," Garrick said. "But Jaston and Hort were fishermen who lost their boat in a storm and couldn't pay their debts," he said with a glance toward two sandy-haired men who looked like brothers. "Kurt ran the betting games at the Wicked Goat until the owner found out how much of the winnings he was skimming." Not surprising, the Wicked Goat was a rough bar in a bad part of Castle Reach known for cheap liquor and poxy whores.

"Ernest was a longshoreman with a weakness for stealing from the cargo," Garrick added, nodding toward a large, dark-haired man with tattoos on his thick neck. "Carl and Jame were butchers who got caught stealing horses for meat." He looked over to a knot of men rolling dice. "Edger, Torr, and Bickel over there worked at the shipworks. Torr was a wagon driver, and the other two did some carpentry work, if I recall. No idea what got them sent here, but all it takes is pissing off the wrong person," he added.

"Coan and those five who toady after him were ruffians, members of the Red Blades gang," Verran supplied. "You don't need to remember their names; just remember that they're trouble."

"Then there'll be blood, because three of our group were Curs before they got sent here, and I know there are Badgers in some of the other barracks," Dawe said in a low tone. Castle Reach, the capital of Donderath, was home to a wide range of residents, from the well-appointed villas and comfortable homes of the merchants and sea captains at the top of the hill below Quillarth Castle's walls, down to the gritty harbor front and its cramped tenements. In the worst of the ginnels and closes where the desperate struggled to survive, gangs like the Curs, Red Blades, and Badgers fought for scarce resources and offered bare-knuckles protection. Old grudges and long-standing vendettas among the gangs were common.

"What about your group?" Blaine asked. "Other than Stefan and Piran."

"Piran and I were on the boat from Donderath together, about six months ago," Dawe said. "Nearly everyone's here for theft or brawling—or debt. Jakk, Roz, and Delf, the ones playing cards, were stable hands who got blamed when a couple of the horses got sick and died. Tadd got caught stealing coins from the shrine to Charrot," he added, indicating a balding, thin man with dark, close-set eyes. "Albert and Horace were sailors who got on the bad side of their captain. Bincy cheated the king's tax collector, One-Eye stole rabbits, Shorty tried to loot a guardsman's saddle-bags out behind a bar. Foss lost more than he could pay playing cards. Whinney sounds like a horse when he laughs. He stole a donkey and got caught when the damn thing refused to let him ride it." He grinned. "Got kicked in the nuts for his trouble, too."

Dawe shrugged. "Evan was a cook until someone got sick and blamed the food. Peters was a mean drunk, and Eddles didn't pay his taxes. That's everyone except Stefan, but he's a mean son of a bitch and his buddies are trouble."

"Do they move the barracks assignments around like they do the work crews?" Verran asked.

Dawe shook his head. "Nope. You're stuck with us until you earn your Ticket or drop dead—whichever comes first." He raised an eyebrow. "And don't take this the wrong way, but one of those is a lot more likely than the other."

DOWN IN THE MINES

BLAINE'S DREAMS WERE DARK. *HE WAS BACK AT GLENREITH, HIS family's manor. The night was dark, and the wind was cool. Blaine heard his boots crunch on the gravel path as the wind tugged at his cloak and hair. The old formal garden hadn't been properly tended for years, but the bones of its structure still remained: overgrown boxwood hedges that had once formed a neat maze and pathways that still wove in and out to make a complex pattern.*

The flowers were dry husks, and overhead in the trees, dead leaves rustled with the cold wind. But Blaine was listening for just one sound—footsteps, behind him and growing closer.

He picked up his pace, moving deeper into the garden. A broken statue stood beside a stagnant reflecting pool dark with algae and fallen leaves. Blaine pressed on, shivering as the wind made the hanging bells of a garden decoration shimmer and ring. This night, they sounded like a dirge.

The steps behind him were not far away. Ahead of him was the old garden gazebo where he had often taken shelter as a child and hidden from his father's tempers along with Carr and Mari.

Just as Blaine reached the shadows of the gazebo, the footsteps caught up to him. Strong arms seized him, spinning him around to face his attacker. The features were nearly obscured in darkness and fog, but Blaine knew his father's eyes and recognized the malice in them as a hand tightened around his throat.

Old reflexes took over. Blaine swung hard with his right hand, landing a solid blow to his attacker's chin. His left hand slammed palm-out against his father's face, breaking the nose and gouging at the eyes. The man's hand loosened its grip on Blaine's neck, and Blaine bucked and twisted, throwing his attacker off-balance and then tackling him and wrestling his assailant to the ground.

He woke in Velant's barracks on the floor, with his hand around Coan's throat. His blanket and cloak had been kicked clear in the struggle, and the rest of the men were awake. Verran and Garrick tried to pull Blaine off of Coan, while Dawe and Piran warned for the men to stay quiet and disperse.

"What in Raka is going on?" Piran demanded. "Do you want to get us all thrown in the Hole?"

"If I were you, mate, I'd ask what Coan is doing out of bed," Verran retorted. "No good reason for him to be over here, anywhere near Blaine."

"Well?" Piran demanded as they pulled the two combatants apart.

Somewhere in the tussle, Blaine had gained a split lip, but Coan had definitely taken the worst of the fight. Coan's nose was bloody and in worse shape than before, and a bruise on one cheek looked like it might blacken his eye. Moonlight streaming through the barracks window cast the room in shades of gray and deepened the shadows.

"He tried to throttle me while I was sleeping," Blaine said, glaring at Coan.

"He had it coming!" Coan protested. "I had to get back some of my pride."

Piran cocked an eyebrow and looked at Coan. "Looks like you got taught a lesson twice in one day," he observed. "Best keep to your own bunk, on your own side of the room," he warned.

Coan's glare let Blaine know the matter was far from settled. Garrick and Dunbar grabbed Coan and hauled him toward his assigned bunk, throwing him onto it for good measure. Blaine sat up, rubbed his bruised, bloodied knuckles and twisted his neck to work out newly sore muscles.

"Damn!" Verran muttered, careful to keep his voice down. "You've got good reflexes. I didn't hear anything."

"Yeah," Blaine replied. "Something I learned the hard way," he added, unwilling to mention that his skills had been gained fighting off his own father more times than he cared to recall.

"Might be best to have someone sit watch, at least for tonight," Garrick said when he returned. "I'll take the next candlemark, and rouse someone else after that. We'll all take turns for the next couple of nights until things settle down."

Blaine nodded and rubbed his neck where Coan had gripped hard enough to bruise. "Yeah. Count me in—tomorrow night." Wearily, he climbed back into his bunk, but he did not expect to sleep well, maybe not for the duration of his time in Velant.

———

Despite the uncertainty of his new surroundings and valid worries about being knifed in his sleep, Blaine woke with a start a few candlemarks later to the banging of a drum. It was still dark outside, but then again he reminded himself, it would be dark for months. Dark, cold, and far from home.

"Move it! Move it! There's work to be done, you malingering dogs!" The guards at Velant appeared to be chosen for their sheer size, surly disposition, and lung capacity. Blaine and the others stumbled from their bunks, pulling on their boots and grabbing their cloaks as they ran to comply.

"Half of you are going to the mines," Captain Jumon shouted above the wind. "The other half will go to the farm." He slashed with his arm to denote where to cut the group of assembled prisoners. "Make it easy on yourselves. Don't give my men any reason to make an example of you."

Blaine was in the group chosen for the mines. He looked around to see who else was with him. Verran and Dawe were in the farm group. *Probably just as well,* he thought and wondered if Dawe's smithy skills might keep him out of the mines for good. Piran was in Blaine's group, as were Garrick, Dunbar, Torr, and Ernest—and Coan. Fortunately, half of Coan's group of toadies were assigned to the farm, but in exchange, Blaine noticed that several of Stefan's hangers-on were assigned to the mines. That made the odds of an "accident" in a dangerous place higher than they already were.

They trudged a mile through the cold to get to the mine entrance. It was outside the main fortifications of Velant, but a wooden stockade had been erected on either side of the wide road, just in case any of the reluctant miners got ideas of escape. *At least the fence blocks the wind.*

"Hold up!" Chester, the mine foreman, shouted as they neared the entrance. "Here's where you get your chains—and your breakfast. Line up!"

"What's going on?" Blaine muttered to Piran, just loudly for him to hear.

"They chain us together by the ankles," Piran replied. "Once

we're down in the mine, some poor sap comes around with food
and water twice a day—you can pretend it's breakfast and lunch.
We have dinner back in the barracks."

"Rowse! Shut up. I'm not telling you again!" Chester yelled,
and Piran grinned. This was apparently a long-standing source of
consternation.

Blaine took a deep breath to quell his anger as one of the
soldiers clamped a leg iron around one ankle. Several feet of
heavy chain connected him to Piran, and an equal length of chain
connected Piran to Ernest.

"You three—down below," the soldier said, pointing to
Blaine and then to the tunnel mouth. Other soldiers shouted
orders to different groups of men. A wide area outside the mine
mouth was filled with dozens of heaps of rock. Soldiers handed
out pickaxes to the men assigned to the rock heaps, separating
the rubies from the rock to make for a more compact load on the
ships back to Donderath.

"Don't worry; you'll get your turn there, too," Piran
muttered. "We all do. Can't say that one's better or worse than
the other—they're both miserable."

The men on the rock piles stayed above ground, where the air
was likely better, and they were spared the claustrophobia of
going below. But Blaine had used a pickax back on his family's
lands, and he knew that wielding one took strength and stamina.
Going into the mine was likely to require just as much effort in a
smaller space. The miners would be out of the wind and perhaps
warmer, but the air in the cramped tunnels was likely to be foul
with sweat and smoke. *This is Velant,* he reminded himself.
There are no good choices here, only worse ones.

Blaine was the tallest, which meant he had to duck as he
entered the mine entrance. Piran moved with a halt-and-go gait
that told Blaine his new barracks-mate was no stranger to the
mines. Ernest was brawny and wide-shouldered, and he cursed

under his breath as he tried to fit his broad frame through the hewn passageways.

Lanterns hung at intervals from pegs sunk into the rock, lighting their way and darkening the top of the tunnel with greasy smoke. Blaine hunched, trying to keep from breathing the fumes.

"That's the good thing about being short, like me," Piran quipped. "Air's better down here." Though he only stood a head shorter than Blaine, his comment was likely true, Blaine thought resignedly.

"Don't know how they can get mules in and out of here, let along men," Ernest muttered.

"They don't bother with mules down in the mine," Piran replied. "They've got us. The only mules are topside, to take the wagonloads of ore to the ships."

As they wound through the maze of tunnels, the ceiling grew lower. Moisture condensed on the rock overhead, dripping into their hair and sending rivulets of cold water down their backs. Later, that might feel good once they worked up a sweat, but now it made Blaine shiver.

The lanterns were barely enough to light the way, and the rocky path made it easy to stumble. Finally the tunnel opened into a larger room deep beneath the surface of Edgeland. A huge area had been carved from the rock, leaving stone pillars as large as a man in places to hold up the ceiling. Pickaxes awaited them, and the experienced prisoners shambled off toward their stations and began to dig at the rock walls.

"Over here," Piran said with a jerk of his head. They let Piran lead the best they could, trying not to trip over each other or their chains. The fetters were just long enough to allow them to station themselves about arms-length distance apart but made it necessary for Blaine and Ernest to shorten their stride so as not to jerk Piran long with them or bring themselves up short.

"Why here?" Blaine whispered as Piran led them to an out-of-the-way corner.

Piran looked to one side and then the other before replying in a tone so low they could barely hear him. "Air's a little better, and there's a vein of rubies that's just been tapped, so we'll have more to show at the end of the day. Trust me, it matters."

Boot steps alerted them to a guard coming up behind them, and Piran hoisted his ax and shouldered into the work. They fell silent until the guard had made his rounds.

"Watch and learn," Piran said. "Do what I do."

Blaine hefted his ax and mirrored Piran's stance. "Swing with your hips, not your back, or you won't be moving tomorrow," Piran advised. "Take it out in little hunks. Less work for you, less work for the blokes up above, and it all weighs the same in the end." He flexed his hands. "And I'd advise bartering for some leather gloves when you can," he added. "Keeps the ax handle from ripping the skin off your hands."

With that, Piran turned to his work and began to whistle a tavern tune Blaine vaguely recalled, popular for its catchy melody and its bawdy lyrics.

"Rowse! Stop yer whistlin' or I'll knock out your teeth!" Coan yelled. Other prisoners shouted Coan down.

"Do another one, Piran!"

"Can you whistle *The Hand of a Lady*?" someone else called out.

"How about *Sailor's Lament*?" For the next few minutes, one miner after another yelled out requests, while Coan turned back to his work in a huff as his companions, Vogo and Rall, argued him out of making good on his threat. To Blaine's amusement, Stefan also looked seriously annoyed.

Piran did his best to accommodate, switching frequently among songs from a well-known dance melody to a dock-yards work song, and then back to a ditty that was a favorite of tavern minstrels for its many verses, each more creatively obscene than the last.

"Not bad, Rowse!" another prisoner yelled. "Mostly on tune today."

"Thank the gods he isn't singing," someone else put in, which got a hearty enough round of chuckles that Piran's ears reddened, but he kept on whistling.

Deep in the mine, there was no way to tell how much time had passed, or whether it was morning or afternoon. The air grew stifling with the exertion of dozens of men, and the cavern stank of sweat and unwashed bodies. Blaine found himself growing light-headed with the work, even though he tried to pace himself by matching Piran's rhythm.

Finally, two men came around, one with a bucket of water and a dipper, and the other with a basket of food. The men moved slowly from one grouping of prisoners to another. More than once, heated words were exchanged but too quietly for Blaine to catch what was being said. Finally, the two reached Blaine's group.

One of the men was just taller than Piran, and even more muscular. He had a head of graying brown hair tied back in a queue and squinted as if the dim light did not suit him. On his left was a thin, hunched man whose gestures reminded Blaine of the rats in Castle Reach. "Got some nice cold water for ya—and some buns and sausage for breakfast," the big man said.

"But you've got pay for it," the rat-man added with a sly twitch of his mouth, not quite a smile, less than a leer.

"Bugger off, Welton. You too, Tanner," Piran snapped. "The guards sent you down here with that food. It's not yours to sell."

Tanner, the big man, gave a nasty grin. "You know better, Rowse. The guards don't care what happens to it, once we're out of their sight."

"They'll care plenty when men can't finish their shift for

hunger when you were supposed to be feeding them," Piran returned, letting his voice rise enough to carry.

Welton, the rat-faced man, made a gesture for silence. "Don't cause trouble, Rowse. You know how it works. Pay us in coin or pay us in food." He leered at Blaine and Ernest. "These your new friends? You don't want trouble, Rowse. Just pay up."

"This is their first day," Piran snapped. "What do you expect them to pay with? They haven't been here long enough to earn any coin."

Tanner chuckled, a ghastly, wheezing noise. "Then I guess they pay with half their rations, like everyone else, unless you want to cover their share and yours too."

Blaine kept his face neutral, though his stomach growled. He had no idea how prisoners earned coin, and what manner of coin they earned, but he had nothing in his pockets of value except for the knife Verran had stolen the night before.

Piran cursed creatively. "All right, just this once," he muttered. He dug into a pouch on a leather strap beneath his shirt and pulled out a coin. "Here," he said, holding it up in the faint light. "Enough to cover our food today—breakfast and lunch."

Tanner elbowed Welton, who reached for the coin, but Piran snatched it back. "Oh no," Piran said. "Not until we've got our food."

Welton grumbled, and his eyes narrowed in a glare. Tanner elbowed him again, and Welton dipped out water for the three men and shoved three meat pasties into their hands. "Here, pox take you. Now give me the coin!"

Piran flipped the coin so that Welton had to grab for it, nearly taking himself and Tanner off balance as Welton dove to catch the coin and his chain dragged Tanner with him. Welton pocketed the coin and muttered to Tanner, and they shuffled off toward the next marks.

"I'll pay you back," Blaine said, wary of Piran's generosity and of being indebted to anyone at Velant, but too hungry to argue.

Piran shook his head. "Don't mention it."

"Thank you," Ernest said, taking a bite of the meat pie.

Piran looked both ways and dropped his voice. "No, seriously. Don't mention it. That coin was counterfeit."

Blaine ate his food quickly before Tanner and Welton had a chance to come back for it. When they were back to working on the rock ahead of them, he looked over to Piran. "If the food is from the prison, how do they get away with selling it?"

Piran let his ax rise and fall. "Tanner pays a percentage to the guards. The piggy-faced one keeps a tally book."

"And Prokief lets them get away with it?" Ernest asked in a whisper.

Piran shrugged. "For all I know, the guards give Prokief a percentage. That's how things work here."

"How do prisoners earn coin?" Blaine asked, taking a chunk out of the wall.

"Usually for jobs no one wants, like digging latrines or burying the dead," Piran replied, and this time, his swing bit into the wall a bit deeper. "Even prisoners have their limits, and Prokief must have figured paying out a few coins was cheaper than putting down riots." He shot Blaine a sidelong glance. "Oh, and Prokief's snitches get paid, too."

"Spies?"

Piran nodded. "You'll figure out who's who soon enough. No use killing them, because someone else will just take the job. Easier to tell them what they want to hear and be on your merry way."

Blaine kept an eye on Welton and Tanner as they made their way around the room. Most of the new prisoners had no choice but to give up part of their meal, which the two thieves then re-sold for extra coin. When Tanner and Welton had finished their rounds, they reported back to one of the lieutenants, a pig-eyed, pock-faced man with one ear.

"That's him," Piran said, following Blaine's gaze. "He's the one they report to." And as Blaine watched, Pig-face accepted a bundle from Tanner and marked something on a bit of parchment in a pouch on his belt. "He's mean as a stuck pig and just about as dumb."

Late in the afternoon, a messenger arrived for Pig-face. He passed along a piece of parchment sealed with wax, which Pig-face accepted gravely.

"That can't be good," Piran said under his breath, with a glance toward the overseer, who was carefully reading the parchment. "Orders from Prokief never turn out well. Wish I knew what that said."

"Trouble?" Ernest asked.

Piran nodded. "Usually, men get reassigned because there's another crew that's short workers. You think the mines are bad, but there are worse duties."

"We've got enough pickpockets around," Blaine said. "Have someone lift the paper, read it, and put it back. Then we'll know."

Piran gave him a look. "Stealing the paper isn't the hard part. Reading it is. Most of the men in here can't sign their names." He paused. "I can read, but I can't distract Pig-face and read the paper on the sly at the same time."

"I can read," Blaine said, driven by an intuition that the message was important. "Get me the paper, I'll read it, and tell you what it says after the thief returns it."

Piran eyed him as if debating the plan. *He's probably trying to figure why someone who can read ended up here,* Blaine thought. *Then again, there've got to be other people here, like Dawe, who could read and figure sums enough to run a business.* He had already decided to leave his old life behind him, one of the reasons he introduced himself as "Mick" and said little about the circumstances of his exile. *If you wanted to seem like just another convict, you've blown your chance.* But deep down, he had the sense that finding out what the message said was urgent.

"All right," Piran said. "Let me work this out. Just be ready for it when it comes, and you'd better figure out how to get a look at what it says without anyone seeing you, or we'll all be headed to Raka before nightfall."

Over the next few candlemarks, Blaine followed Piran's lead, intrigued that Piran and the other prisoners seemed to have a silent language of subtle hand signals to convey messages. As Blaine and his two shackle-mates trundled over to the main heap with their cart, Bickle, Torr, and Dunbar joined them a few moments later.

Piran bent over to unload the rocks, which put him very near Bickle's ear as Bickle did the same. "Get the paper to Blaine," Piran murmured. "Tell Shorty he's got to put it back again so no one notices."

Bickle gave a barely perceptible nod and moved away as if nothing had happened. Piran glanced at Blaine and raised an eyebrow, with a quirk to his lips that showed he was enjoying the game.

Blaine concentrated on his work, afraid he might give the whole thing away if he glanced too often toward Pig-face. About a candlemark after Piran alerted Bickle, Blaine heard Dunbar shout for the overseer.

"Have a look at this," Dunbar yelled. "I think we've got some green stones in with the rubies."

Everyone turned to look at him, and Pig-face hustled over. "Where?" he demanded.

"In that pile—the last few chucks I pulled out," Dunbar said. "Over there."

Pig-face followed Dunbar and his shackle-mates to the pile.

Bickle and Torr crowded so closely behind Pig-face that they
nearly knocked the overseer onto the rock pile. "Get back, you
idiots," Pig-face ordered. Dutifully, Bickle and Torr backed away
as far as their chains would permit.

"I don't see any green stones," Pig-face said, glaring at
Dunbar.

"Right there," Dunbar insisted. "Can't you see them?"

Pig-face picked up a chunk of rock and held it closer to the
nearest lantern. "I see red," he replied, irritation in his voice.
"Not green. Not blue. Red. Like rubies—and damn few of
them."

Dunbar shrugged and rubbed his eyes. "Maybe it's the light. I
could have sworn I saw green. They'd be mighty valuable if they
were green, wouldn't they?"

"They're not green," Pig-face snapped. "Now get back to
work, the lot of you, or the red you'll see will be blood. Your
blood." With that, he stomped off to his usual post.

Once again, Piran, Blaine, and Ernest shuffled over to the
main pile with their load of rocks. Bickle, Torr, and Dunbar
brought a new load up just as Piran turned to leave.

"Hey, watch it!" Piran complained as Bickle bumped him.

"Sorry, mate. Tripped on the chain," Bickle said with a
hapless shrug. Piran gave him a glare and then turned back to
their spot along the wall.

"Be quick," he muttered under his breath to Blaine. "No
telling when the overseer might notice it's missing."

"I've got to take a piss," Blaine said, loudly enough he
figured Pig-face would hear. A trench along the wall that had
already been mined-out served as a latrine, adding to the stink of
sweat and dirty bodies. Being shackled to two other men yielded
the unfortunate consequence that everyone had to go along when
one person needed relief. Taking a leak was one of the few times
neither Pig-face nor anyone else was likely to be watching too

closely. Blaine positioned himself facing the wall, while Piran and Ernest turned around, facing out. The light was bad and the position awkward, but Blaine managed to read the paper by the dim light and relieve himself for veracity's sake. When he turned back toward the others, the paper was hidden once more.

Pig-face glared at them, silently hurrying them back to work. Blaine ducked his head, hoping he looked duly chastened. When they returned to their place, Piran sank his ax into the wall with a mighty crack, and a large chunk of rock came loose.

"Whoo-ee! Look at that!" Piran crowed. "Don't know my own strength! And ain't those rubies pretty!"

"Break that thing up and get it to the center pile before the last load goes up," Pig-face ordered. Piran shot Blaine a conspiratorial wink, and then he brought his ax down several more times until the big chunk was a more manageable heap of stones. Together, they trundled their load to the central collection point just as Shorty, Albert, and Tadd were about to head back. Blaine palmed the parchment and barely brushed against Shorty, who took it before Blaine realized it was gone.

Shorty's group had barely made it back to their place before Tadd groaned and clutched his chest. He gave a deep, hacking cough, and drew his breath in with a painful wheeze. "You'd better take a look at him!" Albert urged.

Pig-face's expression made it clear that Tadd was welcome to die so long as he did it quietly, but he headed over. Tadd was red-faced, gasping for breath, and his eyes bulged alarmingly.

"What's wrong with him?" Pig-face demanded.

Tadd gestured, but the hand motions were impossible to decipher. They were, however, interesting enough to distract Pig-face as Shorty brushed against him, returning the parchment. Tadd gave another wheezing inhale. Albert moved around behind him and brought both his fists down hard between Tadd's shoulder blades. Tadd let out a belch that echoed in the close confines of the rock cavern, and collapsed onto his hands and knees, breathing normally once more.

"Swallowed wrong," he managed, looking convincingly like a man who had nearly choked to death. "I'll be all right."

Pig-face glared at him. "Get back to work," he snapped. "Best you all make up for the time you spent standing around gaping."

For a few candlemarks, the mine room was quiet save for the steady clink of pickaxes against rock. Coan's trio of miners were closest to the rock pile in the center of the room, which meant Blaine had to cross their path with every load. So far, Coan had ignored them. But as Blaine, Piran, and Ernest ferried their biggest batch of rocks to the main pile in metal scuttles. Coan wheeled just as Blaine neared, swinging his ax with lethal force right at Blaine's head.

Blaine managed to raise his own ax quickly enough to deflect the deadly strike, though barely in time. Piran swung his full scuttle at Coan's face, forcing Coan to dodge. Ernest swung his bucket lower, catching Coan right between the legs. The big man went down with a groan. Vogo and Rall, the other two men in Coan's triad, moved forward to fight. Before they could move far, Shorty, Albert, and Tadd closed in.

The point of Shorty's pick rested threateningly against the base of Vogo's neck, while Tadd's ax was between Rall's shoulder blades. "Think twice," Piran said. "Accidents happen."

Vogo leveled a murderous look at Piran. Tadd's lip curled, but he said nothing. The sound of footsteps in the tunnel and the possibility of Pig-face walking in on the situation ended the confrontation. Vogo helped Coan to his feet as Blaine, Piran, and Ernest backed away.

"This isn't over," Coan growled.

"It is for now," Blaine replied.

Shorty's group edged closer to where Coan and his shackle

mates worked, making it unmistakable that Coan and his friends were being watched. For the rest of the shift, Shorty, Albert, and Tadd paused to monitor Coan every time Blaine and his group brought another load to the pile, and Blaine's trio did the same to protect Shorty and the others.

A few candlemarks later, Welton and Tanner showed up with dinner rations. Piran had covered both rounds with his coin, and he reminded the pair loudly of the fact. But as Welton and Tanner made their way down the line, some of the newcomers were not so lucky.

"I just got off the damn ship," one of the miners protested. "How in Torven's name am I supposed to have coin?"

Welton shrugged. "Not my problem. You can still eat—half rations."

"You son of a bitch." Tired, hungry and already on edge from everything that had gone before, the new miner swung his fist at Welton. Welton dodged, and Tanner struck back with what looked like a metal weight inside a cloth sling. Tanner's sap hit the miner, and the man went down. Welton pulled a knife as Pig-face's guards streamed into the room.

"Keep away," Welton warned the others. The guards took in the situation and stood back, doing nothing as Tanner kicked the downed miner hard in the side with his boot, then caught him again in the face, breaking the man's nose. The guards remained silent and motionless, but the message was clear that any who might move to help would receive no support and would be open to the same abuse.

Finally, when the miner lay motionless in a pool of blood, Tanner stepped back, breathing hard. Blood spattered his shirt and his shoes, reddening his fists and arms. "Better get him up before the Overseer spots him," Welton gloated. "All we have to do is say you were in on it," he said with a smug grin, "and the

Overseer will have the guards beat the shit out of you, just because."

The bloodied miner was barely conscious as his shackle mates got him on his feet, putting him with a shoulder to the mine wall so he could remain standing. The guards ushered Welton and Tanner out. Once they were gone, many of the others traded low whispers. Piran had grown dangerously quiet. It only took Blaine one glance at the ice in Piran's gaze to know that they were both thinking of revenge.

———

By the time Blaine and the others finally trudged back to the surface at the end of what he guessed was at least twelve candle-marks, it was still dark. Even darker, if possible, than when they went underground.

"How do you like the Long Dark?" Piran asked as the guards removed their leg irons and the exhausted men lined up to return to their barracks. His tone was affable, though his eyes had not lost the hardened glint that Blaine knew meant Piran had not forgotten the altercation in the mine.

"It'll take some getting used to," Ernest admitted.

"I don't think I'll ever get used to it," Piran replied. "One more damnable thing about this place."

When they reached the barracks, the line had already formed for dinner. Blaine found that he no longer cared whether it was the same meager stew and hard bread they had the night before so long as it was warm and not too awful to keep down.

Verran and Dawe joined them at one of the tables. "I guess you made it out in one piece," Verran said. Even his energy seemed to be flagging. "I've seen enough of livestock and their shit to last me for the rest of my life," he complained. Blaine sniffed the air and realized both men carried a definite smell of the stables with them.

"Go on, mock us," Dawe said, noticing Blaine's reaction. "We mucked out stables, and cow barns, and goat sheds, and chicken coops...if it shits, we shoveled it," he added. "And tomorrow we get to shoe the horses and mules, which are positively murderous because the guards aren't gentle with them. So if I don't come back, it's because some godsdamned mule put an iron shoe through my forehead."

Blaine took another look at Verran and Dawe. Both men sported new bruises on their faces and held themselves as if they had been injured. "Have a run-in with one of those mules?" he asked.

Verran said nothing, focusing his attention on his food. Dawe grimaced. "Stefan had friends out in the barn. They jumped Verran and got him pretty good before a couple of us waded in to chase them off. Made it pretty clear they would be back for more."

"Sounds like the mines," Blaine added, his tone grim. He glanced around to assure himself that Coan and his buddies were out of earshot before filling them in. "Looks like this is going to be a problem."

Piran bent forward as if tucking into his food. "What did the note say?" he asked so quietly that Blaine barely made out his words.

"Prokief needs more men to hunt wolves and bear," Blaine recounted, with one hand in front of his mouth as he added a cough. "Six more, as soon as the quota is filled for the week."

"Damn," Piran said. "That's bad. Practically a death sentence to go out on the ice like that."

"How will he choose?" Blaine asked.

"Probably whoever he dislikes most at the moment. Could be

any of us." A dangerous gleam came into Piran's eyes. "Unless we give him a nudge in the right direction."

"You have an idea?"

"I'm working on it."

Their friends had increased the volume of their conversation to cover for them, trusting that Blaine and Piran would share their secret in good time. Then Blaine and Ernest recounted their experience in the mines, while Piran shoveled his dinner and looked about in the unlikely case others had not finished their portions. Verran's head came up when Blaine recounted the food extortionists.

"Wait, did you say Tanner?" Verran said. "Big guy, squints a lot, never leaves himself open on his left side?"

Piran leaned forward, looking around to make sure no one else was listening. "Yeah. That's him. Why?"

Verran grinned. "I know Tanner. And I know why he guards his left like that. Can't see worth a damn out of that eye. I should know. I nearly put it out for him."

A slow smile spread across Piran's face. "Gentlemen," he said in a whisper, "I think I have an answer to our problem."

5

BRIBES AND PAYBACKS

"MOVE OVER. THIS IS OUR AREA NOW." COAN GAVE DUNBAR A shove, nearly causing the tall, skinny man to tumble over the pile of rocks he and his two shackle-mates had mined.

"How do you figure?" Dunbar replied, coming back from the shove with a push of his own, his temper rising. "We've been here for the last three days. Go back to your own spot."

Torr and Bickel were chained to Dunbar's left. Each of them outweighed Dunbar by double, and Blaine suspected that they were doing more than their share to mine enough each day to meet quota. Both men stood beside Dunbar, looking ready for a fight.

"I say this is my spot now," Coan repeated, backed up by two equally large men who pushed Torr and Bickel out of the way.

"That's enough!" Pig-face, the overseer strode over. He glanced at the pile of rocks and saw several chunks glittering red with rubies. "Looks like we've got a good vein. You three, get to it," he said, pointing to Coan and his allies. "And you three— take over where they were," he said with a jerk of his head to indicate that Dunbar, Torr, and Bickel should exchange sections with Coan's team. Coan gave them a nasty smile of triumph as they grumbled and went their way.

That's one move in our favor, Blaine thought, suppressing a smile. Coan would find out soon enough that Piran and the others had spiked the rock pile with extra rubies, knowing the possibility of a rich strike—and the potential for a reward from Prokief—would be more temptation than Coan could withstand.

Half-way across the large mining room, Tadd, Albert, and Shorty dug away at a section of wall near where Stefan and two other men were working. Since the fight in the barracks three nights ago when Blaine and the others first arrived, Stefan and Coan had gone out of their way to cause just enough problems for the others to make everyone miserable without actually getting themselves in trouble.

"Hey!" Tadd said, turning on Stefan and his two partners. "Quit taking our rocks! We mined those, you lazy ass!"

For an instant, Stefan looked dumbstruck, but his quick temper got the best of him. "What in Raka are you talking about? Rocks are rocks." He made an obscene gesture, and his shackle-mates added equally rough comments.

"By Torven's horns! You've been kicking our rocks over to your pile so you get more credit for the day's work," Tadd accused. "We're taking them back!" Albert and Shorty walked the length of their chain and began helping themselves to rocks from the pile nearest Stefan.

"Give those back!" Stefan shouted, fists balled, and started toward Tadd before he remembered his chains, which brought him up short.

"We mined them; they belong in our pile!" Tadd retorted, standing his ground.

Pig-face waded into the fray, brows furrowed. "That's enough!" He rounded on Stefan, who had already raised the overseer's ire once that day by being too slow to begin his work.

Pig-face eyed Stefan, then the pile of rocks, and the smaller pile where Tadd and his fellows worked.

"Since when have you ever mined more than them, Stefan?" Pig-face asked.

Stefan took a step back. "We had a good day," he replied, sulking. "Ain't no crime in that, is there?"

Pig-face's expression made it clear how unlikely he thought it was that Stefan and his mates had increased their production. "You want their rock pile? Then take the whole thing—and their spot with it. Switch places, and no more out of either of you or there'll be a whipping!"

Pig-face glowered at the two chained teams as they switched places. Albert's foot caught on a rock and he stumbled into Stefan, pushing him into Pig-face.

"Watch where you're going, you big ox!" Stefan growled.

Pig-face gave Stefan a push, knocking him back into Albert, who managed to angle his body so his shoulder caught Stefan in the face. Stefan gave a feral cry and grabbed for Albert, but Pig-face hauled him back.

"That's enough," he snapped with a warning glare at both men. Tadd exchanged a glance with Piran as the miners resumed their work. Piran gave a nod to Blaine. *Everyone's in place,* Blaine thought.

It had taken three days for Blaine, Piran, Verran, and the others to work out their plan. Secrecy was difficult in the crowded barracks and trying to keep plans hidden from Stefan and Coan and their toadies made it doubly hard. Blaine forced himself to keep his attention on the stretch of rock wall he was digging. *Maybe prison isn't as different from court as I imagined,* Blaine thought. *Both are consumed by petty jealousies and small grievances that become the reason for revenge.*

Tanner and Welton made their rounds as they did each day. Piran alternated paying them with real coins and counterfeit to make his deception more difficult to spot. Most of the newcomers and some of the old hands paid half their rations for the privilege of eating. The two extortionists had no problem finding willing buyers for the extra food among the miners, prisoners who always seemed to have a few coins on them. Most of them were spies, Piran had told Blaine. Some volunteered for extra duties, hoping to send money back to relatives in Donderath, but the likelihood of anything actually reaching its intended destination was slim. By the end of the morning rounds, Tanner and Welton had collected a fat bag of coins.

All the better, Blaine thought, as they waited for the right time to spring their trap.

They worked steadily through the rest of the shift, biding their time until Tanner and Welton came around for lunch. The arguments of the morning had been staged to maneuver participants into position or move problem people out of key locations.

"Time for lunch!" Tanner boomed, his voice too loud for the confines of the underground room.

"Rowse. McFadden. Colling. Pay up—one way or the other," Welton looked like he enjoyed his job extorting money far too much.

"Here—but it's the last time I've got coin this week," Piran said, making a show of paying for food with a real coin.

Welton looked disappointed, as if he was looking forward to taking half of Piran's lunch just for fun. Piran groused and rumbled but dutifully handed over his payment.

"You're getting soft, Rowse," Welton gloated. "Ain't like you not to put up a fight."

"Take your money and get out of my sight," Piran said, eyeing Welton and Tanner with loathing.

Welton moved to leave. He guarded Tanner's blind left side. Ernest tripped Welton, which threw Tanner off balance and into

Blaine, who managed to stagger from the collision in such a way as to come down hard on Welton's knee.

"Yow!" Welton shrieked. "Get off my knee, you oaf!"

"Sorry, sorry," Blaine apologized, hoping he looked sincere. He had intentionally not hit with his full weight so that Welton's knee was sore but not broken. Welton's limp put him a step behind his boss, leaving Tanner's blind side open.

Welton hobbled behind Tanner as they moved on to the next group, the last of the convicts to get their meal. Normally, that would have been Coan and his crew, but thanks to the change, Torr, Bickle, and Dunbar were in that spot.

"You're a bloody louse, that's what you are," Torr ranted when Tanner demanded payment. "You're a tick on a mangy dog."

"Do you want to eat or not?" Welton demanded. "Pay your coin or split your food. We ain't got all day."

Torr sprang toward Welton, fists flying. Bickle moved to pull Tanner back, as Dunbar bumped against Tanner nearly hard enough to knock the big man over.

"Sorry, mate," Dunbar mumbled, trying to keep Tanner from falling over. He gave the big man a gratuitous pat on the chest in goodwill as Tanner growled and rumbled like an angry bear, pushing Dunbar away.

"Get away from me," Tanner snarled, striding off so quickly that he nearly dragged Welton with him.

Coan and his crew had stopped to watch the scuffle. "See, that's what I mean," Dunbar said, loudly enough for those around him to hear. "Coan wouldn't know hard work if it hit him on the head. Look at him slacking! That proves he stole our rocks!"

"You lying son of a whore!" Coan roared and launched himself at Dunbar.

"Your mother was a clap-eaten poxy trollop," Dunbar

returned, as Torr and Bickle stepped up, helping Dunbar have the space in his chain to block Coan with his shoulder without being dragged off balance.

Torr wrestled Coan backward, fighting off interference from his two partners, while Bickle tackled Coan from the front. The six men went down in a pile of flying fists, clanking chains and kicking feet.

Tadd, Albert, and Shorty were carting scuttles of rocks toward wheelbarrows near the room's entrance as Pig-face noticed the fight.

"Break it up!" Pig-face shouted. The convicts had moved away from their stations to watch the fight, and Pig-face had to move around Tadd's men in order to get close enough to do anything about the fight with Coan.

Pig-face tripped over Tadd and stumbled, flailing to keep his balance. Albert ducked out of the way, dragging Tadd with him, compounding the problem. Shorty grabbed at Pig-face in an effort not to fall. The four men ended up tangled together atop the wheelbarrow. Pig-face righted himself first, adjusting his uniform.

"Get out of my way!" he stormed, red in the face at the indignity of the collision. Shorty, Tadd, and Albert ducked their heads in obeisance and backed away. In the process, Shorty backed right into Stefan, barely avoiding knocking him over although they staggered, leaning on each other for support.

"Sorry, mate!" Shorty apologized. Stefan looked angry enough to throw a punch, but his friends pulled him back, arguing for a cool head now that Pig-face had waded into the fray.

Just then, Tanner felt down his shirt front with both hands. "My coins are gone!"

"Where did you put them, you big oaf?" Welton snapped. "That's a full day's work gone missing!"

Tanner searched his pockets and his person frantically. "It's gone! My coin pouch is gone! Someone stole it!"

Pig-face had managed to break up the fight between Coan's triad and Dunbar's group. The six men stood a few feet away from each other, bloodied and brooding, with dark glares that made it clear the fight would continue in the barracks that night. It looked as if Pig-face had taken a fist to the cheek at some point in the altercation, since one side of his face was red and swollen.

"Look again, Tanner," Pig-face said. "Are you sure it didn't fall on the ground?"

Tanner and Welton looked around themselves frantic to find the coin purse. "It's gone," Tanner moaned. "I've been robbed!"

An odd look came over Pig-face as he slipped a hand beneath his own jacket. "I'm missing something as well," he snapped. "We have thieves among us!"

"Imagine that," Piran remarked. Pig-face gave him a killing glare.

"Turn out your pockets, all of you!" Pig-face ordered.

The miners grumbled, but each in turn emptied their pockets. "Hey, he's got my coins!" Tanner roared as Coan reached into his pocket to withdraw two small pouches.

Coan stared at the coin bags in disbelief. "I don't know how they got in my pocket," he said, shaking his head.

"Two bags of coins?" Pig-face noted. His tone had gone flat and hard. Blaine took his meaning immediately. Welton and Tanner had been holding out on Pig-face.

"I report the whole amount, honest!" Tanner yelped, eyes wide with fear. "Just didn't have one bag big enough."

Pig-face was counting out the coins from both bags. He swore under his breath. "That's twice what you reported yesterday," he grated.

"It was a good day," Welton protested. Pig-face's expression made it clear he was not convinced.

"I know how the bags got there!" Tanner growled. "His thieving hands put it there! You misbegotten thief!" Tanner hurled himself at Coan, arms outstretched, meaty hands grasping. Welton was hauled along for the ride, squealing in protest as the chain dragged him smack into the middle of a fight between men more than twice his size.

Before Pig-face could move to break up the fight, he saw Stefan make a clumsy attempt to hide something. "Show me what's in your hand," Pig-face demanded.

"Nothing but trash," Stefan retorted, but beneath the insolence, he sounded scared.

"Show me!" Pig-face bellowed.

Reluctantly, Stefan held out a worn piece of parchment with markings on it. "That's mine!" Pig-face snatched the paper from Stefan and grabbed him by the collar, lifting Stefan off the ground. "How did you get this?" He gave Stefan a vicious shake. "You stole it from me! Confess!"

"I didn't take nothing," Stefan protested. Pig-face gave him another shake, hard enough to rattle his teeth. "Liar! This was inside my jacket. Now it's in your pocket. Explain that!"

"I don't know how it got there," Stefan argued. "I didn't take it."

The overseer had grown red in the face. "I don't believe you," he snarled. "And by the gods, I'm sending you and your thieving mates out on the wolf hunt for the rest of the month." He turned to where Coan and his two partners were being dragged back from Tanner and Welton, who were bruised and bloody. "You as well," Pig-face snapped, glaring at Coan's group and then at Welton and Tanner. "If you've got the energy to fight, you can fight wolves and bears."

With that, Pig-face waved over two more guards, who forced Tanner, Welton, Coan's group, and Stefan's triad out of the mine chamber and up the tunnel toward the surface. Through it all,

Piran had carefully kept his attention on the stretch of wall he was mining, as did Blaine and the others. After a few shouts from the guards, who by now were surlier than usual, the other miners returned to work as well.

A few of the miners gave sidelong glances in Piran's direction, and Blaine heard murmurs as the prisoners speculated on the day's events. Blaine kept his head down and avoided eye contact with anyone, but he felt himself sweating harder than usual, and his heart pounded. His mind raced, imagining scenarios in which their plot was discovered and ruthlessly punished.

At court, the politics were just as deadly, he reminded himself, *it just came wrapped in a prettier package. Losing favor with the king might mean not being invited to parties—or being sent to exile. Political enemies have managed to be the death of many a courtier, either indirectly, with a few words to the right ears to reduce a man to starvation, or straightforwardly, with poison or an assassin. Why am I so surprised?*

Piran took up whistling again. Blaine glanced at his co-conspirators, but none of them appeared to have concerns beyond making their quota of rocks for the day. Blaine hoped his expression did not betray him.

Many a man has had to swallow his pride and bend his knee to a tyrant—not much different from the way Prokief's set himself up to rule this little ice realm. And we're the court, maneuvering for advantage, competing for favors—and slipping a shiv in someone's back to clear a path for advancement. I never liked court, but I understand it. So I guess I understand Velant better than I expected.

No one spoke until the miners finished up their shift and shuffled toward the cold, fresh air aboveground. Once they had been freed of their shackles, the men headed toward the barracks in small groups. Bits of conversation drifted across the still air.

"…Coan had it coming. Got what he deserved."

"…never liked Stefan. Probably won't make it long against the wolves. Good riddance."

"…why he'd be stupid enough to steal from the overseer…"

"…Tanner's a greedy son of a bitch. Welton's just as bad."

Piran clapped a hand on Blaine's shoulder. "Nice work, Mick."

Blaine shrugged. "Just glad that today it was us and not them."

Piran nodded. "That's the way it goes up here. You caught on quickly." He punched Blaine in the shoulder. "I think you're going to do just fine here."

ICE BOUND

1

BELOW

"STOP WASTING TIME! WE'VE GOT RUBIES TO DIG, AND I WANT to see that new vein dug now!" The prison guard assigned to overseeing the miners brought a whip down hard across the back of the nearest man. Shackled at the ankle to two other inmates, the unfortunate miner could barely shift his position to escape the blow.

"It's going to bring the roof down on us!" Piran Rowse shouted back stubbornly.

"Just an excuse not to do your job." The overseer's broad features and snub nose had earned him the nickname of Pig-face among the inmates. His face was flushed with anger, and he lifted his whip to strike again, snapping the leather against another inmate at the rear of the group.

Blaine "Mick" McFadden was shackled between Piran on one side and Ernest on the other. They were in the middle of the large underground room being mined for rubies, one of the most profitable exports that the prison colony of Velant sent home to the kingdom of Donderath. Some of the men were toward the back of the room, while others were closer to the opening that led off the tunnel connecting this section to other parts of the sprawling mine deep beneath the arctic ice of Edgeland. And in Blaine's opinion, Piran was right.

Tadd, one of the prisoners near the back of the group, turned to face the overseer. "You get us killed bringing down the roof, and you're sure to miss your quota this month," he said defiantly.

Pig-face's eyes flashed with malice. He signaled to the guards, who closed in on Tadd. One of them landed a hard punch to the gut, doubling the prisoner over, while another brought his knee up sharply, breaking Tadd's nose. Tadd's shackle-mates, Bickle and Albert, were fastened by chains to each other's leg irons. They could not move far enough away to escape being drawn into the beating. The guards' fists and their short wooden staves flew, thudding against flesh and bone. The prisoners dared not defend themselves, nor did the others dare intervene without bringing down even worse on themselves.

After a few moments that seemed to last forever, Pig-face called off his guards. Tadd was bleeding from his nose and mouth, and one eye was nearly swollen shut. Bickle and Albert had not fared better. But none of the injuries was severe enough to stop them from mining. In the six months Blaine had been a prisoner in Velant, he had quickly learned that the guards were experts in inflicting pain in ways that did not compromise an inmate's ability to work. *Usually. Unless they hate the son of a bitch too much to care and lose control. Another reason why Piran should watch his mouth.*

"This is your last warning," Pig-face shouted. "Get to work, or you'll work under the lash, by Charrot!"

Blaine and the others turned back to their pickaxes and the rock walls from which they dug out the rubies. He and the others were all exiles, convicts condemned to a lifetime in the far north for crimes real or imagined. They were expendable, and their lives were far less important to Pig-face or Commander Prokief, the warden, than the rubies they mined.

Blaine's pickax rose and fell in the rhythm he had long ago mastered. Busy enough to spare him from Pig-face's whip, but not any more industrious than absolutely necessary.

Rubies were highly prized among the nobility back in Donderath, and valuable for trade with the Cross-Sea Kingdoms and the Lesser Kingdoms. While the herring that was caught, salted and packed into barrels by Edgeland's fishermen were largely for consumption within Donderath, rubies brought new money into the kingdom.

"He's going to be the death of us, one way or the other," Piran muttered, moving as slowly as he dared without drawing Pig-face's ire—and whip.

"*You're* going to be the death of us, if you don't stop pissing him off," Blaine replied.

"You know Tadd's right. We've all been saying it. We're going too deep. There should be more pillars left to hold up the roof. It's a bloody death trap," Piran added.

"Not much choice either way," Ernest, the third man shackled in their trio whispered. "Get buried alive when the roof falls in, or get beaten to death by the guards—who will take any excuse they can get. One of those ways is faster than the other; maybe less painful, too."

Ernest had a point. Velant's guards were as much prisoners as their charges, assigned to the arctic penal colony in order to get rid of men who were too brutal to be tolerated in regular society. So they were transferred to Velant where they also enforced the law both among the prisoners and those who earned their Tickets of Leave to become colonists. None of them were ever going back to Donderath. Not even Prokief, Velant's warden and the "governor" of Edgeland.

Prokief had won King Merrill's gratitude with a series of

military victories in a previous conflict with Meroven. But those victories had been gained not by outstanding strategy but through sheer brutality, earning Prokief the nickname of the "Butcher of Breseshwa." When the fighting was over, the ruthlessness and willingness to commit slaughter that had won the day became a liability to the king, who "honored" Prokief with the "promotion" and shipped him off with the rest of the exiles.

Feeling the guards' gaze on them, Blaine fell silent and returned to his work. Each triad of miners worked a different section of the rock all around the perimeter of the large, manmade cave. Periodically, they would fill a cart with their results and dump the chunks of rock into a large pile in the center, where other prisoners would haul the pieces to the surface. There, more inmates labored to break up the biggest chunks and separate out the rubies so that the cargo returning to Donderath would be as compact—and profitable—as possible.

Piran began to whistle. Half of the miners hated his whistling. The others were inclined to whistle along, or occasionally, sing. That alone might account for the disapproving glares and catcalls Piran received. Piran's whistling tended to be more on-tune than the singing, and while Blaine did not mind, some of the others wasted no time making their annoyance clear.

"Pipe down, Rowse!"

"This ain't a whorehouse—more's the pity."

"Stop your damned noise, or I'll close your mouth for you!"

Piran kept on whistling, switching frequently among tavern songs that everyone knew even if they only partly remembered the words. Between his own ability with his fists and the presence of the guards, Piran was not worried about retribution, and the grin on his face made it clear he relished tweaking those who disliked his music.

On good days, Blaine lost himself to the rhythm of the pickax, blanking his mind and stilling his thoughts. On bad days, memories crowded in on him; of his home at Glenreith, his brother Carr, and his sister Mari, his Aunt Judith, and his beloved Carensa. All of them were lost to him now, just as he was dead to them. No one returned from Velant except for the sailors onboard the ships that brought prisoners and supplies north and carried holds full of rubies and herring back.

It would be spring in Donderath. Trees would be green once more, farmers would be busy getting crops in the fields, and Glenreith would be bustling with all the tasks necessary to run a manor and its lands. That would be true even for a manor of reduced circumstances, thanks to the scandal Blaine's murder of his father caused. *I did my best to save them from one horror and plunged them into another. But to stop Father from hurting Mari, I would do it all again, consequences be damned.*

Sometimes, he wondered whether Carensa would hold to her vow never to forget him. Part of him appreciated her declaration of undying love. But most of him wished better for her than a life of loneliness in pursuit of a lost cause. Much as he hated the thought of her in another man's arms, it pained him worse to think of her ostracized for her association with him, alone for the rest of her life.

Resolutely, Blaine tried to push those thoughts from his mind. They served no purpose, and life in Velant was unrelentingly grim enough without dwelling on what could not be changed.

Piran whistled a tavern ditty. Across the way, Dunbar, one of the other miners assigned to the same barracks as Blaine and Piran, picked up the tune in a tolerable baritone voice, with lyrics which grew increasingly obscene as the song progressed. More of the inmates gradually joined in, off key and tone deaf, and for a while, the rhythm of their digging matched the beat of the song.

There was scant comfort to be had in Velant, but small shows of solidarity, like this, provided what little there was. While Blaine had earned his banishment as an unrepentant murderer, many of his fellow prisoners' crimes were hardly worthy of exile. Petty theft, unpaid debts, embezzlement, and cheating on taxes were among the most frequent offenses. Others, like their bunkmate Dawe Killick, were the victims of trumped up charges by business rivals, jealous lovers, or someone who envied their land, lover, or possessions. They had been spared the noose, but Blaine was certain that he was not the only one who often wondered just what sort of "mercy" that provided compared to the prospect of a quick, nearly painless death and an end to suffering.

And yet we still dodge the blow that would kill us, Blaine mused. *Death's close enough here every day. We all know how to die. Attack a guard. Defy orders. Attempt to escape. Break the rules once too often on a day when a guard is in a bad mood. It's so easy to die here. We could all have it over with any time we choose, if that's what we really wanted. But every time death gets close, we flinch away. Funny, how that works.*

A sudden cracking noise silenced the whistling and song. Then thunder filled the mine as the roof of the back section collapsed in an avalanche of rock that clouded the air with dust and blotted out the dim light of the oil lanterns. Blaine tried to get out of the way, pulling with all his might on the chains that connected him to Piran and Ernest, stumbling and choking as grit filled his lungs and made his eyes tear until he could not see.

Guards were shouting, but Blaine could not make out what they said above the crash and rumble of the collapse. Men screamed in pain and fear. Some of the shrieks cut off suddenly, while others fell to low moans, the cries of the dying. No one was heeding the guards as a press of men pushed toward the exit, pressing against each other as they tripped on their shackles.

Guards blocked the doorway to the tunnels leading out of the mine. Pig-face stood behind them, and their fear of the overseer obviously outweighed their fear of dying from the cave-in because the guards stood their ground, using their whips and batons to push back the desperate prisoners who surged toward them, trying to escape.

"Stay back!" Pig-face roared. Whips cracked in the air for emphasis, lashing at the prisoners who dared to get too close to the line of guards. "No one is leaving."

"The bloody roof's caving in!" Ernest shouted. "What's to say it won't all fall in on us? Then who's going to mine your bleedin' rubies?"

"Silence!" Pig-face shouted. One of the men launched himself at the guards, dragging his hapless shackle-mates with him. The guard hit the man with his baton so hard it cracked his skull, and the prisoner went down in a heap, bloody and still.

"Try to push past the guards, and I will see you lashed to the posts in the yard and whipped senseless before dinner!" Pig-face yelled. He was red in the face, eyes glinting with lunatic intensity. Blaine wondered if the overseer was more irate over the challenge to his authority than by the prospect of imminent death from the cave-in.

Just then, the next section of roof collapsed.

A curtain of falling rock crushed men beneath it, wiping out two rows of frightened miners. Their blood leaked from beneath the tumble of stone, mingling with the dust. Most of the lanterns had gone out, leaving the survivors in near-darkness. Behind them, they could hear the cries of the dying and the pleas of those trapped but not yet dead.

Instinctive fear of being buried alive outweighed Pig-face's intimidation, and the terrified miners surged forward again, striking back at the guards in blind terror, ignoring the blows of the batons and the sting of the whips in their unthinking frenzy to escape certain death. As the rock continued to fall, the guards' line broke and even they retreated into the corridor, heedless of Pig-face's increasingly hysterical threats.

Men fell as their chains tripped them. Others stampeded over them, crushing flesh and bone beneath their boots as they struggled toward the corridor.

Blaine, Piran, and Ernest dodged to one side, between one of the largest pillars and the natural rock wall, a place Blaine hoped was least likely to collapse. It got them out of the frenzied press, where they were as much in danger of being trampled underfoot as they were being smashed by falling stone.

Finally, the roar of falling rock slowed, then stopped. Blaine found that he was holding his breath, both to keep out the choking dust and in mortal fear that the stone overhead might collapse. For a moment, the silence seemed as deafening as the thunder of the cave-in. The cries of the dying and trapped men had grown faint. Those lost in the first collapse might well be dead by now, and those in the successive cave-ins were muted by the additional volume of stone that buried them.

Dust covered everything. It clung to the inside of Blaine's nostrils, coated his skin, and turned his chestnut hair gray. In the waning light of the remaining lanterns, Piran looked as ashen as a corpse. Ernest was wide-eyed with terror and looked like he held onto control by a thread.

Bodies littered the floor. Some of those caught in the stampede were still alive, calling out for help. Others lay still, crushed beneath the press of their fellow miners. Cutting through the choking dust was the smell of blood and shit, the stench of death.

"You think it's done?" Ernest dared to whisper after a few more moments passed without another collapse.

"Maybe," Blaine murmured, keeping his voice down as if he feared that even so slight a noise might trigger another avalanche of stone.

Piran was cursing loudly, practically daring the gods to take them. Out in the corridor, Blaine heard the buzz of many voices. And above it all, Pig-face's nasal drone cut through the confusion.

"Take the men who got the farthest toward the mine entrance and tie them to the posts in the yard," Pig-face ordered. "I will personally see to their lashing when I get to it, and if they freeze before then, so be it." Stones crunched beneath his boots as he headed back toward the room where Blaine and a few other triads huddled against the wall.

"Send two guards to get wooden posts. We'll brace what's left of the ceiling. As for the other prisoners, I want them back in here. They'll need to dig out the bodies, pull out anyone who isn't dead, and haul the rocks above ground for the rubies."

"Rubies!" Piran exploded. "Men are dead. Men are crushed. And you still want the rubies?"

Pig-face landed a roundhouse punch that caught Piran square in the jaw, sending him reeling back against Blaine and Ernest.

"By the gods, Rowse, if we hadn't lost so many men, I'd kill you for that," Pig-face growled. "King Merrill expects his tribute. No one cares how many scum like you die in the process."

Fear had become anger, and Piran would have lunged at Pig-face if Blaine and Ernest had not held him back. Ernest clapped a hand over Piran's mouth for good measure. Pig-face glowered at them but said nothing more, abruptly wheeling to give more orders to the guards, walking across the bodies of the trampled miners to leave the area.

Piran struggled against Blaine and Ernest, but they held him firmly. Ernest let out a yip of pain. "Damn, Rowse! You bit me!"

Blaine tightened his grip on Piran and bent close to his ear. "Run your mouth, and you'll get us all killed. I am not in the mood to die today. So either you agree to shut up and not do something stupid like taking a swing at Pig-face, or I hold your nose while Ernest holds your mouth until you pass out."

Piran gave Blaine a murderous glare, then nodded. He stopped fighting them, and they gradually relaxed their hold. Ernest removed his hand from Piran's mouth and shook it, revealing a welt in the middle of his palm where Piran had bitten him.

The dust had settled enough for Blaine to get a good look around. Half of the mining chamber was gone. In its place was a huge mound of rock in pieces that ranged from the size of a fist to boulders that would take several men and a lever to prise out of place. A rough dome rose into darkness above the mound from where the stone had fallen. Now and again, more pebbles fell as if to warn them that there was more rock to fall. *All the lumber in the world can't shore that up safely,* Blaine thought.

"You really don't think that once he's cleared it all out, he'll expect us to mine in there again, do you?" Ernest whispered.

"Wouldn't put it past him," Blaine returned.

Piran, usually the cynic, shook his head. "It's a toss-up. There've been cave-ins before, and after they took out what they could salvage and whatever survivors they could reach, they sealed up those the worst of those rooms." He gave a bitter smile. "He's right that no one gives a damn about 'scum' like us. On the other hand, Prokief only gets so many new prisoners every so often, and he needs all of us to keep this place running and make his quotas, or else Prokief and the guards don't get their full pay. So they've got to have a little care with killing us off too quickly."

Grudgingly, the miners who had escaped the cave room returned, grumbling under their breath and sparing baleful glares for Pig-face and the guards. Even the guards looked uncertain about coming back, and only their fear of the overseer convinced them to return.

They set up a line of shackled prisoners to hand rocks out from one person to another. Out in the tunnel, more prisoners hauled carts full of rocks topside and brought emptied carts back to be refilled. The air was foul with dust. Pig-face shouted to the guards, who brought a few more lanterns, but there was little they could do to illuminate the scene.

The first bodies to be removed were those of the men trampled in the doorway. A few of the miners on the top of the heap twitched and moaned, still alive despite their injuries. Pig-face ordered guards to release the injured men from their shackles to better separate the living from the dead, and to carry out those who were still breathing to the barracks. His orders included no mention of calling for healers. The dead were hefted atop the carts that carried the rock to the surface, their broken bodies just so much refuse.

Blaine and the others bent to the work. Blood seeped out from beneath the rock pile, mingling with the dust to create a sticky goo beneath their boots. The rough rocks cut Blaine's hands, and he knew that his back and arms would protest tomorrow from the constant bending and turning. Some of the rocks took two or three men to lift. The cave-in made it a tight fit to get enough men into the room to pass the rocks out.

"We need a pickax over here," Piran yelled. "This one's too big to move. Probably can't get the bloody thing out of the door if we could move it."

The other men passed a pickax down the line and took a few steps back to give Piran room to swing it. A few well-aimed blows, hitting with the full fury of Piran's anger, and the big rock crumbled into more manageable pieces.

"What was that?" one of the other miners asked. Blaine and the others froze, listening. In the distance, down one of the many dark tunnels, they heard scrabbling, like claws on rocks.

"Guard dogs?" Ernest suggested.

Piran shook his head. "Doubt it. Not sure what it is, but I don't want to meet it, whatever it is."

Blaine had already learned the normal mine sounds—footsteps echoing, the clink of metal on rock, the scrape and squeak of heavily-loaded carts. He heard the noise again and shuddered, agreeing with Piran.

Blaine's stomach rumbled. Their meager breakfast was candlemarks ago, and lunch had been forgotten amid the chaos of the cave-in. His mouth was parched, but Pig-face looked too intent on clearing the room of potentially valuable rock to see to the needs of the survivors.

Piran handed out a chunk of rock the size of a large melon, and beneath it, Blaine glimpsed a man. "We've got someone!" Piran shouted. Garrick was trapped near the edge of the pile, his face smeared with blood and dust.

"You alive, mate?" Piran asked, as Blaine and the others crowded close to begin the delicate process of removing enough rock to free Garrick without causing more stones to fall on him from the large, unstable pile.

Garrick moaned. "Leg's bad. Ribs hurt. Get me out!"

"Easy," Blaine said. "We're going to have to take some more chunks off from the top so they don't slide down on you. Stay still."

Garrick's fear was plain in his face. Carefully, Blaine and the others lifted rocks from the pile as if it were a huge puzzle, holding their breath when moving one stone triggered a slide of smaller rocks.

"What's taking so long? Pick up the pace!"

"We've got live ones underneath," one of the men shouted back. "Trying to get them out."

Pig-face swore. "Be quick about it. They won't hold your dinner for you in the barracks, you know, if you're late, and we *will* stay here until that pile is topside."

Piran looked as if he meant to make a remark, but Blaine brought a hand down hard on his shoulder with a warning shake of his head. Piran glowered, then turned back to his work.

"Hold on," Ernest said. "We're almost down to you."

"Dunbar and Albert are under here, too," Garrick managed as they worked to clear the rocks away from his body. One leg was bent at an unnatural angle, and Blaine could see bone poking through Garrick's stained and torn pants.

"One thing at a time," Piran said through clenched teeth, pausing for a moment as the rocks shifted. When the slide stopped, they continued working, passing the stones hand to hand out of the room until more of Garrick's form had been unburied.

"I see another foot," Blaine said.

"Dunbar was next to me," Garrick said as Piran and Ernest moved away the last rocks pinning him. "Albert was chained to him."

"We need to unlock his leg irons," Piran shouted over his shoulder to the guards.

Grudgingly, one of the guards came and unlocked the iron cuff on Garrick's broken leg. Blaine, Piran, and Ernest lifted Garrick as gently as they could, but the movement still raised a cry of pain.

"Easy, mate," Piran said. "You're on your way out now."

Garrick's hand clutched at Blaine's sleeve. His fingers were cut and bloodied. "Get them out," he croaked. "Don't leave them down here."

Blaine nodded. "We'll do everything we can," he replied. "See you back at the barracks."

They followed the chain to find Dunbar's leg. Removing the rocks above him was a painfully slow process. "We need to take some off the other side and the top, or it's all going to come crashing down," Blaine called to those working on the other part of the pile. The fallen rock was heaped between the rock walls of the mine room, going from wall to wall so that only a portion could be accessed.

Grimly, the other miners nodded, and the process of passing stones out hand to hand brought the top of the heap lower and worked away at the side where Dunbar lay. After what felt like forever, Blaine and Piran moved the last of the rocks that covered Dunbar's body.

"He's breathing, but I don't think he's conscious," Blaine shouted. "And we're going to need to unlock him." The chain that led off from Dunbar's leg ran beneath the biggest part of the rock pile. Garrick and Dunbar had been lucky enough to be at the pile's edge, where the weight would be lightest. Even so, their injuries looked bad. Blaine held little hope for those caught under the heaviest portions of the cave-in.

Dunbar's moans were faint as they moved him. Enough blood stained his clothing that Blaine could not guess at his injuries, or whether all of the blood was really Dunbar's. He watched the guards carry Dunbar out, wondering whether he would still be alive when they returned to their barracks and feeling a pang of guilt that he and his triad had survived relatively unscathed while some of their friends had not.

"This isn't going to be good," Piran muttered, as the next stone he removed was covered with blood.

Half a candlemark later, they uncovered Albert's blood-soaked body. His skull was crushed, and the weight of the rocks had broken his ribs and limbs. Blaine flinched as the soldiers tossed the limp form on the top of the rock cart. *One more of us who's finally free of this place. At least it's over for him.*

2

AFTERMATH

BLAINE HAD LOST ALL TRACK OF TIME WHEN HE, PIRAN, AND Ernest finally stumbled to the surface where their leg irons were removed. The cold air was a welcome change from the stench and dust below. Blaine was bloodied to the forearms, with his own blood where he had been cut in dozens of places from the sharp rocks, and from the blood of the men whose bodies they had removed from the cave-in.

"A dozen dead," Piran muttered. "All because Pig-face wouldn't get us out of there."

"He made sure he got his precious rocks, bloody or not," Ernest added.

The harsh, unending daylight of the White Nights had taken the place of the unremitting darkness of the Long Dark. Blaine squinted as his eyes adjusted.

"Looks like he made good on his threat about the whip-pings," Blaine said with a nod toward the posts in the middle of the parade yard. The bodies of three men hung from ropes that bound their wrists. Stripped to the waist, their backs had been cut to bloody ribbons. Though it was officially spring in Edgeland, the temperatures were still cold enough that the whipped men were likely to die from exposure if Pig-face left them out in the elements for long.

I guess Pig-face worked off his frustration about the cave-in on their hides, Blaine thought. *He's likely to get called to account by Prokief if his output is down. Maybe he's afraid of ending up just like them if he displeases his commander. Gods! This place is worse than Raka.*

The sight of the whipped men drew a roar from the crowd of miners as they emerged from belowground. Some of the men still carried their pickaxes, and the adrenaline was high from their close brush with death. Most had seen friends or work partners killed, watched the efforts to remove the rock prized far more highly than the men whose bodies were crushed below.

Shock, pain, blood, and fear combined with a deep, long-standing hatred of Pig-face and his guards. It reached the boiling point as the men came up from the horrors they had witnessed underground to see the bloodied bodies of men whose only crime was trying to escape a cave-in.

"Move your asses!" one of the guards shouted as the men slowed to see what had become of the miners taken for punishment.

"Move your own ass, you bloody bastard!" Kelsen, a miner from one of the other barracks, gave a battle cry and went running toward the guard, tackling him and taking him to the ground as fists and feet flew in a fight.

Like a spark to tinder, the mob of miners surged forward, attacking the guards in teams of two or three, able to move and fight since their shackles had been removed. Those with pickaxes still in hand swung the tools like deadly weapons. The guards were armed with short knives and batons, since swords were useless in the close confines of the mine. That gave the miners an advantage, since they already outnumbered the mine guards.

"Death to Pig-face!"

"Kill the guards!"

The crowd near the mouth of the mine became a melee. Blaine barely missed being punched by an irate miner aiming for the guard behind him. Piran ducked another blow, pivoted, and planted his boot on a guard's rump, with a kick that sent the guard sprawling, where he was tackled by two miners who beat the man senseless.

"We've got to get out of here!" Blaine said, looking for a way to escape the mob.

"The party's just getting started!" Piran's grin was malicious, and he eyed the action, weighing the chance to wade in for some well-deserved retribution.

"You can't win!" Blaine said, as the mob surged around them. "We outnumber the mine guards, but the rest will come running. Come on!"

Ernest needed no urging. Blaine grabbed Piran by the collar and dragged him off to the side. Piran fought him, and Blaine threw Piran up against the wall of one of the barns.

"Get your hands off me!" Piran snapped.

Blaine backed off a step, hands raised. "Fine. Go get yourself killed. Once Prokief sends in more guards, the rioters will get the Hole—or worse. You can't win this fight."

Piran was breathing hard, his blood already high for the fight. But before his exile, he had been a military man, and whatever the reason for the court-martial that sent him to Velant, Blaine suspected that Piran had been an officer, not just a conscript. Blaine could see Piran struggling for control as the riot raged yards away in the parade grounds. Piran's hands unclenched from fists, and his jaw relaxed, although he still gave Blaine a baleful glare.

Already, Blaine could hear the piercing alarm whistles and the ringing of the bell that called out soldiers for emergencies like fires—or uprisings.

"If they catch us here, it won't matter whether we were fighting or not," Ernest said with a nervous glance over his shoulder.

With a growl, Piran pushed away from the barn. For a second, Blaine thought that Piran meant to join up with the rioters. But then he turned away and motioned for them to follow him.

"This way," he said. "It'll keep us out of the guards' sight, and we can move in the barn shadows most of the way back to our barracks."

Several times along the way, they flattened themselves against the outbuildings, scarcely daring to breathe as soldiers ran to put down the rebellion from wherever they had been stationed. Piran's knowledge of the camp proved valuable, as he led them in and out of barns and sheds to keep from being seen, crossing the camp with practiced stealth, enough to tell Blaine this was not the first time Piran had taken such a route.

Sweat streaked down through the gray dust on their faces and arms, and whether or not they were injured, their clothing was covered with blood. Every muscle in Blaine's body ached, his head pounded, and his eyes stung from fatigue and the irritation of the rock grit that covered his body. Yet after the horrific injuries he had seen, he could not complain. By Velant standards, they had gotten off lucky.

They washed up quickly in the ice cold water of a half-frozen horse trough, trying to get the worst of the filth off of their bodies before going in for dinner. The cold helped focus Blaine's thoughts and wake him up, and it was a welcome relief to get the grit out of his eyes and nose. It was a sorry substitute for what Blaine really wanted, but the luxury of a hot

KING'S CONVICTS • 115

bath was not to be had in Velant, except perhaps by its commander. Blaine had no doubt that Prokief enjoyed many of the luxuries Blaine had once taken for granted, and would never see again.

It sounded like a battle in the parade ground. Men shouted and cursed, bellowing battle cries and screaming in pain. The clang of the alarm bell echoed in the cold air, loud enough to reach all corners of the camp. Soldiers commanded the miners to stand down, and the miners replied with jeers and obscenities.

"Over here!" Piran hissed, motioning for them to follow. He led them to a small storage shed against the wall of their barracks in the back, where the food was prepared. A bit of metal flickered and twitched in Piran's hand as he picked the lock on the door, and then they were inside, and Piran manipulated the lock with practiced skill to look as if it had not been jimmied.

Light filtered between the boards of the shed walls, just enough to maneuver. Piran went around to the back, the actual barracks wall, and moved an empty barrel, then knelt and gentled a section of board out of position.

"Get in!" he whispered. "And be quiet."

Blaine went first, on his hands and knees, crawling through the darkness to find himself against another wall. Remembering how Piran had opened the passage, Blaine jiggled the section of boards in front of him and found them loose. A finger-hold kept the boards from dropping out onto the floor and making noise. Blaine emerged, wary for a trap, and saw that they were in the barracks pantry. Ernest and Piran followed, and Piran carefully replaced the boards.

"Now what?" Blaine whispered.

Piran squeezed past him and waited behind the pantry door, ear pressed against the wood. He eased the door open, then signaled for the others to follow as he tip-toed out of the pantry. It was past dinnertime, and the preparation area should have been bustling with activity, but Blaine guessed that everyone had gone to the windows to watch the riot in the parade ground.

Piran flashed them a triumphant smile, and they slipped out of the back room and mingled with the prisoners as if they had never been gone.

All of the prisoners crowded around the windows, and Blaine guessed more were at the windows upstairs as well, straining for a view of what was going on. Dawe and Verran startled when Blaine came up behind him, but a shake of his head silenced their questions as to how the three men had suddenly appeared.

"Time to eat!" one of the kitchen prisoners shouted above the murmur of voices. "You know how that fight's going on end."

Unfortunately, they did, Blaine thought. While he sympathized completely with the miners' anger, they were not numerous enough nor well-armed enough to win against Prokief's soldiers. He only hoped that reprisals did not affect all of them.

Sooner or later, Prokief will overplay his hand, Blaine thought. *Maybe I won't live to see it. But someone will find a way to take him and his guards down.*

The cauldron of stew tasted as if it had sat waiting for a few extra candlemarks on the fire, but Blaine and the others were too hungry to complain as they lined up for their portions of stew, hard bread, and *fet*.

"You made it out." Dawe looked both worried and relieved as he took a seat near Piran and the others.

Blaine nodded. "Yeah. But some of us didn't."

"Not our day to die, I guess," Ernest said, putting into words what they were all likely thinking.

"We know," Verran said. "Prokief pulled prisoners from other duties to help haul out the rock and move the bodies."

"Where did they take Garrick and Dunbar?" Piran asked.

"Infirmary," Dawe replied, his voice tight. "The mage-doctors will look them over, decide whether to heal them or just kill them."

"What?" Ernest asked, eyes growing wide.

Piran nodded. "That's how it works here, mate. A bit like deciding whether to try to cure a horse or put it down. Actually, I imagine they'd try harder for the horse. Fewer of them to be had up here. There's still plenty of us."

Dawe and Verran were assigned to the same barracks as Blaine and the others, but they had been assigned to farm work instead of the mines. Dawe had blacksmithing skills, and Verran was too slightly built to be much use with the heavy work of mining.

"Albert and Tadd are dead," Piran reported, his voice flat. "So's Horace, and ten blokes who weren't from our barracks. Squashed like a bug under all those damn rocks, and all Pig-face could think about were the rubies." There was no attempt to hide the bitterness in his tone.

"I heard that they didn't get many gems from the rock anyhow," Verran reported. He was a musician by trade, but petty theft had earned him exile in Velant. Though Verran, like Blaine, was a newcomer to the prison, somehow he always managed to know more about what was going on than might be expected.

"I heard the guards talking," Verran continued. "Said that the room had been pretty well mined out. The rock up above that fell wasn't the right sort to have rubies in it or something like that."

Piran growled curses under his breath, and his fist clenched. "Pig-face had to know," he said. "It's his business to know, and he's been here long enough to tell one kind of rock from another. That means those men are dead or crippled for nothing—not even Prokief's godsforsaken rubies."

Ernest shrugged. "Agreed. But there's nothing to do about it. You've said it yourself; that's how it is here."

"I'm not ready to leave it like that," Piran muttered.

Blaine gave him a look. "Think, Piran. We've already been flogged once because we got on the wrong side of the guards. I don't relish another turn at it. Be glad we haven't ended up in the Holes." The Holes were shafts cut down through the ice and rock which Commander Prokief used as oubliettes.

Angry as Blaine was about what had happened in the mine, he had no desire for another flogging. From what they had glimpsed of Prokief's response to the miners' riot, there would be swift, brutal repercussions—perhaps for all prisoners, whether or not they were part of the uprising.

"Let me think on it," Piran said. "I'll come up with something."

After they had eaten, they trudged up to the bunk room. Blaine saw that the least injured of the miners had been brought back to the barracks. Prisoners he did not recognize were moving from bunk to bunk, binding up wounds, preparing poultices, and administering doses of a liquid with a smell that made Blaine wrinkle his nose.

Who are they?" he asked Piran.

"Hedge witches," Piran replied with a shrug. "Healers. It's the best the likes of us get."

"I didn't think Prokief allowed magic," Blaine replied.

Dawe gave Blaine a sidelong look. "He doesn't. What's that have to do with it?"

"The warden-mages can't sense the power?" Blaine asked.

"What do you think they're doing?" Piran replied with a nod toward two men, one on either side of the room, who stood by, chanting quietly. "Best I understand it, they mumble like that, and it puts up some kind of screen the warden-mages can't easily see through, at least, if they're not looking hard."

"We're not talking about strong magic," Dawe added. "Most of these folks were village healers who got sent here because they couldn't save everyone, and they were unlucky enough to have a powerful patient die. Family wanted someone to punish, so here they are."

"On the other hand, several of them got sent here for poisoning an enemy or a rival, so even I try not to get on their bad side," Piran said.

The healers were nearly done making their way among the bunks. They turned their attention next to the returning miners, spreading salve on the cuts on their hands and arms, or closing scalp wounds from falling rocks. Blaine accepted their help gratefully. He had seen men die from wounds gone sour, and even in Velant, it was a bad way to go.

"What do you think will happen to the rioters?" Verran asked.

Piran snorted. "Nothing good. Doesn't matter whether they really rioted or just didn't want to get crushed to death. They defied orders—and around here, that's as good as a death sentence."

3

REPERCUSSIONS

Late that evening, the guards came hammering on the door to the dormitory. "Out! Out! Out!" they shouted. They were armed with whips, and now they wore broadswords. Some carried battle axes and morning stars. It was all the evidence Blaine needed that Prokief considered himself to be at war.

Clutching their cloaks and hopping as they tried to put on boots, the prisoners roused from their beds and filed out for inspection. Even the wounded hobbled out, fearful of repercussions if they did not show up to be counted.

The wind was cold, and Blaine blinked against the glaring perpetual sunlight of the White Nights. Three guards instead of the usual solo soldier came down their ranks to make a count, and repeated the action twice more, either to assure themselves that no one was missing, or to make it clear to the prisoners that they were being scrutinized.

Commander Prokief and Warden-Mage Ejnar stood in the center of the parade ground, gazing expressionlessly over the ranks of assembled prisoners. In front of them knelt twenty-five miners, under the watchful gaze of a dozen guards armed as if they were about to ride into battle. The men wore iron bands around their necks, to which ran the chain from the manacles on their wrists. Equally heavy chains ran between their leg irons. Most of the miners were bloody and badly injured; clearly Prokief had given the guards free reign to take out their frustrations.

Once the guards were finished taking account of the prisoners, all eyes turned to Prokief.

"Last night, these prisoners rebelled against the king's authority," Prokief boomed. "They caused a riot that damaged the king's property, and dared to raise their hands—and weapons —against the king's duly appointed officers."

Piran, Ernest, and Blaine exchanged surreptitious glances. A chill ran down Blaine's back as he realized just how close they had come to being among the doomed men.

"Under normal circumstances, disobedience to the law of the king is punishable by death," Prokief continued. "But as you know, here in Velant, we do not have 'normal' circumstances. We are constrained by our distance from the kingdom to make good on our duty to the king with fewer workers than the task requires."

Blaine was skeptical that despite Prokief's words, any mercy would be forthcoming. The commander's next words proved him right. "Because of that, we cannot execute all of the miscreants as their treason warrants. But because of the danger they posed to the survival of this prison—and this colony—I will not permit their deeds to go unpunished."

Prokief looked as if he barely hid a self-satisfied smile. "Therefore," he announced, "five of these men will be executed, as a reminder to all of you what happens to those who dare to challenge King Merrill's authority."

The guards roughly jerked five of the shackled prisoners to their feet. Terror was clear in their wide eyes.

"Three of these men will hang," Prokief continued. The guards led the three doomed men toward the gallows that was an ever-present reminder of Prokief's power of life and death over all those on Edgeland. Nooses hung from the scaffolding, swaying slowly in the wind. A drummer began a slow military cadence as the guards escorted the condemned men to the bed of a wagon beneath the nooses.

At least all those iron chains will make quick work of it, Blaine thought. He had gone out of his way to avoid the public executions which some considered to be entertainment back in Donderath. Those he had witnessed had not always been a quick death. If the hangman did not tie the noose just right, or the drop was not calculated correctly, the hanged men could strangle slowly, a painful, lingering death.

Then he noticed that the guards were removing the three men's chains and binding their wrists with rope. "There will be no hoods," Prokief's voice carried in the cold air. "It behooves you to look on their miserable end, and contemplate that your lives hang by a fragile thread of your obedience to orders." He paused. "Warden-Ejnar will make certain that their end is prolonged, to give them—and all of you—full time to contemplate what happens to those who disobey."

The drummer continued his measured cadence, the same that Blaine recalled from hangings back in Castle Reach. He steeled himself as the nooses were placed around the men's necks. The drumbeats reached a crescendo as the hangman signaled the wagon driver, who snapped the reins, causing the horse to bolt and jerking the platform from beneath the condemned men's feet.

The prisoners fell, dangling a few feet above the ground. Denied a quick death, their bodies bucked in a macabre, desperate dance as their faces blackened and their eyes bulged. Prokief watched as discomfort, shock, and horror rippled through the audience of prisoners, continuing the spectacle for at least a half a candlemark until he was assured that his point had been made. Ejnar made a motion with his hand, and the tortured prisoners finally went still.

Blaine fought down his rising gorge. A few of the prisoners at attention were not so lucky, turning to the side and retching. Two men fainted. Blaine kept his eyes on Prokief, whose satisfied smile fueled a cold, lethal hatred deep in Blaine's gut.

"In case that warning is easily forgotten," Prokief continued, knowing well that it was likely to remain in the survivors' nightmares for the rest of their lives, "two of the insurrectionists will go into the gibbets. They will remain there until they are dead from hunger and the elements, and once they are corpses, the crows will feed on their remains." He paused. "But once again, Warden-Mage Ejnar will prolong their lives as a lesson to all of you, so that you will look on their misery and be reminded of the virtues of obedience."

No one dared say a word, but Blaine could read defiance and hatred in the stiff stances of his fellow prisoners, the clenched jaws and white-knuckled fists. Fury burned so bright in Piran's eyes that Blaine feared his friend would forget himself, but whatever vengeance Piran planned, military discipline enabled him to keep control.

"Now what of these twenty rebels?" Prokief asked. "They have put all of you at risk. It would be within my charge as the representative of the king to levy punishment on all of you for the deeds of these few." He paused, letting that sink in. "But I can be merciful," he said after a moment. "And I am a good steward of the king's resources, mindful of our duty to send him the quota of goods our charter requires. Therefore, no reprisals will be taken against prisoners who did not join the uprising."

Prokief's hand swept through the air to indicate the twenty kneeling men. "These men, however, must bear the consequences of their actions, which constitutes treason against the king by defying the appointed agents of the king's authority." Blaine noticed that Prokief took every opportunity to link himself and King Merrill, when in reality the king considered Prokief a dangerous embarrassment and was well rid of him. *Then again, I'm probably the only one close enough to court to realize that,* Blaine thought.

"I sentence these men to the deepest levels of the mines," Prokief boomed. "They will labor there for the rest of their lives without ever returning to the surface. They will not see daylight or fresh air again, and they will toil without stopping until death alone releases them from their sentence. And Warden-Mage Ejnar will prolong their lives to give them time to contemplate their bad judgment, and make up for the lost time their willful destruction of property has caused."

Once again, the drummer struck up a death march cadence. Prison guards marched the doomed miners into the mouth of the mine, until they disappeared from sight.

When Blaine and the other prisoners turned back, the two remaining miners had been placed in the gibbets, man-sized iron cages roughly the shape of a person, which would allow them almost no freedom of movement. The gibbets were raised by chains until they swung twenty feet off the ground, far too high for their occupants to have hope of escape, but not so far that the men on the ground could not make out the utter terror in the prisoners' expressions.

"Dismissed."

Back in the barracks, the men gathered in small groups of two or three. Some sat or lay on their bunks, staring at nothing. Although Blaine was one of the newcomers, he still felt the loss of those who had died in the cave-in or been sentenced to death.

"Kurt's tied out there on that damn post," Ernest said, his expression bleak. "He was the first person I met when I got onboard the *Cutlass*. He didn't deserve to die like that, just for trying not to get killed by the rocks."

"None of them *deserved* to die," Verran said, his voice bitter. "Just like half the people in Velant don't *deserve* to be here for what little they did. But it's the way things are." Verran walked away to the farthest corner of the room, dropped down to sit on the floor and played his pennywhistle softly. Blaine had seen him do that often on the ship from Donderath and figured that it helped him deal with the situation.

"They're gone! I saw them die!" Everyone's attention turned to Jame. He was a short man, not much taller than Piran but not so strongly built, and before he had been a convict, he had been a groomsman. Like the rest of them, dust grayed his hair and clung to his clothing, but Jame's eyes were wide and wild, and his skin was pallid.

"We were chained together. And Carl had just said something to me. I moved to get a better angle to hit my rock and then... there was a jerk on the chain...and they were gone."

Dawe eased toward Jame. "We know," he said gently. "I'm sorry—"

Jame backed away, unreasoning terror in his eyes. "No. You don't know. You weren't there. They were crushed under that rock. I heard...bones snap. Hort screamed, and he kept on screaming, and I tried to dig him out, but the guards made me move. They dragged me by my chain. I just wanted to dig them out." He held out his bloodied hands, skin badly cut by the sharp rocks.

Dawe advanced another step while the rest of the men either gave ground or looked up to see what was going on. "Easy," he said as if gentling a spooked horse. "Just calm down—"

"I can't calm down!" Jame snapped. "Their ghosts are going to be trapped down there forever. If I hadn't moved, I'd have gone down with them, and I wouldn't have to remember the blood. So much blood."

Blaine had heard tell of soldiers who returned from battle mad with grief for their fallen comrades and guilt that they had survived when others did not. He had no idea what was going on in Jame's mind, but it was clear from the man's wild eyes that he had been completely overwhelmed by what he witnessed.

"It's over," Dawe said quietly. "It's done."

"It's not over! I have to…make it right." From somewhere, a small knife appeared in Jame's hand. Dawe saw it and cautioned Blaine and Piran to stay where they were when they moved to intervene.

"How can you make it right?" Dawe coaxed. "How can you undo what's done?"

"You just want me to forget. But I can't forget. I can't ever forget," Jame howled. "I see them when I close my eyes, bleeding and dying. Oh gods above, I see them. How can I sleep?"

Dawe had made eye contact with Shorty and Whinny, who were closest to where Jame stood. The two thieves moved fast. One grabbed Jame from behind, holding him as he thrashed and bucked. The other wrestled the knife away and swung a punch that caught Jame in the jaw and dropped him in his place.

"Put him in his bunk," Dawe said tiredly. "Maybe he'll have calmed down come morning." He rubbed his temples as if the whole situation had given him a headache.

"Nice wrangling," Jakk said. Blaine recalled that Jakk had been a stable hand before he was sent to Velant, so he had probably calmed his share of panicked horses.

"Not exactly successful, since we had to knock him out," Dawe replied. "But at least he didn't hurt himself—or anyone else."

"Was he close with Carl and Hort before, back home?"

Ernest asked. Blaine struggled to remember who had congre-
gated together on the ship over. Certainly since their arrival,
Jame, Carl, and Hort had been a tight group.

"No idea," Dawe said, massaging the back of his neck.
"Maybe it's just that he was standing right there when it
happened, and he barely missed dying." He went back to his
bunk and swung his long legs in, lying down and closing his
eyes, as if the matter was settled.

Blaine turned back to Piran, who had known more of the
doomed men longer. Piran was handling the loss better, but
Blaine could see the struggle in his eyes. *Of course he's handling
it better. He was a soldier. If he's seen battle at all, he's seen
death. It doesn't make death any easier, but it builds up scars
after a while.*

"One-Eye and Peters were in the group to go Below," Piran
said, pacing between the bunks. "They were on the ship with me
from Donderath. They never made any trouble. Now, they'd
have been better off if they'd been crushed, like the others."

Blaine couldn't argue Piran's logic. Since he questioned the
king's "mercy" in granting them exile to this miserable place, he
was already unsure whether staying alive—no matter what the
situation—was actually preferable to death. He doubted that,
especially in the case of the poor bastards sentenced to dying by
slow torture in the gibbets. At least the corpses that still hung
from the gallows were well and truly dead, though the warden-
mages had made their end as painful as possible.

"That's it?" Blaine asked. "You're dead, and it's over?"

Piran looked at him quizzically. "You were expecting ghosts?
Yeah, I suspect we've got more than a few of those."

Blaine shook his head. "No. I mean, what about a decent
burial?"

Piran gave a mirthless chuckle. "The blokes out there won't
be anything except bones by the time the foxes and crows are

done with them," he said. "There's not much sentiment in Velant —in case you hadn't noticed. Most of the time, the dead are hauled up to that big platform you might have seen beyond the wall. Keeps the wolves away, lets the vultures and crows have their fill. Then the bones get dumped in a break in the ice somewhere, I imagine."

He shrugged. "Once in a while—especially if what killed someone might be catching—they'll burn the bodies. Ground's too hard most of the year to dig a proper grave the animals couldn't get into. Don't know what the colonists do. Probably a mixture of all those things."

Blaine thought he had reconciled himself to the idea that his body would never return home to Donderath, and his family would not know what became of him. But learning the harsh truth that his bones might not even find a resting place in the ground started up a familiar ache deep inside.

"And there's no one who says a prayer or makes a sacrifice to the gods or anything?" Blaine asked, now that Velant had once again unmoored him from his notions of how the world worked.

Piran sighed. "If we did that, Mick, we'd be singing songs for the dead nearly every damn day," he said, not unkindly. "After a while, you learn to let it go."

"What about their families? Will Prokief send notice home?"

Jaston, one of the other men in the barracks, gave a derisive snort. "You think Prokief would bother sending a notice to a prisoner's family? By Torven! He'd be more likely to send a bill for lodging!" A few others laughed at his joke. Blaine recognized that kind of dark humor; he and his brother Carr had engaged in enough of it themselves to keep sane around their father.

"Like as not, they've got no family—least none that wants anything to do with them," Dawe said quietly. "Most of us don't." He gave Blaine a questioning look. "If you do, well, I'm sorry, mate."

"Just another thing at Velant that's a lie," Shorty said from where he lay on his bunk, staring at nothing. "Officially, we're supposed to be able to get letters from back home and send them out on the return ships—assuming you and anyone you know can read or write." He shook his head. "I don't know many people who've heard from someone in Donderath. A few have tried to send letters back, but there's no way to tell if they arrived or if Prokief just tossed them into the sea."

It took all of Blaine's composure not to show how deeply Shorty's words hurt. He had only received a few letters from his Aunt Judith or his sister, Mari, during his time in exile. The letters were damaged and incomplete, but he treasured them regardless. Then, the letters stopped coming. He had no expectation to hear from Carensa, not since he set her free of their betrothal. But deep inside, he had hoped Judith or Mari would tell him how Carensa fared, whether or not she found a suitable husband, and reassure him that she had not been too badly tainted by his scandal.

Then again, maybe it's kinder for them if I "died" when I got on the convict ship, Blaine thought. *What good can come of hearing from me, when I can never come home? How much longer does it keep the pain alive, if I learn that they've gone on without me? No. It's better like this. They did their duty with a few notes. Now, they've made a clean break, sharp as the grave. At least, for them.*

"There's something else I heard," Shorty said. "Got it direct from one of the blokes who was on the front line getting the rubble out of the cave-in. They couldn't find all of the bodies."

"So? Some of them probably got crushed to jelly," Piran said. "That was a lot of rock that came down."

"You don't get it," Shorty snapped. "The bodies weren't smashed—they were missing. And from what this guy said, they could see bloody streaks where something had been dragged off."

"Dragged off, where?" Blaine asked.

"Into the caves," Bickle replied. Everyone turned to look at him. "There's a rumor that there are caves below the mines. Natural caves. No one's gone down there—at least, not and come back up again."

"Caves don't drag off bodies," Piran said, paying closer attention that Blaine expected.

"No," Bickle said. "But monsters do. And the miners who've been here the longest say there are monsters out under the ice."

"What kind of monsters?" Blaine recalled the strange noises he had heard in the mine, and the odd glimpses of shadows other miners whispered about seeing.

"Monstrous monsters," Bickle snapped, irritated. "I can't draw you a picture. If you're close enough to see one, you don't live long enough to describe it. All I heard was that they have big teeth and sharp claws, they move really fast, and they're white as drowned men."

That last detail caught Blaine's attention. "White as drowned men? That's odd."

"Not really." Until now, Verran had been quiet, sitting in a corner with his pennywhistle. He had not been in the mines when the cave-in happened, and since he and Dawe were assigned to the farm, they had not been on the clean-up crew. But he had known the dead and injured men, and the sudden, random deaths seemed to hit Verran hard.

"I spent a bit of time down in the tunnels below Castle Reach," he admitted. "Not where you meet the better sort, but then again, I'm not the 'better sort.' Most of those were dug out, but some were natural, or at least very old. And there were some really strange things that lived in them, especially down at the lower levels. Pale white bugs the size of my thumb—or bigger. Odd looking lizard-things that glowed in the dark."

"We checked out some caves when I was in the army," Piran said. "I've seen the same kind of thing. Strange—but not monsters, and nothing that could drag a body away."

"Things up here have been left to themselves for a long, long time." Shorty did not usually have a lot to say, but now, everyone turned to look at him.

"Think about it. Donderath hasn't had a colony—or a prison —on Edgeland for very long. A few decades?" Shorty said. "Don't know that anyone else lived up here to go poking around in the dark places. And now here we come with all our miners and pickaxes, banging around. Most of the time, the things in the caves leave us alone. But once in a while, when the mine breaks through to a cave—"

"The monsters come out," Piran finished.

Bickle nodded. "That would account for the stories that get passed down from one group of prisoners to the next. Sure, maybe the guards want to give us one more thing to be scared of. But the truth is, they don't like the mines either."

"Did anyone see a break-through to the caves, when the ceiling came down?" Blaine asked.

"There was a hole in the back wall of the room," Shorty added, not moving from his bunk. "One that wasn't there before the ceiling came down. I heard that the bodies that went missing were closest to that hole, and that's where the blood trail led."

"Did the guards see anything?" Piran asked.

Shorty turned away. "One of them got snatched. Quick as you could blink. They heard a strange noise, there was a pale white…something…and one of the men gets pulled in before the others could do a thing about it."

"Are you sure this isn't a tall tale, mate?" Verran asked.

"Because I've heard some strange things from drunken men in my day."

"Find me a drunken man in Velant," Shorty challenged. "I can't say for certain it's true. But it's what I heard, from someone I know was there. And usually, he tells the truth."

"Well, damn," Piran said. "Monsters. As if we didn't have enough to worry about."

———

That night, Blaine's dreams were dark. His memories took over, and he was back at Glenreith once again, on the day when everything changed. *Blaine headed for the manor's front entrance at a dead run. Judith was half-way down the stairs. "Blaine, think about this. Blaine—"*

He flung open the door so hard that it crashed against the wall. Blaine ran down the manor's sweeping stone steps. A full moon lit the sloping lawn well enough for Blaine to make out the figure of a man in the distance, strolling down the carriage lane. The smell of his father's pipe smoke wafted back to him, as hated as the odor of camphor that always clung to Lord McFadden's clothing.

The older man turned at the sound of Blaine's running footsteps. "You bastard! You bloody bastard!" Blaine shouted.

Lord Ian McFadden's eyes narrowed as he saw the sword in Blaine's hand. Dropping his pipe, the man grabbed a rake that leaned against the stone fence edging the carriageway. He held its thick oak handle across his body like a staff. Lord McFadden might be well into his fifth decade, but in his youth he had been an officer in the king's army, where he had earned King Merrill's notice and his gratitude. "Go back inside boy. Don't make me hurt you."

Blaine did not slow down or lower his sword. "Why? Why

Mari? There's no shortage of court whores. Why Mari?"

Lord McFadden's face reddened. "Because I can. Now drop that sword if you know what's good for you."

Blaine's blood thundered in his ears. In the distance, he could hear Judith screaming his name.

"I guess this cur needs to be taught a lesson." Lord McFadden swung at Blaine with enough force to have shattered his skull if Blaine had not ducked the heavy rake. McFadden gave a roar and swung again, but Blaine lurched forward, taking the blow on his shoulder to get inside McFadden's guard. The broadsword sank hilt-deep into the man's chest, slicing through his waistcoat.

Lord McFadden's body shuddered, and he dropped the rake. He met Blaine's gaze, his eyes, wide with surprise. "Didn't think you had it in you," he gasped.

Behind him, Blaine could hear footsteps pounding on the cobblestones; he heard panicked shouts and Judith's scream. Nothing mattered to him, nothing at all except for the ashen face of his father. Blood soaked Lord McFadden's clothing and gobbets of it splashed Blaine's hand and shirt. He gasped for breath, his mouth working like a hooked fish out of water. Blaine let him slide from the sword, watched numbly as his father fell backward onto the carriageway in a spreading pool of blood.

"Master Blaine, what have you done?" Selden, the groundskeeper was the first to reach the scene. He gazed in horror at Lord McFadden who lay twitching on the ground, breathing in labored, slow gasps, and finally went still.

Blaine woke in a cold sweat, although the bunk room was warm by Velant standards. He ran a hand through his hair and realized he was trembling.

Father's dead. He can't hurt anyone else ever again. I'm not proud of what I did, but it had to be done, like putting down a rabid dog. I wish Merrill had just hanged me and gotten it over with, but maybe the gods want my penance. To Raka with all of them. I'm not going down easily, and if I can do anything about it, I'm going to earn my Ticket of Leave. That's my revenge— living out the rest of my days as a colonist. I'll make it that long. I swear it.

Gradually, the shaking ceased. His heartbeat slowed to normal, and his breath grew regular once more. He'd been told more than once that only a fraction of the prisoners consigned to Velant survived their three years to earn their Ticket of Leave and become a colonist. And Blaine suspected that the odds were already against him, since Prokief knew he and Piran always seemed to be found wherever there was trouble.

I got the best of father, and I'll beat Prokief at his own game. Just watch me, Blaine vowed.

He heard rustling and eased out of his bunk to see what was going on. Though it was the middle of the night, during the Long Dark the sun never set. The prisoners had hung scraps of material they had scrounged as makeshift curtains to keep out the light, but enough shone around the edges and through the weave of the material to make it possible to see.

Dawe knelt next to the wall, and as Blaine moved closer, he saw that his friend was marking something with a bit of charcoal he had taken from the fireplace on the first level. The drawing was of three figures. In the center was a being with the features of a woman on one side of its body, and the features of a man on the other. Although Blaine was hardly observant in his religion, even he recognized Charrot, the High God.

The female side held out a hand to another male figure that was slightly smaller. The male figure was horned like a goat, and beneath his feet were waves like the sea. That was Torven, one of Charrot's consorts, god of the Sea of Souls, where souls at peace dwelled after death, and Raka, where the rest wandered in darkness.

The male side of the central figure held out a hand to a smaller female figure. Around her feet were sheaves of grain, sheep, and fruit. This was Esthrane, Charrot's second consort, goddess of the ground and all that grew on and in it, and mistress of the Unseen Realm, where the spirits wandered who were not fit for either Raka or the Sea of Souls.

Dawe was so intent on his drawing that he startled when Blaine came up behind him. "Oh, it's you," he said, looking relieved.

Blaine hunkered down beside him. "What's that for?" He noticed that Dawe had placed a crust of bread in front of the drawing as an offering. A small gesture, but all the more potent given that the prisoners were constantly hungry.

Dawe sighed and looked sheepish. "Nothing much. I'm hoping the guards won't notice, since they almost never come up here. I just felt like...after what happened today in the mines...I needed to do something." He let out a long breath. "It's not like I'd known Albert and Tadd long, but I liked them. They didn't cause problems, and they got along with everyone. They hadn't done anything truly bad enough to deserve being here, let alone dying. But now they're gone."

Blaine nodded. He personally had an uneasy truce with the gods of Donderath's pantheon. Though Dawe's drawing didn't show it, the seers and temples of Donderath counted many lesser gods in addition to Charrot and his consorts. The constellations in the night sky were named for the more important gods and goddesses, like Vessa, bringer of fire. Every household claimed its own minor gods and guardian spirits, from the elaborate shrine in Quillarth Castle Blaine had glimpsed when he had visited with his father years ago, to the more modest altars in noble houses. He had heard that even the poorest homes had a place to make offerings, to beg the favor of the gods.

Blaine's mother had kept a shrine to Esthrane at Glenreith,

and made offerings, beseeching the goddess to deliver them all from Ian McFadden's rages. She died putting herself between Ian and Blaine during one of Ian's furies, and on the night she was buried, Blaine dismantled the shrine and threw the pieces into the creek.

"Maybe you shouldn't have done that, Blaine," Mari had said. Of course she had followed him, as she always followed Blaine and Carr.

"Didn't do mother any good," Blaine replied, his voice choked. "Either the goddess wasn't listening, or she's got a mean sense of humor if that's how she reckons deliverance." He had watched the pieces of the shrine float away, blinking back tears.

Mari took his arm and stood next to him. "It might bring bad luck on you."

Blaine swallowed hard before answering. "This is a bad luck house. I don't see how it can get worse."

She looked up at him earnestly. "Don't say that, Blaine. Please. You're tempting the gods. Father's off at court for a month. Maybe he'll stay longer. Maybe the king will send him back out with the army, and he'll be gone a long time."

Blaine gave a harsh, bitter chuckle. "Maybe one of the court whores will slit his throat, or he'll get a shiv in the back in some dark alley, or his horse will throw him off and break his bloody neck."

"Blaine!"

He turned to her. "Don't you dream about that? Pray for it? How much better it would be if he were gone?" He turned back to the creek. "I do. I just wish it happened before this, before he killed her—"

Mari's fingers dug into his arm. "Please, Blaine. Don't do anything foolish."

He looked in her eyes, saw her fear and worry, and managed a comforting smile. "Don't worry," he lied. "I won't do anything stupid. Someone has to look out for you and Carr."

He had stopped believing in the gods that night. The gods had not heard Blaine, or they had declined to listen, and he did not think he had it in him to ever pray so hard again. Aunt Judith had come to manage the manor in Ian's absence, and if she made offerings to the gods, she did so in her own rooms.

"Not much for the gods?" Dawe asked, and Blaine realized he had gone quiet.

Blaine shrugged uncomfortably. "What can I say? They got me where I am today."

Dawe slid him a sideways glance confirming that he read the sarcasm in Blaine's tone. "I heard you talking to Piran, about no one saying a prayer for the dead." He managed a sad smile. "I will. And maybe someday, someone will say one for me when the time comes." He sighed. "For all I know, it's just a comforting habit," Dawe said, putting the finishing touch on his drawing for the evening and sitting back to look at his work. "But comfort's hard to come by up here, so I'll take what I can get."

Dawe wasn't the only one to feel that way. Blaine knew that many of the convicts made amulets for luck or protection, scratching half-remembered runes into bits of wood or metal and carrying them in a pocket. Blaine sometimes envied them their faith, but he could not muster it for himself.

"Put in a good word for Piran and me," Blaine said. "We seem to need it more than we should."

Dawe chuckled. "This is a bad place for honest men," he replied. "You two will make good colonists, if you don't get yourselves killed first."

Blaine clapped Dawe on the shoulder and went back to his bunk, but despite how tired he was, sleep proved elusive.

4

SOUNDS IN THE DARK

"WAKE UP!" PIRAN SAID, BANGING HIS FIST AGAINST THE SIDE of Blaine's bunk. "We've got new orders. No one's in the mine today."

Blaine roused slowly, having barely fallen asleep after bad dreams and old memories made him restless most of the night. He rolled out of his bunk and pulled on his clothing and boots, giving Piran a bleary-eyed glare. "What? Why?"

Piran gave a lopsided grin. "Word has it that Prokief wanted a word with ol' Pig-face about how many prisoners got killed. Seems even the Butcher of Breseshwa thought it was overkill, especially after Pig-face left those three on the whipping posts to die." He jabbed a thumb toward the window.

Blaine moved the fabric aside to see, squinting at the light. Though it was technically spring, temperatures still got killing cold this time of year. Guards were just removing the bodies of the hapless miners from the whipping posts.

"Is Prokief going to do something about him? Doesn't benefit us any if not, because he'll just be twice as mean and looking to take it out on our hides." At least, that had been normal for Ian McFadden, who found a way to make his family, servants, and livestock pay for any frustrations or slights he encountered.

"Don't know," Piran replied. "But Prokief ordered the guards to go in and figure out what needs to be done to shore up the roofs of the other mine rooms with timber, and then he's going to put together crews to do it. I heard the miners aren't to go back in until he's examined the reinforcements personally." Piran gave a nasty smile. "Want to bet he's still going to hold Pig-face to his usual quotas?"

Blaine scowled. "He's not the one who'll have to mine two days' worth of rock in one," he pointed out. "What are we supposed to do in the meantime? While they figure out how we're supposed to prop the roof back up."

Piran threw him his cloak from where it hung on a peg on the wall. "Chop wood. Fetch water for the kitchens. Raise a barn. Pretty much whatever needs a strong back." He grinned. "But no leg irons."

That alone was worth celebrating, Blaine thought as he took his cloak and followed Piran and the other men downstairs. Garrick and Dunbar were still sleeping off their injuries and were likely to be unable to do much for a few more days. But if Prokief had come down on Pig-face for "wasting" his prisoner resources, that meant the odds were good the overseer would grudgingly give the injured miners at least some time to recover, rather than risk incurring Prokief's further ire.

Breakfast was a bit of smoked meat and a chunk of bread with a cut of salty cheese. A cup of hot, black *fet* washed down the food. Outside, the air was a little warmer, a pleasant change from the bitter cold of the recent winter.

Dawe, Verran, and some of the others headed off for the stables. Guards came to collect the miners and put them to work.

"Rowse and McFadden. There's a woodpile over there. Split

it and stack it. We'll bring more," he said, pointing to a huge mound of wood.

"Bickle and Torr," he continued, "go join the bucket brigade. The kitchen needs water to cook some food for your worthless asses." Blaine and Piran headed off toward the woodpile as the guard continued, sending some of the miners to lend a hand with chores, including several who were sent out to the fields now that planting had begun.

"Not too bad, considering the choices," Piran said as he rolled up his sleeves. Blaine did the same, and then rolled a thick length of wood into position as he took up his ax. He had cut plenty of firewood back at Glenreith, partially out of necessity, but often to work off his rage at Ian's latest offense. He had always found the repetition and the visible results to be gratifying.

Blaine had not realized how much he missed sunlight. The mines had not been bad duty during the Long Dark, when it was nearly as black outside as it was deep below the ground. But now, in the White Nights, being in the darkness of the mines during the day and coming up to the unending sunlight in the evenings turned the natural order of things upside down.

"You think they'll keep us in the mines for the duration?" Blaine asked. He and Piran had been silent for a while, content to settle into the steady rhythm of the axes.

"Thing is, they could put us out on farm duty, but they can't very well put most of the farm prisoners into the mine," Piran said. He had been at Velant for six months longer than Blaine, and had seen more of how the camp operated. "So yeah, it's possible." He paused to bring his ax down with a crack on a thick chunk of wood, splitting it neatly.

"Later this spring, we might get pulled out onto the herring boats," he added. "Not sure you'd see that as better than the mines. It's cold, wet work, you can't get the fish stink off your skin for days, and the only thing worse than eating herring is gutting them."

"You know, I've been thinking about the cave-in," Blaine said. "I'm wondering if in all the confusion, anyone ever accounted for all of the tools."

"Doubtful," Piran replied. "And I'd bet some of them have been hidden and spirited away, for use at a more convenient time."

Blaine raised an eyebrow. "Then how come you didn't steal one?"

"If you recall, we were lucky enough to survive," Piran pointed out. "I was concentrating on getting out of there alive. I'm betting the ones with the best shot of taking tools are the clean-up crew. They can always say the missing shovels and axes were destroyed." He paused. "They'll be the ones to loot the bodies, too, what's left of them. And I know for certain both Carl and Hort had small knives. Wonder where they'll turn up?" Hort and Carl had been among the convicts already established in the dormitory when Blaine and his group arrived. Piran had known them fairly well, but Blaine had never spoken to them outside of the usual comments down in the mine.

It was easy to lose track of time, since the sun never dipped below the horizon on the White Nights. Blaine's stomach had been rumbling for a while before he spotted a dark-haired woman heading toward them with a bucket of water and a basket.

"Food—if you're quick about it," she said, but although her tone was terse, her blue eyes softened the sting.

Piran and Blaine accepted several dippers full of water gratefully, thirsty even in the cold. "It's bread with a bit of meat and cheese stuffed inside," she said, pulling back a cloth to reveal what was in the basket. "All the cooks were in the mood to fix, I guess. Mind that you only take one each!"

Her stern tone did not match her face. Blaine guessed that she was close to his own age, with dark hair cut short for prison. Though her face was smudged with soot and dirt, she was pretty in a worn way.

"Do you always stare at the people who bring you food?" she challenged.

Piran guffawed. Blaine elbowed him and felt his cheeks redden. "No. Sorry. It's just that—"

"You're new, aren't you?" she interrupted. "And you haven't seen a woman since you got off the ship. Sorry, mate. This is as close as they'll let you get."

"What's your name?" he asked.

She seemed to find his interest amusing, perhaps because it was utterly hopeless. "Selane," she replied, casting a glance over her shoulder in case a guard was looming. "And I'd better keep moving if I know what's good for me—and I usually do." She seemed to relent. "What's your name?"

"Mick," Blaine replied. "And this is—"

Selane rolled her eyes. "Everybody here knows Piran Rowse. He's a bit like the pox—popping up everywhere, like it or not."

"Hey!" Piran objected. "I don't have the pox!"

Selane gave him a measured head-to-toe glance. "Mind I said 'pox,' not 'clap,'" she retorted. "I might believe you about the pox."

"Thanks for the food," Blaine said before Piran could manage to steal her complete attention.

"I'm usually in the laundry," Selane said. "But things are crazy enough today, they sent us around with food. I probably won't see you again."

"You never know," he replied, although he suspected she was right. She gave Blaine a shy smile, made a gesture as if to swat Piran out of her way, and headed down the line with her bucket and basket.

"Just for the record," Piran said indignantly. "I do not have the clap."

"What do you know about her?" Blaine asked, following Selane with his gaze.

Piran chuckled. "Stop mooning. I've seen her once or twice. The women don't get out of their building much. Probably not a bad idea, considering. All I know is one of the people who was on the ship with her from Donderath said she swore she was innocent. Shop girl, I think. Someone said she stole something— wouldn't matter whether it was true or not, if it's the owner's word against yours."

He hefted his pickax to get back to work. "She's right, you know. You probably won't see her again—at least, not unless you both survive to make it to the colony."

"How about the colonists?" Blaine asked, glad to leave the topic of Selane behind. "Do you know anyone who's gotten his Ticket?"

Swish-crack. Another piece of wood fell, neatly split. "Some. Not many. Most people leave Velant feet-first." *Dead.* "But there've been a few. Can't say that the colonists have it much easier, although they're not quite as far under the guards' thumbs."

"The guards still patrol Skalgerston Bay," Blaine said.

Piran nodded. "Yeah. And ultimately, Prokief is still boss. But Bay-town isn't the whole colony. If you make it long enough to earn your Ticket, you get a pouch of coins and a grant of ten acres of land." He barked a laugh. "Now, that's ten acres of Edgeland land, which isn't like the farms back in Donderath. It's hard-scrabble. But people manage. They build a house, buy some chickens and goats, grow whatever they can. Sometimes, people go in together to make a common homestead and work it together. That's the way to do it. Most folks only go into Bay-town for supplies or news, so I hear," Piran said. "The homesteads are out beyond the town. And the guards hardly ever go out there." He gave a knowing grin. "The guards know they're only safe in packs, where there are plenty of witnesses. Out on the farms, far from town, anything could happen, and no one would be the wiser."

Piran fell silent as one of the guards strode toward them. "Move the wood you've cut out behind the kitchen and laundry. There's a pile out there. Be quick about it; the Overseer expects you to finish the rest of this stack today."

Blaine and Piran loaded up armfuls of wood and headed behind the nearby row of buildings. The woodpile was set back from the buildings for fire reasons, closer to the high stockade fence than to the laundry and kitchen. There was already a large neat "wall" of stacked cordwood that came almost to the top of Blaine's head. But when they rounded the corner, Piran frowned and stopped, warning Blaine with a shake of his head to halt and say nothing.

Slightly warmer temperatures had softened the ground. And in the mud behind the laundry, a confusing muddle of footprints appeared to have been caused by a struggle. One set of footprints led away, onto rocky ground.

Piran and Blaine quietly set their wood down and followed a rustling noise out behind the woodpile. They split up, one to each side, moving silently. *No one can see the space between the woodpile and the stockade,* Blaine thought. *It's hidden from the buildings, and there's no guard post close by on this stretch of the fence.*

When Blaine came around the woodpile, he saw a red-haired woman struggling against a muscular guard. Blaine and Piran started forward to help, since it was clear what the guard's intentions were. The woman twisted in the guard's grasp, and pulled her attacker off balance, forcing him to tumble across her shoulders. He had barely landed on the ground before she had a knife in him.

Blaine and Piran stopped in their tracks. The guard's eyes bulged and his face purpled. His mouth moved as if to scream, but only a hiss emerged from his lips. He moaned in pain, and his whole body went rigid, then he collapsed and lay still.

The woman was bent over the guard, and she raised her head with an angry hiss when she realized she was discovered. Blaine saw a knife glint in her hand.

"Do you need help getting rid of that?" Blaine asked, holding up his hands, palms out to show he meant no harm. "He looks heavy."

"Did you just say what I think you said?" Piran asked.

Blaine shrugged. "I figure we all benefit if the problem disappears as quickly as possible."

A bemused smile touched the woman's lips. She was slim and short, but clearly stronger than she looked. Her red hair was pulled back in a braid, and her face was smudged with dirt— maybe blood—but her green eyes suggested intelligence.

"Over there," she murmured, with a nod of her head.

Blaine went to lift the dead guard while Piran stood watch. The woman walked a few more steps to where sparse grass partly covered a wooden door set flush with the ground. She gave a tug and opened the door part way, to a passage that loomed into darkness.

"Put him in," she said, and then added, "please."

"What is that?" Blaine asked, lugging the body to the opening and rolling him inside. The man fell like a sack of rocks, and Blaine did not hear him hit bottom.

"Old dry well. Convenient for these kinds of things."

"Are you done yet?" Piran hissed.

"Are you all right?" Blaine asked. He didn't need an explanation to figure out why the guard was dead. The woman was pretty and alone. He could guess most of what happened next.

She gave a curt nod. "Better than he is, that's for certain." She gave him a sidelong look. "You look familiar. I'm Kestel Falke."

Blaine shook his head. "I don't think we've met. I'm Mick. McFadden."

She glanced toward Piran. "Him, I know. Everyone knows Rowse. You'd better get out of here."

Piran glanced from Kestel to where Blaine had thrown the body. "This gives me an idea," he said quietly. "How did you do it? That little knife shouldn't have killed him."

Kestel flashed a proud grin. "Poisoned blade. He had it coming. Tried to get too friendly."

Piran gave her a cagy look. "You owe us, since we helped out here."

"And you'll get us all caught if you don't get out of here," she said, hands on hips.

"I want some of that poison," Piran said. "Consider it hush money."

Kestel rolled her eyes, but she dug beneath her bodice and pulled out a small folded bit of parchment. "Here," she said. "I can make more. Mind you don't get it under your skin, or you'll be the dead one. Works best on a blade. Doesn't need much of a cut, but deeper is better. Works pretty fast." She eyed Piran. "You have someone in mind?"

Piran grinned. "Oh yeah. And he's definitely got it coming."

"You're kidding—an assassin?" Blaine questioned as he and Piran headed back to the woodpile, after stacking the cordwood behind the laundry and kitchen. Just for good measure, they had made certain to muddy the footprints so that no one would notice one man's boots never walked away.

Piran nodded and glanced around to make certain they

wouldn't be overheard. "Yeah. Spy, too, from what they say. And the most popular courtesan in King Merrill's court. Not like I was ever anywhere near the royal court, but we heard stories in the army from some of the officers. It was quite a big deal when she got caught. Apparently, she worked for some pretty powerful nobles—maybe even the king himself. They couldn't let her go, but she had the money and the connections to finagle exile instead of hanging, so here she is."

Blaine's mouth went dry. *She thought I looked familiar. Could she possibly have remembered me from court? I didn't go often, but often enough, perhaps. But I was nobody important, no one worth remembering.* Another possibility occurred to him. *Unless my father bought her services—or one of his enemies did, and I got to him first.*

That raised disquieting possibilities. Blaine decided to put them out of his mind—for now.

"What do you intend to do with the item you got?" Blaine asked in a low voice as they returned to finish chopping wood.

Piran gave him a look as if he were a simpleton. "What do you think?"

Blaine rolled his eyes. "I didn't mean *what* so much as *who*."

Piran cocked an eyebrow. "I think you know. But the bigger question is how. That's going to take some planning."

"You've never heard the saying 'better the wolf you know than the wolf you don't?'"

Piran chuckled. "You mean a replacement could be worse than the original."

"It's certainly possible, given where we are."

Piran gave Blaine a look as he thought for a moment. "You killed someone to end up here, didn't you?"

Blaine had not shared the details of his story with anyone in Velant, but the branded "M" for "murderer" on his forearm made some things public knowledge. "Yeah. But you knew that already."

Piran nodded. "Are you sorry about it?"

"Not in the least," Blaine replied without stopping to think about it.

"Even though you'll pay a price for it for the rest of your life?"

Blaine grimaced as he saw where Piran was going with his logic. "I get it," he said. "But have a care. I thought what I did brought judgment on me alone. I discovered that my actions affected a lot of other people who might not think I did them any favors."

"You think it can get worse than it is?"

Blaine inclined his head toward one of the bodies in the gibbet. "Ask him."

———

"It figures that Prokief would put us on the crew to prop the damn roof back up," Piran muttered.

"I suspect that we're near the top of his list when it comes to expendable prisoners," Blaine replied.

Two days had passed since the disaster, enough time for Pig-face and the other mine bosses to be sure the collapse would not trigger a series of cave-ins before they sent a team of miners into the wreckage.

"Keep it down!" Pig-face snapped from where he stood in the safety of the corridor. "There's work to do. Your quotas haven't changed. The longer it takes to shore up the roof, the more you'll have to mine to make up for lost time."

Shielded from Pig-face's view by his body, Piran made an obscene gesture at the overseer, a futile but satisfying defiance. Bickle, Torr, and Shorty had been sent into the mine with them.

Now, as Blaine looked around the debris-clogged room, he hardly knew where to begin.

"We could use some light," Piran yelled over his shoulder. "The cave-in took out half the lanterns. We can't dig out what we can't see."

Pig-face gestured to a cart full of tools and equipment. "So, put up sconces. There are torches in the wagon."

Blaine and Piran exchanged a glance. "Commander Prokief forbade torches because of the firedamp," Blaine replied. "Firedamp" was what miners called the bad air that sometimes seeped into mine chambers. It was highly explosive.

"We don't have lanterns to spare," Pig-face said. "Use the torches or do without."

"I don't fancy surviving a cave-in to be blown sky high," Piran muttered.

Pig-face might not have heard Piran's actual comment, but he must have suspected the intent. The overseer strode into the room and backhanded Piran hard enough that Piran had to take a step to avoid being thrown off balance.

"Don't try my patience, Rowse," Pig-face growled. "There'll be a new boatful of convicts soon. Plenty of muscle for the mines. Don't think you can't be replaced."

Pig-face shouldered his way back to the tunnel. Rage burned in Piran's eyes as his gaze followed the overseer, but for once, Piran kept his tongue.

"Let's get the torches in place. Sooner we can see, the sooner we're done," Blaine said.

Before long, the torches blazed, illuminating the room. "What a mess," Bickle sighed, taking in the full extent of the damage now that they could see.

Rock dust was thick over everything. A huge pile of rocks lay where the roof had collapsed. Some were stained dark with dried blood. The task was monumental. It would take five men days to clear the rubble—assuming the dust didn't ignite and cause a second explosion.

Blaine and the others bent to their task. Pig-face hovered the doorway. "McFadden! Pick up the pace," Pig-face ordered. "All of you—no lunch or water until you clear to the first pillar." He leaned against the wall of the tunnel with a satisfied smirk and took a long, noisy drink of water from his canteen, taunting the thirsty men as he let the precious water drip from his chin.

The torn leather gloves Blaine wore came from Tadd's meager possessions, but they were of no use to a dead man. Even with the gloves, the rough rocks tore his skin. Time and again they were obliged to take up pickaxes to break huge rocks into rubble small enough to lug over to the wheeled cart.

After a candlemark, two guards came in with large buckets of water. Blaine and the others, thirsty and tired, looked up expectantly. But instead of providing them with drinks, the guards used their dippers to soak the rough rock in the central pile, the walls and floor. In the process, a good bit of the water soaked the miners, though none of it was given for drink.

"Keeping the dust down, like you wanted," Pig-face announced.

Piran's glare was murderous, and even Bickle made a low growl in anger. Pig-face's expression made it clear that he relished the chance to exact his petty revenge.

For the moment, the soaking felt good, washing away some of the sweat and grime. But soon enough, the mine's chill would make damp clothing miserable, despite their hard labor. Blaine clenched his jaw so hard his teeth ached, but he kept on working. *Finish up. Get out. That's what matters,* he told himself.

The miners worked in shifts, trading off between breaking up the big rocks, hauling chunks to the cart, and pushing the heavy cart out of the mine. Pig-face made a show of lounging as they worked. He could have assigned watching them to a guard, but it was clear the overseer was enjoying the situation.

Torch light flickered across the walls, making the shadows dance. More than once, Blaine cast a nervous glance over his shoulder as movement caught his eye. He kept on working, focusing his attention on the pillar that was their milestone. Blaine's stomach rumbled and his throat was parched, but he consoled himself with the thought that they were closing in on their objective.

Finally, they cleared the last of the rocks from the first pillar. Much more of the room remained, but the tired, thirsty miners brought the last arm-load of rocks to the cart and dropped them with a clang and a thud into its dented depths.

"All right," Piran said. "We've reached the first pillar. How about some food and water?"

If it were up to Pig-face, Blaine wouldn't have been surprised for the overseer to force them to work until they dropped from hunger or dehydration. But Prokief monitored the mines like a business, and if too many miners were injured, the king's quotas went un-met. Prokief's need to keep King Merrill happy was the miners' only security.

Pig-face clapped his hands, and two guards brought buckets of water and a large basket of hard bread and dried meat. "Eat fast," he snapped at the prisoners. "There's more work to do."

Blaine gulped down the water as a guard ladled it into his mouth, already feeling woozy from dehydration. The food helped, though both food and water were too little, after too long a wait. Everyone fell silent, eating as quickly as they could.

In the quiet, Blaine heard a strange scrabbling noise, and an unnatural squealing that sent a chill down his spine.

"What's that?" Piran demanded. "That noise—what's making it?"

"Not your concern," Pig-face retorted, though it looked to

Blaine as if the overseer was frightened. The guards in the tunnel cast wary glances toward the darkness and readied their weapons.

"There's something down there—or your men wouldn't have drawn their swords," Piran pressed.

Pig-face's fear became rage. He came at Piran and Blaine wild-eyed, just barely hanging onto control. "Get back to work," he growled, "or by all the gods, I will send you down that tunnel without a torch and you can find out for yourself what's down there—and whether it's hungry."

———

The rest of the miners returned to their work the next day. The mood was darker than usual. Three bodies still swung from the gallows, and two more languished in the gibbets. Rumors spread about the men who had been sent to the depths of the ruby mines without hope of ever seeing the sun again.

"I heard it goes so deep, it gets hot again," one of the men said to the miners in earshot. "You know, where all that liquid rock is that spews out of the volcano now and again." Estendall, a large volcano, sat several miles off the coast of Edgeland. It had not erupted for quite some time, but stories abounded, passed down from one group of convicts and colonists to the next.

"They say there are creatures in the deep places that eat men," another miner ventured. "Horrible things that can't stand to be in daylight or breathe the air up above."

"If there are monsters in the deep, why don't they ever come up and snatch the miners up above?" one of his fellows challenged. "What do they eat?"

"How do you know they don't snatch a man or two, now and again?" his companion argued. "Men go missing down here. The guards blame it on bad air or falling into a hole. Who's to say they're not lying?"

"Has anyone ever seen these monsters?" Piran leaned on his ax for a moment. "Well?"

"If you got close enough to see them, they'd see you and eat you!" The miner's two companions nodded in agreement. Blaine remembered what Carl had told them, and suppressed a shiver.

"You heard something about the monsters on the lowest levels?' Blaine asked.

"Heard about monsters…not sure where," one of the men replied. "Just that they go real deep, and only come up now and again. Maybe all the blood from that cave-in made them hungry."

His friends guffawed, and Piran's jaw clenched. Blaine was sure Piran was thinking of their bunkmates who had been killed or injured. "Maybe the monsters are a story they tell to keep us in line," Piran replied, taking up his pickax again. "We've seen enough monsters above ground." But something flashed in Piran's gaze, for a moment, just long enough for Blaine to know that Piran had an idea. Most likely, a dangerous idea.

Despite Piran's bravado, Blaine could tell that the last few days wore heavy on his friend. Piran's gaze followed Pig-face and the guards, and Blaine knew him well enough to see the desire for revenge still burned hot.

Blaine and his friends were back in the room where the cave-in had occurred. He suspected Pig-face enjoyed sending the same teams into the area who had already survived the collapse, knowing that fear of a second disaster would increase their discomfort. He and the others worked in groups of nine, three triads of shackled men to a room, in areas that were much smaller than the cavernous area that had collapsed.

"We're behind on quota," Pig-face shouted, striding through the room. His whip was coiled on his belt, but he carried a flail, and brought it down hard on the neck and shoulders of men he considered to be moving too slowly.

"Fewer miners means more for each of you to mine," Pig-face taunted, taking Prokief's support as confirmation that he was supreme in his authority down below. "Teach you to be more careful. It was shoddy work that brought down the ceiling, and I won't have any more of that! We lost access to valuable ruby rock because of carelessness. And if you don't know the punishment for carelessness, have a look at the gallows and the gibbet on your way topside."

Piran's hands clenched around his pickax white-knuckled. Blaine felt his teeth grind in frustration. *Those men were executed for a show of power and dominance,* Blaine thought. *The only one who was careless was Pig-face. Our lives are worth less than a horse or a mule to him, because the animals still have worth back in Donderath—we're just refuse they threw away.*

"The next time you're tempted to be careless, think of your friends in the deep," Pig-face gloated. "They'll never see daylight again. The work's even harder down there, because fewer miners have dug it out—yet. That might change," he added with a smirk, a threat no one could mistake.

"On the other hand, they don't have to worry about dying, like you do," he added. "Oh, they could be crushed or dismembered, that's true. But not much else will kill them. The warden-mages saw to that." His grin was ugly. "Not 'till I'm done with them. If they can crawl, they'll mine."

Piran made a low growling noise. Blaine brought a hand down on Piran's shoulder, warning him, and Piran shook free with a look of irritation. *Pig-face is baiting us. He'd probably love to have more miners to torture and use up below—especially Piran and me. But that's not in my plans,* Blaine thought.

"I want my Ticket of Leave," Blaine muttered, just low enough for Piran to hear.

Piran gave him a murderous look, and Blaine stared him down. With a curse, Piran looked away and went back to his digging with renewed zeal, no doubt picturing himself putting his ax into Pig-face's head with every swing.

Blane made sure Pig-face had no reason to use his flail on any of their triad. He and the others worked at a steady pace, enough to produce a pile of rock that compared favorably to the output of any other group, but not so quickly or productively as to raise the expectations for them all. It was a tactic Blaine's father, Ian McFadden, had frequently accused the farm hands on their land of employing, usually in terms just as contemptuous as those Pig-face used.

Those were free men, not prisoners, not even bound to the land, Blaine thought with a sigh. *But they were smart. Father would have used them up and burned them out, just like Pig-face, if they had let him control the pace. This is good enough to get us by. Once we've got our Tickets and our homestead, we'll see how hard we can really work—for ourselves, not some damn overseer.*

Blaine was well aware that the odds were against his surviving Velant and earning the chance to become a colonist. Those odds were particularly bad considering his friendship— and shackle-partnership—with Piran Rowse, who seemed intent on causing trouble.

Piran's quick with his fists, but almost always with good reason. I've never seen him fight just to trounce someone weaker. Usually, he takes on blowhards his size or bigger. I suspect it's something left of his military days. He hates a bully even more than I do.

Blaine tried to lose himself in the mindless rhythm of the rise and fall of his pickax. But when that was impossible, he pictured just how he would set up his homestead, once he earned his Ticket of Leave. In the months since he had arrived in Velant, since he had first learned of the possibility of "graduating" from the prison to become a colonist, Blaine had tried to learn as much as he could about the process. Many of the convicts dismissed the possibility out of hand, as a cruel dream dangled by Prokief and the overseers to keep prisoners from committing suicide in a mass riot that took the guards to the grave with them.

Yet Skalgerston Bay and its colonists were real, and since no one came to live on Edgeland except as convicts, that meant some of those prisoners did survive Prokief's rule to earn their Tickets of Leave. Blaine was resolved to be among them when his three years were up—assuming he could keep Piran from getting him killed.

"You're thinking about your homestead again, aren't you?" Piran said, and shook his head.

Blaine shrugged, and Ernest chuckled. "It's a nice change. What do you think about?"

"Food, mostly," Ernest replied. "Beer. And the comforts of a pretty brunette I was forced to leave behind." He sighed, and his regret was only partly affected.

Piran raised an eyebrow. "I'm compiling as long a list as I can of creative ways to kill someone," he replied, and while he did not elaborate, they were all certain who that "someone" was.

Blaine rolled his eyes. "I've done that. It's overrated." He had spent much of his childhood imagining ways his hated father might die in accidents and not come home. The list had been varied and imaginative, but none of the scenarios had prepared him for what actually happened.

"Looking forward to something makes it twice as good," Piran replied.

"You're a sick bastard, you know that?"

Piran chuckled. "Up here, that's a compliment. And a survival trait," he added, cocking an eyebrow.

Despite Piran's heckling, Blaine found refuge in mentally

designing the small house and necessary outbuildings for his someday homestead. Back at Glenreith, he had helped out in the fields out of necessity, and to stay out of his father's way. It was probably not seemly for the lord's son to take off his shirt and toil with the laborers, but the exertion had likely bought Ian several more years of life by working off Blaine's anger.

Now, that experience stood him in good stead. He had helped to raise barns and build storage sheds. His homestead would need both, as well as a cabin for him to live in. He knew enough about farming from helping with the harvest that he felt confident about raising a garden, and as a child, he had loved tending to the livestock. Ian McFadden might have been noble, but the family's best days were behind them even before Blaine's scandal. Perhaps the scion of better-off nobility would never have soiled their hands in the barns or fields, but necessity gave Blaine little choice. Now, those hard experiences might come in handy.

"So what are you going to do, if you get your Ticket?" Ernest asked, sincerely interested. Blaine guessed that fantasizing about the future—anywhere but Velant—might be a common escape.

"We get some land, and a bag of coins as our portion when we leave the prison," Blaine said. "I figure that money has to mostly go for seed and livestock and tools. I can cut down trees for lumber. And I know a bit about raising crops and keeping chickens. A cabin can't be too hard to build. It can't be too big, or there's no way to keep it warm. And then a shed for the tools and livestock. I figure it'll be small to start. I can always make it bigger."

"I hear some of the colonists pool their portions with friends to get a better start," Ernest said. "That way, more people help with the building and the crops and the animals."

"Worth a thought," Blaine said. If he had to make a list of people he might trust to go in on a homestead together, Piran would be one of them. Dawe Killick and Verran Danning might be good choices, too. Solid, steady Ernest wouldn't be a bad option, either.

"Colonists don't just have to farm," Piran said. "They can earn a living in Bay-town if they have the skills."

"I thought you didn't pay any attention to things like that?" Blaine joked.

Piran shrugged. "I hear things. You'd be surprised."

"Like what?" Ernest asked. Mining was boring work, and talking whiled the time away. The mine was dimly lit with lanterns, stuffy despite the cool air outside, and thinking too hard about being far below ground could make any man claustrophobic. Idle chatter kept Blaine's mind busy so that it didn't run to darker territory.

"There's always need for good blacksmiths and talented whores," Piran said, flashing a rakish grin. "Beyond that, I expect it's like any village. They'll need bakers and hedge witches, fishermen, net-makers, carpenters, coopers, and cobblers. Seamstresses and tailors, too, since I figure not everyone can make clothing."

"And candle-makers, wagon-makers, and wheelwrights," Ernest said. "Plus sail-makers and boat builders for the fishing fleet."

"And don't forget someone to brew the beer and distill spirits," Piran added. "I hear that the Crooked House is the best tavern in Bay-town, but sailors are a thirsty bunch. Someone with a talent could probably do well."

It was odd, thinking of a "normal" town on the edge of the world, Blaine mused. But the Bay-town residents would need all the same necessities—and long for the same comforts—as the people back in Donderath. *I was born noble. I never learned a trade, since I was supposed to inherit Glenreith someday. So I'd best pick mates with skills to bring in money if I partner up with*

*my homestead. And I guess that means I'm going to be fishing
for a lot of herring.*

"So what do you want, if you get your Ticket?" Blaine
asked Ernest, knowing Piran would give him a flippant
response.

Ernest considered the question. "I wouldn't mind a place of
my own, or with some friends," he said finally. "Never had any
elbow room growing up with ten brothers and sisters. Build a
little place, find a wife, settle down." His gaze became distant as
the pickax in his hand rose and fell.

"I've been around boats all my life, so the herring fleet
wouldn't bother me. I might like that, though I suspect the
weather up here gets a lot worse than back home. Still," he
mused, "a boat's a boat. I'm pretty good at patching boats, even
made and mended some nets now and again. So maybe that
would give me a trade over in Bay-town."

"Don't get your hopes up." Pig-face's voice was nasal and
grating. "None of the likes of you are going to earn a Ticket.
'Least not to anything except the burying yard." He laughed
heartily at his own joke, poking Piran in the ribs on his way by.
Piran stiffened and looked as if he might take a swing at Pig-
face, then with great effort took a deep breath and thought better
of it.

Pig-face's comments had exactly the effect he intended,
dampening the mood. Exile itself was not the worst of being sent
to Velant, nor—at least to Blaine's mind—was the scandal of
being a criminal. He had accepted the responsibility for his
actions. The hardest part to live with was the petty mean-spirit-
edness of overseers and guards who enforced a pecking order
within the ranks of the damned.

*Maybe it's better in Bay-town when the colonists aren't so far
under the guards' control every waking moment,* Blaine thought.
For some space to do what I please without someone watching

over my shoulder, I'd take the homestead farthest from town, convenience be damned.

To Blaine's right, Torr's pickax hit the rock wall and sank in deeper than usual. "What in Raka?" he muttered as he struggled to pull his ax free.

"Looks like you broke through to another room," Shorty observed as Torr's pickax came free and the rock fell away to reveal a dark hole.

"There isn't another room on the other side of us," Whinny said. "Overseer told us we could mine the whole way across Edgeland from here."

"Well, there's something," Piran said, intrigued. He signaled for Bickle, Torr, and Shorty to watch the doorway, and led Blaine and Ernest over to have a look.

"Cool air," Torr observed. "I wonder if it's true that there are caves underneath parts of Edgeland."

"If there are caves, either Pig-face doesn't want us to know about them, or he doesn't know," Ernest observed quietly.

"Not likely to do us much good," Bickle said. "Even if we got into the caves, and even if they went somewhere, you can't run away up here at the top of the world. There's nowhere to go."

"Maybe that's why Pig-face isn't worried," Whinny replied. "The monsters will get you first."

"Too bad the monsters don't get Pig-face first," Bickle said.

Piran met Blaine's gaze without saying anything. Blaine felt a chill go down his spine.

———

That night, Blaine was on kitchen crew, washing out the tin cups and plates afforded to the prisoners. Each one had to be accounted for every night, lest someone steal one and fashion it into a weapon. The three-person group to which he was linked in the mines was the unit to which he was assigned elsewhere in the camp, at least for now. Piran cleaned up garbage, while Ernest brought new plates for Blaine to wash, then carried away (and counted) the clean plates.

A scratching at the door made Blaine glance in that direction. "Did anyone else hear that?" he asked.

Piran and Ernest nodded. Carefully, Piran headed toward the door. He grabbed a cord of wood and held it like a bludgeon as Ernest swung the door open wide.

Kestel Falke dodged inside in a swirl of black cloth and red hair. She moved in a blur that put Piran on his back, still clutching his cord of wood, and sent Ernest across the room. "I came to warn you," she said.

Blaine glanced over his shoulder toward the common room. Piran got to his feet and went to stand guard by the door, while Ernest immediately began shuffling tin dishes around to make the maximum noise possible to hide their conversation.

"You shouldn't be here," Blaine said.

"Well, I'm here," Kestel replied, hands on hips as if she was daring him to make something of it. After seeing her put Piran on his back with apparent effortlessness and send Ernest reeling, Blaine had no desire to pick a fight.

"What's going on?'

"Pig-face is out for you," she said. Considering the severity of the punishment if she were to be caught with them—for all of them—she looked cool and unruffled. *Maybe the rumors about her being a spy and assassin are really true,* Blaine thought. "I overheard two of the guards talking. He wants an excuse to either kill you or send you Below."

"Why?" Blaine asked.

Kestel gave him a scathing look. "I don't know. Probably your natural charm." She pushed a bit of torn fabric with markings on it into his hand. "I've got to get back. But you did me a good turn. We're even."

"Thanks," Blaine said, but she was already out the door before he spoke.

"Well, damn," Piran said.

Ernest looked a little dazed from the surprise visit. "What's on the rag she gave you?"

Blaine looked down at the scrap of fabric and frowned. "It looks like a map," he said. "But it doesn't look like the mine tunnels we use."

Piran came over for a look while Ernest watched the door. "Those don't look like just mine tunnels. I think it's showing the caves."

"Caves." Blaine echoed.

Piran nodded. "Yeah. Guess those rumors are true." He stared at the map. "So she came here to warn us, and gives us this, knowing what we already have."

"No real surprise, but nice to get a warning," Blaine observed. "Pig-face has been out to get us for a while."

"Then we're going to have to do something about Pig-face," Piran said in a low voice, "before he does something about us." He smiled. "And I think she was giving us a suggestion on how to make him disappear."

5

MONSTERS

BLAINE, PIRAN, AND ERNEST WENT BACK INTO THE MINE THE
next day. Guards shackled them at the ankles near the entrance to
the mine, and they shuffled in.

The cold air was not frigid enough to keep the bodies of the
dead men in the parade yard from decomposing. The stench
carried on the air, and even the wood smoke from the chimneys
could not mask the smell. Crows and vermin picked at the
bodies, making the corpses swing from the nooses, and tearing at
those who remained suspended against the whipping posts. The
men in the gibbets moaned like the spirits of the damned, denied
the relief of shock or death by the warden-mages.

Most of the prisoners ducked their heads as they passed by
the corpses or the gibbets. It was impossible not to see the
bodies. Some of the miners who had been friends with the
murdered men refused to look away, as if bearing witness to the
deaths was a tribute to their fallen comrades.

Gone, too, were the men sent Below. They had disappeared
as if they never existed without even leaving behind a body to be

mourned. All that remained were the scant personal items left behind in their bunks that vanished soon after without a trace.

One of the murdered miners had been from Blaine's barracks, and two died in the cave-in, while two more were sent Below. Their bunks would go unfilled until the next ships came with new prisoners from Donderath. Until then, the empty spaces were a constant reminder of Pig-face's vicious temper.

"Didn't deserve that…"

"…supposed to just stand there and be crushed?"

"…pox take his wretched hide."

Men muttered about the deaths once the guards were out of earshot. Even that was courting disaster, since there was always the chance that one of the prisoners might sell information to the guards for favors. The tension in the air was new, potent and dangerous, different from the underlying, ever-present sense of frustration. It reminded Blaine of how it felt in a thunderstorm, right before lightning struck nearby. Tempers were combustible, and it would not take much to fan a spark into a conflagration.

Since Kestel's warning the night before, Blaine felt jumpy. He wasn't sure which had him more on edge; Pig-face's scheme to get rid of them or Piran's intention to kill the overseer first. *This could end badly either way*, he thought. *Pig-face could lock us away for the rest of our lives in the Deep. But if we kill him and get caught, Prokief will kill us as slowly and painfully as possible. Damn. There are plenty of ways to lose and only one chance to win.*

Once they were inside the mine, Blaine realized that Piran had managed to move them a bit from their previous spot. All the mining teams gradually moved to reach new areas of the mine room walls, and the change in position was slight, but it placed Piran slightly behind one of the posts holding up the ceiling, where he was out of the guards' line of sight for some of the time. This room was small with only nine miners: Bickle, Torr, and Shorty were one team, Jaston, Eddles, and Jame were the second triad, and Blaine, Piran, and Ernest made up the last group.

No one but he and Piran knew of the map. "Cover for me," Piran murmured. Blaine and Ernest shifted their positions to better hide Piran from view. Every few strokes, Piran struck to one side. *He's looking for a way into the caves,* Blaine thought. *From what the map shows, they've got to be off to the side and below us somewhere. It's amazing the mine hasn't broken through to them more often.*

Then again, it was likely that the original mine had begun in natural caves. *If that's true, then many of these rooms might be part of the cave system. So there are bound to be tunnels or passageways nearby.*

At any other prison, Piran's zeal would have been part of a plan to escape. But on Edgeland, escape was nearly impossible. Even if they could elude the guards, tracking dogs, and warden-mages, the colonists could not afford to risk Prokief's wrath by sheltering them, and without the protection of the colony, death was all but certain from the harsh terrain, unforgiving weather, and scarce resources. But Piran wanted something else—a place to hide a body.

Bickle's group worked steadily, and whenever Piran began to whistle, theirs was the first triad to pick up the song, however badly off-key. Torr and Shorty moved with the rhythm of long practice. Whinny had come down with a fever too high even for the guards to ignore, and so Jame was shackled in his place.

Jame's movements were jerky, and he seemed ill-suited to the work. The pickax was too heavy for him to lift properly, and Blaine winced just watching the awkward way Jame swung the tool. *It'll be a wonder if he can move tomorrow, if he doesn't put the point of that pick through someone's foot before then,* Blaine thought.

Jame struggled with the pickax, but his mind did not seem to be on his work. His eyes darted from one side to the other, and he licked his lips frequently as if gathering his nerve.

"Bend your knees and swing from your hips," Torr suggested. "It'll save your back."

"I'll do as I please!" Jame snapped. His eyes seemed a bit too wide, his voice a little too thin. *Maybe he's panicking about being belowground,* Blaine thought. Some miners struggled in their first days deep in the mines. *Best if you don't think how far down you are, how much rock is over your head, how easily it could all come crashing down.*

"Easy!" Bickle said, with a bit of an edge. "Just trying to help."

"I don't need your help."

Bickle and Torr exchanged a glance. "Yeah. Tell us tomorrow when you can't get out of your bunk. But go ahead. Don't let us stop you." They went back to their work, doing their best to stay out of Jame's way. That was difficult with a length of chain binding them together.

We're all on edge, Blaine thought. *Pig-face saw to that. Jame looks like he could snap at any moment. And no matter what he does, it won't be good.*

They worked throughout the morning, and by the time the men came around to ladle out soup and hand everyone a piece of bread, Piran had tested half a dozen spots and found nothing but rock and a few rubies to show for it.

"Just a little farther," Piran grunted, sure this time he had found a weak spot. His next swing opened a small hole the size of a coin that led into darkness. Cool air rushed through the opening, stuffy, moist, and filled with a musky scent.

Before Piran could do more, Pig-face sauntered in, with one of the guards behind him for protection.

"I would have thought you'd have more by now," Pig-face observed, looking down at the pile of rock. "Pity." Without warning, he wheeled, bringing his lash down hard against Torr's back, who was closest to him.

"Leave him alone!" Jame lunged like a madman, slashing his knife across Pig-face's throat in one wild movement that left them all spattered with blood.

"Damn," Piran muttered. He moved fast and buried the blade tainted with Kestel's poison into the guard's back who had come in with Pig-face.

"Open it!" Piran hissed to Blaine as he wrestled the dying guard to the ground. "Everyone—be ready!"

Blaine swung his pick and broke through the weak spot, opening a larger hole. Something rattled in the deep dark, and the sound made Blaine's skin crawl. He swung again, and the hole opened wider. This time, he glimpsed movement in the shadows.

Before he could ready for another swing, a creature exploded from the darkness, crashing through the rock. It burst through with a blast of strength, throwing rock shards in every direction, and landed on six powerful, reptilian legs with feet that had dangerous, sharp claws. A second monster followed just seconds later. Screams sounded, echoing from the rock. In the distance, Blaine could hear the running boot steps of soldiers.

The monster's scaled skin was as white as a drowned corpse, and its eyes were red and slitted. The broad, flat head looked from side to side, and its nostrils flared, scenting for blood.

Blaine and the shackled prisoners backed away as fast as they could, although the small room gave them little maneuvering space. Behind the broken wall, Blaine heard claws skitter on stone. *There are more of those things. And if they come through, we're dead men.* He and Ernest held their picks aloft, ready to kill anything else that came through the hole.

"Stay still!" Piran ordered, his pick lifted in case the monster came after him. But it was blood the thing was after, and Pig-face was awash in it, as was the guard who lay at his side.

Some things won't eat food that's already dead, Blaine thought. The white lizard monster had no such compunctions, perhaps because food in his darkened world was scarce. It moved with frightening, fluid speed to grab Pig-face in its toothy snout, shaking the body once or twice with enough force to snap a neck. The movement splattered more blood across the chamber, covering the walls and ceiling with flecks.

Guards appeared at the entrance to the mine room, then drew back when they saw the monster.

"Stay out!" Piran shouted. "It's already attacked the overseer and his guard! There's no telling what it'll do next!"

The monster turned at the sound and fixed its red, slitted eyes on Piran. Piran spread his legs wide, squatted down to be on eye level, and let out a roar from the core of his being. Startled, the creature clamped its jaws down on Pig-face's body. Its companion did the same with the bodyguard, who gave a weak moan until the long, sharp teeth sank into his flesh, nearly biting him in two.

The red eyes turned to Piran as if daring him to object, then glared at each miner in turn. The room smelled of blood and sweat. For a moment, everything was quiet. The guards outside in the corridor had no desire to risk their own safety. None of the prisoners dared move. Pig-face and his bodyguard were beyond caring.

"Git!" Piran shouted, charging toward the monsters, his pick raised. Blaine and Ernest were dragged along, following his lead. That cleared a path to the hole to the darkness. With a toss of its head, the monster holding Pig-face raced for the break in the wall, moving with lethal grace. Its companion followed, so quickly they almost blurred. Blaine dove for the opening as soon as the monsters were gone, bringing his pick down hard on an overhang of rock, praying to all the gods that it would fill the gap instead of enlarging the entrance.

Rock tumbled down, closing the hole in the wall. Blaine looked down at his hands and saw the pick shaking in his grip.

"What…in Raka…was that?" One of the guards said, from just outside the doorway.

All of the men looked pale and shaky. "*That*," Piran replied, "was a monster. One we haven't seen before. Damn fast. And in case you didn't notice—it ate the Overseer."

"Is it gone? Can it come back?" the guard asked. Blaine noticed that the man did not step into the room, and guessed the guard was all right with sacrificing the nine prisoners to save his own skin.

"We sealed off the hole," Blaine replied. "Might not want to mine too deep in here. There are more of them down there: I heard them."

Belatedly, the guard found his nerve. "How did you all get covered in blood?" he demanded.

"We fought the thing." Ernest was the most unlikely liar, and therefore, the one with the most potential to be believed. He was genuinely frightened, and that added to his veracity. "It came through the wall so fast we barely saw it, and it grabbed the Overseer. He fought it, and so did the guard who was with him, but it was all over in the blink of an eye. None of us even had a chance to do anything before it was over." He shuddered, and Blaine believed Ernest's horror was entirely real.

"That's what you all saw?" the guard challenged, looking from one man to the next. Blaine held his breath. One by one, they nodded. Even Jame appeared to be in possession of himself again. *He still looks jumpy,* Blaine thought. *But if he doesn't say anything, that might get figured as a reasonable response to a very bad situation.* Jame had the presence of mind to hide his knife, and his gaze was focused and sane.

"Damn," the guard said. "I'm going to have to explain this to the commander. Where's the hole?"

Blaine led him to the spot where rock blocked the entrance to the caves. "There were more of those things," Blaine said.

"I heard them." Ernest nodded.

"They went away because they had all the food they could carry—for now." Blaine nodded toward the pile of rocks that sealed off the hole. "I wouldn't trust those stones to keep those things out if they wanted more meat," he added, daring to meet the guards' gaze. "They were big enough to carry off two large men easily. They're used to the deep places. I bet they could dig through those stones before we knew they were coming." Blaine saw fear in the guards' eyes.

"Gather up what you've dug today," the lead guard ordered. "We're going to need to make a report of this to the Commander. Until then, this room is sealed."

To his credit, Piran managed to keep a smirk from his face until they were headed out of the mine, each man carrying as much rock as he could handle. Blaine's gaze warned Piran not to say a word. Ernst looked like he was in shock, now that the immediate danger was over. Torr and Bickle were ashen and silent. Shorty feigned boredom, like Piran, but Blaine bet that the bloodshed and terror had touched both of them, though they covered their reactions well. The others just looked haggard. They were all covered in blood, and from the smell, someone had soiled himself.

"Prokief will have questions," Blaine muttered as the guards ordered them to the surface.

"Count on it," Piran replied, looking smug.

"He's not likely to believe us."

"The guard saw the monsters," Piran replied. "The monsters ate Pig-face and his bully boy. We all saw it. There's nothing left to say."'

Blaine hoped Piran was right. But he doubted Prokief would be as easily satisfied, even with the guards' testimony. Nothing went easy in Velant.

6

RETRIBUTION

"Lies! All lies!" Prokief backhanded Blaine across the face hard enough to split his lip. "I want to know what happened to my overseer and his guard!"

"He was eaten by a monster," Piran snapped. "What in Raka else is there to tell you?"

Prokief wheeled, punching Piran in the face, breaking his nose and splattering blood across the snow. "I know you're lying. I want the truth, or you'll all stay here until you freeze!"

The nine surviving prisoners knelt in the snow in Velant's parade ground, hands bound behind their backs. The other convicts were confined to barracks, but the interrogation took place in view of all of the buildings, designed to be a demonstration for the rest to take to heart. As angry as Prokief was about Pig-face's death, Blaine was also sure the commander was furious that he and Piran had not been caught among the rioters, which would have given Prokief the excuse for condemning them to death.

"The monsters are real," Shorty protested, drawing off Prokief before he could strike Blaine or Piran again. "Your guards know it. You have to know it, too. That's why you sent the rioters to the deep levels."

Blaine and the others had been out in the parade ground for several candlemarks, long enough that Blaine's feet and hands were numb. The cold quickly clotted the blood on his lip and slowed the swelling. A glance at the others suggested that the frigid temperatures were taking their toll. Bickle was shivering convulsively. All of them were red-faced from the wind and cold, and if Prokief kept them out much longer, they were likely to lose a few fingers and toes to frostbite, if not a nose or ear.

Prokief clubbed Shorty with his fist so hard that it knocked the prisoner to the ground. "You know it's true," Shorty replied defiantly. "We were lucky to get out alive."

Commander Prokief was a bear of a man. He was unusually tall and built large and solid, ham-fisted and thick-necked. He mocked the weather by wearing no hat, and the arctic wind tossed his dark hair like a storm cloud around his head. Blaine guessed that Prokief weighed at least as much as he and Piran together, but Prokief had the solid muscle of a bull. Tales abounded of Prokief's rages, times when he had beaten one or more inmates—or guards—to death with his bare hands.

The spark that fueled those rages usually bore little connection to reality. At his best, Prokief was coherent but cruel. Raging, he was beyond reason, caught up in his own fury. It was clear from his repeated questioning that he did not accept their report of what had happened, and Blaine had no idea what version Prokief wanted to hear, or whether anything they said could appease his temper.

One glance at the guards who had also survived the monsters' attack told Blaine Prokief would not be easily appeased. They stood at attention, faces bruised and eyes blackened, a sure sign that Prokief had made his disappointment clear.

Prokief gave a feral growl and stalked toward Shorty, and the look in his eyes was murderous. Shorty was bleeding from one ear and the side of his mouth, but he lay where he fell, staring down Prokief as the commander headed to deliver more abuse.

Prokief snatched Shorty from the ground and shook him like a rag doll. He slammed Shorty to the dirt and landed a savage kick to the ribs. Shorty grunted a curse but dared not fight back, though with his hands bound there was little he could offer in his own defense.

"What if we killed the monsters, would that satisfy you?" The words were out of Blaine's mouth before he had time to think. He just wanted to save Shorty's life—and get the rest of them out of the freezing cold and away from Prokief's beatings.

"Are you mad?" Bickle muttered.

"Maybe," Blaine allowed. "But if we do it, will that be enough for you?"

Prokief glowered at him, contempt and hatred glinting in his dark eyes. "For now," he snarled, "this time."

With a wave of his hand, Prokief signaled for the guards to cut the prisoners' bonds. Blaine and Piran helped Shorty get to his feet, while Torr and Jame steadied Bickle, who looked like he was already succumbing to ice sickness.

Once they got inside the barracks, Dawe, Verran, and the other convicts moved to help Shorty and Bickle, bringing strips of rags for bandages and cups of hot water to drink.

Jame and Ernest rounded on Blaine. "Are you trying to do Prokief's work for him?" Jame demanded. He advanced on Blaine as if he intended to take a swing. Blaine's fist balled to defend himself. Piran stepped between him.

"Shut your mouth, or by Torven, I'll shut it for you," Piran growled. Blaine moved up beside him.

"Prokief was going to keep us out there until we died from the cold or he beat us to death," Blaine retorted. "We didn't have any chance out there."

"And you think that going hunting for those monsters gives us a chance?" Ernest argued. "No one's seen the men who got sent to the deep places."

"Pretty sure they're dead," Piran replied as if the thought did not disturb him. "Pretty sure Prokief knows it, too."

"I think Prokief was so angry because he does know there are things living in the deep places. That's what got him scared—he has no idea what to do about it," Blaine answered. "We can go on the way we've been going, and have a man get picked off now and again, until we're all gone—"

"Or we can just march down like pigs to the slaughter and make it easy for them," Jame finished. Jaston and Eddles had come to stand behind Jame.

"What if we got rid of the monsters once and for all?" Blaine suggested. "So that we didn't have to worry about them anymore —and neither did Prokief and the guards."

"How are you gonna do that?" Jaston demanded.

Blaine and Piran exchanged a glance. "We've got a plan," Blaine replied. "And it'll solve the problem—but maybe not in the way Prokief expects."

———

Two days later, Blaine and the other survivors of the attack headed back into the mines, accompanied by the guards who had also seen the monsters. It was clear the guards intended to do as little as possible, resolutely stopping just inside the mouth of the mine.

"We wait here," the lead guard said. "You can tell us all about it if you come back out."

The other guards laughed, and the sound echoed down the dark corridors.

"If Prokief doesn't believe in monsters, how come he pulled

the rest of the miners out today?" Piran muttered. His nose had been set, but it was badly swollen, which made his voice sound muffled.

"He believes," Blaine said. "He's just hoping that we'll kill the monsters and the monsters will kill us, solving two problems at once."

"What about the men Prokief sent down here to die?" Jaston's voice sounded thin with fear. "We've just volunteered to join them."

"That's not part of the plan," Piran said, clapping Jaston on the shoulder. "We've got every intention of getting back out." Jaston gave Piran a look that made it clear he was unconvinced.

"Grab your packs." Blaine nodded toward the bundles of torches, rag-wrapped lengths of wood. They had four lanterns among them, safer in the depths of the mine than open flame, but the trade-off was the brightness of the light and the size of the area illuminated. The lanterns shielded the fire, reducing the risk of explosion, but provided a dim light that did not extend far ahead of them.

"And your picks," Piran added. Despite the danger, Prokief had refused to issue weapons of any kind, so the group was armed only with their mining pickaxes. Jame and Piran had their knives, and Blaine was certain his friend had some of Kestel's poison, along with a few other bits of contraband Blaine was counting on to turn the situation in their favor.

This mine was one of three on Edgeland and the largest of them all. Blaine had worked in the mine for most of his time in Velant and never gone beyond the second level. Prokief no doubt expected them to follow the path of the doomed men into the mine's depths, but Blaine and Piran had other plans.

"What's Piran looking at?" Jame asked once they were out of earshot of the guards.

eserv01 line

"Where'd he get that map?" Bickle was close enough to look over Piran's shoulder.

"Doesn't matter where it came from," Piran said. "What does matter is what the map shows. Caves. And if this is right, we don't have to go all the way down to get to where the monsters live. We can do it right through here," he added, leading the way into the room they had cleared of the cave-in.

"We think the monsters move through the caves," Blaine explained. "We see them when the mine tunnels break through into their caverns."

"So instead of hunting through miles of dark tunnels, we go where we're sure the monsters are—because it's where they lived before there was a mine," Piran finished. He moved around the room, holding his lantern in one hand and rotating the map with the other, aligning the two.

"Dig here," he said, pointing to an area of the wall where they had previously broken through.

"How do we know the air in there isn't bad?" Bickle asked.

"We don't," Blaine replied. "In fact, I'd expect it will get that way, the deeper we go."

"You really are trying to kill us," Torr grumbled.

Blaine turned to face Torr. "You want to go back and face Prokief and finish freezing to death on the parade ground? Fine with me. He's not going to believe us until we bring a couple of those monsters back dead, and we can convince him we've gotten rid of the threat. So what'll it be?"

Torr turned back to his work with a curse. Piran held his lantern aloft and positioned the other lanterns, so they illuminated the area as they worked. It did not take long for their picks to break through in the place Kestel's map indicated.

Piran dug in his pack and removed a small handmade cage with two brown mice inside. "Here," he said, handing the cage to Ernest. "If the mice start to act funny, we're getting into bad air."

Torr and Bickle eyed the mice as if Piran had lost his senses. "Mice?" Bickle said incredulously.

Piran nodded. "Velant's not the only place with mines, you know. Got them back in Donderath, too. Some of the men I soldiered with worked in the mines, and they told how the crews would take a bird or some mice down with them to tell when the air was getting bad." His lip twisted. "Of course, Prokief wouldn't spare a rat to save any of us."

"We're kicking up some dust," Blaine observed. Fine dust and bad air were a recipe for combustion. "Mind you keep the lanterns closed," he warned the men.

Piran nodded. "If anything's down here, it's going to know we're coming."

After about a candlemark, they had a large enough opening to step through into the cave. Blaine went first, lantern in one hand and pickax in the other.

"Torven take my soul," Ernest murmured in awe as he stepped through behind Blaine, close enough to remain in the lantern's glow. He held the caged mice at arm's length and clutched his pickax with his other hand.

Their lanterns barely made a dent in the gloom, but what they could see astonished Blaine with its unexpected beauty. Unlike the rough-hewn walls of the mine, the cave's contours were sculpted by water and time. No harsh ax-marks marred the stone. Crystals sparkled in the lantern's light, star-like clusters of ice that covered the cave's roof and outcroppings.

"Do you think anyone else has ever been here?" Bickle asked in a voice just above a whisper. Despite the danger, the sight was breathtaking. Shorty and Torr followed, looking around themselves as if they had entered another world.

"Someone drew the map and got it back out," Piran observed, bringing up the rear. He pointed to a dark streak, likely blood from the men who were dragged away by monsters. "Let's keep our wits about us, so we can live to tell the story."

They moved forward cautiously, careful not to outpace their light. Blaine had explored a few caves as a boy near his home at Glenreith, and he remembered more than one close call with a sudden drop-off or the dark water of a hidden, depthless pool.

"Something's been through here," Ernest said, bending to examine the rock floor. He directed the light downward for a better view. "Look," he said, pointing out what looked like partial tracks in the fine dust on the cave floor.

The mice chattered nervously. "Keep moving," Blaine urged. "We need to find evidence of the monsters."

"Evidence is fine," Jame replied. "But I'd just as soon not find the monsters themselves."

The cave floor sloped downward sharply in places, forcing them to move carefully to avoid a misstep. Piran ventured away from the cave wall, raising his lantern over his head to give them a better sense of the cave. The vault was perhaps a dozen feet over their heads, but the far walls were lost in shadow.

"Don't stray too far," Bickle warned. "You're the one with the map."

Blaine led them through a second, smaller chamber. Unlike the first room, this section had fewer ice clusters and was hardly wider than a tunnel. But as Blaine neared the entrance to the next room, he paused, sniffing the air.

"Firedamp?" Torr asked, worried.

Blaine shook his head and held a finger to his lip, then raised his pickax. The others readied their weapons in response. He hoped that he was wrong about the stench, but it smelled to him of rotting meat.

They stepped through the entrance, and their lanterns reflected from white outcroppings on the floor of the cave room.

"Those aren't rocks," Ernest said quietly. "They're skulls."

"I think we found the men Prokief sent down here," Bickle added, his voice unsteady.

Instinct warned Blaine to turn just as four pale reptiles emerged silently from the shadows. Their strange, musky odor combined with the sickly-sweet smell of decomposing flesh, and Blaine forced himself not to retch.

The corpse-pale lizard-things were large, each the size of a boar. They raised their flat, scaled heads to scent the air, and their eyes glowed red in the lamplight. No audible signal passed among them, but as one, they charged.

"Now would be a good time to set your trap," Blaine called to Piran as he swung his pickax at the nearest cave monster. The lizards were fast despite their bulk, and sharp claws scrabbled on the rock floor as they moved. The flat, snake-like heads hid mouths with rows of sharp teeth, and their long, flexible necks gave them a viper's agility to strike.

Teeth snagged Blaine's sleeve, narrowly missing his arm. Blaine danced backward, just seconds ahead of the reptile's claws. His pickax's heavy iron head struck a glancing blow, ripping into the smooth, white scales and tearing a crimson gash. The giant lizard hissed in pain and slithered back out of range, moving with a snake-like grace that sent a chill down Blaine's spine.

"We need to kill one of those things to prove we were here," Piran yelled, fending off one of the monsters. His pick hit hard enough to break bone, and the huge white lizard gave an ear-splitting shriek of pain as it scuttled back. "And someone needs to cover me, because I can't fight and do what I need to do."

"I've got Piran," Ernest said, setting the caged mice atop a rocky shelf and moving into position in case the injured lizard tried to attack. Piran dug into his rucksack, withdrawing a coil of tightly wound cloth twisted into a thin cord, and then dumping his pack of torches into the center of the room.

Blaine barely had a chance to put his lantern on an outcropping when the next lizard sprang at him, moving with terrifying speed. Torr and Bickle held their lanterns as they fought, and the light swung crazily with their movements, casting wild shadows across the cavern.

"Watch those claws!" Torr yelped, exacting vengeance with his pick for the four deep gashes that scored his shoulder where one of the reptiles had lunged from the darkness.

Out of the corner of his eye, Blaine saw Piran run for the bundles of torches the others had dropped. A yellow-white lizard slithered from the darkness, striking out with its extendable neck.

"Piran, watch out!" Ernest yelled, as he brought his pick down in a deadly arc, sinking the point deep into the monster's skull.

"Finish it off!" Piran shouted as he dumped the torches together and began to feed out the coil of cord. "We need one of those things for proof!"

Ernest ripped the pickax forward, cleaving the lizard's skull almost in half. The big reptile shuddered and then fell over. Ernest approached it carefully, freeing his pickax only to bring it down again, severing the head from the neck. "That thing's body has to weight as much as any of ours," he said. "I'm not carrying more than the head out of here."

Bickle cried out as another of the snake-lizards scuttled out from behind a pile of rocks, and the teeth snapped on his left thigh. He struck the creature with his ax, sinking the point deep into the creature's shoulder and nearly pulling away one of its legs. Shorty ran to help, hacking furiously at the reptile, ripping his pick through the creature's flesh in bloody furrows.

Jame was locked in combat with another of the white lizards, one with a half-moon shaped blaze on its head. More of the creatures began to edge from the shadows. "They've got friends!" he yelled. "We can't hold them all off!" He was bleeding from a set of deep gouges on one thigh, and his left arm hung useless, savaged by a bite from one of the creatures. He lunged and dodged erratically, fighting more from rage and madness than with clear intent, or perhaps the bad air was pushing him over the edge of sanity.

"Get in a good shot and get out!" Ernest urged.

"I can finish him," Jame snapped, breathless, continuing to circle the monster, which watched him with baleful red eyes.

"Time to fall back!" Piran shouted.

Blaine was feeling the exertion of the fight. He felt light-headed and the stinking air burned in his lungs. His head pounded, almost making him a target when one of the lizard-monsters remerged from the shadows, moving like a white blur. Blaine swung his pickax again, shattering the creature's right shoulder.

The huge lizard lunged at him despite its damaged leg, snapping at him with a maw full of sharp teeth. Blaine dodged the creature's mouth and brought the full force of the sharp pick down on the lizard's spine. The monster screeched as its body collapsed, shuddering and twitching. Two more lizards slithered forward, more intent on fighting each other over the body of their fallen comrade than in attacking Blaine, who backed up quickly to get out of their sight.

Bickle and Torr were fighting one monster, while Shorty held off the other. "Get in one last hit, and we've got to go!" Blaine yelled.

Jame and his opponent were so intent on each other that neither seemed to notice what was going on around them. Jame was bleeding in half a dozen places, and so was the lizard, but they were both still standing and each looked determined to see the battle through to the end.

"Jame! Give it up. We're leaving."

Jame did not reply. He and the lizard had locked gazes, shadowing each other's movements. The intensity in Jame's face was no longer sane. The lizard lunged, and Jame feinted, then he dove forward, and the lizard dodged.

"Come on!" Piran yelled.

"This one's mine," Jame growled.

Jame and the lizard both launched themselves at the same time, colliding in the middle. The monster's maw closed over Jame's midsection as Jame's pick sank deep into the reptile's underbelly and tore out its entrails. They fell together in a spreading pool of blood, rolling to gain advantage. Jame pounded on the creature's head with his fists, gouging out its red eyes, as the maw continued to chew on his torso, feet kicking to do more damage with their long claws. The other lizards fell back from Blaine and the rest of the party, unable to resist the allure of so much warm, fresh blood and such an easy feast of flesh.

Blaine reached for the lantern and Ernest grabbed the mouse cage. The mice lay still, barely breathing.

"Bad air!" Blaine shouted. "Move out now!"

Bickle was limping badly, leaning heavily on Torr. Ernest and Blaine led the way back out of the caves, followed by Jaston and Eddles as Piran fed out his homemade fuse, and Shorty took the rear guard position. The air was getting to them all, and Blaine knew in a few more moments, they would be in no better condition than the mice.

"How long will it take for the fuse to burn?" Shorty asked.

"With luck, slower than we can run." Piran stopped when they reached the room where the cave-in had been. "Get the others out of here," he said to Blaine. "And the guards, too, I suppose. I'll see you out there."

"You had damn well better," Blaine said, clapping a hand on his shoulder. He turned to the others.

"Run!"

Shorty and Torr lifted Bickle off his feet and ran with him

suspended between them. Ernest came next, with the monster's severed head in one hand and the caged mice in the other, and then Jaston and Eddles. Blaine was right behind them. The guards startled as they came into view.

"What's going on?" the lead guard demanded.

"Firedamp. Monsters. Run!" Blaine shouted. He nearly bowled one of the guards over, then reached down and grabbed the man's collar, dragging the guard with him toward the door.

"You can't just—" the lead guard protested as Piran came running at full speed up the tunnel.

Piran did not stop to argue. He punched the guard in the face, dropping him like a sack of rocks, then hauled the man's body over one shoulder and kept on going. The third guard took one look at the monster's head and the prisoners' bloody wounds and took off running.

Just as they reached the mine entrance, a boom like trapped thunder rolled up from the depths, echoing in the vast caverns and mining rooms, amplified in the narrow stone tunnels. Blaine threw himself to the ground, taking the guard with him, and threw his arms over his head. A blast of sound, smoke, and dust billowed after them, deafening in the quiet of the arctic night.

For a few moments, Blaine could only lie still, barely conscious, stunned by the blast concussion. His ears rang, and he gasped in the cold, fresh air like a drowning man. Gradually, as his wits returned, he felt the pain of his injuries and a pounding headache from the caves' foul air.

"Sound off!" he shouted, anxious to see if the others had survived. The sound of his own voice made his head ache as if he had been struck.

"Jaston"

"Eddles"

"Torr"

"Ernest—and Bickle," Ernest yelled back.

Piran muttered a creative obscenity, ending in "Here!"

"Shorty, and two guards." That was everyone except for Jame.

Blaine had just gotten to his knees when he saw Prokief and a dozen guards heading their way. "Shit," he growled. "I am in no mood to get murdered after I just escaped getting killed."

"You blew up the mine!" Prokief was so incensed that his voice went up a note from its usual pitch.

"And the monsters," Blaine replied, too exhausted and injured to give a damn about anything.

"You destroyed the king's property."

"We *are* the king's property," Blaine snapped.

"Look here, if you don't believe us," Ernest argued, holding aloft the monster's head. Prokief's guards exclaimed in horror and fell back a step.

"The monsters were in the caves," Blaine said, keeping his voice level although it took all his willpower not to lash out. "They killed the men you sent to the deep mines—and Jame. The air was bad. A torch set it off. We all nearly died, but we got ahead of the explosion." He had no intention of confessing that Piran had made a fuse, and trusted the others to keep mum on that detail.

"They dragged us out, sir," the lead guard said, getting to his feet to stand belatedly at attention. "Warned us and then pulled us to safety. They could have let us die."

Prokief eyed the monster's head, then shifted his attention back to the prisoners. It was apparent from their torn clothing and bloody wounds that they had battled for their lives.

"You'd better hope that all you did was close up the caves, or there'll be Raka to pay," Prokief grumbled. "If it's closed off good ruby shafts, you'll be digging them out with your bare hands."

For a long moment, no one spoke. Blaine's heart was still

thudding from the fighting and the run out of the mine, and he was so jumpy from the adrenaline that there was no margin left for fear. *Let Prokief kill me and get it over with, if that's what he's going to do. I'm done with being afraid.*

"You'll be part of the clean-up detail," Prokief said abruptly. "And until we've made up the production lost from this nonsense, everyone will work longer shifts." His eyes narrowed. "Rowse and McFadden, I'm watching you. Step out of line again, and you'll be lucky to survive the consequences." At that, Prokief turned on his heel and strode away, surrounded by his bodyguards.

"That's a tale to tell in Raka," Piran said, his voice colored with satisfaction. "We beat the monsters."

This time, Blaine thought. *But monsters are hard to kill, and they have very long memories.*

NO REPRIEVE

1

THE HOLES

"NOT BAD ENOUGH THAT IT'S SO COLD IT WOULD FREEZE THE nuts off a wolf," Piran Rowse grumbled. "Not bad enough that we've got these bloody shackles. Does it have to be dark for half the year, too?"

Blaine McFadden—Mick to his fellow inmates—grunted in reply. "That's the point, Piran," he said. "If you recall, we were exiled because they weren't fond of us."

Piran's curses were spectacularly creative. "I seem to remember exile was supposed to be better than a noose. Some days, I'm not sure about that."

It was up for argument whether it was colder and darker outside Velant's ruby mines or down in their depths. *At least in the mines*, Blaine thought, *there wasn't the constant, cutting wind, nor the threat of the wild bears and wolves that prowled the wilds up top.* Predators of another type ruled the deep places.

The crack of a whip stung Blaine's shoulder. "Stop talking and keep digging!" The guard glared at Piran and Blaine as if he were hoping they would be foolhardy enough to reply.

Piran held his tongue until the guard was out of earshot, and then began a muttered litany of expletives that was remarkable even for him.

"Shut up, Piran," Blaine said. "For some reason, you mouth off, and I feel the lash for it."

Piran shot him a crooked smile. "Just one of my many talents."

Chok, the guard, moved on, only to stop several paces farther down the tunnel to lash another prisoner who was not mining the rubies quickly enough, though Blaine suspected the inmate was near to his breaking point. Velant was Donderath's garbage heap, its dumping ground for people it considered useless for anything except brutal labor. The prisoner went down with a whimper. Chok cracked him over the head with his staff for good measure, a sickening muted thud. This time, the prisoner fell silent. Most of the Velant guards were dangerous. Some were worse than others. Chok was one of the monsters.

"You won't get out of here that easily," Piran said. "If anyone kills you up here, it's likely to be Prokief himself."

"Compared to you, who've annoyed the shit out of nearly everyone, so you've got a line waiting to do you in," Blaine replied, but his grin took the sting from his words.

If I had to be shackled at the ankle to a fellow prisoner, there would be worse partners than Piran, Blaine thought. They had been paired by the guards because they were relatively equal in their reach and stamina, meaning they could swing their pickaxes and sledgehammers efficiently without knocking each other off balance, and march in and out of the mine without tripping each other.

Three months ago, Blaine had been a free man, the son of a down-at-the-heels noble back in Donderath. But when his father, Lord Ian McFadden dishonored Blaine's sister Mari, Blaine killed him in a cold rage born of years of abuse. Blaine had expected to hang for his crime. But King Merrill knew of Ian's penchant for violence, and he had granted Blaine the "mercy" of exile, to the arctic wilds of Velant on the island of Edgeland at the top of the world.

Even now, Blaine felt no remorse, though he often thought that a quick death at the end of a noose would have been preferable to the prospect of spending the rest of his natural life in a frozen wasteland under the thumb of Commander Prokief and his vicious guards.

"Just three years," Blaine said. "We only have to survive three years before we can get out of this godsforsaken pit and earn our Tickets."

Piran barked a sharp, bitter laugh. "Keep on believing that, mate, if it gets you through the night. You know how many convicts survive three years? Not many. Not bloody many at all." Tickets of Leave were granted to convicts who served their first three years without further crimes. It meant they became colonists instead of inmates, but no one returned home, not even the soldiers, who were as much prisoners as their charges.

Despite the persistent cold, mining was hard work, and sweat beaded Blaine's forehead, running in rivulets down his grit-streaked face. Although he had done physical labor on his father's estate, nothing had prepared him for the relentless hard work demanded from Velant's inmates. Prokief made it clear that his first priority was making a profit for the homeland with the rubies they mined, and the herring fished out of the bay by the colony's small fleet of boats. Whether or not the inmates survived the effort was of little consequence to Prokief or anyone else.

Piran had started singing a popular tavern song, making up additional verses that were as obscene as they were amusing. The guard glowered but said nothing, since both Blaine and Piran swung their pickaxes in time to the off-key melody.

"Better get those rock chunks broken up smaller than that, or there'll be grief," Blaine advised the third prisoner in their shackled trio. Ford nodded, too winded to speak. Ford stood a head shorter than Blaine, with the slight build of a boy not yet a man. Only fourteen years old, he had been exiled for stealing, not uncommon when a thief made the mistake of pickpocketing a powerful victim.

Too late.

"What kind of rubbish work is this?" Chok said as he made another pass down the long mining tunnel. He kicked at Ford's rock pile, scattering the pieces. "Pick those up."

Ford bent to comply. The guard brought his knee up into the boy's face, and Blaine heard a snap as Ford's nose broke. "Now look at the mess," the guard chided as blood flowed down Ford's face. "Someone's gonna have to wash that blood off the nuggets. Who's gonna do that? Huh?"

Ford snuffled a reply, doing his best to stoically bear the pain and humiliation. Malice shone in the guard's eyes. Piran had a reputation for a hot temper, and the branded "M" on Blane's forearm that marked him as a murderer gave the guards pause. But Ford was easy prey.

"I asked you a question!" the guard thundered at Ford and slapped him hard across the face. "Well?"

"Me, sir," Ford stammered, scrambling to gather the blood-splattered ruby nuggets.

The guard's foot shot out, catching Ford in the stomach. The boy crumbled with a muted "oof."

"On your feet, boy!" the guard snapped. "Lazy ass. Get up before I drag you up by your hair!" He gave another savage kick, and Ford's body jerked with the force of the blow.

Blaine's temper was at the breaking point, and he knew from Piran's stance that his partner was already past that. With barely a glance between them, Blaine and Piran moved at the same instant, closing from both sides on the guard.

"Leave the boy alone," Piran growled, landing a right hook that connected with the guard's jaw hard enough to break bones, as his pickax swung low, busting the man's ankle. Blaine had already learned how to use the chain of his shackle to trip an attacker, and he swung one foot in an arc and then jerked the chain back hard, pulling the guard's good leg out from under him. The soldier fell, and Blaine swung his sledgehammer into the guard's shoulder with a satisfying crack.

"Don't think you'll be busting up any children for a while," Piran gloated. "And it's a shame about your jaw, but I don't think you'll be telling the commander any tales until it heals up." The guard sputtered angrily, sending a spray of blood flying. "Not that you'll be much good for anything with a bum shoulder and a bad leg, but the healers might fix you up enough to clean out the latrines."

Blaine knelt next to Ford. "Come on," he said. "Get up. We'll pay Raka for what we've done." But Ford's breathing was shallow and uneven, and he was moaning in pain. *That last kick hit him hard. Maybe hard enough to break something inside. Damn.*

Blaine looked up at Piran. "Got any other bright ideas?" he asked, glancing at the guard who was trying to grab at Piran with his good hand. Piran stayed just out of reach.

"Not really," Piran replied. "But he had it coming. And it's not like we were going to get out early for good behavior."

Running footsteps echoed in the rock tunnels. Blaine heard guards shouting as they barged their way through the miners, alerted if not by the sound of the fight itself then by one of Prokief's many informants among the prisoners.

"Get him up!" a guard ordered, regarding Ford with disdain. "Or we'll haul him up ourselves." Blaine muttered an apology as he lifted Ford as gently as he could, wincing as the young man cried out in pain and doubled over.

"Rowse! Should have figured you were causing trouble. Tell your tale to the commander," the second guard said. "Out with you."

Two more of Prokief's soldiers came to help the downed guard, who let out a bleat of pain as one of them jostled his broken shoulder.

"Not so tough now," Piran mocked, then cursed as one of the soldiers gave him a shove toward the mine exit hard enough to drag Blaine off balance.

"Shut up, Piran," Blaine muttered. But it was far too late for that to matter. Fights between the convicts and the guards were common, and when the guards won—which was often—the matter went unnoticed by the prison's commander, even when convicts turned up dead. Blaine was under no illusion that their transgression would go unpunished, especially since Velant's commander seemed to have taken a particular, personal dislike for both Blaine and Piran.

Ford was barely conscious as they made their way up the narrow rock tunnels toward the mine entrance. Blaine was supporting most of the boy's weight. Normally, a healer could put an injury right most of the time. But Prokief rarely wasted healers on convicts, unless he was short on labor for a needed task. Blaine doubted that the little bit of healing magic and hedge witch cures the prisoners provided for each other could save Ford if the guard's attack had damaged his innards. Then again, that particular guard wouldn't be damaging anyone else for a long while. The satisfaction of that knowledge was almost enough to temper Blaine's fear of the punishment that awaited him. Almost.

Other prisoners glanced up as the guards hustled them out of the mine. Some gave bored stares, and Blaine guessed they were glad that this time, the guards were focused on someone other than them. Others eyed them with anger, certain that Blaine and

Piran's misdeeds would lead to harsher conditions for all of them.

A few looked at them with grudging respect. It was rare to win against the guards, all the sweeter for being a fleeting victory. But if the time ever came that Prokief's warden mages lost their ability to enforce the commander's harsh discipline, Blaine doubted there were enough guards to hold off the inmates' pent-up rage.

A blast of frigid air hit them as they stepped out into the perpetual twilight of the Long Dark, the half of the year when the sun barely rose above the horizon. Edgeland's temperatures barely rose enough during the "summer" months to enable the colonists and inmates to go outside without heavy cloaks and hats. The dark winter months felt interminable, and the temperatures plunged to bone-chilling cold that even the thickest furs would not warm.

Piran continued to hum the bawdy tavern song, a small show of defiance. Still, Blaine could see a glint of fear in Piran's eyes. Blaine felt his gut tighten at the prospect of Prokief's revenge. They might have saved Ford, or perhaps merely avenged him, but there was a good chance that they would die for their efforts.

"Unlock the boy," one of the guards ordered. "Take him back to the barracks," he said to two of the other guards. It would be useless to request a healer, since the guards would only laugh. Maybe one of Blaine's barracks mates could help Ford, or at least ease his passing if there was naught that could be healed.

"You two aren't getting off that easy," the guard gloated, as Ford was dragged away, hanging limply between the two soldiers.

"Is the commander having a dull day?" Piran asked cheekily. "No small children to drown? All out of animals to torture? Did the Butcher of Breseshwa get bored?" Prokief had commanded an army that turned the tide at Breseshwa, a border city where there had been an uprising ten years prior. When the fighting was done, the rebels were dead, and so were every man, woman, child, and animal in Breseshwa. King Merrill had "awarded" Prokief his position as warden of Velant.

"Shut up, Piran," Blaine muttered, but it was far too late now.

Commander Prokief's headquarters was squat and ugly. Unlike most of the buildings in the prison camp, the commander's building was made from hewn rock. Convicts still whispered about the number of men who had died quarrying the stone and hauling it into place. The prisoners' barracks, the laundry, the storage barns, and the camp's other buildings were made mostly of wood, but Prokief's building was his own personal fortress, against the elements and the inmates.

"I hear the commander's waiting for you," one of the guards said, with a nasty chuckle. Few prisoners who attracted Prokief's personal attention were seen again.

"If we'd have known that, we'd have dressed better," Piran said. Blaine elbowed him, but Piran only grinned more broadly.

The commander's headquarters was the anchor for King Merrill's authority on Edgeland's godsforsaken ice. The royal seal was painted over the doorway into the sentencing chamber. A pennant with the insignia of the King's army hung down one side of the entranceway, and a battle flag from Prokief's former unit graced the other side. The two guardsmen at the doors wore uniforms that were reminiscent of the king's guards back at Quillarth Castle, though Blaine knew that even the soldiers assigned to Velant had been given the choice between exile and death for their crimes.

Even the tall, wide wooden doors appeared to have been designed to intimidate, carved with the seals of the noble houses of Donderath. There, near the bottom, was his own family crest, the mark of the House McFadden, lords of Glenreith, for all the good it would do him. Blaine had left that history, that identity, behind when the convict ship left Castle Reach. The king had stripped him of his title. He had disavowed his heritage. Here, he was just Mick. *Probably for the best. Prokief would probably enjoy slapping me down even more if he knew who I used to be.*

"Enter." Commander Prokief's deep voice was flat and cold. The guards shoved Blaine and Piran into the sentencing chamber, then forced them to their knees. Prokief was a bear of a man with the manner of a brawler, tall and broad-shouldered with a cloud of unruly dark hair and a full dark beard.

"McFadden. Rowse. Again. I am not patient." Prokief glowered at them. He was known for his brutality on the battlefield as much as for his effectiveness. Prokief had been useful to the king up to a point, but he had long-ago crossed the threshold that made him an embarrassment.

"You fought a guard. Struck a soldier. Caused him bodily harm. Disobeyed direct commands. Do you deny this? There are witnesses," Prokief said.

"Your attack dog savaged a young boy for the fun of it," Blaine snapped, at the end of his patience. "We're convicts, not monsters."

Prokief's laughter was a low rumble. "No? So…righteous… considering the crimes that brought you here." He looked to the well-armed guards. "Remove their shackles," he ordered. "Then restrain them on the floor." He jerked his head toward the cuffs and manacles set into the stone. "And bring me the whip."

Prokief removed his uniform jacket and slowly turned up the sleeves of his shirt. The look in his eyes gave Blaine a sick feeling, as he recognized that Prokief relished delivering the punishment. He drew a pair of black leather gloves from his belt and slowly fitted them onto his beefy hands. Then he reached out to take the whip from the guard who had retrieved it from where it hung on the wall, among many instruments of Prokief's "discipline."

"Bind them."

Guards pushed Blaine and Piran toward the iron restraints. They were stripped of their clothing and spread-eagled face-down on the cold stone, bound wrists and ankles. The ropes stretched the skin on their backs tight, in preparation for the lash. Blaine worked at keeping his face impassive. Even Piran stopped wisecracking.

Rough rope bit into Blaine's wrists. The cold stone floor leeched the heat from his body, and Blaine knew that the restraints would tear at his flesh when he began to shiver. Prokief swished the knotted leather whip through the air so that Blaine and Piran would hear it. He cracked it, chuckling when they flinched, although this time, he did not strike them. He was enjoying their fear, just like he would relish their pain.

Showing them the whip had been part of the performance. The whip sang through the air, and its first strike slashed across Blaine's back. He gritted his teeth, refusing to give Prokief the satisfaction of hearing him cry out. The second strike lanced open Piran's skin shoulder to hip. Piran cursed, jaw set, eyes narrowed.

"One."

Prokief was no novice when it came to administering the lash. He was skilled in making every blow count, opening new skin with each strike, cutting across muscle and sinew in a way calculated to make the victim's every movement exquisitely painful.

Blaine forced himself to breathe and closed his eyes. Prokief did not know that Blaine's father had long ago taught him how to take a beating, had trained him to hide his pain and force down his killing rage. And while Blaine's father had not whipped him, he had laid into Blaine often enough with his fists or walking

KING'S CONVICTS • 203

cane that Blaine knew how to go far away in his mind, to his own imaginary fortress, where he would wait out the assault.

"Two." The lash fell twice, once on each of them.

"Three." Blood spattered as Prokief raised the thin, merciless leather cord and snapped it once again, spraying with them with droplets. Forty lashes would kill most men, Blaine knew. On occasion, the flayed body of a prisoner had been tossed out in the snow of the parade ground until it froze solid, where it remained until the thaw, a warning for the rest of them. Blaine wondered how far Prokief would take their punishment, whether he and Piran would become Prokief's next cautionary tale.

"Four."

After ten lashes, Blaine's vision swam. His body cramped from the unnatural positions in which the manacles stretched him, but every twitch and shiver tore at his bonds or pained his bloodied back. Piran stopped cursing, and his face had paled. Blaine's jaw clenched so tightly against the pain that he feared he might crack a tooth.

"Fifteen."

Blaine grunted and bit into his lip. The lash fell, again and again, each time striking in a new spot. He lost count, slipping in and out of consciousness.

Blaine gritted his teeth. His silence enraged Prokief, who brought the lash down harder as the guard counted. "Sixteen... Seventeen...Eighteen...Nineteen...Twenty."

When the last lash fell, Blaine lay still, lost in pain and shock.

"Douse him with salt water," Prokief commanded.

A guard went to grab a bucket from near the wall. The weight of the water hurt as much as the salt that stung in the fresh, raw wounds, and Blaine barely bit back a cry.

"Take them to the Holes. No food or water. Three days." He paused. "Ejnar, come here."

Dimly, Blaine heard the swish of the warden-mage's gray robes as the man's soft boots stepped around the rivulets of blood on the tile floor. "Commander?"

"Use your magic to keep him from dying. I want him alive when he leaves here, even if he's barely breathing."

"Done, Commander."

Blaine could hear the satisfaction in Prokief's tone. "Give him something to remember me by while he's down there. Fever and cramps, eh? It would be pleasant to hear him beg for death."

"As you wish, Commander." Ejnar paused. "And Rowse?"

"The same."

"With pleasure." Ejnar had no sooner spoken than Blaine felt a wave of fire building inside his body. A moment earlier, soaked to the skin and spread-eagled on the ice-cold tile, Blaine shivered uncontrollably. Now, he felt sweat breaking out on his temples, only to subside a moment later with shuddering chills. His gut clenched, and the pain would have doubled him over had the ropes not kept him flat against the floor. Blaine's breath came in shallow gasps as the pain hit again. He writhed, twisting against the ropes that held him until the skin at his wrists and ankles were raw. Every movement stretched the savaged skin on his back, yet it was impossible not to move. After only a few moments, the scream Prokief coveted tore from Blaine's lips.

"Make sure he remains conscious." Prokief turned from Ejnar to the guards. "When his time's up, drag him out when the prisoners are in the yard. Let them see the price of insolence."

"Unlock the cuffs," Prokief ordered. The commander made no effort to hide the gloating tone in his voice. "Get them dressed and give them each a woolen cloak. Then throw them in the Holes."

Blaine forced himself onto his knees, refusing to give in to the pain of every movement. Pulling the rough-spun cloth of his shirt over his savaged back hurt enough to make him pale.

"Three days in the Hole," Prokief repeated, settling his gaze on Blaine with satisfaction. "Perhaps you'll remember who's in charge."

The Hole. Prokief's oubliette. Blaine felt his hopes, briefly raised from surviving the whipping, plummet. Deep holes cut into Edgeland's ice held prisoners Prokief wanted to make sure never forgot the 'lesson' he wanted them to learn. Usually, the prisoners were beaten first, or whipped, before being dropped into the icy, solitary darkness until Prokief remembered to send someone to get them out. Some survived. Many did not.

One of the guards shoved Blaine, intentionally placing his hand to press against the fresh wounds that seeped blood through Blaine's homespun shirt.

Blaine bit back a curse. He had no desire to go into the Hole with broken bones, something a vengeful guard could easily arrange. Even Piran restrained himself to a murderous glare.

The snow crunched beneath his feet as the guards dragged Blaine and Piran to the oubliettes. Blaine saw an unbroken expanse of white that stretched into the gray horizon, and more snow falling from slate-colored skies. He shivered as the snow fell on bare skin where his ragged prison uniform did not protect him from the cold.

A soldier on either side dragged him, one on each arm, with Blaine between them as dead weight, too injured to stand. Blood dripped from Blaine's mouth into the snow, leaving a crimson path of droplets. Red stains trailed behind him from his injuries as the guards dragged him across the snow. The gritty ice burned against his raw wounds until his skin grew numb from the cold.

Blaine and Piran exchanged a glance that spoke volumes. Solidarity. Shared suffering. Acknowledgment that it might be the last time they saw freedom. And above all, an unspoken vow that someday, somehow, they would be avenged against Prokief and their attackers.

One guard removed the lid from the Hole, then the two guards heaved Blaine into the darkness. Blaine tumbled down, deep into the ice, as they replaced the lid and left him in blackness. He landed hard.

Blaine lay where he had fallen, breathing hard from the pain, alone in the darkness. *Will Ejnar really meddle to keep us from dying down here? It would be like that bastard Prokief to want the chance to torture us longer. Gods know, Piran and I have earned his ire a dozen times over.*

After he caught his breath, Blaine forced himself to his knees and began to feel around the ice to discover the bounds of his prison. To his relief, Prokief's sadistic humor had not included tossing in a wolf or some other predator to finish Blaine off.

Of course not, Blaine thought. *That would be too easy. Merciful, by his standards. And if he had intended a blood fight, he would have left the lid off, so the soldiers could watch.*

It would not have surprised Blaine to find the frozen corpse of one of the oubliette's prior occupants. Then again, Prokief liked to make sure all of Velant's inmates saw the evidence of his brutality to remind them that their lives and deaths were wholly under the prison commander's control and subject to his whims.

Blaine permitted himself a grunt of pain. The fall had winded him. His back hurt badly enough to bring tears to his eyes, but he swallowed down his pain and forced himself to pace the circumference of the oubliette.

He could stretch out his arms and reach both sides. That meant his prison was too small for him to stretch out. On the other hand, cold as it was deep in the ice, he was out of the wind and snow. Still, freezing to death was a real possibility. Prisoners found it difficult enough not to die from ice sickness in the normal course of their work, when they could retreat to the relative warmth of the barracks and the heat they could coax from the scant rations of firewood.

The oubliette contained no food, and certainly no means to build a fire, and no draft to vent one. Once again, the dubious mercy of Prokief's punishment was clear.

Blaine eased down to sit, tucking his cloak around himself to conserve as much body heat as he could. His gut still clenched spasmodically and he alternated between chills and fever.

I never really expected to survive Velant, Blaine thought. *No matter what Prokief told his mage this time. And none of us will ever return to Donderath. Piran's right; the chance of living long enough to get out of this damned prison and become a colonist was slim. A sucker's bet.*

And yet the colony of Skalgerston Bay was populated by the Velant colonists that had survived the hardships of Prokief's prison. Those who earned their Ticket of Leave received a small amount of acreage and a pittance sum of coin to build a cabin for themselves and start over as a colonist. Most returned to the jobs they had held in Donderath, coopers and blacksmiths, whores and tradesmen. The herring boat fleet made fishermen of all able-bodied colonists, and sometimes if the food ran short, some of the convicts as well. Everyone did some farming, since the shipments from back home did not come as often or as regularly as needed to keep people fed.

How much life can change in just a short period of time, Blaine thought. *I managed to trade Father's brutality for Prokief's. At least back at Glenreith, I had a bed to sleep in and hot meals most of the time.*

Still, he knew that given the choice he would not change the course of action that brought him to Velant. *Not if it meant that Father continued to beat Carr and abuse Mari. If I hadn't killed Father, he would have had to kill me. So perhaps death was looking for me either way, though I cheated King Merrill's noose.*

Three days, Prokief said. Do I believe him? If I fall asleep,

I'll likely die down here in the cold—unless Ejnar can actually keep me alive and torture me at the same time. Freezing to death isn't that bad of a way to go, considering the options. No more pain, or hunger, no more being the guards' target. I can fight to stay awake. Maybe I'll even manage to last that long. But did he mean it? Will he really haul us out then, or did he just say that to raise false hopes? What's to say he won't change his mind?

Cramps bent him over from time to time. Fever raised a sweat, then chills shook him to his core. But after a time, Blaine felt some strength return. He did not trust Prokief's word or Ejnar's magic to assure his survival. The cold, not his wounds, was the biggest threat. He resolved to keep moving as long as he could.

Blaine struggled to his feet and forced himself to pace the oubliette, then reverse course and pace again. He rested, leaning against the icy wall, and traced the path once more. The pit was cold, dark and silent except for the scrape of his boots against the ice. Blaine felt jumpy, as if energy tingled through the darkness and the ice, catching him in its flow. *Just my imagination,* he thought. But he had heard whispered rumors, back in the barracks, that magic coursed beneath Edgeland's snow and rock, out through the bay to Estendall, the volcano that sometimes rumbled and sent plumes of steam into the cold air. Rivers of magic flowed through certain places, some of the hedge witches said, things they called "meridians." Legends and wives' tales, Blaine thought. But in the darkness, he wondered.

Most people in Donderath had at least a flicker of small magic, and they used their talent for everyday tasks— healing a sick cow, making crops grow faster, finding where to drill a well. Blaine found his own talent of limited usefulness. In a fight, he had a second of forewarning of where his opponent would strike, sensed even earlier than signaled by the movements or expression of the other fighter. It was a secret Blaine had long guarded, since it gave him his only edge against his father. Here, it had enabled him to best other convicts who had tried to put him in his place. But against the ice and cold, it was useless.

Alone in the darkness, memories returned vivid and unavoidable. For the first time since the awful days about the convict ship, he let himself think about Carensa. The anguish in her eyes when King Merrill passed sentence had been almost too much for Blaine to bear. He remembered the touch of her skin and the scent of her hair, and her last, desperate visit to him when he awaited exile in the dungeon. Despite his pleas, she had been there on the dock when the Cutlass sailed from Castle Reach, a silent witness. *We would have married just a few months from* now, he thought. *If I hadn't ruined everything.*

To stay awake, and to blunt the pain of his injuries, Blaine counted his steps as he walked. Even so, his mind wandered. He thought about Glenreith and realized that the only truly happy times he could remember were when Ian McFadden was gone at court, sometimes for months. Only then had Blaine and the rest of the family been certain that they would not bear the brunt of one of Ian's rages. A few golden moments were crystallized in memory. His mother Liana, before the awful night Ian's temper had taken her life. Carr, his brother, when he was young enough to escape Ian's fists, when Blaine had been able to draw off Ian's anger and protect Carr and his sister Mari. It had been worth every bruise to see them safe. Then Blaine had grown too tall and strong for Ian to beat, and he had turned his attention to the others. Blaine had not always been able to protect them. Carr turned sullen and angry. Mari grew quiet and hid. When Blaine finally discovered why Mari tried so intently to vanish from her father's gaze, when the depths of Ian's debauchery had finally been exposed, Blaine had taken the matter into his own hands and run Ian through.

Five hundred steps. Walking keeps me warm, but eventually

I'll tire. No food to replenish my energy. Sooner or later, exhaustion and cold will even crowd out the pain. And then it will be over.

It was cold enough that the blood on his back froze to his shirt. Every movement ripped his shirt free from the ice-scabbed lacerations. Fever melted the ice, and blood trickled down his back, only to repeat the cycle again and again. For now, Blaine welcomed the pain. It proved he was still alive. When it dulled, his life dimmed with it. He focused on the pain like a beacon.

Five thousand steps. Only a few candlemarks had passed, but Blaine was growing tired. Before the fight in the mine, and the ordeal in Prokief's headquarters, Blaine had already been exhausted from the hard labor in the ruby mines and at the edge of starvation from the prison's scant rations. That left few reserves on which to draw, now that his body began to register the full trauma inflicted on it. Uncontrollable shivering cramped bruised muscles and tensed broken skin, jerking him awake every time the tremors made him shake from head to toe.

At least I won't die of thirst, he thought, using the buckle from his belt to scrape off some chips of ice. But even that was folly. Eating ice would lower his body temperature. Sooner or later, whether from cold, hunger, exhaustion, or thirst, he would die in the darkness. Weaponless, he lacked the means to shorten his suffering.

Twenty thousand steps. Blaine sank to the floor, unable to push his weary body further. He wondered how Piran was doing, whether Piran was shouting curses in the darkness or trying to climb the slick walls of his oubliette, or surrendering to the finality of the situation.

One hundred thousand. One hundred thousand and one. Blaine kept counting, though he had stopped walking candlemarks before. He was resigned to the numbness in his fingers and toes, the growing stiffness in his bruised body. He huddled in his rough blanket, trying and failing to warm his burning cheeks and ears.

If I'm still alive when they haul me out of here, what will I lose to the cold? A hand? The tip of my nose? My ears? Toes? Just in the few months Blaine had been in Velant, he had seen his fellow convicts lose a bit of themselves to the awful cold. Frostbite was relentless. Blaine had helped hold a man down as the hedge witch cut off two toes that had already gone gangrenous, frozen dead by the cold.

That's what we have to look forward to, if we survive. Dying by inches.

Blaine kept on counting, but the pace grew slower. Now and again, he lost his place and had to back up to the last number he remembered. It gave him a focus, but he was tiring. Even something as simple as counting became difficult to maintain. He counted to keep from sleeping, but when the dreams and nightmares finally claimed him, it did not matter.

Sunlight warmed his skin. The meadow down the lane from Glenreith was yellow with spring flowers. Mari ran through the blooms, shrieking with glee. She gathered a fistful of blossoms and presented them to Blaine with a wide smile. Her face and dress were grass stained, but her eyes were alight. Innocent. Untouched still by the horrors to come. Blaine reached for the flowers, but Mari pulled them away and with another gale of laughter, turned and ran across the field.

"Come back!" he shouted, starting after her. It occurred to him that he should be counting his steps. Why? He wasn't sure. It had been important. He knew that, but not the reason, and so as he ran, he kept a silent count with each footfall, as the tall grass sliced at his skin, leaving traces of his blood behind on every razor-sharp blade.

"Mari!" She only laughed harder and ran faster. Surely he could catch her, but she remained far ahead of him. They were

leaving the meadow and its brilliant sunlight, heading into the darkness of the forest. Blaine called for Mari to stop, but she ignored him, or perhaps she was too far away to hear his warning. The forest was dark and cold, filled with danger and predators. Wolves. Bandits. Monsters.

In the shadows of the tall trees, Blaine lost sight of Mari. He could hear her laughter, but he could no longer see her. A glimpse of her white shift sent him running in one direction, and the sound of her voice made him veer off. Mari was everywhere and nowhere, and it was growing dark. He had lost count of his steps, and now he would not find his way out of the forest.

Blaine shouted Mari's name, but silence answered him. His bootsteps pounded on dry leaves and crunching on the sticks and pinecones that littered the forest floor. Nothing mattered except finding Mari and leaving the woods. He stopped, lost. Her laughter was gone. A wolf howled. He heard her scream, this time in fear.

"Mari!" he shouted, starting to run again. Shadows gave way to darkness. So dark beneath the tall, old trees. Cold, too. Snow began to fall, thick and heavy, blanketing the ground. The wolf howled again. Another scream. The forest melted away, and Blaine ran through knee-deep snow. Up ahead he saw Mari. Her shift was no longer grass-stained white, but crimson, and she stood over the wolf's body, holding a bloody sword. Blaine shouted to her, terrified for her safety, angry that she had taken on the wolf herself, but Mari only stared at him as if in a daze, then began to shake her head.

Blaine lost his footing and crashed down into the snow. The cold blackness swallowed him. Mari and the wolf were gone, and only the dark remained.

The sound of a pennywhistle pierced the darkness. Lost, Blaine followed the music. He could barely hear it at first, but gradually, the notes grew louder, closer.

"What in Raka is he muttering?" a distant voice asked. The music stopped.

"Sounds like he's counting to me," another voice replied, just as far away as the first.

"Why in Esthrane's name is he counting?" the first voice sounded, closer now.

"Ask him if he wakes up," the second man replied.

For a time, the voices faded into darkness. The pennywhistle took up its tune again, a jaunty tavern song that reminded Blaine of home. When the shadows parted again, Blaine heard the steady cadence of a boot tapping against rock.

"Are you back yet?" The voice was one of the speakers he had heard before, familiar, but not yet someone he could place. "Because it's bloody boring sitting vigil."

With a struggle, Blaine opened his eyes. Even the dim light of the lantern hurt. It took him a moment to recognize the sparse surroundings of the prisoners' barracks. "Verran?"

"Thank Torven! He's stopped counting!" A chair scraped against the floor, and then Verran Danning stood over him, looking down with an expression that mingled annoyance and concern.

"How long?" Blaine croaked. His throat was parched, and his body felt leaden.

"Three days in the Hole, two days since then," Verran snapped. "With Dawe and me playing nursemaid, trying to get food down your sorry gullet and warming you up slowly enough, so we didn't have to chop off all the small bits from the cold."

Blaine had met Verran on the ship from Castle Reach. He and the minstrel-thief had struck a deal to watch each other's back on the long journey, and that had deepened into friendship when they had been assigned to the same barracks. Dawe Killick, one of the other prisoners in the same section as Blaine and Piran, had also become a good friend.

"Piran?" Blaine managed.

"He's alive," Verran replied. "Probably refused to die just to annoy the piss out of Prokief. Not in much better shape than you, but at least he didn't mutter numbers in his sleep."

Counting. Steps. The oubliette. Cold darkness. Little by little, memories flooded back. Pain. Dreams. Blaine shifted his weight and realized he lay on his own bunk. He winced, then realized that moving did not hurt as much as he expected.

"Got Tellam the hedge witch over here to save your sorry ass," Verran said, slipping his pennywhistle into his pocket. "Said he'd settle for a quarter of your next ration, if you survived, for his trouble. He closed up the stripes on your back and kept them from souring, and then he eased the ice sickness the best he could."

"Thanks," Blaine said.

"Dawe and I agreed. It was better to keep you and Piran alive than have to get new bunkmates," Verran replied. "We're used to how bad the two of you snore, and how you both wake up fighting in your sleep."

"You'd prefer counting?"

Verran barked a laugh. "No. Definitely not. Snore all you want. Just no more bloody numbers."

Blaine went back to sleep. After a time, he woke again. Verran was gone, but Dawe dozed in a chair nearby and startled as Blaine roused. "Good. You woke on your own. Thank Charrot and the spirits." Dawe unfolded his thin, lanky body from the chair and bustled over to the small brazier that kept the chill away and let them warm snow for water and make tea from the dried berries and leaves they plucked from the hedgerow.

He helped Blaine sit up and forced a chipped cup of hot tea into his hands. "Drink this. The healer said it would help." Blaine glanced across the small room and saw that Piran was also sitting up. They nodded to each other, in recognition of the shared triumph of survival.

"Prokief sent a guard to say you're back to the mines tomorrow," Dawe said. He shrugged as Piran let out a half-hearted barrage of curses. "Hey, I'm just the messenger. Guess you're bloody lucky he didn't throw your carcasses to the wolves when they fished you out of the Hole.

"What about the guard we thrashed?" Piran asked, his voice rough.

Dawe gave an unexpected chuckle. "Yeah. About that. Turns out his fellow soldiers didn't much like him, either. I hear he turned up dead, with his throat slit and his pay missing. One of the guards tried to blame it on you, but there were enough witnesses to what happened in the mine that didn't work out so well. Blaine came out of the Hole, he went in. Not sure Prokief means to fish him out."

Blaine sipped his tea and looked away. Tomorrow would bring new horrors. Maybe, if he survived long enough, he would earn his Ticket of Leave. It was little enough to live for, but it was something. He closed his eyes, and at the very edge of his memory, he heard a child's remembered laughter. Worth the price.

COLD FURY

1

DARK WATER

"I HATE THE SEA." BLAINE "MICK" MCFADDEN LEANED forward and then pulled back hard, dragging the heavy fishing net over the side of the herring buss.

"I don't mind the sea. I just hate the herring." Piran Rowse was on the other side of the net, pulling with all his might along with Blaine.

"That, too." Blaine was soaked despite the heavy oiled canvas topcoat and pants issued to all the fishermen. His boots were as sodden as his clothing, and he was chilled to the bone.

"Look at the bright side," Piran added. "It's almost the Long Dark, and there'll soon be too much ice for the boats to do much fishing."

Blaine slid a glare in Piran's direction. "Not helping. I hate the Long Dark even more than herring, if you can imagine that."

Piran clucked his tongue in mock amazement. "I don't believe I've ever heard you mention that." They both knew Blaine commented on his dislike for the arctic night on every dark day.

The fishing boats fought choppy waters off Edgeland at the

top of the world. Blaine, Piran, and the rest of the men on their small herring buss were convicts, sent north to the infamous Velant Prison for crimes real or imagined. After two and a half years, Blaine had seen all he wanted of Edgeland's brutal winters, knowing that he was condemned to deal with them for the rest of his life.

The lights of Skalgerston Bay, the harbor town that served the colony of Edgeland and the Velant Prison, were barely within view as the boat bobbed on the waves. It was as bright as the day would get this time of year, with the sun just at the horizon. In a few more candlemarks, the sun would sink from view. Blaine hoped they were off the water by then. The rough gray sea was formidable enough in daylight. In darkness, its vast expanse and cold depths were terrifying.

"Keep moving!" Carson, the ship's overseer, yelled as he slapped a flail against the boat's mast for emphasis.

Blaine and Piran worked together to empty their net onto the boat's deck. Half of the men on this shift manned the nets, while the others sat on crates in the middle of the deck cleaning and cutting the fish that were then salted and packed in barrels. Some of the herring would remain in Edgeland for winter provisions. Even Blaine had been hungry enough in the dead of winter to welcome a meal of herring. Most of the fish would find its way back to Donderath, the kingdom that exiled both the prisoners and their jailers.

In good weather, the men often sang to keep a rhythm throwing and pulling the nets. The cold, damp air made voices rough and throats sore, so the crew worked in silence save for the slap of nets and the clunk of knives. Blaine let his thoughts drift as he matched Piran's movements. They had been working on the boats for two weeks, and he had gotten past the worst of sore muscles and aching tendons from the hard work. Rough as the work aboard the herring boats was, it didn't compare to the ruby mines where Blaine and the others usually toiled. Convicts provided cheap labor to provision Donderath with fish and gems, and the irony was not lost on Blaine that the herring they caught was going to the kingdom he and the others would never see again.

Jaston and Hort were two of the other prisoners from Blaine's barracks. They had been fishermen back in Donderath, sent to prison for debts they could not pay. The two men seemed to be the only ones enjoying the fishing voyage. They worked together as if they had been gathering in nets all their lives, with an economy of movement borne of long practice. When it was their turn to gib the fish, their knives flew faster than anyone's, and Blaine noted that the two men were the only ones not complaining about the smell.

"I figure most of the men on the ship are thinking about what they're going to do once they earn their Tickets of Leave," Blaine said, grabbing hold of the net.

"I'm not worried about it," Piran replied. "It's all what you're used to," he added as they drew back to hurl their net out into the waves. "That's what makes a place feel like home." He grinned. "Set me down in a tavern anywhere, with the smell of good ale and pipe smoke, and I'm happy."

Blaine rolled his eyes. "Didn't you leave out the part about 'willing whores'?"

Piran shot him a look. "Included in the word 'tavern' mate. It all goes together." He paused. "How 'bout you? What will it take for Bay-town to seem like home?"

"Nothing special," Blaine lied. He had gone to great pains these three years in Velant to hide the fact that he was noble-born, although his family had not been especially wealthy or powerful. Glenreith, his family's manor, had not been well-off for years, long before Blaine's exile plunged the family into scandal. And while Blaine cherished a few good memories of his

222 • GAIL Z. MARTIN

late mother, his sister, brother, and aunt, too much of his life had
been marred by the violence and abuse meted out by his father,
Lord Ian McFadden, the man Blaine had murdered, the reason
Blaine was a convict in Velant.

"You're not pulling your weight!" Carson's voice cut above
the wind, and his leather flail sang through the air, catching
Mason, one of the convicts, across the shoulders. Mason winced
away, but since he was dragging on a net with all his might, he
could not escape the beating.

"I'm doing all I can!" Mason argued. He was a slightly built
man who stood shorter than Piran, ill-suited to the hard work of
the boats. Though his features suggested a man in his thirties, his
build was more like that of a teenager, long and thin without the
bulk of muscles. How he had been selected for herring duty,
Blaine did not know, unless one of the Velant guards had it in for
the man. Petty vengeance was more likely than just bad luck.

"I've had enough of your malingering!" Carson railed and
brought the flail down again. This time, its knotted ends cut into
Mason's work-mate, Teodor. Teodor gave Mason a murderous
look but kept his peace, unwilling to draw Carson's attention to
himself.

"I can't do more than I'm doing," Mason protested. Blaine
suspected he was telling the truth. Mason's hands were raw and
bloody, cut from the rough nets. He tried to remember Mason's
usual duties in the prison camp. *A tailor, isn't he?* Blaine thought.
*Sewing uniforms for Prokief and the guards. One of the few
'light' duties they don't give to the female prisoners.* Mason's
long fingers and uncalloused hands looked used to fine work, not
the heavy lifting of the mines or the farm. *I wonder who he
pissed off enough to get sent out here.*

"Pick up your pace, or I'll throw you overboard myself,"
Carson growled. For emphasis, he boxed Mason hard enough on

the ear to send the man staggering into Teodor, who gave him a rough shove back to his place.

"Don't look at me for sympathy," Teodor muttered when Carson was gone. "I'm doing my half and part of yours, too."

"I offered to gib," Mason sulked. "I'm better suited to cutting fish than hauling them."

"Carson'll gib you if you don't watch out," Teodor said.

Carson strode up and down the deck with his flail at the ready, cuffing those prisoners who weren't moving fast enough to suit him, or who merely raised his ire. "Rowse!" Carson shouted, stalking toward where Piran and Blaine worked their nets. "Stop lollygagging and get to work!"

Piran and Blaine exchanged a glance, then brought their net over the side with one well-timed lurch. The full net splashed cold salt water across the deck, drenching Carson from head to toe, and just for good measure, a few of the fish Piran flung loose from the net angled dangerously near Carson's head.

"I can have you whipped back at the camp for that!" Carson sputtered. He rounded on Piran with his flail, but Piran turned just at that moment with a large fish in his hand that was solid enough to absorb the blow meant for Piran's head.

"You could, but you won't because Mick and I here pull in twice as much fish as almost anyone other than the monger boys over there," Piran said with a nod toward Jaston and Hort. "And we mine more than our share of rubies, too. We're profitable. So bugger off."

Few prisoners could get away with Piran's bravado, but Carson just gave Piran a vicious look and moved away. *Piran's here from a court-martial,* Blaine thought. *Carson and the guards are soldiers. I wonder how much they know about why Piran was sent here—and whether his reputation protects him.* Piran was tight-lipped about what had landed him in Velant, but he had a hot temper and a hard fist. Few of the prisoners or guards gave him trouble more than once.

"Try not to get us thrown in the Holes again," Blaine muttered. "You've got a few weeks until you earn your Ticket of Leave." Piran had arrived at Velant six months before Blaine, in the same shipload of convicts as their friends Dawe and Kestel. They would be earning their Tickets shortly, while Blaine still had half a year to go.

"Prokief's going to be glad to see the back of us," Piran said with a grin as they emptied the last fish from their net and cast it into the gray waves. "He's had three years to kill us if he really wanted to."

Prokief's a sadistic son of a bitch, Blaine thought. *Just like Father. I wouldn't put it past him to stick shivs in our backs as we walk out of the prison gate, just for spite.*

"What's the first thing you're going to do as a colonist?" Piran asked, shifting the conversation.

"Buy a new shirt that doesn't stink," Blaine replied, guiding the net as the boat rode the waves. "You?"

Piran grinned wider. "Buy some time with a pretty lass, and all the beer I can drink."

They had played this game for years, imagining what they might do when they were finally granted their Tickets. Many prisoners did not live long enough to last the three years it took to win the qualified "freedom" of moving from the prison to the colony where they were still forever exiles from their homeland.

"We stick to our plan," Blaine said. "Pool our coin and land, build a homestead and run it together. You, me, Dawe, Verran, and Kestel. We'll make a good team."

Each prisoner who earned his Ticket got a small bag of coins and a few acres of hardscrabble, icy land in the wilds behind Skalsgerston Bay. The idea to pool resources had developed over time, along with the unlikely friendship that bound the five of them together. Verran Danning and Dawe Killick were assigned to Blaine and Piran's barracks. Dawe had been framed for murder by a business rival, while Verran was an unapologetic thief. Like Blaine, Verran still had six more months to go.

"Why do you think Kestel was so keen to join our homestead?" Blaine asked as they strained to pull the net back toward the boat. It was hard enough hauling in a net full of fish, but the sea was fighting them more than usual, getting rougher by the candlemark.

Piran grunted as he wrestled the net over the rail and sent a cascade of flopping fish across the deck toward the gibbers. "You mean besides our charm and good looks?" he said, with a grin. Piran had a boxer's squat, muscular build and he kept his head shaved even in the dead of Edgeland's winter. His nose had been flattened enough times to give him the look of a brawler, but his wit managed to get him out of as many scrapes as his big mouth got him into.

Blaine stood a head taller than Piran, and two and a half years of hard work in Velant's mines had put more muscle on his frame. His dark chestnut hair framed regular features and blue eyes, and his beard protected him, at least a little, from the arctic cold. "Yeah," Blaine said. "Besides that."

Rumor had it that Kestel Falke had been a courtesan in King Merrill's court, as well as a spy and an assassin before her fall from grace. She seemed to enjoy the gossip and the protection of a dangerous reputation, so she neither confirmed nor denied the stories, and no one could gainsay her. From a few encounters Blaine had witnessed, Kestel's fighting skills were easily good enough for her to at least be an assassin. She had helped Blaine and Piran on more than one occasion, and asked only one thing in return, for them to include her when they created their homestead.

"Well, it might be that she values our witty conversation and good breeding," Piran said, letting out a yell as he hauled with all his might.

"Doubtful."

"Dawe says he's a good cook," Piran supplied. "Maybe she wants a good meal."

"Probably not."

"Then maybe it's Verran and his damn pennywhistle. No accounting for music lovers," Piran suggested with a grin. Verran often plied the bunkhouse audience with tavern tunes and dance songs, but he was more likely to play for his supper and ale in a tavern than amuse an audience that wasn't already well into their cups.

"Highly unlikely," Blaine replied. "The only thing I can come up with is that despite what the rumors say, none of us have any designs on trying to bed her."

Piran raised an eyebrow. "I fancy my nuts where they are, thank you, not served to me on a platter." He shook his head. "Don't get me wrong—Kestel's good looking, and I lay my bets that she plays her looks down intentionally to avoid the wrong kind of notice." He grimaced. "Too many people go missing, someone will get wise," he added so that only Blaine could hear.

Blaine and Piran had met Kestel when she was in the midst of throwing a body down a well. They had given her a hand with the task, and in exchange, Kestel provided valuable information. That was nearly two years ago, and while male and female prisoners had little opportunity to mingle, the three of them had forged a profitable friendship. Still, Blaine had been surprised by Kestel's request, not in the least because he still had no idea how she knew that he and the others had even been planning to go in together.

"If she ever was in the courtesan business, I don't get the impression she's of a mind to go back to it, once we're colonists," Blaine observed, dumping out his side of the net.

Several fish flopped toward the rail, and he slid them toward the gibbers with his boot. "She was pretty clear about that."

"Have you seen the likes of what comes through Skalgerston Bay?" Piran asked, giving Blaine a look that questioned his sanity. "Sailors and former convicts. Quite a come-down from lords and dukes and fancy palace balls. Makes me a bit worried about the quality of evening ladies I'll find once we're free men."

We may get out of Velant, but we'll never be free men again, Blaine thought and put his back into the next net full of fish. It had been almost three years since Carensa, his betrothed, had watched the convict ship sail from the docks in Castle Reach. Blaine had watched from the porthole until her figure disappeared from view.

Carensa's probably married by now, he thought, forcing down the pang that brought. He had released Carensa from their vows when he was taken to the dungeon for the murder of his father. Blaine had begged her to forget him and go on with her life. He doubted that would be so easy, and feared his scandal might have reduced her opportunities. *I tried to save my family and ended up destroying them.*

"Hey, don't worry. I'm sure there'll be enough 'company' for both of us," Piran joked, mistaking Blaine's sudden quiet. "Although I get the prettiest ones." Blaine forced a smile. Piran's idea of a night out held little appeal for him. *But there was that one girl I met, from the laundry. Selane. I'd like a chance to get to know her better—*

"Move faster!" Carson's flail cut across Blaine's back and shoulders, painful even through his clothing. The knots on the leather strands opened bloody gashes where they tore the exposed skin on his neck and cheek.

Blaine hunched away, knowing better than to make a reply. Even Piran settled for a deadly glare. They were moving as quickly as the rough sea permitted, and Carson likely knew that. *He's either worried that we won't bring home enough fish and Prokief will hand him his ass, or he's just a sadistic son of a bitch, and he beats people up for fun. Or both.*

Even Jaston and Hort were not spared Carson's insults and blows, though the two fishermen moved with the ease of long practice, hauling in nets nearly full to bursting. Carson seemed to save the worst of his spleen for Mason, who staggered under the load of the heavy net he and Teodor fought to guide over the rail.

"Lose those fish, and I'll have you whipped to the bone," Carson shouted at Mason, who looked terrified out of his wits. The net slipped, spilling some of the fish back into the water, and Carson rained down a hail of blows as Mason tried and failed to get the net back under control.

"Keep that up, and we'll lose the whole thing," Teodor snapped. "I can't move this bloody net without him!"

Carson gave Teodor a baleful look and stepped back. Blood mingled with rivulets of sea water on Mason's face where Carson's flail had opened a slice on his cheek. Mason dove at the net as if he intended to wrestle it aboard all by himself, channeling his anger into strength.

Carson glared at Teodor. "You want to protect him? Fine. But if your haul is low, you'll both go to the Holes for this. Maybe then you'll try harder next time." Carson strode away, paying no attention to Teodor's murderous stare. The Holes were oubliettes sunk deep into the ice where Prokief put prisoners who resisted his authority. Many who were sent to the Holes died of exposure. Those who survived were often maimed by frostbite. It was no idle threat.

"Hear that?" Teodor growled at Mason. "I'm not going to the damned Holes over you, so you'd better move your worthless ass."

"I don't like the look of those clouds," Piran said with a nod of his head toward where the moon was nearly hidden, breaking Blaine's train of thought.

"Doesn't make much difference—we're out here until Carson says otherwise," Blaine muttered. He was trying not to think about how choppy the water had gotten, or how the boat bobbed like a cork out in the middle of a vast, dark expanse.

Captain Davis, commander of the *Petrel*, left the wheel to his first mate and walked over to where Carson stood. Blaine and Piran were too far away to catch much of what was said, but Blaine could hear enough to get the gist of the conversation.

"...don't like the look of the sky..." Captain Davis argued.

"...when we reach our quota..." Carson returned.

"...to Raka with your quota...this is my ship." Davis's jaw was set. Carson was unmoved.

"...orders from Commander Prokief..." A wave lifted the boat and let it drop just then. Blaine didn't hear more of the argument as he and Piran struggled to hold onto their net and manage not to be thrown overboard. *Not hard to figure out the rest,* Blaine thought. *This might be Captain Davis's boat, but the colonists are nearly as far under Prokief's thumb as the convicts. Backed by Prokief, Carson outranks Davis, even here. That's got to rankle.*

By Blaine's count, this should be the last day of the ship's run. The crews worked day and night, taking turns sleeping and working. If it weren't for the bitter cold wind and the salt spray that chilled him to the marrow, Blaine might have welcomed the change of scenery along with the fresh air. Edgeland's ruby mines were dank and dark even during the White Nights of summer, stifling with the smell of sweat and unwashed bodies. *We're just as dirty and just as sweaty on the boat,* Blaine thought, *I just can't smell anything except the damned fish.*

The *Petrel* rose and fell as waves washed over the decks. Fish flopped and slid across the boards, and the gibbers were thrown from their seats with the violence of the last wave. Blaine and Piran were knocked off their feet and went sliding, though they managed to hold onto their net in the process. The deck pitched one way and the other, requiring Blaine and Piran to crawl back to the railing.

"We're not finished yet!" Carson shouted above the wind. He brought his flail down on the back of the nearest fishermen, a convict named Trad who was doing his best to stay on his feet.

Rain began to fall, gently at first, then harder as the wind picked up. The clouds hid the moon. Gusts of wind snapped the sails and drove the rain sideways. *If this gets much worse, being under quota will be the least of our worries,* Blaine thought. *We'll be at the bottom of the sea and so will Carson's precious barrels of herring.*

The ship lurched again as Blaine and Piran cast their net, throwing Piran off balance. He yelped as he started to go over the rail. Blaine grabbed for Piran's belt and pulled him back. The ship dropped down as the wave fell to a trough, ripping the net from Blaine's hand and nearly breaking his fingers. Blaine hung on to Piran with one hand and the railing with the other. They teetered on the rail, and for a moment Blaine feared that they would both fall overboard. Strong hands grabbed them from behind, pulling them back to safety as the other fishermen pitched in.

"Thanks, mate," Piran shouted. "Thought I was a goner."

I thought we both were, Blaine thought. He crawled to one of the masts in order to get to his feet. They had lost their net, and by the look of it, the other fishermen had reached the point where they were more afraid of the sea than of Carson. Carson had gone to argue with Captain Davis, and Blaine realized that despite the overseer's orders, Captain Davis had turned the boat back toward Skalgerston Bay.

Carson may be willing to drown to avoid disappointing Prok-

ief, but Davis appears to have other thoughts on the matter, Blaine observed.

He could barely see the other herring boats, just shadows on the water. The wind was gusting hard, and while the fishing busses were sturdy, Blaine could hear the wood creak and strain as the sails struggled to propel the ship faster than the choppy waters would permit. The sails filled and bore them forward, all the while heaving like a wild bull as the sea rose and fell beneath them. Some of the men retched, but no one dared go to the rail. The hungry, dark water was much too close for comfort.

"Watch out!" Piran shouted. In the next instant, a wall of water crashed over the deck. It would have hammered them to their knees if they had not lashed themselves to the mast with their belts. Icy water hit them like a body blow, and for a moment, Blaine could not breathe as the water engulfed him.

The wave hit them hard enough to knock a man from his feet, and pulled back with the force of a giant's hand, inexorably taking everything with it. Men flailed and screamed as they tried to find something solid to anchor them, or as the wave's force tore them lose, breaking hands and arms as it dragged them into the sea. When the wave receded, the men on deck climbed to their feet, warily watching for the next wave to hit.

One of the convicts had been thrown against the mast by the force of the wave. He lay at the base, his neck broken. Several of the prisoners sputtered and choked as others pounded on their backs, trying to clear the seawater from their lungs. *I never thought I could drown without leaving the boat,* Blaine thought.

Blaine had no idea where Carson had been when the wave struck, but he looked bedraggled, which fouled his mood even more than usual. He began to stride around the deck, counting the prisoners. Those who were below, lucky enough to have the sleep shift, were spared nearly drowning, though Blaine wondered if the boat was watertight enough to keep them entirely dry. *It clearly wasn't my lucky day.*

"Where's Mason?" Carson demanded.

"He was right there when the wave hit," Trad replied.

"Mason washed overboard," Teodor said, shaking the water out of his hair like a spaniel. "We got the worst of the wave when it hit, and we both slammed the deck pretty hard. Then the wave pulled back, and it was all I could do to hold on. I thought I saw him in the water, but if it was Mason, he wasn't fighting, just sort of let the wave take him." He glared at Carson. "Don't completely remember, since I was drowning."

"There! I see him!" Jaston pointed to the water near the side of the boat.

Blaine squinted, barely making out a form on the water, floating face down. If he had not known a man went overboard, he would have thought he was imagining things. The ship rose with another swell and sailed down into the trough. The man was gone.

Carson was drenched to the skin, which only served to highlight his sharp, bony build and the hard angles of his face. He stalked toward where Captain Davis fought with the boat's wheel. "You've cost me a prisoner!" Carson shouted above the wind.

Davis did not look up. "Go to Raka. You insisted we stay out here. It's on your head."

"The Commander can rescind your Ticket," Carson threatened, shaking his flail as if he meant to beat someone with it.

Captain Davis wrenched the wheel to the right, trying to steer the herring buss between the worst of the waves. "That's only a concern if we survive the storm," Davis snapped.

"I want one of your men to replace the convict I lost," Carson demanded.

"Shut up and get out of my sight," Davis ordered as he used

all his weight to wrest the wheel in the other direction as the sea surged. "I have a ship to steer."

The ship shuddered violently, with the sound of wood grating against something hard and solid. Blaine and the others struggled to keep their footing. He exchanged a worried glance with Piran.

"Icebergs," they said in unison.

"Wonderful," Blaine muttered. He strained to see out over the choppy waters, but it was too dark to make out much of anything. Icebergs were a hazard to ships near Skalgerston Bay. In good weather, the fishing captains had little trouble steering around them, and every boat had large poles to help push the bergs away from the hull. Even at night, the spotters on the bow, armed with lanterns, did amazingly well at avoiding the large chunks of ice.

"This is all Carson's fault," Piran growled. Blaine had been thinking the same thing. Carson had insisted the boat stay out longer than Captain Davis advised, and since theirs was the lead ship on this expedition, Carson's stubbornness had meant none of the other boats made for shore, either. Now they had not only the storm sea and wind to navigate, but dozens of chunks of ice, some as big as wagons, being hurled at them with all the fury of the ocean.

A cold knot settled in the pit of Blaine's stomach. For the first time, he realized that they might not make it back to Edgeland alive.

"Man the poles!" the first mate shouted. Blaine and Piran ran for the forward poles, along with Hort and Jaston. The poles were more like pikes, long and sturdy with a blade at the tip to maneuver chunks of ice or other debris out of the way of the ship.

"Spread out along the sides and keep an eye out for ice!" It was difficult to walk on the pitching deck, but Blaine went to one side while Piran went to the other. Hort and Jaston took the midship position, while Teodor and Torr went aft. The high waves had extinguished their lanterns.

"This is like poking boulders with a stick," Blaine muttered. Pieces of ice were difficult enough to spot in daylight, since most of their bulk was submerged. By night without lanterns, it was an impossible task.

By the time Blaine could spot one of the small icebergs, it was nearly too late to shove it away. Blaine thrust his pike at one of the chunks that neared the hull, trying to slow its approach if he could not deflect it completely. The pole bowed as if it would break, fighting the resistance of the weight of the ice and the drag of the water.

Blaine could see the prow lanterns of the other herring boats as they battled the storm to return to port. From their erratic courses and the frequent changes in direction made by Captain Davis, Blaine guessed they were all dodging floating obstacles. He caught a glimpse of white against the dark sea and jabbed at it with his pole, but the iceberg must have been bigger than it looked because it caught the bladed tip of the pike and nearly took Blaine and the pole with it as the waves shifted.

Blaine's heart thudded as he fought to pull the pike free. He wrested it clear, but the effort almost put him over the railing. The rain had turned to sleet, its crystals sharp enough to make tiny cuts as they hit exposed skin. Blaine's beard and brows were icy, and a thin film of ice on his canvas coat cracked and crunched with every movement. His breath was a white cloud, and the sea spray burned his eyes, making it harder to see.

"If this ship is damaged, I'll see to it that you all hang!" Carson screamed above the wind. Blaine noted coldly that Carson had not found it necessary to grab one of the poles himself. *He's as scared of dying as we are,* Blaine thought as he managed to deflect another chunk of ice. *Maybe more so. Guaranteed to make a mean son of a bitch even meaner.*

A deafening crash reverberated through the entire ship as the boat's forward motion stopped abruptly, throwing everyone off balance. Blaine grabbed for the railing and slid on the sheen of ice, barely managing to stop himself from going over. He had made a make-shift safety line with his belt, but he did not trust it to hold against the full strength of an angry sea. The waves had grown fierce, and as the ship struggled to maneuver around the iceberg that had glanced off its prow, a wall of water bore down on the fishing boat.

"Hang on and duck!" Blaine shouted. He crouched, waiting for the deluge and the chunks of ice it would carry.

Boom. A sound like an explosion nearly deafened Blaine in the instant after the wave slammed down on the deck. He could hear men's screams and cries, muted by the water that washed over him and strained against his safety line. Blaine clung to the railing with his full strength. The line felt as if it might tear him in two as it pulled back against the sea.

When he could finally see and breathe again, Blaine felt cold terror fill him. A huge hole had been torn in the center of the deck where a berg had come crashing down on the *Petrel*, and the herring buss had started to list.

"Get the men out of the hold!" the first mate shouted. Half of the convicts aboard the *Petrel* were below, though whether or not anyone had been able to sleep was questionable given the rough sea.

Frightened men were already climbing up out of the hold looking as sodden as if they had been on deck. "Hull's cracked," one of the men yelled. "We're taking on water."

"Can't find half a dozen of the men," someone else shouted.

"Do something!" Carson shrieked.

Teodor wheeled and sank the blade end of his pike right through the overseer's heart. "I've had about enough of you," the big man rumbled. He pulled his pike free from Carson, who was still gasping, and heaved Carson over the rail.

"If I'm going to die, I'll die happy," he muttered. Given the likelihood they were all going to drown, Carson's death would be one more fatality.

"Grab anything that floats!" Piran yelled, as the *Petrel* listed starboard. The first mate had retrieved a lantern from below decks and was flashing a desperate signal to the other boats, though Blaine doubted the rest of the fleet would risk turning around to save them, even if the storm made such a maneuver possible.

I've made it this far just to drown? Bitter disappointment warred with primal fear.

"Come on," Piran said, grabbing Blaine by the arm. "Climb up the mast. We've got to stay out of the water as long as we can." Piran shinnied up the mast like a born rigger, while Blaine struggled against the icy handholds and slippery footings. They dared not climb too high for fear of capsizing the listing ship, and reached a point of equilibrium, shifting their weight one way and the other to keep the boat where it was while it remained afloat.

The worst of the rain appeared to be over, and the wind had stopped gusting. *Too little, too late,* Blaine thought.

The *Petrel* was riding lower in the water, and the frightened men shifted toward the highest sections of the deck. The hold was already heavy with casks full of fish, which was likely to hasten their trip to the bottom of the sea. Blaine strained to see the lights of Bay-town. It was still too far to swim, and the icy water would be sure death to anyone foolish enough to try.

"Never liked the damned water," Teodor said as he climbed atop the barrels at the base of the mast. More barrels rolled across the deck, and still others remained in the netting that held them ready for the gibbers.

"We can't stay up here much longer," Piran said as the ship shuddered beneath them. "We're running out of time."

"I've got an idea." Blaine dropped down from the mast and sloshed through the shin-deep water on the deck. He grabbed one of the empty herring barrels and a net. "Grab the empty barrels and all the nets you can find. We're going to make rafts."

Blaine's idea beat waiting to sink, and the convicts seized onto the possibility, gathering up as many of the unused barrels as they could find and dumping fish out of the full barrels when there were no more empty ones to be found. Even the herring boat's crew pitched in, since it was clear to everyone that the *Petrel* was beyond saving.

"Don't know how long we'll last in those waves," one of the sailors said as they used rope to secure a net over a dozen barrels.

"A damn sight longer than we'd last without the rafts," Teodor replied. The group managed to put together eight rafts before the doomed *Petrel* listed sharply.

"She's going over!" Captain Davis yelled as he abandoned the wheel. "Grab anything that floats!"

The barrel rafts were unsteady, so the men lay flat across them to keep from capsizing. There was barely enough space for all the survivors, and a few of the rafts had bodies piled two deep. No one complained, given that the alternative was the ice cold water.

Unless those ships come back for us, we've just prolonged the suffering, Blaine thought as he clung to the sodden net. His hands were cramped, his skin stung from the salt water, and he was already soaked through. Some of the men around him were shivering uncontrollably, one of the first signs of ice sickness. Blaine had seen men succumb to cold in the prison, and he knew that wet and cold, they had precious little time left.

"Watch out for ice!" Hort yelled and kicked at a chunk that

banged into their raft. The sea had calmed, so they had less risk of being swept away in the waves, but without paddles or a rudder, there was no way to steer themselves to shore. They were at the mercy of the current.

"There's a light!" Josten raised up enough to point. Two bobbing lights seemed closer than before. Blaine could not tell whether the other herring boats had come back for them, or whether it was his imagination, the wishful thinking of a dying man.

"It's a ship!" Piran yelled. "Over here!" he screamed at the top of his lungs, nearly deafening Blaine, who was right beside him. The others took up the cry, and the lights grew close enough that Blaine could see the prow lanterns on two ships.

"Remain on your rafts. We'll throw you a line and tow you in," a man's voice boomed across the dark water.

"I've never been so glad to see a boatload of convicts in my bleedin' life," Piran said, rising up to be able to catch the rope thrown by the nearest ship.

"Let's just hope that the townsfolk feel the same," Blaine replied. "Because it looks like that's where we're headed."

2

NEWS FROM HOME

COLONISTS LINED THE HARBOR FRONT IN SKALGERSTON BAY
when the herring boats limped back to dock. Bedraggled and
shivering, Blaine and the others had to be helped from their
makeshift rafts, and they stumbled their way ashore like drunken
men, their bodies too cold and stiff to move.

Blaine expected to be packed into wagons and hauled back to
Velant, so he was surprised when he and the other survivors—
along with the crews of the returning boats—were welcomed
into one of the big warehouses on the wharf front. Inside,
lanterns lit the cavernous space and fires burned in metal barrels.
The light and heat were a godsend after the long hours onboard
the boats, and Blaine shuffled his way toward the fire, hoping
that his body would function normally again after he was warm.

"You've all had quite an adventure out there," one of the
colonists said. He dropped his voice, mindful that some of Prokief's men were aboard the ships that did not founder. "Pox take
the idiot that sent you out in this weather. We knew storms were
coming."

"There's soup and bread to help you warm up." One of the

female colonists, a plump woman in her middle years, gestured toward a large cauldron and a table piled with loaves. "Best we could do on short notice."

Blaine was painfully aware of how shabby he and the other convicts must look, clothes dirty and sodden, unwashed, unshaven, and hair matted. He expected the colonists to shy away from them and was astounded that the Bay-town residents had bothered to turn out to see them come ashore, let alone welcome them with fire and food.

The man who had greeted them seemed to guess Blaine's thoughts. "We've all been convicts, you know," he said with a wry smile. "It's not the kind of thing you forget."

Blaine was shivering so hard it took more than one try to get the cup of soup to his lips. "Thank you," he managed.

The tall man watched him with a distant look in his eyes. "Fishing this time of year is a fool's errand," he replied. "Our men won't go out once the icebergs get bad. You can see why."

Blaine nodded. "So it's true?" he said, glancing around the warehouse. "Some convicts make it out alive?"

The man chuckled. "Yes," he replied. "It's true. In fact, don't let Prokief lie to you. If you survive three years in Velant, it's the king's law that you be released to the colony. *If* you survive." He paused. "I'm Ifrem, owner of the Crooked House—the best damn tavern in Bay-town."

"Quit yer braggin'," another colonist bantered.

"It's true," Ifrem admitted with a grin. "Not exactly the Rooster and Pig, but not too far off the mark." Everyone knew the Rooster and Pig, a garishly painted tavern on the waterfront in Castle Reach, the main harbor city back in Donderath. The Rooster and Pig was famed far and wide for its bitterbeer. Even King Merrill sent servants to fetch its beer, while sailors spread the tavern's fame far and wide.

"I'd give a lot for some of that bitterbeer right now," Blaine replied, wishing he could stop shivering so that his voice no longer trembled with the cold.

"We brought ale as well as soup, but we figured you should eat something first, warm up a little," Ifrem said. He watched Blaine sip the soup as if it were elixir. "How long until you earn your Ticket?"

"Six months," Blaine managed. "If I live that long."

Ifrem did not take his comment as humor. "Be careful," he advised, dropping his voice. "The commander doesn't let go of his prisoners easily. Especially if you've drawn his ire."

"If we hadn't before, we will now, coming home one boat—and all that herring—short," Piran said. He had begun to get his color back and managed not to look half frozen despite his bald head. "And I suspect we're not on his list of favorites to begin with."

That, Blaine knew, was putting it mildly. He and Piran had managed to be a thorn in Prokief's side for the entire span of their internment and had the scars to prove it. Piran's mouth caused a good bit of trouble, but Blaine and Piran had also surfaced as unlikely leaders who had earned a reputation among the prisoners for challenging the most brutish of Prokief's underlings.

"We'll go out when the sun hits the horizon and bring in whatever barrels we can find," Ifrem said. "Some of them should be floating out there if the current doesn't take them. We'll send them up to the prison. That might ease things a bit, if the boat's load wasn't a total loss."

"Some of our men drowned," Blaine said. "It was bad out there."

Ifrem nodded. "I'm not keen on fishing, but I've had my turn out there when we needed all hands to provision for winter. It's a dangerous business. Those rafts were a smart idea. A man doesn't last long in the water, cold as it is."

Blaine could feel the soup warming him, and his fingers and toes ached as sensation returned. He was punchy from the adrenaline and exhausted from the long shifts aboard the boat, but tired as he was, one question was uppermost in his mind. "What news do you have from home?"

"Before I answer that, I'll get you some ale," Ifrem offered. "Sit down before you fall down."

They sat. All around them, the convicts huddled around the fire barrels, gratefully eating the food the colonists provided. Blaine heard some of Prokief's overseers arguing with the boat captains, trying to rush getting the prisoners back to Velant. The captains were colonists and disinclined to give in to the overseers after being forced to stay out longer than prudence dictated, at the risk of their ships. At the moment, both sides appeared to be at a standoff.

Ifrem returned with the ale, which Piran and Blaine accepted thankfully. He sat down across from them. "We don't hear as much as we'd like," Ifrem said. "The ships only come every three months. Getting a message delivered costs coin to bribe the sailors, and sometimes coin to get them to release a letter someone already paid to send up here," he added, his face twisting in annoyance.

"But you get some news?" Blaine pressed. "Some letters?"

Ifrem nodded. "Yes. Prokief allows very little mail into or out of the prison—it's part of how he keeps you under his thumb," he said quietly, glancing over his shoulder to make sure the overseers were out of earshot. "But out here, we get news from the sailors and some news from our families—at least, those that want to acknowledge we're still alive."

Blaine had heard little from his Aunt Judith or his sister Mari since his exile. After the first year, the letters stopped coming altogether. He had tried to reassure himself that they had not completely forgotten him or disavowed him, but as the years passed without word, it was difficult to keep believing. *After all this time, if I could get a letter to them, should I do it? Maybe it's better to let the dead stay dead.*

"The news isn't good, unfortunately," Ifrem continued. "The border skirmishes with Meroven have been going on for a while, but it's escalating. The border areas are battlefields, there's talk that the army might start taking conscripts, and the longer the fighting goes on, the more of a burden falls on everyone."

Meroven was the kingdom to the north of Donderath, a proud land with a long history of bad blood and broken treaties with its neighbor to the south. "Are we winning?" Piran asked, leaning forward, his soldier's instincts at the fore.

Ifrem swore. "Meroven's king is a madman. He's reckless, land-hungry."

"But are we winning?" Piran pressed.

Ifrem sighed. "It depends on whose letters you believe," he replied. "I'm sorry—you've been without news for so long, and now I can't offer you good tidings." He looked at Piran and seemed to size him up.

"You fought?" Ifrem asked.

Piran nodded curtly. "A while ago."

"Count yourself lucky you're not back in Donderath," Ifrem said. "The first letters we received were nervous about the fighting but confident it would be over soon, and in Donderath's favor. Lately, that's changed."

"Do you know why?" Piran's tone had an unusual urgency to it. Blaine wondered how many of Piran's friends still fought under the king's colors, facing the Meroven threat on the battlefront.

"Anything we hear is third-hand, at best," Ifrem replied. "It's not a sea war, so the sailors don't know anything. We get the gossip that makes its way to Castle Reach, after it's been passed through who-knows-how-many tale-tellers. Some things might grow with the telling. But I don't think they're exaggerating the odds. No one's winning, and it's been dragging on a long time."

"What about the Cross-Sea Kingdoms?" Piran asked, hungry for details. "Or the Lesser Kingdoms to the south?"

Ifrem shrugged. "I wish I could tell you, but we're not hearing from the soldiers themselves. Just what reaches their mothers, sisters, and wives. I don't know anything else."

Piran nodded. "It's more than we knew before. Thank you." Piran was rarely reflective, but he had a pensiveness to him Blaine suspected had more to do with the news of the war than their near brush with death.

There were so many questions Blaine longed to ask about the colony, now that leaving Velant was almost a reality. "How does it work, when convicts are released?" he asked, pleased that his voice no longer shook with the cold.

Ifrem stole another look over his shoulder. The dispute between the guards and the ships' captains had grown louder. Blaine wondered how far the captains would push their luck, since Prokief was the colony's governor as well as commander of the prison garrison.

"You walk out of the prison with your papers and your coin and the clothes on your backs," Ifrem said. "We usually know when to expect a new group. The colony has an unofficial governing body, a Council of Citizens. We try to assign each new colonist a guide, someone to help you make the change. There's a lottery for land parcels. When you build your house and barns, we get a group together to make the work go faster. Same with planting and harvest."

A note of pride colored Ifrem's voice. "We watch each other's backs, for the most part," he said. "More than back home, that's for sure. If there's hunting or fishing to be done, we all pitch in. More hands make for less work."

Blaine had another question on the tip of his tongue when the shouting started.

"Our orders were to bring them back immediately," one of the overseers argued, his voice pitched to be heard above the buzz of conversation. It was clear that the overseers were out of patience. *Or perhaps, they're as afraid of Prokief as the prisoners are,* Blaine thought.

"Let them finish eating," the plump woman cajoled. "We have food enough for you, too."

Blaine wondered if it galled the colonists to extend their hospitality to the overseers. Surely they too had experienced the casual cruelties of Prokief and his guards when they served their time in Velant. Yet there was no undercurrent of bitterness in the woman's voice. The overseers were just as miserable as their sodden charges tonight.

Reluctantly, the overseers accepted rations of soup and bread now that all the convicts had been fed. "Lady, you don't understand," one of the overseers said. "If we don't get them back soon, the Commander will send the warden-mages."

The room went silent. Everyone turned to look at the overseers. "We're overdue," one of the guards said, regaining his bluster. "They might be on their way now."

There was no mistaking the fear in the eyes of the colonists. It mirrored the terror of the convicts. Prokief's warden-mages were a law unto themselves, brutal and sadistic. That the guards also feared them was a measure of how much power they wielded.

"Of course," the woman said, seeming to shrink in on herself. "You've got to get back. We didn't mean to cause any trouble."

"You'd better go," Ifrem said, standing, indicating that Blaine and Piran should do the same. "If the gods are with you, we'll see you here soon."

Blaine and Piran set their cups aside, murmuring their thanks. After all of the colonists' generosity, they had no desire to bring hardship on them. A scuffle outside made Blaine wonder if it was already too late.

A gust of frigid wind swept through the warehouse as a dozen Velant guards burst through the door. They had their swords in hand and looked as if they welcomed a fight. The colonists and prisoners stepped back, hands raised. They had more than enough experience with Prokief's guards to know how volatile the soldiers were, and how much latitude they had in meting out punishment. Even the overseers looked frightened, and Blaine wondered whether Prokief would weigh the loss of a ship and its herring as more grievous than their disobedience in not returning immediately to the prison. *Prokief's not likely to pay much attention to extenuating circumstances,* Blaine thought.

"There's no need for a fight," Ifrem said, moving to the fore. The soldiers said nothing and stopped in a line along one side of the warehouse. A man dressed in the gray robes of a warden-mage strode through the doorway. The room fell silent.

"Commander Prokief does not take kindly to disobedience," the warden-mage warned with a glance toward the overseers. He raised his hands and intoned a chant. The overseers fell to their knees, arms clutched around their bellies, doubled over in agony. Blaine and Piran exchanged a nervous glance. That particular malicious spell seemed to be a favorite among the warden-mages given how often they employed it for even trivial infractions. Prokief's warden mages were masters at inflicting pain without doing permanent damage, thereby denying the respite of shock and death. Blaine and Piran had both been on the receiving end of the warden-mages' cruelty, and the memory of the searing pain still haunted Blaine's dreams. He felt his gut clench as he watched the overseers topple to the floor.

"Explain," the warden-mage snapped, glaring at the colonists.

Ifrem paled, but he held his ground. "One of the fishing boats was struck by an iceberg," he said, his voice calm and measured. "The storm almost swamped the other boats. All the men nearly drowned." He glanced toward the disheveled prisoners.

"They were half-dead from exposure. If we hadn't brought them in to warm them, you would have lost many of them by the time they reached the prison." Although Ifrem's voice was carefully neutral, there was a hint of challenge in his eyes as he lifted his chin and met the warden-mage's gaze. "Surely the Commander desires live workers to meet your quotas."

Clever, Blaine thought. *Remind the warden-mage that the king expects his due, and it'll be that much harder to deliver the more of us Prokief kills for spite.*

The warden-mage barely glanced at the tortured overseers, but he made a gesture with his right hand, and the spell lifted, leaving the overseers lying spent and gasping on the floor. The guards hauled the men roughly to their feet, though a few of them looked like they might pass out from their ordeal.

"Rowse! McFadden! Is this true?" The warden-mage's gaze fell on Blaine and Piran. He wasn't the lead mage, Ejnar, but he had inflicted punishment more than once at Prokief's command when Blaine and Piran had managed to draw the commander's ire. It was not a good thing that he recognized them, and Blaine saw concern—and curiosity—in Ifrem's gaze.

"Exactly as he said, sir," Blaine responded, managing to keep the bitterness out of "sir." "We were on the water in the worst of the storm, in the dark, and the icebergs broke our hull. Only half the crew made it to shore. Our overseer, Carson, died in the wreck."

"The colonists saved us, which wouldn't have been necessary if those bloody overseers hadn't kept us out in a storm past full dark," Piran snapped. Blaine repressed a sigh. Piran never could leave well-enough alone.

A wave of the mage's hand sent Piran across the room to slam into the warehouse wall. "I do not like your tone," the mage observed. Piran rose and shook himself off. His lip was bloodied. For once, he kept his comments to himself, though his gaze was murderous.

The mage's eyes narrowed, and he turned back to the overseers, who shrank back in fear. "Interesting," he said, stretching out the word as if pondering each syllable. "The commander will not be pleased that your bad judgment cost a ship, its load, and several prisoners. We will discuss this when we return to the prison. The commander will want to know."

Perhaps Blaine should have felt satisfaction in the fear he saw in the overseers' eyes after the harsh treatment they had received at Carson's hand. Earlier in his imprisonment, he might have been inclined to gloat silently. Now, he knew that whatever punishments the overseers endured—however well deserved—would just result in even worse conditions for the prisoners.

The warden-mage looked to Ifrem and the colonists. "I will let Commander Prokief know that you intervened to reduce the loss of his assets. He may reimburse you your supplies." His voice turned cold. "You also violated the prohibition of fraternization with the prisoners. Commander Prokief may refuse your reimbursement as punishment for disobeying the rules. Until he makes his decision, I am placing a tenth-bell curfew on all colonists within the sound of the Bay-town bell tower, effective immediately. Those who violate the curfew will be held accountable."

By the set of Ifrem's jaw, Blaine could see that the punishment rankled, but Ifrem ducked his head and nodded. "Understood." The tension among the colonists unmistakable, and Blaine wondered what hardships the curfew would cause them and whether they anticipated having their good deeds incur the wrath of Prokief and his lackeys. Ifrem sensed Blaine's gaze and caught his eye, and gave a brief shake of his head. *They knew, and they came anyway.*

"All of you—in the wagons!" the warden-mage ordered.

The prisoners fell in line, reluctantly leaving the warmth and welcome of the warehouse. There was no mistaking the hatred in their eyes for the warden-mages, yet they all knew that there was no chance to go against Prokief's word. *But if the time ever comes that Prokief and his mages are vulnerable, watch out,* Blaine thought.

The convicts kept their heads down, queuing up for the wagons. Outside, it was bitter cold, and their canvas coats from the ships were still wet and of little use shielding them from the cold.

"Rowse!" the mage said as Blaine and Piran moved to climb into the wagon. "As punishment for your insubordination, you and your friend will walk." His lips quirked in a hint of a vengeful smile. "If prudence won't shut your mouth, perhaps when your folly inconveniences your friends sufficiently, they'll impress on you the need for discretion."

Blaine glared at Piran as the guards tied their wrists with rope and fastened the ends of their tethers to the back of the wagon. If the weather were better, Blaine might suspect the mage meant to have them dragged, but given the sleet and mud, the wagons would be moving at a fraction of their normal pace.

Piran managed a defiant grin as the horses started forward, nearly pulling him off balance. "Don't say a word," Blaine growled, trying to keep his footing in the muddy ruts. "You're not my favorite person right now."

The wind had picked up again, and though the rain was not as heavy as it had been when they were out to sea, the icy mix of sleet and hail cut their skin and clung to their clothing. The wagons lurched and struggled on the up-hill path so that in addition to keeping their feet, Blaine and Piran had to watch out that the wagon did not slip back and run them over.

Half-frozen ankle-deep mud threatened to pull their boots from their feet with every step. Their ropes were long enough to give them a few feet of leeway, but every time the wagon gained traction and surged forward, it jerked them hard enough that they staggered. More than once, both men slipped and fell into the muck. Ice frosted their brows and beards, forming a brittle skin over their coats and gloves, and hanging in little icicles from their hats. The rough rope bit into their wrists, cutting into their skin then freezing to the blood and pulling free with every movement.

They did not waste their breath talking. Blaine was already tired from a full day of fishing, and the hardship and danger of the shipwreck pushed him into exhaustion. It took all Blaine's waning strength to remain on his feet and stagger after the wagon, and by the time they saw the torches along the prison walls, Blaine's teeth were chattering so hard that he thought he might break a tooth. Piran looked equally miserable. The fresh blood on his lip was frozen, and his face was bruised where he had hit the wall. They were both shivering so violently, the warmth and welcome of the colonists might have been a fever dream.

The wagons stopped in front of the barracks. Blaine and Piran fell to their knees, utterly spent. Two soldiers came to cut their bonds. "Get up," one of the soldiers snapped, giving Piran a kick in the ribs to underscore his order.

"We'll get them inside." Teodor and Torr jumped down from the back of the wagon. Teodor got a shoulder under Piran's arm, while Torr helped Blaine to his feet. It was all Blaine could do to force his legs to keep moving and his knees not to buckle. The guards did nothing to help or hinder them, but Blaine did not trust their luck until he and the others were inside their barracks and the door shut behind them.

"By all the gods!" Dawe Killick was the first to spot Blaine, Piran, and the others. Dawe grabbed Verran Danning by the arm. "Come on!"

Garrick and Dunbar also came running. Ernest gave a shout to rouse the rest of the barracks. During the Long Dark, Piran had trouble keeping track of time, but the smell of food filled the lower floor of their bunkhouse, suggesting that dinner was not long past.

Five of the men on the herring boats were from Blaine's barracks; the rest were drawn from other buildings. They had been spread among the ships, so luckily, not all had been aboard the *Petrel*. All of Blaine's bunkmates had returned. Mason and the men who drowned were from other barracks.

"To Raka with the overseers," Hort said as he collapsed onto one of the benches near the small stove.

"I second that," Josten said, dropping onto the floor a few feet away. Blaine and Piran had practically been dragged from the wagon to the barracks, and it took Dawe and Verran to help them over near the heat.

"You look like you've traveled the Unseen Realms," Dawe observed worriedly. "Have you eaten?"

Blaine tried to answer, but he was so cold that all he could do was nod. Piran leaned against the wall, eyes shut, barely conscious. Verran ran to get blankets, and conversation waited until all of the men moved close to the stove and had blankets to warm themselves.

Verran put a pot on the stove to boil. "Tea" in Velant was just a collection of plant leaves for flavoring, but Blaine could think of nothing he wanted more in the whole world, except perhaps a slug of good brandy.

"It'll take a bit to warm up," Verran said apologetically.

"Dinner was a couple of candlemarks ago. We saved your grog rations for you," he added.

"It's been a bad run," Josten said and began to tell the others what all had happened during the herring expedition, including the last, doomed battle with the sea. Hort jumped in from time to time with more details. Blaine let them do the telling. He was utterly exhausted. But as bad as he felt, Piran seemed worse, and Blaine watched his friend with concern.

"You might want to get some of the grog into Piran," Blaine said finally, when he had warned enough to attempt to talk. "He had the worst of it from the warden-mage."

"Pox take his soul," Verran muttered. "I meant the mage, not Piran," he clarified, as he rose to get the grog. Verran returned with a bucket of watered rum and tin cups. The other men waited until Blaine and the returned fishermen had drunk their rations. Blaine could tell the others were desperate for any news of the colony or life outside the prison walls. He just wished he had better tales to tell.

"So Carson's dead?" Ernest asked. "I can't say I'll miss the blighter."

"There'll be someone to take his place," Shorty, one of the other bunkmates, said. "There always is."

"Unfortunately no one thought to push him overboard before the damage was already done," Piran muttered, and Blaine was certain it was no idle threat. They had already agreed on the raft that they would keep the details of Carson's death—and Teodor's role in it—to themselves.

"And if you had done it earlier, the catastrophe wouldn't have happened, and no one would praise you for it," Dawe said, sipping a cup of tea as he listened. "Warnings are all well and good, but sometimes the damage has to be done before anyone will actually listen."

Blaine knew that Dawe was right, but it still galled him that

Carson's stubbornness had nearly cost them all their lives. "Captain Davis knew better," Blaine said, his voice rough and halting. "Carson wouldn't listen."

"Of course not," Verran said, contempt thick in his tone. "He's an overseer. They know everything, or think they do."

"If the colonists make good on their promise to bring whatever barrels back they can reclaim, Prokief might not have quite a big a fit over it," Shorty commented. "After all, it was his man who got you into the mess."

Dawe slid a sidelong glance at Shorty. "Do you think that will matter?" he asked. "The Commander might be even more upset because it *was* his person who caused the shipwreck. He knows we know it, and that's going to gall him."

"I'm afraid Dawe's probably right," Blaine said. The cold, wet air had made his throat sore, and he could barely speak loudly enough to be heard. His voice sounded like a croak to his own ears, and he hated to think of how it must sound to the others. "Prokief's men shamed him in front of us and the colonists. The boat captains are going to make an issue of it, and regardless, it can't be undone. That's going to rankle with Prokief. He'll get even."

"Get even for being wrong? That's rich," Verran muttered. But they all knew the truth of it. Right or wrong, Commander Prokief was always "right." The overseers who survived Prokief's discipline for disappointing him would be out for revenge as well, since the warden-mage had called them to account in front of an audience.

"Nearly makes me wish I hadn't tried so hard to survive," Hort said. "I suspect there'll be Raka to settle with."

"What did you hear—about home?" Dawe asked. He looked from Blaine to Piran and then to the other men. "You were in the colony for a candlemark. Did they say anything?"

"I heard that the Crooked House's ale is almost as good as the Rooster and Pig's," Hort said.

Verran gave him a skeptical look. "Hard to believe," he said.

"Wouldn't count on it," Blaine croaked. "We were talking with the owner. He still went on about the Pig's bitterbeer."

"The lady who brought me my soup said not to be fooled," Josten said. "Said that the Commander will try to lie to us about our Tickets, but that the king himself demands we be sent to the colony if we survive three years."

"Truly?" Dawe asked, perking up.

"I imagine there are a few exceptions," Hort said. "But that's what the colonists told us. They seemed a bit urgent about it, like they knew we hadn't heard it from Prokief. Apparently, he likes to make out that he has to give permission."

"If so, then I have some hope of getting out of here," Piran rasped. They all chuckled, but Blaine and the others knew it was true. Piran had been enough of a thorn in Prokief's side that the prison's commander was likely to throw up whatever obstacles were available to him to keep Piran from going "free." *And since we've been partners in crime for most of his incidents, that goes for me, too,* Blaine thought.

"Donderath's on the brink of war," Piran spoke up. It hurt to listen to him, his voice was so raw.

The other men looked at him wide-eyed. "What did you hear?"

"Let me tell it," Blaine said, since he had more voice left than Piran. Piran nodded, bowing to the circumstances. He told the anxious listeners what Ifrem had recounted, emphasizing that the news was third-hand at best and likely out of date.

"Still, it's something," Verran said, uncharacteristically serious. "By Torven's horns! We haven't heard anything in almost three years. Wish it could have been better."

"Almost worth nearly drowning to get," Piran said.

Blaine slid a reproving glance toward him. "I don't imagine the drowned men would agree."

Piran grimaced. "No, I suppose not," he replied. "But any fight you walk away from—"

"—is a good fight," Blaine finished.

"What do you make of the news? The fighting?" Dawe asked. He looked right at Piran. "You were a soldier, even if you don't like to talk about it."

"Not much to go on," Piran said quietly, his voice thready. "Who knows what was left out by the time the stories made it all the way up here? Right now, it's still a border conflict. It won't be an easy win if it becomes an all-out war. Meroven trains good soldiers. They'll put up a hard fight."

"You're worried." Garrick met Piran's gaze.

Piran looked away and shrugged, but Blaine sensed his tension. "Maybe," Piran croaked. They're well-provisioned. Their commanders are sharp. They don't accept failure. They're your worst nightmare." He frowned. "This could go badly. We're too well-matched."

"What would happen to us, if we lost?" Dunbar asked. They all turned to look at him. He raised his hands placating, as if they questioned his loyalty. "I hope we don't. I hope it never gets that far. I just mean, what if we did? Would Meroven bother sending ships?"

Dawe leaned back, considering the possibility. "Gods, I hope it doesn't come to that. But you've got a good point. If this becomes a real war and Donderath loses, how long would it be before Meroven even remembered we were up here?"

"The ships wouldn't sail without pay," Ernest pointed out. "If there's a war, no one might care about rubies, but they might still want the herring."

"They can have mine," Blaine muttered. He had disliked the salty fish before he nearly died retrieving it. He doubted he would ever be able to eat herring again without remembering the fishing accident.

"If Meroven won, they'd want to lay claim to all of Donderath's territory," Shorty said. "Including us. Rich men always want rubies. Question is—would we have all starved to death by the time they remembered to send provision ships?"

"And would Meroven still keep Edgeland as a prison colony, or let us finally go home?" Verran wondered.

Dawe gave a snort. "Speak for yourself. There's nothing back in Donderath for me anymore. I'm better off up here."

Several of the men nodded. While Blaine suspected that all of them nursed secret dreams of a homecoming; in reality, most had little or nothing left back in Donderath. *Even if I went back, what then?* Blaine thought. *Carensa is likely wed to someone else. I've been nothing but trouble for Carr, Mari, and Aunt Judith. I doubt any of them would welcome me with open arms, no matter how right they might think I was for what I did.*

It wasn't the first time Blaine had been down this line of thinking. By the introspective looks on the faces of many of the men around him, he suspected that they, too, had come to the same conclusion. "This is home now," Garrick said haltingly. The others looked at him, but he drew himself up.

"If we get out of here, I get coin and land. The colonists sound like a decent sort, from what you said, better than my neighbors back in Donderath, that's for certain. I know enough to build a cabin out of logs, and I can hunt and fish for food, earn some coin. It's a hard life, but a damn sight better than what I'd have if I went home," Garrick said, with a note of defiance as if he challenged the others to gainsay him.

"I don't think anyone would be giving land to the likes of us back in Donderath," Verran said.

"Maybe that's because back home, it's actual dirt and not just ice," Piran managed to reply.

Verran glared at him. "Maybe so. But it's a better deal than what anyone was going to do for us in Donderath," he said, "and we'll all be around to watch each other's backs."

"We'll never really be freemen, not while Prokief's around," Hort pointed out.

Verran gave a snort. "Can't say that I was all that 'free' back home, if 'free' means having choices. That's what got me where I am today. Up here, I might be able to eat without having to thieve for food."

"Play that whistle of yours at the Crooked House, and they'll throw food at you to make you stop," Ernest said with a grin, deliberately provoking him.

Verran rolled his eyes. "I'll have you know, I earned a mostly honest living playing for my dinner in more than one tavern," he said, drawing himself up with a show of righteousness belied by the gleam in his eye. "At least, as far as anyone knew," he added with a broad wink.

I was noble, and hardly "free," Blaine thought. *Carr and Mari and I lived in constant fear of Father's tempers. I didn't feel very free being beaten for the old man's whims or sneaking around in my own house to avoid his rages.*

Curfew fell, and the guards banged on the door, warning the men to go up to their bunkrooms. Blaine helped Piran stand, but Piran waved off further assistance, limping on his own to the ladder and managing to climb unassisted on sheer, cussed will. Blaine was exhausted, and while he had regained feeling in most of his fingers and toes, his skin burned, and his eyes still stung. Every muscle protested, and he was wretchedly tired. He had no idea what duties Prokief would invent for them come morning, and for once, he was too exhausted to worry about it before he fell asleep.

3

THE HUNT

"I can't believe he's sending us out on the hunt." Blaine flexed his left hand, still trying to regain all of the sensation in his fingers after nearly freezing aboard the herring boat. "Ifrem was right—Prokief is going to make it as hard as possible for us to earn our Tickets of Leave."

"I can't believe that still surprises you." Piran's tone made no secret of his loathing for the commander. "He's a sadistic son of a bitch."

It was the second day after their disastrous run on the herring boats, and well into their second day of confinement. A day's confinement was normal when prisoner work crews changed assignments, moving from the mines to the herring fleet, or from the farm fields to lumbering. Two days was unusual, and it made Blaine wonder if Prokief might still be sorting out the debacle with the fishing boats.

"What Mick means is, he can't believe Prokief would want to be stuck with the two of you any longer than he has to be," Garrick said, and the others laughed.

"Prokief doesn't lose well," Dunbar added. "Letting prisoners leave Velant alive might seem like losing to him. But he can't kill all of us. King Merrill wouldn't get his herring or his rubies. He might notice." He shrugged. "Prokief's a madman. Who knows why he does what he does?"

"I didn't survive all this time just to get killed on a hunt a few months before I earn my Ticket," Blaine muttered.

"Then get revenge. Don't die," Garrick replied.

Blaine hoped it would be a simple as it sounded. Wolf hunts were a necessity when Edgeland's wolves grew bold and ventured close to the prison stockade and into the farmyards of the colonists. During the White Nights, when prisoners worked in Velant's fields and headed to the forest for lumber, teams of wolf hunters made regular forays to cull the packs and weed out the most aggressive hunters. During the Long Dark, the prisoners had fewer reasons to venture outside the stockade, but it still benefitted both the prison and the colony for the wolf packs to be held at bay.

Stuck in their barracks, there was little to do except sleep, wager, or talk. After almost three years together, none of the men, not even the thieves, would play Piran at cards. Some of the men huddled in small groups betting on dice. Verran leaned against the wall playing tunes on his pennywhistle. Of late, Blaine noticed Verran's songs tended to be tavern ditties popular before they were exiled, and he wondered if it was Verran's way of readying himself to earn extra coin playing at the Crooked House once they were released.

Verran paused his playing and looked up. "Prokief must be pretty desperate to let the two of you have weapons," he said. "Even with precautions."

"I suspect that's why he's made it very clear the rest of you are a surety," Piran grumbled. Blaine, Piran, Carl, and Bickle had been assigned to the wolf hunt which would leave in two days. Many of them neared the end of their sentence at Velant, as did a few of their bunkmates. When Prokief announced the roster of hunters, he made it extremely clear that any attacks on the soldiers who accompanied the hunting parties or attempts to flee once outside the stockade would bring harsh reprisals against the prisoners left behind, and earn a noose for the miscreants when caught.

"I can't tell you how uncomfortable I am being the guarantee of your good behavior," Dawe replied with a sidelong glance at Piran.

"Don't worry," Blaine said. "We both want out of here badly enough to toe the line. It's only a few more weeks for Piran." In reality, the colony was still under Prokief's control since the commander was also the governor, but increased distance gave an illusion of freedom, and Blaine was wholeheartedly ready for the change.

I'm surprised Prokief is sending Adkin and Twain," Dawe said. "It's likely that he hates them even more than he has it in for you and Piran."

"I thought of that, too." Piran looked up from what he was doing. "I think Prokief's up to something."

"How can anyone have possibly been more irritating than Piran?" Blaine asked, and Piran glared at him.

"It's different with them than it is with the two of you, I think," Dawe said, hesitating as he figured out how to put his thoughts into words. "You and Piran challenge Prokief's authority. You defy him just by refusing to break. And he knows others look up to you, which grates on him all the more." He paused.

"With Adkin and Twain, they're the kind that attract bullies," Dawe said finally. "They're easy marks. And for a sadistic son of a bitch like Prokief and his guards, that's like honey to flies."

"I've heard the wolves are worse than usual this season," Ernest put in. He leaned against the wall, watching a group of men bet at dice. "Some of the soldiers were talking. The colonists are angry about the wolf attacks, and so the problem with the herring fleet just made things worse. They're supposed to receive protection from Velant's guards, and gods know, they get enough grief from the guards and the warden-mages—they deserve what they've been promised."

"All of which is going to put Prokief in an even worse mood than usual," Piran replied. "Lovely."

They were downstairs in the common area, permitted longer in the large, open room due to the lockdown. Though it was the middle of the afternoon, the Long Dark meant the sun was barely visible, and the room was dimly lit even with the help of the lanterns. The men talked in hushed voices, always mindful that guards and their spies were nearby.

Blaine was edgy. After his near brush with death aboard the herring boats, he thought he might want to sleep for days. He had availed himself of the opportunity to sleep and heal but found that two days was a long time to try to sleep even after all they had endured. His dreams had been dark, full of portents and warnings, none of which he could clearly make out. *A veiled warning is as useless as no warning at all*, he thought. Blaine was sure he would not rest easy until he had his Ticket of Leave safely in hand. The hunt worried him. Too many things could go wrong. *I'm sure that's what Prokief is counting on*, Blaine thought.

The barracks door slammed open in the wind, and three guards stepped inside. "Rowse! McFadden! And the rest of the wolf hunters. Come with me."

Blaine and the others rose to their feet, exchanging questioning glances with each other. "What's going on?" Piran challenged, never one to leave well-enough alone.

"You're to get your provisions, so you're ready to leave first thing in the morning," the lead guard replied. "Everything but your weapons—you'll receive those after you're outside the prison gates."

Blaine followed Piran and the others out of the barracks, hoping that provisions included warmer clothing than the standard issue for those who worked the mine or the farm. Blaine doubted his heavy wool cloak would be enough out on the windswept open land. *Unless the wolf hunt is just a pretense, and Prokief means for us to die of exposure in the forest. Finishing off what he started on those damned herring boats.*

The guard led them toward the laundry building, usually off-limits to male prisoners because it was one of the areas reserved for female convicts. The women made all of the prison-issued clothing for the convicts while tailors made the uniforms for Prokief and his guards. Blaine hoped this meant they were going to get the heavy outerwear they needed to survive.

The guards led them into a large room lined with tables. "Start on your left, move to your right," the lead guard ordered. "Find a coat that fits you on the first table. Woolen shirts and heavy pants are on the second. Third table is socks, hats, gloves, scarves—you'll need them where you're going. Take care of what you get—they'll be your colonist clothing if you come back from the hunt."

In two and a half years of hard labor, Blaine had received new clothing only twice. What he was currently wearing was ripped and threadbare, little protection against the bitter climate. The canvas overcoats and water gear they had worn aboard the herring boats had been borrowed. "Maybe Prokief means for us to survive, after all," Carl murmured.

"Or he wants to make sure it looks good if the king ever questions why so many of the convicts die before they leave," Piran replied under his breath.

"Quiet down!" the guard yelled. He gestured for Blaine and the others to begin to file along the tables. On each table, piles of clothing lay separated into rough sizes—large, medium, and small—and one or two guards stood watch to assure that no one took more than his share. The coats were tanned hide with the fur turned inward. Blaine was pleased to find a coat that fit his tall frame reasonably well. They moved to the next table, where they found homespun woolen shirts and pants, much warmer than his current clothing. The final table held hats and gloves pieced from the bits of hide and fur along with woolen scarves. Blaine searched among the gloves for a pair long enough to fit his hands and retrieved a pair from the pile.

"I think you'll find these will be a better fit," the guard said, making eye contact with Blaine. That alone was curious, as was the guard's intervention. *Kestel's got to have had something to do with this. I wonder what she's up to?*

Blaine took the pair of gloves from the guard and put his hand in, finding a small bit of parchment in one of the finger sections. He gave no indication that anything was unusual and nodded to the guard. "These will do fine," he said, still wondering how Kestel had managed to get the guard to do her bidding.

She was a spy and an assassin—and a courtesan, he thought. *I suspect she has her ways.*

Piran gave him a questioning glance as they headed back to the barracks with their provisions. Blaine gave a nod, confirming that Kestel had made contact. He waited until they were back in the barracks and the guards had locked them in before he pushed his hand back into the glove and withdrew the small rolled piece of paper.

"1 bell" the paper read. "That's it?" Piran asked, looking over his shoulder. "What does that mean?"

"I suspect it means she's going to get us a full message at

first bells," Blaine said quietly, rolling up the paper and slipping it back into the glove. "And I guess she means to find me."

Piran raised an eyebrow. "In a locked-down barracks? What is she, a blinkin' ghost?"

Blaine shrugged. "If the rumors are true, she was the best at what she did."

"Until she got caught," Piran said. "Or she wouldn't be here."

"Everyone makes mistakes," Blaine replied. "Let's see what she thinks is important enough to be worth the risk."

Although Blaine knew he would need his energy for the first day of the hunt, sleep did not come easily. He heard the camp bells toll midnight and lay awake for a candlemark until he heard first bell. The barracks was quiet except for the snores and muttering of his barracks mates. Wind made the roof creak. He thought he heard a noise near the door, but just as he was about to move, a hand covered his mouth, and strong arms shoved him back into place.

"Don't move. Just listen." Kestel's voice was barely audible, her lips next to his ear. Blaine could hardly make out her form in the near-darkness and figured she had donned head-to-toe black for the occasion.

"Prokief plays dirty. He really doesn't want to let you and Piran go. He's going to try to frame you on this hunt to have an excuse to keep you in Velant."

"Why not just kill us, if he hates us so badly?" Blaine murmured.

"I don't know," Kestel replied. "It's odd. Maybe it's something to do with Piran being a war hero before he was exiled. You've got to keep Piran in line on the hunt. If you don't do something stupid out there, I've got a plan to make sure you get your Tickets. I'm making arrangements to trump Prokief's hand. Trust me."

Blaine raised an eyebrow at that, but Kestel shook her head. "Not now. I'll tell you later. Just don't give Prokief anything to use against you."

"Anything else?" Blaine's chances to connect with Kestel were extremely limited due to the prison's strict separation of male and female convicts. It had taken all of their ingenuity over the last two years to make plans for after their release, stitched together from snippets of conversation and cryptic notes.

"Keep your head down, keep Piran's mouth shut, and we may all get out of here," Kestel said. She heard a noise and glanced sharply over her shoulder. "Got to go."

Blaine looked in the direction of the sound, and when he turned back, Kestel was gone without a trace.

————

Soldiers came to collect Blaine, Piran, and the other hunters at sixth bells. The Long Dark made morning and evening nearly indistinguishable, but rising in darkness never put Blaine in a good mood. They received their meager breakfast rations along with their packs for the journey, filled with enough provisions to tide them over until they could trap their own food on the trail. Blaine and the others marched out of the camp behind the soldiers, taking turns in teams of two pulling a sledge with their provisions and weapons.

"Tell me again why we couldn't have horses for this?" Piran growled, shouldering into the rope harness.

"I guess they figure the wolves will smell the horses," Blaine replied, taking his place next to Piran.

"And you think they won't smell us?" Piran asked, incredulous. "Mate, even after the dunking we got in the harbor, we're all rank as day-old fish. The question isn't 'will the wolves smell us?' The real question is whether they think we're carrion."

They trudged forward, changing places with Carl after a candlemark, and then Blaine and Bickle took a turn, then Aiken and Twain. The forest was farther than it appeared, and a crust of icy snow covered the open stretch of land between the prison and the tree line.

"I'd kill for a cup of *fet* right now," Piran muttered. The black, bitter drink was in short supply for prisoners, though the guards seemed to have plenty to keep themselves alert, and enough ale or grog to relax after their duties.

"I've heard the colonists get *fet* with the shipments from home," Blaine replied as they trudged behind the wagon, out toward the forest at the edge of the darkened fields.

"Here's hoping they have some whiskey worth drinking, too," Piran said wistfully. "I'm a tad dry after all this time."

Blaine suspected that Ifrem's Crooked House was more likely to brew its own ale and distill its own spirits than have the bulky items shipped from Donderath, but after three years in Velant, Blaine doubted he would be particular.

"I want proper sausages," Carl said with a sigh. He had been a butcher before he was caught stealing and sent to Velant. "Once we're out of here, I'm are going to go work for the butcher in Bay-town, or start my own."

"There's always work for carpenters," Bickle said, referencing his former trade. "Houses to be built, barns to be raised—coffins to be assembled."

"Aren't you cheery," Piran grumbled.

Bickle shrugged. "It's true. The only man guaranteed steady work is the gravedigger."

"I plan to see if the cooper needs extra hands," Twain said. "All those barrels going out with the herring fleet and back on the ships—someone's got to build them. Might as well be me." Twain was Piran's height but not as muscular, with shaggy, light brown hair.

"I was a cobbler," Aiken said. "And the first thing I intend to do when I get out is make myself a decent pair of boots." Aiken was stout and stocky, with a reddish beard and thinning, curly hair. Blaine remembered what Dawe had said, guessing about the reason for Prokief's dislike of the two men. He could see what Dawe was talking about. Twain was soft-spoken, reluctant to make eye contact, and hung back from the others. Aiken was awkward, trying to joke with the others and not quite succeeding. *Show weakness around Prokief and you're fair game.*

"What about you, Piran?" Carl asked. "What are you planning to do once you're out? There's no soldiering to be done that the guards aren't doing, and much as you're suited to it, I can't figure you can make enough from boxing to survive, even if you could find anyone dumb enough to fight you."

"I probably could," Piran replied, refusing to take offense at his friend's jibe. "But my nose has been rearranged enough, thank you. I figure there's always work for something with a strong back."

"And a thick head," Bickle joked. They chuckled despite the cold and dark. Bickle looked to Blaine. "How about you, Mick?"

Blaine had asked himself that question ever since he got off the convict ship. As the son of a lesser noble, he'd had some experience working with horses and helping the workers bring crops in from the field. But where Dawe could do smithy work, and Verran could play his music to earn coin, Blaine had no skills other than what he had picked up from the mine, farm and herring fleet as a prisoner.

"I imagine I'll figure something out," Blaine replied. "Probably out doing whatever jobs need to be done, along with Piran."

They fell silent. The light from the torches on Velant's walls was far behind them, and the dim moonlight revealed little of their path. The forest loomed in front of them, dark and impenetrable.

"When are they going to give us our bleedin' weapons?" Piran muttered. Blaine had shared the essence of Kestel's message with his friend before the guards came, so Piran was on what for him counted as good behavior. Blaine understood his impatience to have a weapon in hand.

"You don't think it was all just a set-up, do you?" Carl said nervously. "Get us out here where no one can see, and kill us all?"

Blaine dared not let them in on Kestel's warning. Instead, he shrugged. "Maybe. But it seems like a lot of work for something Prokief could have done just as easily back at the prison."

Kestel had been certain Prokief was indeed laying a trap, and equally certain that Blaine and Piran were the intended victims. *He's had three years to kill Piran and nearly as long to do me in. If he hates us so much, why are we still alive?* Kestel's theory that Piran's war record conveyed some immunity intrigued him, but every attempt to find out more about Piran's time as a soldier was aptly deflected. Prokief was a law unto himself in Edgeland, and Blaine could think of no other reason he would stay his hand. *Perhaps a benefactor, high up in the military, with enough clout to make Prokief restrain himself?* Blaine wondered. He would likely never know, unless Kestel wormed the secret out of Piran.

"We'll camp here." One of the guards, a thin man with a hawk-like nose, gestured for them to stop. The prisoners had dubbed him "Beak." A second guard had the long face of a hunting dog, and was nicknamed "Hound." "Flat-nose" looked as if he had gone a few rounds too long in a boxing match. "Knacker" was perpetually glum and quiet. Six prisoners and four guards made up the wolf team to which Blaine and the others were assigned. Two other teams of equal size had veered off a while back, aiming for other wolves' territories. *Either there's a big problem with wolves, or Prokief has a long list of people he wants rid of,* Blaine thought.

"You said you'd give us weapons once we got out of camp," Piran spoke up. "Well—we're out. And before we camp on the edge of a forest in wolf territory, we need our weapons." The others moved to stand behind Piran.

"There won't be time to hand out weapons if the wolves attack in the middle of the night," Blaine said. "You're as likely to die as we are if that happens. We want out of here. No one's going to do anything stupid." He very carefully did not look at Piran.

Beak was the lead guard. Hound and Knacker moved over to speak with him, casting glances now and again toward the prisoners. After a moment, Beak moved forward. "Line up, single file," he ordered. "You get a blade and a crossbow with twenty quarrels. If you shoot an arrow, retrieve it. Misuse your weapons against us or your fellow prisoners, and you'll go back to Velant in chains. Understood?"

Blaine and the others grunted assent. They queued up, and the guards reluctantly passed out the weapons. The swords were likely discards from what the soldiers used to train. They did not look like they had been battle-ready in a long time, and while they had an edge and a point to them, Blaine would have given a lot for a whetstone to hone them if he was expected to carry one of the weapons into a fight for his life.

The crossbows were equally hard-used. Piran had the most experience with such things, and he examined his bow and quarrels once they had returned to the fire. "What a bunch of trash!" Piran muttered, eyeing the swords with contempt.

"I notice the blades and bows the soldiers have look newer and in better shape," Carl said, with a nod in the directions of the guards' fire.

"The sight on the crossbow is crooked, the tension seems off, and the arrows are badly made," Piran grumbled, not keen to be talked out of his annoyance so easily. "As for the swords—if you can call them that—the balance is off and we'll beat the wolves to death with them before we slash anything with those dull things."

"Would you rather have sticks and rocks?" Blaine asked, giving Piran a glare to remind him of his promise to not cause problems.

"Maybe," Piran huffed. "They probably wouldn't be worse."

Blaine was as disappointed as the others in the conditions of their weapons, but he was not going to add fuel to Piran's rant by saying so. *It keeps making me wonder—is this all an elaborate ruse on Prokief's part? Or just stupidity?*

"They're not going to expect us to go wandering around the forest, looking for wolves, are they?" Bickle asked with a nervous look toward the lightless tree line.

"If they're smart, they'll try to lure the wolves close to the edge of the trees," Carl replied. "I've been on a couple of wolf hunts, back in my village. Once we go into the forest, the advantages all belong to the wolves. I don't care how good your equipment is. That's true even when you're familiar with the forest, and we aren't."

"The guards have been on wolf hunts before," Blaine reminded them.

"*Some* guards have been," Carl replied. "We don't know how much experience *these* guards have."

They set up their camp quickly, building lean-tos from saplings near the forest's edge and covering them with army canvas tarpaulins. Once they got close to the tree line, Blaine could make out the rough roads that led into the forest, likely from the logging teams who kept Velant and Edgeland provisioned with lumber.

"How about some lanterns?" Piran challenged.

Beak glared at him. "I've got a few in my pack," he said, jerking his head toward the rucksack he carried over one shoulder. "Don't want to use them if we can help it."

Blaine had learned quickly that the "Long Dark" as they called the six month period of polar night, was not pitch dark. Tonight, a luminous deep blue settled over everything. The snow-covered ground reflected some of the light, which along with the moonlight made it possible for them to see their way. Overhead, faint ribbons crossed the sky, "Spirit Lights" the guards called the phenomena. The odd blue glow and the strange overhead lights gave the empty, cold land an eerie feel. Out here, the twilight was enough to see relatively well once their eyes adjusted. Inside the tree line, it would be darker. Blaine eyed the forest warily. It was not much of a stretch of the imagination to believe they were being watched.

Beak grabbed a canvas pack from the sledge. "Rowse, McFadden, Aiken, Twain. Grab your weapons and come with us," he ordered as Knacker came to join him. "The rest of you are on the other team."

The prisoners traded wary glances. It was clear to Blaine that they did not want to split up. On the other hand, ten people were unlikely to sneak up on a pack of wolves. Small groups had the best chance of success. *Let's just hope we all come back out of the woods—with or without a wolf or two to show for it.*

"What's in the bag?" Piran asked quietly as they followed Beak down the rugged logging trail. Knacker brought up the rear, sword in hand. It was a reminder, as if they needed any, not to get out of hand.

"Bait," Beak replied. "Half a fresh-killed deer. There's a clearing not too far in. We'll set up two blinds, and wait for the wolves."

"We could wait a long time," Blaine observed.

Beak shrugged. "Our men have hunted this section of forest

pretty hard. Most of the deer are gone. If the wolves are still around, they aren't finding easy pickings. They might be hungry enough to take a chance."

"It's not as dark as I thought it would be back here," Blaine murmured. The trees were tall enough that there was little undergrowth, and enough of the large trees had been removed to thin the canopy, allowing the moonlight and blue twilight to permeate even here.

"We're still close to the forest's edge," Piran murmured. "Deeper in, it'll be a different story. We'll need lanterns."

"And we have them, if we need them," Knacker replied. "Now shut up. Wolves have ears, you know."

Beak led them to a clearing that had been logged clean. From the trees remaining, Blaine guessed it had been a stand of large, old growth. The light was better in the clearing, and now that their eyes were adjusted, Blaine could see reasonably well across the whole area. "Up here," Beak indicated, keeping his voice just above a whisper. "We'll have one blind here, and one over there," he said, indicating a spot on the other side of the clearing. Both were on high ground with a good view of the area. Skeptical as Blaine was about the guards' intentions, it appeared that Beak had scouted the area, and knew something about wolf hunting. "McFadden and Aiken stay here with me," he said. "Rowse and Twain go to the other side."

Piran's expression made it clear that he disliked the order, but in a remarkable show of restraint, he managed not to snap out a response. Blaine had already prepared himself for the possibility that the guards might not want the two of them together, especially not two prisoners with the reputation for trouble he and Piran had acquired.

Blaine tried to remember what the hired men on his father's lands said about going after the wolves that occasionally harried the livestock. He knew that wolves were smart, wily opponents, with smell and hearing at least equal to any dog. That meant the hunter had to be stealthier and more cunning than his prey, something easier said than done.

"Sit here," Beak ordered, pointing to one side of a tree on a slight rise near the road. It was a scrubby tree, not worth logging, something to lean on while they waited. "Have your bows ready and your swords at hand," he whispered. "Don't move. Hope you two took a piss before we left camp; we might be here for a while," he added with a malicious smile.

On the far side of the clearing, Blaine could make out Piran, Twain, and Knacker settling into a similar blind. There was little to camouflage either position save some tall, dry grass, but that meant few obstacles to a clean shot. Beak walked into the middle of the clearing and emptied the partial deer carcass from his bag, then buried the bloody canvas beneath the snow some distance away. He cleaned his hands on the ice and returned to where Blaine and Aiken waited.

"So we just wait here for a hungry wolf?" Blaine murmured.

"We'll give it a little time for our smell to fade," Beak said, a note of pride in his hunting knowledge coloring his tone. "Then we'll start. Aiken—you watch the bait. McFadden, keep watch in the opposite directions. I don't want anything sneaking up on us from behind."

They sat in silence for what seemed like forever. Blaine's senses were on high alert, more attuned to the threat from the man seated near him than the fear of being mauled by a wild animal. He struggled not to fidget, but he was wary and restless. Staying still took all of his willpower. The forest, which had grown quiet during their entrance to the glade, began to rustle with the sounds of life.

Overhead, Blaine heard the scrabble of squirrels in the tree branches, and the beat of wings as an owl flew into the gloaming. Not too far away, a twig snapped. Leaves rustled. The forest was waking up, after its thrall at their arrival. And as cold and restless as Blaine felt, curiosity tugged at him to see what the forest held.

"Here we go," Beak replied just above a whisper. He raised his right hand to his mouth and pulled in his breath against the skin on the back. It made an awful squeal, like a dying rabbit. Which was exactly what it was supposed to sound like, Blaine imagined. Beak repeated the sound once, then stopped, and signaled for Blaine to stay still and quiet.

A few moments of silence passed. Then a howl rose on the cold night air. It sounded close, and despite himself, Blaine felt the hackles rise on the back of his neck. Something deep inside him feared the dark forest and the wolves, caring nothing for the sword or the crossbow in his hands. The fear was old as time, older than reason. Primal. Out here, in a fair fight, the wolf won.

"A call," Beak whispered, with a nod toward the blind where Piran and the other guards concealed themselves. Blaine nodded that he understood. The guards were luring the wolves with the simulated cries of their prey and competitors. The howl rose again, and once more, Blaine felt ice slither down his spine.

Beak gave a curt nod. *Now, we wait,* Blaine interpreted.

Out here, they were far from the bells of Skalgerston Bay and the prison watchtower. Without the movement of the sun, there was only the course of the moon for Blaine to gauge time. Movement caught Blaine's eye and he tensed. He had positioned his bow across his knee so that if a wolf appeared, he would need very little movement to strike, providing less opportunity to make a noise that might scare off their quarry. His finger was ready on the crossbow's trigger when a fox loped into the clearing.

The fox stopped and sniffed the air, looking all around. Blaine and the others remained still as statues, not daring to breathe. The fox trotted up to the dead deer and began to feed.

Blaine grimaced, impatient. Beak placed a hand on his arm and gave a warning shake of his head. Blaine let out a quiet breath and forced himself to relax.

After the fox had nearly sated himself on the kill, the animal raised his head warily, sniffed the air, then turned and ran off a different way. Blaine's senses sharpened, and he scanned the clearing.

At first, he saw nothing but shadows. Then, one of the shadows eased forward. Fluid and beautiful, a large male wolf emerged, stepping warily into the clearing. Proud and powerfully built, the wolf was silver gray with darker markings. From its caution, Blaine guessed it had survived more than one season, meaning it was wary and clever.

The wolf advanced slowly on the bait, stopping every few feet to scent the air. Their blinds had been selected to be down-wind as well as for visibility, and the wolf did not seem to find anything amiss. He raised his head and let out a blood-curdling howl to call the rest of his pack.

Zing. A crossbow bolt flew from beside him. Beak's followed an instant later, and Blaine's just after that. The first quarrel took the wolf through the front shoulder. The second missed, and Blaine's shot caught the wolf in the hindquarters.

The dying wolf managed one strained cry before he toppled over. All around them, the pack fled.

Beak turned to Aiken with a murderous look on his face. "Aiken! You palsied goat! You worthless piece of shit! You shot too quickly and lost us the rest of the pack."

Before Blaine could intervene, Beak swung a fist at Aiken, smashing the man's nose and knocking Aiken to the ground. Beak's fists flew, pounding Aiken, who tried and failed to block the blows.

"You're going to kill him!" Blaine said, trying to grab Beak from behind and restrain him before the damage was done.

Beak threw him off. "Mind your own business, McFadden."

Across the clearing, from the sound of it, Knacker was laying into Twain. Piran was having as little luck as Blaine deflecting the guard's murderous temper.

Blaine tried to get between Beak and Aiken, taking the worst of the blows on his shoulders and back as he had done years ago to protect his younger brother and sister from their father. *The trap,* Blaine thought, remembering Kestel's warning. *Prokief knows what got me sent here. He probably knew of my father, heard about his rages. And he certainly knows that Piran and I don't take well to the guards knocking heads together. We're being set up—Aiken and Twain are the pawns in Prokief's game.*

"Get out of my way!" Beak roared, giving Blaine a shove that sent him reeling. Blaine's temper frayed, but he managed to remain in control, knowing that actually fighting the guard would land him in the Holes, or lose him his Ticket of Leave.

Blaine came up with an armful of loose snow and flung it in Beak's face, distracting the guard. Aiken was bleeding from his nose and ears. His breath came in painful wheezes, and Blaine bet Beak had broken the man's ribs.

"I'm going to rip you apart, McFadden!" Beak yelled.

Blaine backed out of his way. "Prokief's not going to be pleased if you've got no wolves and dead prisoners. You'll be the one in the Hole." He stayed out of Beak's range. Dodging a madman's fists was an old game Blaine had mastered long ago. "You can't fight the wolves yourself. They'll be back. You really want to carry Aiken out along with the wolves we shoot?"

Beak glared at Blaine but did not lunge forward to attack. Piran and Knacker were shouting at each other, but they had not come to blows. Knacker reached down and grabbed Twain by the collar, pulling his limp, bloody form behind him like dead weight as they rejoined Blaine and Beak. From the glint in Piran's eyes and the set of his jaw, Blaine knew his friend was only barely restraining his temper.

Knacker kicked at the savaged deer carcass. "Not much left. Won't be much use to draw move wolves—assuming they'll come after all this ruckus."

"We're not leaving without the wolves," Beak replied.

"They won't come back here," Piran argued, his voice dangerously cold.

"Then we'll go to them," Knacker responded. "It's a big forest. And they'll be hungry smelling all this nice, fresh blood."

"Maybe these two can still be useful," Beak said, a cold smile touching the corner of his thin lips as he toed Aiken's unconscious form. He looked to Blaine and Piran. "You want to keep them alive? You carry them. We're going deeper into the forest to get those damn wolves."

Blaine hefted Aiken into his arms. The battered prisoner groaned in pain at being moved but did not regain consciousness. His face was badly swollen, and his lips were cut, dripping blood. *For all I know, the damage is already done*, Blaine thought. *Twain doesn't look in any better shape.* The prisoner Piran carried was also unconscious, dead weight in his arms. A blood trail marked the snow, sure to attract predators of all kinds.

"Here," Beak said, thrusting a dented lantern into Blaine's hands. He lit it with a bit of steel and flint to make a spark and used a piece of straw from his pocket to light the other two lamps he produced from his pack. "Mind you keep the shutters nearly closed," he ordered. "Don't want the wolves to spot the light." Blaine noted that the lantern's glass sides had been tinted with blue dye to dim the light. Even with the faint glow, Blaine stumbled often over roots hidden beneath the snow.

This section of the forest was old and mostly untouched. They had moved a distance from the forest's edge, and here, the huge evergreens' massive canopy would have made it dark beneath it even on a bright day. Thanks to the Long Dark, it was now almost as pitch black deep in the forest as it was inside the mines. Going farther under the circumstances was suicidal. *The guards fear Prokief as much as the prisoners do,* Blaine thought. *Maybe even more than they fear the wolves.*

"We're going too far from the road," Piran protested after they had walked another half a candlemark. "We can't see this far in, like we could nearer the forest's edge."

"Shut up and walk," Knacker snapped.

The forest had grown too quiet. Blaine was certain they were being watched. He wondered whether Beak and Knacker knew where they were going, or whether the guards were just so obsessed with the hunt that they had abandoned all caution.

"Stop here," Knacker ordered after they had walked another half a candlemark. Their lanterns barely made out the clearing, a broader space among the trees.

"Put Aiken and Twain in the center," Beak ordered. "They're bloody enough, the wolves won't have any trouble finding them."

Piran rounded on Beak. "Are you serious? You mean to use them as bait?"

The guard's grin was malicious. "Are you volunteering to take their place? Because frankly, I'd rather see you and McFadden out there."

Blaine caught Piran's eye and mouthed "trap." Piran clamped his mouth shut, though his expression was easy to read. He walked beside Blaine toward the center of the clearing, carrying their two unconscious companions.

"You're actually going to let them do it?" Piran growled.

"Until the wolves come," Blaine replied. "Then we protect Aiken and Twain the best we can, and hope we shoot some of the wolves while we're at it."

"I'd rather shoot Beak," Piran muttered.

"The feeling's mutual. Remember—we've been set up. Prokief isn't really after these two. It's us he wants," Blaine said under his breath as he laid Aiken down on the snow beside Twain.

Neither of the battered men stirred. *Probably for the best,* Blaine thought. As vicious as the beating they took had been, Aiken and Twain might not recover, even if Blaine and Piran managed to save them from the wolves.

If we knew they were beyond hope, we could slit their throats and end their misery. He had seen such things done in his time at Velant. When the guards took matters too far and recovery was impossible, it was the last kindness a prisoner's friends could offer. Blaine considered the option and discarded it. *We might be wrong. They might not be as bad as they look. I have enough blood on my hands without adding more.*

"Hurry it up," Knacker hissed. "Unless you want to be the bait yourselves."

Blaine and Piran went back to the two blinds Knacker and Beak had set up, one on each side of the clearing. Blaine mentally calculated the distance between their hiding place and the injured men, figuring out how long it would take for him to cross the gap.

Better yet, we shoot the wolves before they get to the bait, Blaine thought. *To Raka with what Beak and Knacker want. That gives us dead wolves and live prisoners—maybe.*

They waited. Blaine wondered how they were expected to shoot wolves when they could barely see, since Beak had insisted they extinguish their lanterns except for one which he hid in a crevice in the rocks, with its shutters tightly closed. After several minutes, Blaine could make out shadows in the gloom, darker and lighter shades of gray. The temperature was dropping, and Blaine wondered whether Aiken and Twain might succumb to the cold before they bled to death. From what he could make out, neither man was moving.

Did it ever occur to Beak and Knacker—or to Prokief, since he's the one who set up the trap—that all that blood makes bait out of all of us? Then again, maybe Prokief wanted rid of Beak and Knacker too, and they're too dim to realize we've all been played for fools.

The forest rustled with activity. Sound carried farther in the winter, making it difficult to tell how close the animals were. Blaine heard the *skritch* of claws against ice as small creatures hurried across the frozen snow and the hoot of distant owls. Something rustled in the tree behind him, but when he looked up he saw nothing but shadows. The wind made the bare branches click like bones.

Snow had a smell. Blaine would never have believed that, back in Donderath. Now, after two and a half years in the arctic, he could describe more textures of snow and types of snow-storms than he would have ever thought possible. A light dusting of flakes fell through the air, covering the thin crust of ice that had formed over older accumulation.

We're rank enough, the wolves probably smelled us when we set out from Velant.

Blaine had his crossbow ready. He stretched cautiously, trying to remain limber in the cold. His fingers were growing numb, and he was getting chilled from inactivity. *Sitting around in these temperatures is asking for ice sickness. We'd warm up if we could move around.*

From the movement of the moon, Blaine guessed they had waited for over a candlemark before he heard noises close behind them in the forest. He froze, then reached slowly for his weapon. Beak had heard the sounds too and looked around with wariness verging on panic.

Blaine heard the *swish* of something large padding across the icy snow, a sound almost lost in the wind. *I'm imagining it,* he told himself. He caught a glimpse of yellow eyes, then heard a howl that was answered by another and then another, pack members calling to each other, surrounding them.

Blaine felt a chill that had nothing to do with the temperature, he realized that they had made an important miscalculation.

The pack sounded a lot bigger and a lot closer than Beak and Knacker had reckoned.

The wolves were wary, staying hidden among the trees just out of range. Blaine could not see exactly how many wolves there were, but he was fairly certain the wolves blocked the road, their best way back to safety. These were huge, mature wolves, thickly muscled with heavy, silver coats. Each wolf was at least as long as a tall man, and Blaine guessed that the wolves weighed as much as men, too. That made them exceptionally dangerous opponents—man-sized predators with razor-sharp teeth and claws, and a finely-honed hunter's instinct.

Knacker rose from his blind to take aim on one of the wolves. He had barely reached his feet when a large gray wolf sprang from behind him, taking Knacker to the ground beneath the wolf's solid body. Knacker's crossbow went flying, and he tried to reach his sword.

Piran had his cross-bow ready, but as Knacker fought the wolf, there was no way to take a shot without endangering the guard.

"Help me! Do something!" Knacker shrieked. He twisted away from the wolf and made it to his feet, heading for the trail at a run. He had not gone five strides before a gray-black wolf and its light gray mate closed on the guard, cutting him off from the path. The wolves herded him, nudging him one way and then the next, giving him room in one direction only to encroach from the other side. It appeared as if the wolves were toying with him.

"Get away from me!" he shouted, frightened. He brandished

his sword, swinging it this way and that, too panicked to try to load his crossbow. The wolves growled a low, throaty warning that made the hackles rise on the back of Blaine's neck.

Piran squeezed off a shot at the wolf that stalked Knacker, taking the wolf in its side. The animal howled in rage and pain. Two new wolves broke from cover. One of them attacked the injured wolf while the other snapped at Knacker, sinking its teeth deep into the guard's shoulder. Knacker was bleeding heavily, and his terrified screams seemed to draw the wolves, like the cry of injured prey.

Another wolf was slinking toward Aiken and Twain in the center of the clearing. Blaine shot with his crossbow, and the wolf fell, writhing. Blaine vaulted over the fallen tree that was his blind and ran to cover the two prisoners as half a dozen wolves advanced from the tree line.

A growl warned Piran that he had troubles of his own. Piran was fast on his feet, the legacy of too many brawls. He got in a shot with his crossbow, then dropped it to draw his sword. The wolf lunged at him, and slammed him down on the ground, even as Piran's blade plunged into the wolf's belly and out his back. Pain and anger drove the wolf into a frenzy, and sharp teeth barely missed Piran's throat while claws raked his left arm. Piran and the wolf rolled, and Piran jerked his sword free, trying to stay clear of teeth and claws to get in a deathblow. The wolf's teeth *snicked* just behind Piran's leg. Piran brought his sword down again, and the dull blade got halfway through the wolf's neck and stuck.

"Son of a bitch!" Piran muttered, bringing his boot down hard to stomp the wolf's face to the ground so he could free his sword and swing once more. This time, the blow severed the wolf's head. Piran leaned back, breathing hard, covered in blood. He looked past Blaine and tensed.

"Mick! Behind you!"

Blaine wheeled as a big, dark-furred wolf leaped at him, claws out and teeth bared. Blaine pulled the trigger on his crossbow, but the shot went wide as he dodged aside. The wolf landed and pivoted in the same movement keeping Blaine in his sights, just as a third wolf sprang at Beak.

Beak got off a shot before the wolf tackled him, but the quarrel grazed the animal's shoulder, doing minimal damage. Beak and the wolf fell to the ground, and Beak kept rolling, trying to dislodge his attacker. He had managed to draw a knife, and he sank it between the wolf's ribs, arching back out of range as the wolf snapped at him.

Blaine took a step back and reloaded, never taking his eyes off the wolf facing him. "Let's try that again," Blaine murmured. He squeezed off a shot, and the quarrel *zinged* through the air, catching the wolf in the chest as it started toward him. It dropped in its tracks, but another wolf was already bounding from the tree line to take its place.

Across the clearing, more wolves had emerged. Whether they were reacting to the attack on their pack member or drawn by hunger, they had decided to stay and fight instead of fleeing. Blaine could not spare his attention to note the particulars, but he heard Piran shouting and Knacker scream.

Blaine made a feint toward Beak, hoping to scare off the guard's attacker, but the wolf watching Blaine lowered its head and took a measured step forward, stalking him.

Beak was fighting for his life against the wolf, beating against it with his crossbow once his quarrels were spent. Beak twisted and bucked beneath the wolf, trying to wrest free. The wolf was wounded, its fur matted with blood, but it was not ready yet to give up the fight. The creature was as large and heavy as a man, and much more agile. Nothing Beak did threw the wolf off. The animal's lips drew back, exposing its long, sharp teeth and lunged. Its teeth went deep into Beak's shoulder, crunching through bone.

Blaine risked taking his eyes off the wolf that was watching him long enough to swing his blade down hard on the neck of the wolf that was mauling Beak. He swung harder than usual, compensating for the poor edge on the blade. Blood sprayed as the blade cut through the wolf's pelt, lodging deep in the muscle beneath. A good sword would have taken the wolf's head off with the strength Blaine put behind the blow. The wolf fell to one side, mortally wounded, as Blaine withdrew his sword, and the other wolf used Blaine's momentary preoccupation to close the gap between them.

The second wolf moved fast, leaping as high as Blaine's head, covering at least eight feet of distance. Blaine swung his sword and opened a bloody gash on the wolf's belly. The wolf struck Blaine full in the chest, paws on his shoulders, and they crashed to the ground. Warm blood covered Blaine from the wolf's wound. He wrestled with the wolf to keep its teeth and claws away from his neck.

Blaine brought his knee up, intentionally striking in the wolf's gut wound. When the wolf froze in pain, Blaine used all his strength to throw his man-sized opponent to one side, scrambling to get clear. His crossbow was out of reach, but he still had his sword, and he stood ready for another attack. Even a wounded wolf could be a formidable opponent.

Twain and Aiken lay in a pool of bloody slush, dangerously still. Blaine could smell the coppery tang of their blood; he imagined that to the wolves, the scent must be overwhelming. Despite the dead wolves around him, more came forward.

The lead wolf lowered its head, eyes fixed on its target. Blaine moved forward to get in another blow with his sword, and the wolf sprang. Claws ripped through his heavy coat, tearing through his shirt as well, opening up gashes on his chest. Blaine gasped at the pain and staggered backward. He had the presence of mind to thrust forward with his sword and at the same time, bring his left arm around in a hard roundhouse punch that caught the wolf near its left eye.

The wolf yelped and fell away, bleeding and twitching. Blaine felt blood running down inside his shirt where the claws left gouges. Blaine drew in deep lungfuls of cold air to steady himself and force back the pain, and a moment later, turned back toward Beak. "Still alive?" he yelled.

"Damn wolves," Beak replied, his voice weak. "What about the others?"

"Your buddy is down," Blaine snapped, turning in a slow circle to watch for more wolves. "Piran and I are hurt but standing. Six wolves down. Four others wounded. Don't know how many more are out there."

Piran retrieved his crossbow and shot at the wolves savaging Knacker. Piran's first shot missed, but it forced one of the wolves to let go of Knacker. Knacker got onto his elbows, trying to drag himself away. Piran's second shot felled one of the wolves at it turned to go after Knacker, but the other wolf was fast, dodging out of the way just enough so that the arrow sliced through his flesh without lodging in his body.

Knacker had managed to haul himself a few feet across the ground, leaving a bloody trail. The wolves returned their attention to him with a snarl. The larger wolf sprang for Knacker, planting both forefeet on Knacker's back to pin him down and closing his powerful jaws on Knacker's unprotected neck. Knacker's body went rigid and spasmed as teeth snapped his spine, then lay still.

"I think there are two more, along the tree line to my right," Blaine shouted.

"And two more behind you in the trees to your left," Piran replied. "Big pack."

"Too damn big. Now what?"

"I've got an idea." Piran began to shout and wave his arms, making an awful racket in the quiet forest. Blaine followed his lead, hollering and swinging his outstretched arms. Piran grabbed several fist-sized rocks and hurled them toward the wolves in the trees. The rocks smacked against the trees, sending down a blizzard of snow. Blaine grimaced at the pain from the gashes on his chest as he drew back to throw, but his aim held true.

Their shouts sent a flock of birds flying into the air, and their voices echoed throughout the forest. After a few tense moments, the wolves retreated into the shadows.

"Think they're really gone?" Piran asked.

"For now," Blaine replied. He walked back to retrieve the lantern and opened up the shutters, lighting up the clearing. Twain and Aiken lay in the center. "Aiken's dead," he reported after he bent to check the men. "Twain's got a pulse, but it's faint. I'm not sure he'll make it back to the prison." He walked over to Knacker's body and bent down to check for a pulse. "Dead," he reported. Then he used his sword to cut away two long strips of wool from Knacker's cloak.

"What are you doing?" Piran asked.

"Keep making noise. I've got an idea to get us back to the sledge." Blaine lit the other two lanterns. Then he wrapped the strips of Knacker's woolen cloak around two short, sturdy branches and lit the make-shift torches from the lanterns.

"Here," Blaine said, handing off one of the torches to Piran. "Wolves hate fire even more than they hate all that noise."

"We hope," Piran muttered.

They walked over to where Beak lay. Both Blaine and Piran had been bloodied by the wolves, but Beak looked as if he had taken the worst of it. "Can you walk?" Piran asked. Blaine knew how much Piran detested the Velant guards. But neither of them intended to leave an injured man behind for the wolves.

"Doubt it," Beak managed. The ground around him was red with blood. Blaine wondered whether or not Beak would make it back to camp.

"Well you'd better try, because I don't feel like carrying you," Piran said. He cut a forked branch and fashioned a crutch, and thrust it at Beak. "Use this." He and Blaine got Beak up on his feet. "I've got to carry Twain."

"What do you think we should do about him?" Piran asked with a nod toward Knacker's corpse.

"If we don't take him back with us, Prokief will claim we shot him or some fool thing," Blaine said, with a glare toward Beak. "Isn't that right?"

Beak cursed and looked away, which was all the answer Blaine needed. "You're sure we have to save him?" Piran asked, meaning Beak.

"Not completely sure," Blaine replied, feeling less than generous.

Beak was aware enough to realize his danger. "What do you want?"

"Just your word that you'll tell Prokief the truth about what happened here," Blaine said. He glanced down at the ground. "Don't take too long to make up your mind—you're bleeding a lot."

Beak was too weak to fight about it. He nodded. "All right."

"I want your word, mate," Piran said.

"You have my word," Beak growled.

"What about Aiken?" Piran asked.

Blaine looked reluctantly back toward the dead prisoner. "I suspect his fate was sealed when Prokief sent him and Twain on this hunt, wasn't it?" he said, glaring at Beak. The guard looked away, but not before Blaine read guilt in his expression.

Blaine propped the torch up and walked over to where Knacker lay, then hefted his body in his arms. It hurt like a son of a bitch to put strain on his torn muscles.

"We'll take this one back in case there are questions," Blaine grunted. "So no one can invent stories." He shifted Knacker's dead weight and grabbed the torch. "Come on. Let's get back to camp."

4

LIBERATION DAY

"I JUST KNEW THAT HUNTING TRIP WAS GOING TO COME BACK AND bite us on the ass." Piran paced as he and Blaine awaited the arrival of Commander Prokief, in the cold courtyard with the others. Prokief did not stand on ceremony, and if he was of a mind to get his final vengeance on them, anywhere would do.

"You really have a way with words, anyone tell you that?" Blaine replied. Humor hid his tension, but not convincingly. Piran should have earned his Ticket six months earlier, along with Kestel and Dawe, but Prokief used the disastrous wolf hunt as an excuse to extend Piran's sentence. This was supposed to be their liberation day, the day they earned their Tickets of Leave along with the rest of the inmates who had arrived on the *Cutlass* three years ago, and all those whose arrival had been near that time.

Both men wore the best clothing they had, which wasn't saying much, Blaine thought. Since their new provisions had been destroyed on the wolf hunt, they made do with the prison garb that wasn't in tatters. The morning had started out well. Guards called for the departing prisoners to gather their meager

292 · GAIL Z. MARTIN

belongings and come to the parade grounds, where they would
be formally released and granted their papers.

Blaine and Piran had traded good-natured barbs with the men
who had been their barracks' mates for three years. Garrick and
the rest would soon be their neighbors in Skalgerston Bay. The
colony was small enough that Blaine had no doubt he would see
familiar faces. Though they all tried to play down their anxious-
ness, everyone felt a buzz of excitement at the possibility of their
impending release. *I've waited so long for this,* Blaine thought.
Let's hope nothing goes wrong.

He knew he was not the only one who feared that the long-
awaited liberation would be denied. Blaine remembered how, six
months before, Dawe had spent the night in front of the
makeshift altar he had built, beseeching the High God, Charrot,
and his consorts Torven and Esthrane for their safe deliverance
on the night before he and Kestel were released. Throughout
their incarceration, Dawe had been the most devout of any of the
men, although some stopped by with a small offering of food or
a trinket of whittled wood during the high feast days or when
they needed a favor. He had left his altar behind when he earned
his Ticket. Last night, there had been a near-steady line of men
bringing tribute and stopping to offer a prayer. Blaine had largely
given up on the gods hearing him the night his father had beaten
his mother to death. But even he saved a crust from dinner for an
offering, just in case.

When morning came without incident, Blaine had relaxed, a
little. Piran seemed in good spirits, meaning his cynicism about
the reality of being set free was only slightly modified. Blaine
had felt a weight lift as he walked out of the barracks for the last
time, his paltry belongings tied up in his extra cloak. Even
Piran's whistling hadn't bothered him—and for once, no one else
complained.

Verran was waiting for them at the parade ground, and his

excitement was unmistakable, but beneath it Blaine sensed wariness.

"Where do we stay, until we can build a homestead?" Blaine asked as they waited for their release. "Surely the tavern can't hold all of us."

"It's not the first time Bay-town's gotten a new group of ex-convicts," Verran replied. "I imagine they've figured it out. Maybe in those warehouses they used when they fished you out of the ocean."

"I want a hot dinner that doesn't taste like swill, and a decent tankard of ale to go with it," Piran sighed.

Blaine cleared his throat. "Kestel and Dawe will be waiting for us as close to the gates as the guards allow," he said. "We agreed that once we are out, we separate the money for the homestead and supplies from 'spending' coins."

Verran grinned. "Do this right, boys, and we'll have chickens and eggs and fresh goat meat aplenty, in a house of our own." He gave them a conspiratorial wink. "And I know a thing or two about making berry wine. Stick with me, and you won't have to fork over all your coins at the pub."

"How did Kestel know so bleedin' much about the colony?" Piran asked. "She was locked up in here like the rest of us, wasn't she?"

Blaine shrugged. "Connections. The kitchen and laundry get shipments of supplies from Bay-town every week. The laundry women aren't supposed to talk to the wagon drivers, but the guards couldn't watch them all the time, and Kestel isn't your average prisoner." He grinned. "The wagon drivers are the ones bringing us notes from Kestel with every delivery. She's been working at the Crooked House, getting to know the colonists, and Dawe's been helping the blacksmith. So we'll have some extra coin to buy provisions."

"A few coins here and there go a long way," Blaine added.

He dropped his voice. "One of the wagon masters brought a map of the open land outside Bay-town with him. Kestel says she's put a deposit on a good section. Somehow she got the plot she wanted in the lottery. It's ours as long as we show up with the money and claim it."

"Don't we get a say in this?" Piran asked, raising an eyebrow.

Verran laughed. "Get used to it, Piran. I used to be a married man. I know how these things work."

Piran shot Verran a glare. Blaine suspected that whatever 'deal' Kestel had worked out would be very much in their favor. "It would have been nice to be sent to Bay-town in daylight," Piran fretted.

"I imagine you could stay here until the seasons changed, if you asked nicely," Blaine replied in a droll tone.

"No thanks," Piran replied. "I'll be very glad to see Bay-town, no matter the season. But I'm not going to believe we're really gone until I'm at the Crooked House, having my first real godsdamned whiskey in three and a half years!"

All around them, the would-be colonists talked in low tones, milling about nervously, anxious to be gone. Blaine wondered if they, too, feared that something might interfere with their departure at the last moment. Gods knew, his dreams had been dark for a week. Each time, he had been about to walk out of the prison's massive front gate when the portcullis slammed down, cutting him off from the rest of the prisoners, or guards rushed out to seize him alone and drag him back into Velant.

Just dreams, he told himself. Yet he knew he would not relax until he was in Bay-town and Velant was behind him.

That was when the guards came.

"Uh oh," Piran murmured, directing Blaine's gaze with a nod of his head. Four of Prokief's guards were headed in their direction, walking like they had a purpose.

"Don't give him a reason to deny your leave," Blaine said, gripping Piran's forearm tightly. "If it means taking a beating, take it and keep your damn mouth shut. You're too close to the end to lose it now. Do you understand?"

Piran watched tight-lipped as the guards drew closer. "You're asking a lot."

"Swear it!" Blaine whispered.

"If he doesn't, I'll knock him senseless and we'll sort it out later," Verran muttered.

"Kestel swears she's fixed things. Trust her." Blaine murmured.

His heart sank as the guards stopped in front of them. "Rowse. McFadden. Come with us. The warden wants a private word with you."

Blaine drew a breath to steady himself and nodded. "All right," he said. His heart was thudding, and his palms were sweating. His mind jabbered in near-panic, and he struggled to remain outwardly calm. *Prokief wants us rattled. Whatever game he's playing, we give him the advantage if we let him get to us.*

The set of Piran's jaw and the killing chill in his eyes told Blaine all he needed to know about Piran's mood. The guard had led them into the massive, ugly stone building where Prokief had his office. It was the only stone building inside the prison walls, Prokief's own private keep. The squat, hulking structure bore a resemblance to its occupant. Blaine had no doubt it had been intentionally built to intimidate.

Blaine and Piran said nothing as the guards escorted them through the bleak, featureless corridors. Blaine did his best to keep his expression neutral, hoping he could keep the fear from showing, certain Prokief would see it anyway. Piran looked ready to explode. His hands were balled into fists at his side, white-knuckled, probably clenched hard enough, Blaine thought, for Piran's nails to draw blood on his palms.

Piran's got a temper, but he was an army officer. Let's hope he's got some of that discipline left. Otherwise, we'll be hanging from a gallows by evening bells.

The guards escorted them into an office that was sumptuous by Velant standards. Back in Donderath, it would hardly have been remarkable, let alone a sign of high status. But here at the edge of the world, things like carpets, tapestries, and furniture made in Donderath were true luxuries, and few if any other than the prison commander could acquire them.

"Well, well. Here you are." Prokief sat behind his desk. He was a bear of a man, with a broad chest, thick neck, and powerful shoulders. His war record had won him accolades from King Merrill. His reputation as the "Butcher of Breseshwa" earned him exile in the form of a promotion.

"You asked to see us, sir?" It stuck in Blaine's craw to be polite, but he had spent enough time at court to understand the politics of survival. He managed to not grate his teeth on "sir" although he was certain Prokief understood his deception.

Prokief steepled his fingers, staring at them in silence, a move designed to intimidate. Minutes went by, and Prokief said nothing, ratcheting up the tension. Blaine felt his throat tighten and his stomach clench. *It's a game,* Blaine thought. *A test. Just one of Prokief's sadistic little amusements.* Dealing with his own father had given Blaine many insights into Prokief's tactics.

"Why are you dressed to leave?" Prokief said finally.

Blaine swallowed down bile. "We've earned our Tickets. It's time for us to go, sir," he replied, not trusting Piran to speak.

"Did you receive notice that you had earned your Tickets?" Prokief's voice was flat. His eyes were cold, unreadable.

"Yes sir. The guard came to our barracks and read off the list of names," Blaine answered, hoping his voice sounded carefully neutral.

"And you thought you heard your names on the list? Interesting."

Piran drew a deep breath and held it. Blaine shot him a warning glance. "The guards were quite insistent that we take our things and leave the barracks, ready to go to Bay-town," Blaine said evenly. Inside, Blaine felt cold panic. *This is what Prokief's wanted all along, the bastard. He's had it in for Piran and me for a while, and now he's going to find some half-assed pretense to keep us here while the others go on.* He fought down his emotions, hoping that there might yet be a way to win their freedom.

"You two have been expensive," Prokief said, his voice a deep bass rumble. "Every time there was trouble, you were there. Cave-ins. Sunken boats. Fires. Wolves. Damage. Why should I let you go until you've worked off the debt you've created?"

It was all a match of wits, Blaine knew. All about who would blink first. Prokief held all the power in what was most definitely an unfair fight. *But I am not knuckling under on this, even if I die today,* Blaine thought. He knew Piran's resolve was just as strong. He glanced at Piran and saw that Piran appeared to be biting his lip with the effort not to speak. Blood flecked at the corner of Piran's mouth.

"We pose less of a burden to the prison as colonists," Blaine pointed out, his voice dispassionate. "As colonists, we provide our own food and clothing, our own shelter. The prison still reaps the benefit of the goods we send for trade."

A nasty smile twitched at the corners of Prokief's mouth. "True. Then again, I'd be entirely within my rights to hang you both. That would also satisfy your debt."

Prokief and Blaine's father Ian McFadden were cut from the same cloth. Both were military men used to demanding obedience, who enjoyed using their strength, rank, and privilege to bully those with no recourse. It took all of Blaine's presence of mind not to allow Prokief to goad him into violence. Right now, they had a stand-off. But if Blaine or Piran took action, Prokief would have the excuse he needed to detain them, or worse, send them to the gallows.

"You're aware that Mick and I were two of the most productive workers in this whole damn prison?" Piran asked, and his voice gave no hint of his stress. This was his gambling face, the way he stared down adversaries in a fight. "Mick's right—we're worth more to you as colonists than convicts, and dead men don't earn anything for anybody."

Prokief looked as if he were considering their comments, still regarding them through his tented fingers. "I don't have to release any of you," he said calmly. "I assure you, the king has better things to think about than convicts he's already thrown away."

Technically, that was a lie. Blaine thought, but the king's supervision was likely to be lax so far from home. Up here, Prokief was a law unto himself, and he knew it. Blaine was sure he counted on them knowing it, too.

"Go back to your barracks," he said after another long, nerve-wracking pause. "I'll reconsider your release at some point. Perhaps. If you don't cause me any problems. Make trouble and you'll hang." He gave a cold smile. "I think I'd enjoy watching the two of you dance at the end of a rope."

Prokief was playing with fire. Blaine seriously wondered how long Piran's control would last. If Prokief meant to keep them in the prison—or hang them—then they had little to lose. The white-cold rage he felt inside could easily run hot enough to kill.

A knock came at the door, loud in the silence. "I'm not to be disturbed," Prokief yelled.

The knocking persisted. With a curse, Prokief signaled for a guard to open the door. One of the guards from the parade ground entered with a well-dressed stranger close on his heels. The stranger had the look of entitlement Blaine associated with the noble houses and held a folded parchment in one hand with a red wax embossed seal.

"What is the meaning of this?" Prokief demanded. "Why did you defy my orders to intrude? And who in Raka are you?"

"I am Vilnas, liegeman to King Merrill, the king's new courier." He was a tall man with light blond hair and icy blue eyes, and every gesture indicated he considered himself Prokief's superior.

Vilnas stepped around the guard and produced several more sealed parchment documents from his vest. "I've just come on the *Endurance* from Donderath. The prisoners and supplies have already been unloaded, and I mean to head back when the ship sails. These are your latest orders," he said, placing the documents on Prokief's desk.

"I'm busy. This will have to wait."

Vilnas did not move. "My orders were quite explicit. Lord Pollard emphasized the need to return these items post haste, and Lord Corrender made it clear that you were to read his letter immediately, in my presence, and acknowledge its receipt with your signature."

Prokief regarded him with disdain. "Corrender has no business making demands of me."

Vilnas was not dissuaded. "I am to remind you of your oath, and the provisions stipulated." Prokief seemed to take his meaning immediately, and he grew red in the face.

Prokief swore. "You presume to dictate to me—"

"I suggest you read and sign the papers," Vilnas replied. "They are time-dependent."

Prokief growled, but he shuffled through the papers, signing as he went. He broke the seal on the final document and grew red in the face as he read its contents. "How dare Lord Corrender interfere! He has no authority over how I deal with my prisoners."

"Lord Correnders has received reports from his informants here which might not present matters in the best light," Vilnas replied. "He has assured me that he will withhold those reports if I return with a confirmation that you have complied with his request." His smile tightened. "I'm certain that Lord Pollard and the king would be most interested, should the reports reach their eyes."

"Get out!" Prokief roared, thrusting the papers at Vilnas. "Out! And take these two with you," he added, gesturing at Piran and Blaine.

Vilnas glared at Prokief. "You're wise to remember that the War Council has eyes and ears among the colonists. They are watching you." It was evidence of how far beneath him Vilnas considered Prokief to be that he had not even broken a sweat during the argument. "I believe you have forgotten to provide two additional, important papers."

Prokief cursed and fixed Vilnas with a killing glare. Then he reached down and opened a folio on his desk, withdrawing the two precious documents that granted Piran and Blaine their freedom as colonists.

"Take them and get out of my sight," he snarled, throwing the Tickets of Leave at Blaine and Piran, who hurried to retrieve them.

Vilnas had not moved. "Show them to me," he said, holding out his hand. He looked back at Prokief. "We wouldn't want any mistakes to cause problems later," he added with a patently insincere smile.

Blaine and Piran handed Vilnas their papers, utterly mystified as to why anyone had taken an interest in their welfare. Vilnas glanced at the documents and then advanced on Prokief. "They're. Not. Signed," he snapped. Outside, the tower bell rang. Vilnas raised an eyebrow. "My ship leaves in a candlemark. You're cutting it fine."

For a moment, Blaine thought that Prokief might snatch the papers back from Vilnas and rip them to shreds. Instead, he slammed the papers onto his desk and scrawled an inky line across each, and used sand to blot the ink. With a growl, Prokief handed the papers back to Vilnas, who examined them closely and finally nodded.

"They'll do. Gentlemen…" he said with a disdainful look at Blaine and Piran.

"Get out!" Prokief's face was beet red, and the cords in his neck strained.

Prokief looked as if he would launch himself over his desk. Vilnas turned without saying a word and strode from the room. Blaine and Piran were a step behind him, and Blaine would have been fine with sprinting for the gates.

None of them spoke as they passed through the ranks of guards. Blaine kept his head up and his eyes straight ahead. Piran walked in step with him, shoulders squared and chin up. Vilnas moved through the corridors as if he owned the place, with a look on his face to make it clear he had seen much better.

By the time they reached the parade ground, the portcullis was up and prisoners were making their way in a line four abreast through the huge, fortified prison gates. Verran caught up with them on the way.

"Let's get out of here," Blaine said before anyone could ask a question. "Time to talk later."

His heart was thudding as if it might burst out of his chest as they approached the gate. Blaine took a deep breath and willed himself to be calm, but he could not get the memories of his nightmares out of his mind. Piran had regained his usual swagger. Vilnas moved with the utter assurance of a man who knew the game was rigged in his favor. Verran bounced on the balls of his feet, fidgeting and bobbing.

The walls were dark, shadowed lines in the arctic twilight. Velant was a fortress, built to fend off its own residents more than to withstand attackers from outside. Guards lined the walls, watching in silence as the prisoners streamed out of the gate. The huge, heavy portcullis had been cranked open, and it hung above their heads when they passed through the gates, looming like an executioner's ax.

Velant's walls were twelve feet thick. The passageway was dark, but the blue glow of the polar night seemed all the brighter on the other side. Blaine stiffened, waiting for an arrow in the back, or for the massive gate to come crashing down on them. He took another step, and another without incident.

"We're free." Verran's voice was quiet and reverent.

The press of the crowd carried them forward, down the road toward Skalgerston Bay. Bay-town's lights glowed against the deep blue sky, and lanterns swayed on the ships in the bay, reflecting off the water. It was the most beautiful thing Blaine had ever seen. The cold air stung his cheeks, and only then did he realize tears streaked his face. Piran sniffed, looking like he was fighting back his emotions. Verran blinked rapidly, fending off tears. Vilnas gave them a curt nod of acknowledgment, and strode ahead of them toward the harbor.

"What in Raka do you suppose that was about?" Piran asked, staring after Vilnas.

Just then, Kestel bounded up to them, followed by Dawe. Blaine, Verran, and Piran swept Kestel into an embrace and clapped Dawe on the shoulder.

"It worked!" Kestel exulted when they set her down.

"You said you had 'fixed things,'" Blaine replied. "How?"

Kestel grinned. "I didn't stop being a spy when I became a convict. Both Corrender and Pollard have their spies in the prison and among the colonists, reporting back on Prokief to make sure he doesn't short the king what's due with the rubies and herring."

"How did that have anything to do with getting us our Tickets?" Piran asked incredulously.

Kestel's grin widened. "Once I got out of Velant, I sent a letter to Corrender telling him Prokief was taking liberty on granting Tickets and that I suspected Prokief would try to rescind the Tickets of two of my homestead partners. I asked him to assure that wouldn't happen." She shrugged. "He's always had a soft spot for me."

Blaine closed his eyes. "I wish I had known that beforehand. My heart nearly gave out when Prokief called us into his office."

"It worked, didn't it?" Kestel repeated. "Prokief really is stealing from the king's portion. I made sure Corrender knows it, and since you're here, Prokief must know that someone's on to him, which keeps him in line, relatively speaking."

Vilnas turned. "I will see you safely to town, Mistress Kestel. Lord Corrender sends his regards, and a package which I had delivered to your lodging."

Kestel withdrew a sealed letter from beneath her coat. "Thank you, and thanks also to Lord Corrender. Please give him this for me." Vilnas took the letter, pocketed it, and turned off toward the harbor.

Blaine gave Kestel a questioning look as they watched Vilnas walk away. He knew there had to be more that she wasn't saying.

Kestel scowled. "Fine. I may have also slept with the messenger, to seal the deal. Not exactly sacrificing my virtue, but don't expect me to make a habit of it. Just so you know."

Blaine nodded, still wondering if there wasn't more but he also knew Kestel well enough that it was best to just accept the help and move on.

It felt as if the whole procession of newly-freed convicts

were holding their breath, waiting for soldiers to be dispatched at any moment to haul them back. But the farther they got from the prison without incident, the more tension dissipated. After half a candlemark, Verran pulled out his pennywhistle and began to play a jaunty tune known in every tavern in Castle Reach.

One man began to sing along with gusto, making up for with enthusiasm what his tenor lacked in tone. Another voice, a woman's, joined his, and then more chimed in until a huge, off-key choir made their way toward Bay-town belting out the bawdy lyrics of a bar tune at the top of their lungs.

Piran's singing was notoriously bad, but even he sang along. Verran was fairly dancing to the tune he played as others clapped and whistled. One of the female convicts grabbed Dawe's hand and pulled him into a few dance steps, laughing as they tripped and stumbled. Kestel linked arms with Piran and Blaine and joined in the song. Blaine hummed along, not trusting his voice to hold, feeling completely overwhelmed.

True to their word, the colonists of Bay-town were waiting for them. Ifrem, the owner of the Crooked House tavern, had told Blaine that the colony did its best to welcome the convicts when new groups were released. At the time, Blaine wondered whether or not it was an idle promise, but now, he realized that Ifrem had downplayed the reality.

Hundreds of colonists lined the roadway when the former prisoners made the last turn toward the city. The colonists began to cheer and shout. Some waved Donderath flags or homemade pennants and banners. Others clapped as the newly-released convicts came into view. The bell in the city tower began to peal in celebration. The cold night air smelled of wood smoke and roasting meat, and Blaine realized how hungry he was now that the worst was over.

As Blaine and the others reached the wharves, the colonists moved toward them. The same warehouse that had welcomed

Blaine and Piran and the half-drowned herring fishermen was lit with fires in metal barrels and enough lanterns to illuminate its cavernous interior.

A short, pudgy middle-aged man stood on a crate in the center, clapping his hands for the crowd to hush. "Attention, everyone! Attention!"

The group grew quiet, and the man on the crate motioned for the newcomers to gather around him. The established colonists drew back to line the walls of the warehouse. "My name is Adger. I'm on the Merchant Council—and I run the town's distillery." A cheer went up from the newly freed convicts at that, and Piran was one of those hooting the loudest.

Adger motioned for silence. "Congratulations on securing your Tickets of Leave! I speak from experience when I tell you that we all understand." The colonists along the walls nodded.

"Arrangements have been made to help all of you find your way here in Bay-town," Adger continued. "Tonight you'll sleep here. The colony has a general fund to provide a few necessities like your food and drink tonight and bedding. Tomorrow, we'll match you to suitable work, get you introduced to the people you need to know to make your transition and complete the lottery so you can purchase a homestead."

Blaine looked around the huge warehouse. He wondered how many of the others felt utterly at a loss, as he did, now that freedom was a reality. *All those years, I was so focused on surviving to get my Ticket,* Blaine thought. *The plans we made seemed like dreams, so far out of reach. Maybe I never quite believed it would happen. And now that it's real, I'm not entirely sure what to do.*

Adger looked out over the group, with an expression that made Blaine think the distiller had an inkling of how the new colonists were feeling. "Tonight we celebrate, with warm food and plenty of grog. Many of your new neighbors are here tonight. Ask them questions. Get to know them. We'll be seeing a lot of each other," he added, and the established colonists chuckled. "Then get a good night's sleep. You've got a new life waiting for you."

A group of musicians struck up a merry tune. Blaine was not surprised to see that Verran had joined them. Piran spotted someone he recognized and wended his way through the crowd toward a familiar face. Dawe was already in line for food. Blaine was hungry, but still too wound up from the day's events to eat. While Kestel chatted with one of the Bay-town women, Blaine drifted back toward the warehouse doorway, and slipped outside, into the azure polar night.

The sea breeze rustled his chestnut hair. *Right after I get a good bath, a shave and a haircut are top of my list,* he thought. *It took time to adjust to prison. I never realized that being free again would take getting used to.*

The waters of Skalgerston Bay stretched off to the dark horizon. Far across that ocean lay Donderath, with the home and loved ones Blaine would never see again. He drew in a deep breath of cold, fresh air, letting it revive him. His thoughts were awhirl, his feelings confused. Relief. Uncertainty. Happiness— tempered with concern. Lingering anger and fear of the unknown. All those emotions and more swirled in a mix that made him queasy.

He glanced back as the door opened. Kestel slipped out, drawing her cloak around herself as the wind caught her red hair. "Not hungry?" she asked, coming over to stand next to him.

Blaine shook his head. "I thought I was," he admitted. "But my stomach's off. Too much happening."

She smiled. "Don't wait long. Everyone else looked ravenous." They stood together in silence for a few minutes.

"Thank you," Blaine said quietly. "For what you arranged back at the prison. Prokief really wasn't going to let us go. I'm not sure what would have happened if your man hadn't shown up when he did."

Kestel nodded. "I had a feeling Prokief would try something. That's why I warned you, and why I had Corrender word his letter the way he did and send his emissary to deliver it."

Blaine smiled. "If you were anyone else, I'd wonder whether you knew what you were getting yourself into, homesteading with the likes of us," he admitted. "But I think you can handle it."

Kestel grinned. "Oh, be sure of that. We'll make a good team. Complimentary skills. We'll share the chores. I'll mind the livestock and tend the kitchen garden. Dawe's probably already getting set up with one of the local blacksmiths, and Verran's found his fellow musicians. Mark my words—he'll be playing for coins at the Crooked House tomorrow night. I'm not worried about you and Piran finding work. After breakfast, we'll pay for our land and building materials, so we can start on the house and barn." She let out a long breath. "We're not just going to survive —we're going to do just fine."

"Aren't you worried that people will talk?" Blaine asked. "I mean, you're moving in with four men."

Kestel shrugged. "People will talk no matter what I do. That's the problem with a reputation, and mine breaks the rules in every way possible. They'll figure out soon enough that I'm not a courtesan anymore. They don't need to know about the spying. And if they mind their manners, I'll stay out of the assassin business." She grinned. "If they think the four of you are very lucky fellows, well, it's up to you whether you tell them the truth or not."

Blaine snorted, expecting that he and the others would be open to quite a bit of ribbing and speculation, and not giving a tinker's damn. "Maybe it's a good thing Donderath is so far away," he said, looking out over the harbor lights. "We've got something here we'd never get back home. A chance to start completely over, and see what we can make of things."

Kestel nodded. "Time to stop looking back, stop thinking of Donderath as 'home.' If we're going to make a go of this, really succeed, we've got to leave it all behind. Edgeland is home now, and the people we choose are our families."

"That's going to take some getting used to," Blaine said. "But I think I like the sound of it."

KING'S EXILES

1

HOMESTEAD

"We'll never get this finished before the Long Dark sets in." Blaine "Mick" McFadden stared at the half-built barn and sighed. Here in Edgeland, at the top of the world, winter came early and lasted long. That's what made Edgeland the prime location for Donderath's most fearsome prison and penal colony. Nowhere was farther from home.

"Sure we will. We'll make up for lost time before the herring fleet goes out again. Work in shifts, two at a time." Piran Rowse said, and the wicked gleam in his eye told Blaine that the more unlikely the outcome, the more Piran welcomed the challenge. His fondness for a dare had helped to bring him to this godsforsaken place, after all.

"Kestel and Dawe have the house almost livable, and Verran's bringing in enough money from his music at the Crooked House that we've got coin enough for supplies—put together with what we brought in from the last fishing run. We've got this, Mick. You'll see."

Despite himself, Blaine smiled at Piran's defiant optimism.

His friends might not know the full story behind his exile or his fall from grace as a lord's son, but finding this group of unlikely housemates in the shared misery of Velant Prison was one of the best things that had happened to Blaine. Even if it had to happen here, in Donderath's frozen oubliette.

"Come on," Piran said with a friendly slug to Blaine's shoulder. "Daylight's wasting."

That wasn't exactly correct, because during the White Nights, the sun never set. That created a desperate urgency to do everything that couldn't be done in the long, sunless winter. In the short time since Blaine and his friends had received their Ticket of Leave from Velant after their imprisonment, they had taken every job they could find and pooled the small sum they each received as a released prisoner, combining their acreage allotment to create a homestead where, with any luck at all, they could live out their lives.

Blaine and Piran worked in comfortable silence. Digging side-by-side in Velant's ruby mines and working in the cramped confines of the herring fleet gave them a sixth sense about each other's movements, a rhythm that carried over to the building projects required to have their hard-scrabble land ready for the worst weather.

"Kestel says we'll have new goats coming in a couple of weeks, once the ones she's spoken for are old enough," Piran volunteered as he carried lumber and handed up the supplies Blaine needed to work on the next section of the barn. "Verran's already named the chickens, and now he's trying to convince Dawe not to kill any of them for food."

Blaine snorted. "If the alternative is herring, I've got a thing or two to say about that." The fish hadn't been a favorite before his exile, but here in Edgeland, where herring was cheap and plentiful, he'd had his fill, even before the miserable fishing runs. Then again, food could be scarce, and Blaine had gone hungry far too many times to be picky.

"Maybe this winter, but come spring, when we get the plants in, and the rabbit hutches are full, we won't have to eat herring if we don't want to," Piran told him. "And gods know, I'd prefer not to eat it ever again."

They hadn't finished the roof yet on the barn, which left Blaine with a view of sky and ground, high enough that he could see all the way to Bay-town, and the waters of Skalgerston Bay beyond it. The wind that rustled through his hair wasn't warm by Donderath standards, but for Edgeland, it was almost balmy. If he looked one way, gentle foothills gave way to flatlands that ran down to the harborside. Behind them sprawled tundra and mountains, the true wilderness. And off to the East, high on a cliff overlooking the ocean, were the dark walls of Velant Prison.

Blaine didn't look that direction, not if he could help it.

"You hear about the fight, down at the docks?" Piran seemed determine to hold a conversation, even if Blaine wasn't feeling chatty.

"What now?"

"Kestel and Dawe went into town to help get the new releases situated. A couple of the latest group to get their Tickets decided to celebrate. Went at it a little too hard, and they started to throw punches. Ifrem waded in to stop it before anyone called the guards and got a black eye for his trouble."

"Shit. Are they idiots? The Edgeland guards aren't any better than the ones in Velant. Worse, I'd say, because they think they need to keep reminding us we're not really free."

"Yes, they're probably utter fools," Piran agreed. "And Ifrem did not take it well. Verran said that by the time the customers all piled on, the idiots had been thoroughly pummeled. Ifrem managed to get it contained before the guards got involved, but it could have gone worse."

Much worse. Commander Prokief ruled Velant Prison with an iron fist, and his guards knew they were unlikely to face any consequences for their treatment of the wretches that were shipped to that forsaken place. Blaine and his friends had survived with the scars to show for it. Prokief's reach extended to the colony, and the guards seemed to delight in reminding those who had escaped the confines of the prison that their freedom could be revoked on a whim.

"It's been a while since I've gone down to the Crooked House. Guess I should show up a little more often, even if it's only to help keep the peace," Blaine replied as he nailed a board into place.

"Ifrem told me to remind you that he owes you a drink," Piran said as he loaded more supplies onto a platform and hauled on a pulley to bring it up to Blaine's level. "Something about helping out the last time he ran the still."

Blaine chuckled. "Yeah, that was an adventure. Managed to save the batch without blowing anything up."

Supply ships from home came far too seldom, so the colony had to be as self-sufficient as it could manage. Making its own beer, wine, and rotgut whiskey went a long way toward making exile survivable. Colonists could put up with hardship much better with a way to take the edge off, and a gathering place that reminded them of civilization. The Crooked House was all those things, and Ifrem was a friend. Blaine couldn't get them home to Donderath, but he was resolved to make Edgeland as good a home as possible.

The rest of the morning passed without incident. When Piran wasn't handing off supplies to Blaine, he was beside him to make quick progress on the roof. By the time Dawe brought them lunch, Blaine had to admit that they might be ready in time for true winter.

"You're getting there," Dawe said, tilting his head up to take in their work. His lanky frame always looked underfed, and his dark hair stuck out all over. "It'll be good to have a place to store the harvest. We were out in the garden this morning. For a bunch of first-time farmers, we aren't doing too badly."

"Are you volunteering to help, or did Kestel just send you with lunch?" Blaine wiped his arm across his forehead, warm despite the cool wind.

"Verran and Kestel sat up last night coming up with a list of things that aren't the way they should be with the house," Dawe reported. "I need to spend some time down at the forge this afternoon to make a few pieces—hinges and the like, and I'll bring more nails when I come back, too."

"Yeah, we could use more. We've got enough to get the beams up, but we'll need more to finish the roof," Piran agreed. He grinned. "Lunch?"

Dawe held up a fat piece of cloth, stuffed with food. "Hard-boiled eggs, sausage, and bread, with a jug of ale to wash it down. Nothing very original, but you won't be hungry."

There had been enough times in Velant when they had all gone without. If Blaine had taken any part of his privileged upbringing for granted, he was grateful for every small favor now.

"Just so you know, tread lightly around Kestel when you come in," Dawe warned. "She got pecked by one of the chickens, broke some eggs, and had to chase the rooster to get him back into the pen. She is not in a mood to be bargained with."

"Is the rooster still alive?" Blaine asked.

"Yes. Which is more than many men who've raised her ire can say. Just don't poke the bear."

"Me? Never." Blaine couldn't keep the humor from his voice. Kestel's reputation as a spy, courtesan, and assassin usually settled arguments before they ever started. Apparently, no one had told the rooster.

Working from sunup to sundown took on a different meaning during the White Nights. Still, they were tired and running low on materials by the time the sun had traveled across the sky.

"What did I tell you? Another day like this, two at the most, and we'll have the roof on," Piran predicted. "After that, we can finish the inside without as much pressure." He bumped Blaine with his elbow to win his agreement. "I told you we'd be fine."

"I'll believe it when it's done." Blaine no longer trusted in luck. He stifled a yawn and stretched. Velant had hardened his body with brutal conditions, but homesteading offered daily challenges that earned sore muscles and tested his resourcefulness. "Let's clean up, and go see if there are any livestock we need to chase to spare them the wrath of Kestel."

Blaine and Piran made their way to the square, two-story home they had all pitched in to build. He felt a thrill of pride at what they had accomplished. The house was plain on the outside, a solid construction of logs from the nearby forest, but it was solid enough to stand against Edgeland's harsh weather and had room for their little found family to grow. The temperature had dropped, and the wind picked up, heightening the contrast between outside and indoors.

The house had the bedrooms on the second floor. A large common room and a kitchen with an ample pantry provided what they needed, both function and comfort. They had all pitched in to build the furnishings, and if some of the chairs wobbled or the angles of the table weren't quite true, the satisfaction of making what they wanted counted far more than appearances.

"Oh good, you're here," Kestel greeted them when they ducked inside. "Dawe would have been annoyed if his stew had overcooked waiting for you."

Her red hair was tied up in a functional knot, and the man's tunic and trews she wore suited the hard work of homesteading. Even without the enhancement of rouge and kohl or the fine gowns and jewels she had worn at the palace, Kestel had a fire and beauty that was impossible to ignore.

Which meant that she'd drawn the boundaries of their relationship clearly when she proposed the arrangement of living with four men. Here in Edgeland, she belonged to no one but herself and had no plans to change that, though her housemates were free, she reminded them, to find partners of their own.

"It smells good," Piran said. "Does this mean you sacrificed the chicken that annoyed you?"

Kestel backhanded him good-naturedly with a swat to the chest. She barely came up to Piran's shoulder and was even shorter compared to Blaine and Dawe, but none of them doubted who was in charge.

"The rooster lives. At least for today," she announced with a grand sweep of her arm as if extending an official pardon. "I bartered some cabbage for the hen with the neighbors. Half their patch didn't come up well, and she had a bird to spare."

Blaine and Piran went to wash up in the basin. Dawe filled pottery bowls with stew while Kestel set a pot of water on the fire to boil to make tea or *fet*, a dark, potent brew that could almost wake the dead. By the time Blaine and Piran returned to the table, Verran had joined the group.

"How's the barn?" Verran Danning was dressed to perform at the Crooked House, in his best shirt and pants, boots shined and hair tamed. His slight, wiry build fooled too many people into underestimating him, which served him well at the petty theft that had helped to earn him passage to Velant. Now that he'd left thieving behind, he relied on his music and the touch of magic that swayed the crowd whenever he played and sang.

"It's a big, bloody pain in the ass," Blaine replied, digging into the stew with gusto as he realized just how much of an appetite he had worked up with the construction project. "And if the weather stays mild and Dawe can get us some more nails, we should be done with the roof soon. Then we just need to build the stalls and pens for the livestock, and the bins for keeping winter vegetables and fodder." He sighed. "Plenty of work to go around, for a while yet."

"Good thing we mine some of the iron and copper we need here," Verran said, talking with a mouthful of food. "The supply ship's late again."

"Again?" Piran looked up. "That's the third one in a row. Have you heard anything about why?"

Verran shrugged. "I've heard lots of things. Rumors and theories are the stock in trade of the crowd down at the Crooked House. But anything with real facts? That's hard to come by. Even the sailors who stop in don't know anything except gossip." He tore off a hunk of bread and sopped up the gravy, taking a big bite before continuing.

"The ships are due around the middle of the month. That's always iffy—storms at sea, slow winds, and late departure can all hold them up. But in general, they've always been pretty regular, because they also carry the pay for the guards at Velant and here in town."

"Because there's so much to spend it on up here," Piran remarked.

Verran ignored his friend's sarcasm. "I'm guessing it helps morale. Because the guards can't go home any more than we can." The soldiers that were assigned to Velant and Edgeland usually drew the duty to avoid the noose on account of one infraction or another. "And Prokief made such a big deal about how he sends reports back to Donderath with each ship, to keep King Merrill informed."

Blaine noticed that Verran said "Donderath" and not "home." After almost four years, they had all made an uneasy peace with the fact that they would live out their years in Edgeland.

"Do you think Merrill actually reads the reports?" Piran asked. He washed down a bite of stew with a slug of ale. "I mean, Prokief always went on and on about carrying tales back to the king, but why would he care? The fact that we were up here proves he's already written us off."

"I imagine it had more to do with Prokief keeping his head on his shoulders than anything to do with the convicts," Kestel remarked. She and Blaine had first-hand knowledge about how things worked at court and among the nobility, although Blaine kept his own connections a secret.

"The king owed him for his service in battle, but Prokief was such a brute, they couldn't keep him in the army. Posting him here was a 'promotion' and didn't require killing him." She paused. "And since I was a spy for two of the lords when I was in Velant, I suspect that even if the king doesn't read the reports, some of the lords do."

Verran cleared his throat theatrically. "Back to my story," he said, with a mock glare toward Piran, who responded with an obscene hand signal. "The sailors said that ships were late delivering their cargo to Donderath and that pirates were worse than usual. Apparently, some ships sank, and not from bad weather."

"It could be a coincidence that the ships are late," Piran replied. "And sailors have nothing much to do for weeks at sea except drink and make up stories. The best stories earn them free drinks, because everyone here is starved for news. So there's a reward for telling tall tales, if the truth is boring."

"Have the seers had anything to say about it?" True mages weren't supposed to be shipped to Edgeland, but most people had a glimmer of magic and a minor talent, and sometimes their gifts grew after they came to the arctic wasteland. Blaine had learned to take the warnings of the mystics and seers seriously.

"The seers say plenty—it's always wrapped in riddles so no one's quite sure what they meant," Verran replied, and spooned out the last of the stew in his bowl. He looked up hopefully at Dawe for more. Dawe shook his head, so Verran helped himself to another hunk of bread.

"Like the sailors, the seers love drama," he said. "But there's been a bit too much talk about 'dark clouds on the horizon' and 'dreams of fire and armies' for my liking. If it's not true, they need to hold their tongues. People have enough reason to be on edge here, without made-up tales making it worse."

"You're going into the Crooked House tonight, aren't you?" Blaine asked. He finished his ale and wiped his mouth. The stew had been good, but the portion hadn't been quite enough.

Verran nodded. "The ships that have come in brought enough coin to town that people are spending it, and I figured some of it should come my way." He grinned. "Which of course, I'll bring back here, minus a drink or two, for my efforts."

Kestel rolled her eyes. "Is your magic slipping? Between what Ifrem pays you to play and what the crowd buys to shut you up, you should have all the drinks you need, for free."

Verran struck a dramatic pose. "Ah, my Sour Rose. You wound me to the quick! It is my fragile muse that begs to assuage its sorrows."

Kestel snorted a laugh. "Fragile muse. That's a good one. Your jokes are getting better." The fondness in her voice softened her words.

"I think I'll catch a ride in with you," Blaine said. "It's been a while since I've been to town, and I'd like to hear the gossip myself—or see if Ifrem has anything he'll tell me that he's not saying out loud."

"And perhaps court a certain someone?" Piran inquired, elbowing him in the ribs.

Blaine felt the color come to his cheeks. "Maybe. Selane might not even be at the pub."

"Although a few coins to an errand boy to carry a message could increase your odds," Kestel teased.

Blaine had been thinking that very thing and found himself looking forward to the trip to town, despite the cold, bumpy wagon ride there and back. "We'll see," he replied. "I thought I'd stay at the pub, like Verran does, and we can come back together in the morning." He glanced at Piran. "Don't worry—I'll be back bright and early to start on the barn again. I know you were worried."

Piran gave an exaggerated sigh. "And here I was, just saying to myself that I wondered if I'd be forced to sleep late because your return was delayed."

"I don't plan on being delayed, but if I am, feel free to start without me," Blaine needled. This was one of the things he loved most about this motley, misfit crew that had become his family. They joked, teased, and argued, but never once did he doubt their loyalty or affection.

"I'll be working on the ledgers," Kestel informed them. "Someone has to keep an eye on business."

"We don't have a business yet," Piran replied. "We barely have a farm."

"We have money coming in and money going out. Some of what we buy we use for ourselves, and some goes to make things that we can sell. Eggs. Vegetables. And when we get the forge built, Dawe can not only make what we need but sell to others. And all of that," she added primly, "is a business."

Piran and Kestel helped Dawe clean up after the meal, while Blaine went to change clothing. Minutes later, he shouldered into his coat, because while the long summer days were the warmest that Edgeland had to offer, the White Nights were cold, despite their light. Kestel told him what they needed in town—candles, salt, and thread—and made him repeat it back to assure her he would not forget.

He and Verran had barely made it outside before the wagon pulled up outside. Blaine and Verran crawled up into the bed of the wagon, burrowing in the straw among the goods the farmer took to town to stay warm.

"Selane—you fancy her, don't you?"

"Yes, of course. Isn't it obvious?"

Verran shrugged. "There are all kinds of fancies. Is yours the kind that might mean we have a new resident at the homestead, before too long?"

The hard work of earning the money for materials, clearing the land, and building the house and barn had made Blaine's trips to town less frequent than he would have liked. Yet he didn't feel right about pursuing Selane with serious intent until he could provide for her.

"It's a bit soon to talk about that, don't you think? We might at least get the roof on the barn first. We're barely making ends meet now, what with buying seed and a plow—and share of a workhorse. We'd better get all that squared away before we add new mouths to feed."

Even with the five of them pooling their earnings and effort, starting the household and farm from scratch took all their time, money, and energy. Blaine knew it wouldn't be fair to bring someone new into the mix, especially since even the best match was certain to ruffle some feathers.

"I imagine so," Verran agreed, growing silent as he watched the clouds move across the sky. "I wonder if we'll all bring someone home, eventually. Maybe even Kestel."

"You don't believe her when she says she has her hands full with us?"

Verran shook his head. "I believe she believes that, for now. And I can't blame her for wanting something of her own, given where she's been. Still, it's just an odd idea that we'd have to be thrown onto Donderath's refuse heap to find a mate and a purpose."

Before the day when he'd taken matters into his own hands to deal with his wretched father, Blaine would have said he'd had both a mate and a purpose back home. But his exile had broken his engagement to Carensa, and cut him off from the inheritance of his family lands and manor. So to find meaning and love again, here? That would be almost more than Blaine dared hope.

The wagon driver left them off in town, near the Crooked House pub. One look bore out the reason for its name—the building had a definite lean, as if its builders had indulged too much ale during its construction. Yet despite that, and in defiance of harsh winters, heavy snow and the worst sea storms the ocean could muster, the Crooked House remained the heart of Bay-town life.

By this time, the shops had closed for the day. The Crooked House was the gathering place for those who needed a place to stay in town or merely wanted some cheerful companions and a decent dinner. Over the years, a few other pubs had sprung up in Bay-town, but the Crooked House was the most popular, and Blaine rarely went elsewhere.

Ifrem, the owner, stood behind the bar, pouring drinks when Blaine and Verran entered. The tavern owner was at least two decades older than Blaine, bald with a salt and pepper dark beard. A cheer went up from a handful of regulars who were happy to see the musician, and a few voices called out greetings to Blaine, reminding him that it had been a while since his last visit.

"I see Verran dragged you to town," Ifrem said as they pushed up to the bar. "He says things are going well at the homestead."

Blaine waited for Ifrem to pour him a glass of the strong

homemade whiskey. "The work's coming along. There's still a lot to be done." He lifted his drink in salute, and took a sip, managing not to lose his breath at its potent bite.

"There's always work to be done, until the day you die," Ifrem replied, moving down the line to fill the glasses and tankards of impatient customers. The smell of roasted venison and baking bread filled the air, reminding Blaine that he was still hungry. A board of meat, cheese, pickles, and bread would do nicely.

"What's this I hear about ships coming late?" Blaine asked as the crowd ebbed and flowed at the bar, coming up to have their cups refilled and then returning to their tables.

"Might be nothing," Ifrem replied. "But I have the feeling that things might be rougher back in Donderath than the official news suggests. Just bits I've put together, listening to the sailors talk. Little things that don't seem like much to them, but strike me as strange."

"Like?" Blaine enjoyed the burn of liquor down his throat, warming him from the inside out.

"Comments about the harbor not being as busy as usual, or the trade caravans ordering less from abroad. And mention that more soldiers were moved to the northern border. Nothing that seems important—unless it is."

Blaine mulled that over as he nursed his whiskey. Donderath and Meroven, the kingdom's northern neighbor, had been skirmishing along the border for quite some time, with fault on both sides, or so Blaine had heard. Extra troops might just be a show of power, designed to stop smuggling or prevent a territory dispute. There were several causes Blaine could think of, none dire.

And yet. If the shipping and caravan changes were signs of hard times, it would be a bad time to also have trouble at the border. King Merrill was a decent king, all things considered. He had his faults—and turning a blind eye to Blaine's father's excesses had been among them—but Merrill seemed to be trying to be a good monarch and a fit ruler. He had never been enamored of battle for the sake of pageantry. So if Merrill saw a need for military force, Blaine was inclined to believe there was cause. The question was, what did all that mean for the kingdom and its fortunes?

Whatever the answer, it was unlikely to be found in a bar at the end of the world. Blaine knocked back the rest of his whiskey and put his glass down for more. But his mind kept racing, drawing worrisome conclusions.

Edgeland provided gems, ore, and herring in trade. During the worst of the winter, rough seas and harsh storms could make it too dangerous to bring large ships into port, so the colony had to be as self-sufficient as possible. Still, there were goods that Edgeland either couldn't produce itself or comforts better made back home that filled the portside shops and tempted both guards and colonists alike to part with their hard-earned coin. Some of those comforts included foods that wouldn't grow in Edgeland's arctic weather, spices to make game meat edible, and medicines that the healers here could not make for want of hard-to-find ingredients. Not to mention the sailors themselves, who kept the shops, pub, and brothels busy and supplied the coin that helped keep the colony going. Having fewer ships come into port, or waiting longer between ships, did not bode well.

The clock tower bell reminded Blaine of the time, and he looked around until he saw one of the young men he recognized as being a messenger for the shopkeepers.

"I need you to go to the chandler's shop, and take a message to her apprentice, Selane. Tell her that Mick is at the Crooked House, if she'd like to pass the evening. Go now, and I'll give you a copper for your trouble."

The boy headed out straightaway, and Blaine turned his

back to the bar, leaning back and watching the crowd. Verran played a lute that belonged to the pub, a switch from his penny-whistle. No doubt, when their fortunes improved, he'd probably want one of his very own, Blaine thought. Despite the borrowed instrument, Verran's playing was quite good, and when his magic added to it, the result had the crowd swaying and singing along, forgetting their troubles just a bit more than usual.

Nothing wrong with that. Trouble's what got all of us sent here in the first place. Forgetting's harder than you'd think, especially when you're a world away from where you started.

He watched the door, impatient for the messenger to return. While Blaine would have gladly gone and fetched Selane himself, he had learned the hard way that her mistress, the candle maker, had very strict ideas of propriety, and having a single man call at the back door "like an alley cat" did not meet those ideals. Not wanting to cause Selane problems with her employer, Blaine was resigned to playing by the rules.

Half a candlemark later, the door opened to admit Selane and another woman, Annalise, who also worked at the chandlery. Selane spoke well of Annalise, who was a bit older. The two apprentices had hit it off and got along well with each other.

Selane made her way through the crowd to where Blaine had managed to find them a table in a quiet corner. He rose to meet her and pulled her into his arms for a kiss that was all too brief and far too public. "I missed you," he said, taking in the smell of her hair and the scent of her soap, and the press of her lips again his.

"I've missed, you, too," Selane said, settling into her chair. Blaine knew her favorites and had already ordered, so when Ifrem waved him over, he went to retrieve the warm rolls with honey butter and a glass of ale.

"How's the candle making business?" Blaine asked, realizing

now that Selane was with him how much he had marked her absence.

"Mistress says I'm doing well, but I still don't quite have the art of it," she confessed. "It's not just dipping the candles and making them come out straight and evenly thick—although that's harder than it looks, even with practice. But knowing how to add the tints to turn the wax pretty colors or the scents so they'll smell good when they burn? It's nearly witchery, as far as I can tell." She smiled self-consciously. "Not really, of course. But it seems like it, since I can't quite get it right just yet."

"You will," Blaine told her, reaching across to take her hand. "She saw promise in you, or she wouldn't have taken you on."

"I know. That's what I tell myself. But I want to show her I'm worthy, and I get so discouraged that I'm not a quicker study."

Blaine had met Selane in the early days before they had both earned their Tickets of Leave. She was pretty, which had caught his eye first. But she was also practical and willing to work hard, both qualities required to survive and do better than subsist in Edgeland's harsh reality. He had fallen for her easy laugh and quick humor, which seemed to make even the darkest worries seem less dire.

"And business has been good?" Blaine couldn't help asking, knowing that with a shop near the harbor, the chandlery supplied most of the colonists who hadn't decided to take up candle making themselves.

Selane bit her lip. "I'm not sure. Mistress doesn't say much about such matters. But I think it's a bit slower than it was when I first started. Perhaps it's the season. I haven't really been with her long enough to know." She squeezed his hand and smiled. "I can't imagine you think that's very interesting. Tell me how the homestead is coming along. I want to know everything!"

Blaine found himself talking about how far he and his friends had gotten with the buildings, and recounting some of the funnier mishaps of tending the garden crops. Keeping the chicken and the goats out of the vegetables had been an undertaking, and it had required several versions of fencing before the feathered and furry thieves were locked away from their treasure.

"I know it was probably vexing when it happened, but you make it sound like such an adventure when you tell about it!" Selane said, giving him a smile that warmed him more than the whiskey.

"The livestock is really managed by Dawe and Kestel," Blaine admitted. "Piran and I did the worst of the work getting the garden plowed, and we've taken on most of the construction, although the others help when we need a hand. So if there's anyone chasing down misbehaving goats and stubborn chickens, it's them."

Selane's smile dimmed, just a bit. "I can't really picture that, somehow. I wish Kestel liked me more."

Blaine took her hand in both of his. "She likes you, just fine."

Selane shook her head. "She's friendly enough, and she's never said anything cross. It's just that I get the feeling she's not sure I'm good enough for you."

Blaine hadn't noticed. He knew Selane's impression might just be insecurity. After all, Blaine, Kestel, Piran, Verran, and Dawe had bonded under the worst conditions, not unlike soldiers who had gone to war together. It would be difficult to let a newcomer inside, although eventually, he expected that most or all of them would want to do so. Perhaps this was harder because he was the first.

"She's very protective," Blaine said. "We had to watch out for each other. Kestel's not the trusting type. So it might just take a while for her to decide you won't hurt me." He squeezed her hand reassuringly. "Give it time. She'll come around."

Selane nodded. "I will. I want to be comfortable with your friends." A hint of color came to her cheeks. "I think my mistress approves of you, despite what she said when you came to the door. She's asked me more than once if you had plans to come to town, off-handed like she didn't care, but I know she did."

"Good. I'll win her over." Selane was a little younger than Blaine, and while she didn't need her mistress's permission to marry, it certainly wouldn't hurt to have her employer support their union.

The door from the kitchen flew open hard enough to hit the wall behind it, and Bernard, the cook's assistant, came running in, face flushed and wide-eyed. "Come quick. The potter's shop is on fire!"

Blaine rose to his feet at the same instant at Selane. "Stay here," he warned her. "You'll be safer."

Selane shook her head. "The potter's shop is just on the other side of the bakery from the chandlery. If the fire spreads, our shop could go to—and we have our rooms over the shop." She laid a hand on his arm. "Mistress could be asleep. I need to get her out." Annalise joined them, wide-eyed with fear.

Blane nodded. "All right. But go now, and be quick. I'll help with the bucket brigade, and if we're lucky, the fire won't get that far." He kissed her quickly. "Be safe."

"You, too."

Blaine ran to join the others who streamed out of the pub. Only those whose illness or injury prevented them from doing hard labor stood on the sidelines. The rest joined the line to pass buckets of water up from the harbor to try to douse the flames that were rapidly claiming the potter's shop.

"What happened?" Blaine asked as he took his place, straining to see if he could spot Selane amid the smoke and fire.

"Delancy got out," the man next to him said, naming the potter. "Not sure about his apprentice. Said the kiln exploded."

330 • GAIL Z. MARTIN

He shook his head. "Better not break any dishes. It'll be a while before there are more to replace them."

It was odd that in a place where cold was a constant danger that fire could be just as feared. Bay-town didn't have the resources to build from quarried stone, and what mud there was to be had was desperately needed to grow crops. Brick buildings just weren't feasible, leaving wood as the main alternative. A city made of logs and lumber was kindling waiting for a match.

Smoke billowed from the potter's building, blown inland by the harbor wind. Though this was technically summer, the temperature dropped quickly once night fell. The heat from the flames and the activity of handing off bucket after heavy bucket up a human chain chased off the cold, but Blaine saw the bystanders rubbing their arms and fidgeting to keep warm.

"Oh gods, there goes the bakery roof!" Someone yelled, and Blaine looked up to see where embers caught in the wooden shingles, quickly rising into flames.

He looked down at the long brigade to the harbor and realized that too many people were crammed into too small a space. The number of volunteers was actually slowing the time it took for buckets to reach the front, and at this rate, they'd never be able to douse the potter's shop, let alone stop the fire in the bakery from spreading.

The whole town could burn.

"Form two lines!" Blaine hollered, and his voice carried over the confusion. "Do it now!"

Blaine wasn't a stranger to anyone in town. Many of them had worked beside him on the herring boats, and others remembered him from their years in Velant. He'd earned a reputation for having a level head. Without debating the matter, the lines split, sharing the buckets. Down toward the water, Blaine could hear Verran trying to forge some semblance of order at the dockside, so the buckets filled efficiently. Some people dismissed

Verran because of his penchant for drama, but they overlooked his keen mind and his ability to rally people. Blaine had seen both talents come into play far too often to underestimate his friend when the going got rough.

It did not escape his notice that the town guards, who were all too eager to punish infractions, where nowhere to be seen when a few more able bodies might have been useful.

He lost track of time, falling into the hypnotic rhythm. Turn, take the bucket, turn, pass the bucket. Over and over, and over again. Smoke burned his eyes and made him cough. Being uncomfortably warm was a rare thing in Edgeland, but for the first time that he could remember, sweat poured down his back, and his skin felt reddened by the heat.

The sun never set, but it dipped to hover just at the horizon. In its place was the awful false sunset of the burning buildings that lit up the twilight in shades of red and gold. Finally, when the night was long spent, Blaine mopped his forehead with the sleeve of his shirt and saw that the worst was over.

The potter's building was a total loss, and the bakery had lost its roof and seen damage to its second floor, but the chandlery appeared intact, aside from whatever the smoke and heat might have done to the wax and wares.

The weary volunteers gradually dispersed. Verran joined Blaine on the walk back to the Crooked House. Both of them were soot-streaked, hair wet with sweat and plastered to their heads.

"That was a bit more excitement than we bargained for, eh?" Verran said, exhaustion lacing his voice.

Blaine scanned the crowd around him, looking for Selane. "Yeah. But it could have been a lot worse."

He tried to convince himself that Selane, Annalise, and Mistress Dennison were just hidden from his view by the people around them, but every step he took away from the harbor without spotting them made his heart pound. Had they been trapped inside? Overcome by smoke?

By the time they reached the pub, Blaine had braced himself for the worst. He glanced over the subdued group who gathered there, too alert to go home, exhaustion mingling with shock.

No sign of Selane.

"Ifrem, have you seen—"

Ifrem cut him off. "Selane left word for you. Mistress Dennison had a hard time of it with the smoke, and her nerves got the best of her. I gave the three of them a room upstairs, and Selane said to tell you to come up and see for yourself they were all right."

Blaine nodded as relief flooded through him. But with relief came crushing exhaustion, and he suddenly felt the strain in his back and overtaxed muscles from hours of twisting and hauling. He nearly staggered, bumping into Verran who also looked as if he were having trouble just staying on his feet.

"I've already given my other room to the potter until he can figure out what to do next," Ifrem said. "The rest of the rooms are already taken, and people are sleeping in the meeting room. And of course, there's my boarder." Ifrem's long-term, mysterious boarder was a permanent resident of the Crooked House. No one knew who he really was or what crime brought him to Edgeland, and if Ifrem knew, he wasn't saying.

"But folks who need a place to stay for the night are welcome to sleep in the common room. It's not much, but it beats trying to go home now, and it's warm enough with so many people and a few logs on the fire."

Blaine and Verran nodded their thanks.

"I'll save you a spot," Verran said. "Go check on your lady."

Blaine headed upstairs, and knocked at the door Ifrem had said was Selane's. When she opened it, he bit back a gasp. Selane's face and dress were soot-streaked, and her hair on one side looked like some of it had been burned. Her skin still looked reddened from the heat, and she cradled her bandaged left arm against her chest. Annalise didn't look much better.

"You're hurt," Blaine said, eyes widening.

Selane gave a wan smile. "Not badly. It could have been much worse. Mistress had been sleeping, and by the time she woke, the smoke was thick. We dragged her out, but by then, bits of the ceiling were falling in. 'Twas a close thing, getting down the steps."

"Too close." Blaine drew her into his arms, mindful of her injury, and kissed her. "I'm glad you're all right. All three of you."

"I was worried about you," Selane admitted. "I heard them say some of the people in the bucket brigade were hurt by pieces of the building. That's why I told Ifrem to send you up when you came in. I wanted to wait for you, but Mistress needed to lie down." She glanced behind her. "I'm afraid the smoke hurt her breathing. She doesn't sound good."

"Did you ask for a healer?"

Selane nodded. "Yes. Ifrem put out the word, but I imagine they're busy with more serious injuries right now. I just hope someone comes soon."

"I'll be right downstairs if you need anything," Blaine reassured her. "Just let me know."

She stretched up to kiss him, just a light brush of lips, but enough to convey so many things without words. Selane smiled at him, then closed the door, and Blaine headed downstairs. He spotted where Verran had found spots for them along the wall. Just sitting down felt so good, Blaine wanted to savor the moment.

"Kestel and Dawe will worry," Verran said. "Piran will just figure we drank ourselves soused and needed to sleep it off."

Blaine snorted. "Because that's a very Piran thing to do," he replied. "If they haven't already heard about the fire from someone tonight, I expect they'll know before we get home. This is Kestel we're talking about. Somehow, she'll know."

The toll of the evening hit him full force just then as if he'd finally spent the last of his reserves. Despite the press of people and the low murmur of conversation, Blaine leaned against the wall and let exhaustion overtake him.

ROUGH WATERS

BLAINE HAD HOPED TO FIND A WAGON HEADED BACK TOWARD THE homestead in the morning, but shortly after seventh bells, a ruckus in the street outside the Crowded House made enough noise that even the exhausted firefighters inside could not sleep through the din.

"I'll see what the fuss is about," Blaine said to Ifrem, dragging himself to his feet. "If it's nothing important, I'll get them to move on and take their racket somewhere else."

He stepped over bodies to make it to the door, weaving his way through the press of tired rescuers. The room smelled of smoke, sweat, and seawater, and a film of ashes covered the floor, shed from the hair and clothing of the bucket brigade.

The scent of burned wood hung in the air, mingling with the pervasive odor of fish from the harbor. But the cold wind felt clean, and he took a big breath to clear his lungs. Even his mouth tasted of ashes, and he hoped Ifrem had food and brew on hand.

Blaine joined the knot of colonists who were talking not far from the entrance to the Crooked House. "One went down for sure," Conal Dorin said to the listeners crowded around him. "One's still missing. And two of them came back short-handed."

He didn't need to hear the sadness in Conal's voice or see his sober expression to figure out what had happened. The herring fleet had gone out a few days ago, but it hadn't been his and Piran's turn to man the boats. Now, it sounded like something had gone drastically wrong.

"And the rest came back, just leavin' them there?" The speaker was a red-haired woman, and while Blaine didn't know her name, he did remember that she was married to one of the fishermen.

"There was naught to do, except sink the rest of the boats if we stayed," Conal replied, sounding as if he took the accusation personally. "Haven't seen a storm that bad in a long time. It didn't feel natural. Whipped up out of nowhere, and gone just as fast after it did its worst. We searched as long as we could. They're calling for volunteers to go search for bodies and the missing boat. Not sure they'll find anything."

"We'll be down two full crews, plus the men who went over-board," Tom Makillin said. "Plus however much of the catch was on the boats that didn't come back. There'll be shit from Prokief about meeting quota, mark my words."

Unfortunately, Blaine knew Makillin was right. Prokief would care far more about the lost herring and the missing boats and gear than about the lost crew members. And with the Long Dark nearly upon them, it would be hard to make up for the catch that was lost.

"Who didn't come back?" Vin Jonner asked. He often crewed on the boats, called busses, that Blaine and Piran fished on. Makillin rattled off more than two dozen names, and Blaine felt a stab of loss. He knew all of the missing men. They were good sailors, so if the storm bested them, it had been fierce indeed.

"We're getting up a search party," Makillin said. "I came up here to see if there was anyone at the pub willing to lend a hand."

"I'll go," Blaine found himself saying. Verran would tell Kestel and the others why he was late returning. With luck, it wouldn't hold up progress on the barn by more than a day or two.

"Thanks, Mick. I figured I could count on you." Makillin gave him a look up and down, as if only just noticing the ash and soot. "Oy. Are you up to it, if you were out all night with the fire?"

Blaine shrugged. "You'll be hard-put to find anyone who wasn't out, at least, anyone who could crew a boat. Took the whole damned night, but we stopped it on two buildings."

Makillin nodded. "I saw. Smoke's still rising but didn't see any fire. They say the potter's helper didn't make it out."

Blaine sighed. "Sorry to hear that." When he'd trudged back to the Crowded House in the wee hours, the fate of the apprentice hadn't been confirmed. Bay-town's wise women would be busy arranging the funerals, for the fire victims and those who died at sea.

"How many more do you need for the search boats?" Blaine asked. "The pub's full of everyone who didn't make it home last night."

"Maybe two more," Makillin replied. "We wanted to go out fast before word gets back to Prokief. If we can retrieve anything, it might temper the consequences."

Blaine agreed with the tactic but held little hope that it would save them from Prokief's wrath. Prokief's temper bordered on madness, and it was his wild rages that won him both acclaim on the battlefield and ostracism once he returned to civilized society. Up here, far from King Merrill's notice, Prokief ruled with

338 • GAIL Z. MARTIN

an iron fist, punishing any disappointment—real or imagined —severely.

"The guards are sure to make a report," Jonner warned.

Makillin nodded. "That's why we're going out right away. If we've already sailed, he can't tell us not to."

"Let me see who I can get," Blaine said and ducked back into the Crowded House. Several of the men were already awake, and once he told them about the tragedy, they were quick to volunteer. Verran promised to let Selane and the rest of their homestead know and wished the rescue crew good luck. Ifrem sent them off with boiled eggs baked in sausage and some bread and ale for the trip. Then Blaine headed out with the other volunteers, hoping to get the boats in the water before the guards mucked it up and made a bad day even worse.

———

Clear skies and good winds made a mockery of the savage weather on the previous day. The calm seas taunted them as if nature questioned the truthfulness of those who had borne witness to the storm. Blaine had already grown used to the fickle winds, and the fate that had befallen the unlucky herring crews was one every fisherman on Edgeland feared. Going out in the small boats was like placing a wager in a high-stakes game, and yesterday, the crews had lost their bet. Blaine would have said a prayer for the deliverance of the missing men, and for the safety of the rescuers, but he had long ago decided no one was listening.

Beck Ornsby captained the lead boat. He had been one of the lucky ones who had returned from the ill-fated trip and was determined to return to look for survivors now that they had gotten their injured crew and damaged boats safely to shore.

Despite having little rest since the last emergency, Blaine

found himself running on nerves and wide awake. The brisk wind drove sleep from his eyes, carrying the boats along at a fast clip.

Usually, the colonist crews bantered and joked, compared to the rigid discipline aboard the prisoner ships. But today, conversation was terse, with people speaking only when necessary. Some of the men prayed quietly, others kept their own counsel, staring off into the distance, thinking perhaps of times when they had cheated fate themselves. Blaine looked out over the cold, gray ocean, so large and pitiless, and shivered.

When they reached the area where the men had been lost, the four fishing boats sailed in a line, with sufficient space between to avoid collision but close enough that they would not overlook any barrels, bodies or castaways. Given the vast expanse of ocean, it seemed like a fool's errand, but Blaine knew they owed it to their lost companions to try.

Two of the rescue boats towed empty dinghies so that they could carry back anything they found. Wind, waves, and ocean predators could have spread anything that floated over a large area or pulled corpses and swamped boats to the bottom.

"There's something!" a man aboard the next boat over yelled, pointing to a bobbing speck. As they neared the spot, Blaine saw more flotsam and found himself hoping that it might be survivors. Instead, they found three herring barrels, and then two more. Blaine helped haul the cargo onboard, as voices began shouting from one of the other boats.

"A boat! There's the missing boat!"

Something heavy thudded against the side of Blaine's craft, just below the waterline. He looked over the side and swallowed hard. A corpse floated, face down, and waves rustled the dead man's hair and clothing.

"Poor sot," one of Blaine's companions said with a sigh. "C'mon lads, let's get him aboard."

The lead boat continued toward the missing ship, while the others retrieved a grim catch of bodies and a few more barrels. By the time they caught up, they had found four bodies and three more barrels, all from the boat that had foundered. The others of its crew had almost certainly drowned.

Cheers went up when Ornsby's boat reached the missing craft. As Blaine's crew approached, they could see that the mast of the errant ship had been snapped, and the small boat listed to one side. But there were men aboard the damaged boat, and when the boat came into range, Blaine could see that all but two of that ship's crew had survived.

"Let's get the living into one of the dinghies," Ornsby shouted. "Then we'll tow the *Tailwind* in behind us." That gave them a chance of saving the wreck's cargo, although Blaine doubted the shipwrights could repair the boat itself.

The slow return to Skalgerston Bay gave Blaine time to feel every aching muscle. Sadness for the lost sailors tempered the happiness of finding some of the missing men alive and being able to retrieve a portion of the cargo. The seas were always unpredictable, but this year, they had been worse than ever. Blaine could only hope for good fortune when he and Piran went back out with the fleet.

Onlookers lined the harbor as the fishing boats came in. Some were the partners and children of the missing fishermen, while many of the other men from the herring crews stood in small groups, anxiously watching for the rescue craft to return.

A cheer went up when the sailors from the damaged boat came ashore, but it muted quickly as Blaine and the others carried the drowned men onto the dock. The wails of mourners rose as families claimed the dead. Feeling awkwardly out of place, Blaine and the other men from the rescue boats brought the salvaged barrels to the dockside just as half a dozen guards came striding up.

"What's the meaning of this?" the captain demanded. "Why have the boats gone out off schedule, without permission?" He turned to a woman who hunched beside the body of her dead husband, inconsolable in their grief.

"Stop your caterwauling!" he ordered. The man glared at the assemblage, which had fallen grudgingly silent. "Speak up. I want answers!"

"One of the herring boats sank last night, and another was damaged in a storm and went missing. We went to find the missing sailors, retrieve the king's cargo, and bring home the bodies," Blaine answered.

"McFadden," the captain said with a sneer. "Should have figured that if there's trouble, you and Rowse would be in the middle of it."

Blaine spread his open palms. "No trouble, Captain. Just protecting the king's valuable resources and cargo."

"There wasn't a storm last night."

Could the man be any more stupid? Blaine wondered silently. "Not here on shore," he replied, keeping his tone carefully neutral and avoiding eye contact. He tried for just the right mix of enough confidence to not encourage the bully, but sufficient deference to avoid challenging the captain's pride. "But out on the sea, storms that never reach land come up out of nowhere."

"Boats don't go out without permission."

"It was an emergency," Blaine replied. "We would have lost the boats, all the men, and the rest of the cargo, which would mean not being able to meet our quota. That would look bad on the colony, and on the Commander. We didn't want to disappoint the king."

It was obvious that the captain wanted to find some way to exert his authority, but Blaine's wording had made it difficult to punish the colonists for protecting Prokief's interests. The captain gave the crowd a baleful glare, and everyone seemed to be holding their breath.

"Make sure the boats are fixed, and full crews go out in the morning," he snapped. "You'll be accountable for making up for any lost barrels." With that, he turned on his heel and led his guards back toward their garrison.

Blaine let out a long breath and saw the same relief of the faces of those around him. The widows sobbed quietly, pressing their kerchiefs over their mouths to muffle their grief. Ornsby came up beside Blaine and clapped him on the shoulder.

"Nice work. I thought we were goners for a moment."

For a moment, so did I. Blaine managed a tight smile. "Glad it worked out. If the worst is having to bring in more fish, I can live with that."

The guards operated with impunity as the sole law of the colony, and since Prokief oversaw any reports informing the king or his advisors about Edgeland, martial law remained unchecked. Like any conquered people, the colonists quickly learned subterfuge to survive. Informants went missing, easy to arrange in such a harsh land.

The throng of onlookers dispersed, leaving the families of the dead to carry away the bodies of their loved ones for burial. Blaine helped get the barrels to the nearest warehouse and lent a hand tying up the fishing boats and hauling the damaged craft far enough on shore that the tide wouldn't carry it out and sink it.

"Mick!" Verran threaded his way through the thinning crowd, scanning the faces until he spotted his friend.

"What's wrong? Is Selane all right? Did Mistress Denison take a bad turn?"

Verran shook his head. "No. Ifrem sent me to bring you back and let you know there's a meeting tonight, and he would like you to be there," he replied, dropping his voice so no one else would hear.

"Why me?" Blaine protested. "I've barely gotten my Ticket of Leave."

Verran gave him a look. "We've been out for months, and plenty of people knew you from before. Look—I don't know why, I just know what he said to tell you. So come on," he added, tugging at Blaine's arm.

Blaine cast a look back at the wharf, as the last of the people drifted away. Elation over having saved some of the men warred with sadness at not being able to rescue them all. And beneath it all burned a never-ending anger at Prokief and his guards for making their existence as difficult as possible.

On the way back to the Crooked House, Blaine filled Verran in on what had happened in the harbor, and the last-minute appearance by the guards. Verran swore under his breath, punctuated with some choice obscenities at the guards' mistreatment of the grieving families. Blaine shared his sentiments but saw little use in railing against a situation that couldn't be changed.

The Crooked House's common room had emptied out, with the colonists who had taken shelter during the storm finally returning to make the best of their lot. Blaine had gotten a look at the burned buildings in daylight on the way back from the wharf, and the damage looked even worse now that the smoke had cleared.

The potter's building was a total loss, and the roof and second floor of the bakery were also destroyed. Fortunately, the chandlery next door appeared to have only received some scorching and smoke damage, and Blaine hoped that Selane, Annalise, and Mistress Denison would be able to go back to work and not lose all the candles they had already made.

"Verran gave you my message?" Ifrem asked when Blaine and his friend entered.

Blaine nodded. "Yeah. What's going on?"

"Need to get everyone on board with rebuilding the two

shops that got destroyed," Ifrem replied, wiping up the bar and restocking from the busy night before. "Tempers are a bit frayed lately, what with the White Nights nearly over and people thinking of all the things they need to do before the dark sets in. Makes them prone to forget how we need to work together when things like the fire or the fishing boats going missing happen. It's never convenient, but in the long run, everyone gets what they need."

"All right," Blaine said, taking a seat at the bar. Ifrem put a plowman's lunch in front of him, egg, meat, cheese, and bread, and a cup of hot *fet*. Blaine realized he was starving. He cradled the warm cup, inhaling the aroma, before taking a sip of the bitter stimulant and hoping he could feel it coursing through his veins to revive him after a brutal two days.

"Do I get to sleep before then? Because I can't promise I'll make any sense otherwise."

"Sure. Selane, Annalise, and Mistress Denison headed back to their shop, so I've got two free rooms upstairs. Take your pick and grab some shut-eye. You've got a couple of candlemarks until the meeting."

Blaine shoved some more food in his mouth and washed it down with *fet*. "Why me?"

Ifrem slung his rag over his shoulder and looked at Blaine like he was dim-witted. "Because people listen to you. They trust you. I heard that you stared down the captain of the guard, at the harbor."

News traveled fast in Edgeland, especially if it was bad. Someone must have practically run from the harbor directly to the pub to carry that tale, but Blaine wasn't really surprised. Gossip was plentiful, but events worth discussing were relatively rare. They'd had enough excitement to last for months, packed into two days. Blaine hoped they were in for a long, boring winter. Excitement was almost never a good thing.

Blaine felt almost human again when Verran roused him from his nap. His muscles still ached, and his throat was scratchy from the smoke, but he no longer felt likely to drop over from exhaustion.

When he came downstairs, Blaine expected to see the Council, made up of the community members who had risen to positions of significant authority or influence as the representative for their guilds.

Instead, Blaine found the room full of the laborers and fishermen, tradespeople and worried volunteers, the people whose hands and hard work would rebuild what the fire had destroyed.

"We've got work to do rebuilding two shops and part of another, and the Long Dark is coming," Ifrem continued. Whispers started, and Ifrem held up a hand for quiet.

"I know we all have things that have to get done to be ready for winter. But we also rely on the potter, the chandler, and the baker, and they can't rebuild alone."

"We won't get far in the winter, no matter what, if the ships stop coming from Donderath," a man said from near the back of the room. Heads nodded in agreement, faces creased with worry.

"As concerned as we all about the late ships, that's a separate problem—one we have no control over," Ifrem replied. "If anything, it means we need to pull together tighter than ever, because we may have to find ways to do with less."

"Do with less?" A ruddy-faced man stood up. He had broad shoulders and thick arms from hard work, and Blaine thought he remembered the man working down on the docks. "By Torven's horns! We aren't magicians. We can't make something from nothing! With the ships, it's hard enough. Without them, we won't make it."

A ripple of anxiety fanned through the crowd. It was easy to see people's worry in their furrowed brows and tight-lipped expressions. Blaine shared their concern, but he also understood

Ifrem's point, and practicality needed to be the focus, not fears over things they couldn't change.

"We've made it this far; we're pretty damn hard to kill," Verran observed. That got a laugh, even from the dock worker.

"The reason for the meeting was to come up with work teams, take shifts," Ifrem said, calling the group back to order. "We built Bay-town by pulling together. We can rebuild the same way."

A dark-haired man stood up. His skin was leathery from years of labor outdoors stood. "I want to help. That's why I'm here. But how do we work these shifts and see to our own needs as well?"

Several voices piped up at once, debating various possibilities. Ifrem and Blaine exchanged a glance as if to say "what are you doing to do?" They let the discussion go on for a while, until it was clear the group had reached an impasse.

Blaine cleared his throat. "What if each team that works on rebuilding the shops in town also helps its members in return? So if there are six people on a team, each of the six people gets one day when the team shows up to help them with their own tasks, in repayment? That should speed your projects along, and be fair to everyone."

Heads nodded, and people whispered among themselves, considering the proposal. "If we work three teams in shifts while the White Nights last, we get three days' work done in one," Ifrem added. "And if we have a fourth team that's dedicated to bringing in the lumber, it should go even faster."

"Sounds good." Sven, the speaker, was a short, stocky man whom Blaine had often seen at the Crooked House, and among the wagon masters and day laborers who took on whatever jobs were needed. He seemed to know everyone, and his friends valued his opinion. He'd be a good man to have on their side. "I volunteer to lead one of the crews. I know a thing or two about building houses, enough to be dangerous, at least." The chuckles that spread through the group suggested Sven knew much more than he let on.

That kicked off a rush to form the teams. Blaine didn't commit to lead, but he did sign on to help. Verran walked up to one of the groups, then sauntered over to where Blaine stood by the bar.

"You agreed to help do construction?" Blaine asked, raising an eyebrow. Verran fetched tools and supplies and hammered nails when they built fences and sheds at their homestead, but after a couple of well-intended disasters, they had all agreed to let Verran tend the livestock and the kitchen, while Kestel lent a hand with the building.

"Of course not. I put in Piran's name," Verran replied with a grin.

"You know, if Piran and I have to stay in town to work on the teams, you, Dawe, and Kestel will need to pick up the slack on the barn, or it won't be done by the Long Dark, even with a day of help from the team."

Verran sighed. "It might be the death of me—or someone else, given my lack of talent—but of course, I'll help. I can fetch and ferry, and as long as I don't have to climb, I hit the nails most of the time."

Blaine sent Verran back to the homestead, with a message for Piran to come into town. He figured Verran would regale the others with all of the exciting news, and fill them in on the plan to rebuild the ruined shops. Delaying construction on their own barn bothered him, but Blaine resolved to trust to Kestel and Dawe's ingenuity.

If the weather held, the rebuilding might go quickly. Blaine had seen a barn raised in a day, and while the two shops were smaller, they were probably a bit more complex. Still, working day and night would probably have the task done in just a few days, and then Blaine could get on with readying the homestead for the Long Dark.

In the meantime, when he wasn't working or sleeping, the project gave him an excuse to spend more time with Selane, and lend a hand with the chandlery as well.

His shift didn't begin for a few more candlemarks, and Piran wouldn't get notice and be able to make it into town before then, so Blaine unexpectedly found himself with free time. He decided to make good use of it and walked down to find Selane.

A crew of eight men and women were already at work tearing down the potter's shop and clearing away the wreckage from the bakery. Blaine watched for a moment, noting that the guards stood well back, making no effort to help. Then again, they weren't keeping the crew from their work, which was as much as they could hope for.

As Blaine had expected, the potter's shop was a complete loss. Whether or not they could save the first floor of the bakery remained to be seen. That would depend on how much the fire had damaged the timbers that held the structure up, and the workers might not know until they had cleared away all the debris and seen just how far the flames had gotten.

As the workers swamped over the ruined buildings, the baker hauled sack loads of ruined baked goods out to a wagon.

"How bad is it, inside?" Blaine asked. Dawe and Kestel handled most of the baking for their group, but rare special occasions sometimes warranted a treat, and Blaine had chatted many times with Ronald, the bakery owner.

Ronald's shoulders slumped. His arms and face were darkened by soot, and a sprinkling of gray ash clung to his short, dark hair. "Bad enough." He coughed hard enough to make his eyes tear. "My pans and tools weren't damaged—that's important. Thank the gods. But I had my quarters above, and everything there is gone."

He gestured toward the loaves of bread and small cakes in the wagon. "Can't get the stink of the smoke out of them, or the taste. Might be able to feed it to the pigs, but that's about all it's good for." Ronald shook his head. "That's a day's work of baking, lost. And more days when I can't bake while we clean up the mess. All my flour, too. I don't know what I'm going to do."

"Talk to Ifrem," Blaine suggested. "See if you can use the kitchen and the oven at the Crooked House. He always bought his bread from you, right? You might be able to bake there, just until your place is cleaned up."

A spark of hope lit Ronald's eyes. "I've been so focused on the mess, I hadn't thought that far ahead, but you're right. It's worth a shot." He sighed and glanced up at the charred top floor. "Maybe he'll let me sleep in the kitchen, too. I might as well ask."

Bits of broken crockery and shards of pottery littered the street in front of the wreckage. The potter was nowhere to be seen, From what Blaine could make out, it appeared that the second floor had collapsed into the first, which likely meant that not only were the potter's wares ruined but his equipment as well. It was going to take quite a while for things to get back to normal for him.

Which left the chandler. The roof and upper floor of the building were darkened with soot and smoke, but nothing had actually caught on fire. The door stood ajar, and Blaine went inside, pausing as his eyes adjusted to the dimness.

"We're closed." Mistress Dennison barely glanced his way as she wiped down shelving with a rag. The shop smelled of smoke and creosote, and the ash in the air nearly made Blaine choke.

"I came to see if I could help," he said after coughing. "Whatever you need."

Selane looked up and smiled at him. She and Annalise and their employer were as soot-covered as chimney sweeps, and while they had bound up their hair with rags, Blaine doubted there was any way to keep the black dust from seeping into every crevice and pore.

"You can grab a broom, if you know how to use one," Mistress Dennison replied. "Don't know if we'll ever sweep this place clean, but we've got to start somewhere."

Blaine took the broom Selane offered, and used it on the walls as well as the floor, to get rid of the soot that was everywhere. Meanwhile, as Mistress wiped down shelving, Selane and Annalise sorted through the candles that were already made, setting any that were damaged aside.

"The ones that were open to the air will be gray, no helping that," Selane mused. "But they'll burn as well as ever, and once they're burned they're gone, so it shouldn't affect the price any."

"Did the smoke get to everything?" Blaine asked as he swept, trying to keep his strokes short to not raise new clouds of dust.

"No," Selane said, at the same time Mistress Dennison said, "Enough."

Selane wore a look that clearly said she was trying to raise her employer's spirits. "The wax we haven't molded yet is fine, although the top layer is gray. But if we add some coloring, no one might notice. And besides, people just burn them to a nub, and they'll do that same as always, so it shouldn't matter."

Mistress looked unconvinced. She was a thin woman in her forties, sent away—like Selane—on false accusations of theft. Rumor had it, she'd made her way in Edgeland for nearly twenty years, rendering tallow and purifying beeswax to make candles as good as any Blaine had used back in Donderath.

"I guess we'll see," Mistress replied. She sounded exhausted, and worry showed in the lines around her eyes and the set of her mouth. The gray in her short, dark hair couldn't all be blamed on fallen ash. Small burns marked her hands and arms, a hazard of her trade. "We were luckier than Frederick, the poor man," she added, meaning the potter. "We've still got a roof over our heads."

By the time Blaine had to go for his shift with the rebuilding crew, they had managed to get the front room of the shop in much better shape. Wiping down the windows let in more light and removed the film of smoke and soot. Selane had arranged the candles for sale to minimize the gray cast to the wax. Mistress and Annalise went to start working on the back room, where they made the wax and formed the candles, leaving Blaine and Selane alone for a few minutes, something Blaine knew was entirely intentional.

"I have to go, but I can come back tomorrow," Blaine offered. He wanted to pull Selane into his arms, but they dared not with Mistress likely to walk in at any moment. Instead, he brushed her arm with his fingers and took her hand. "I should have time before my shift."

Selane shook her head. "I'm glad you came today; it really helped." She dropped her voice. "Mistress was worried that the damage might be worse than it is, but I really don't think people will mind the color, and it's only for part of what we have in stock."

She tightened her grip on his fingers, giving him a look that Blaine read to mean that she, too, wished they could do more. But Mistress had her own ideas about respectability, and Blaine had no intention of causing problems for Selane with her employer. Still, he could not deny how much his attraction to her filled his dreams and daydreams.

"And now that we've got the shop fixed up, people can come in and buy, and we can tidy up the back as it suits us," Selane added. "I just don't want her to fret. It's not good for her heart." She glanced toward the other room as if afraid to be overheard. "I worry about her."

That kindness, unspoiled even after false accusation and the harsh conditions of Velant, was one of the things that had drawn Blaine to her. Blaine found himself yearning for Selane's gentleness. He vowed that she would never know the full truth about what had sent him to Velant, because he did not want to see disappointment in her eyes or prove unworthy of her love.

"What about your chambers upstairs?" Blaine asked. "Are they livable?"

Selane laughed. "They're still far better than Velant, or the cell at the prison before that! Just need some airing out, and a good scrubbing. Although my white shirt will never be right again," she added ruefully. Still, she had found the good to be had in the situation, and Blaine was grateful that she and her companions still had a safe place to stay.

The buzz of voices outside told Blaine the shifts were changing. "I need to go," he said and brought her fingers to his lips for a quick kiss. "But tomorrow, maybe I can bring all three of you something to eat, even if you don't need my help."

"I'd like that," Selane said, with an honesty that Blaine had found lacking in many of the young noblewomen he had met back in Donderath. Except for Carensa, his betrothed. Her memory still brought an ache to his heart, but time and the finality of exile had begun to dull the pain. He was as dead to Carensa as if King Merrill had made good on the threat to hang him, and he hoped for her sake that she had forgotten him and moved on.

"Then I'll see you tomorrow," he promised, finding that his step was lighter as he headed out to join the work crew.

———

Four days later, Blaine and Piran found themselves in the back of a wagon headed toward the homestead. Blaine glanced at the sky, noting that just in the time they had been gone, the daylight had grown a little shorter. Soon, the winter dark would be upon them.

"You know, the dark isn't so bad, not really," Piran said as if reading his thoughts. "We have a home this year, a proper one. Food enough that we won't go hungry—although Dawe and Verran aren't exactly good cooks. That's more than we've had for a long while." He grinned and elbowed Blaine in the ribs. "And since you've got an in at the chandler's, we won't run out of candles!"

Blaine chuckled. "I think we might even get a bargain, if we don't mind some smoke-gray ones for a while."

"I don't care, as long as they light," Piran replied. "I'm easy to get along with like that."

This time, Blaine snorted in laughter. Piran was many things, but "easy to get along with" was not one of them. "How many times has your nose been broken?" Blaine asked, raising an eyebrow. "They take bets on your card games down at the Crooked House because of the fights you get into over them."

"Just a little spirited discussion amongst friends," Piran replied, hiding a smile. "And the one thing I can't stand is someone who can't cheat well. Takes all the fun out of it."

"Uh-huh. You just hate it when anyone cheats better than you do."

"Well, of course. Misses the whole spirit of the game."

Blaine shook his head. Piran might never have exactly told his mates what infraction finally got him court-martialed and sent to Velant, but Blaine was certain it had more to do with his mouth and nothing to do with his loyalty. His friend might revel in being rough around the edges, but Blaine and Piran had been in too many tight spots together for Blaine to overlook the courage and determination Piran hid under a joking, foul-mouthed exterior.

He didn't care about the transgressions—real or imagined— that brought his friends to Edgeland. All that mattered was that they had come to a cold and hostile place and found each other, found their family. Even though he swore they would never know about the crime that earned him exile, Blaine felt humbled by their friendship, promising himself that he would overcome the taint of murder—patricide—to be worthy of their trust.

The wagon pulled down the lane to the homestead, and Blaine offered a few coins to the driver as he and Piran jumped out. They had no sooner started to make their way toward the barn when they heard shouting, and ran toward the noise just in time to see Kestel and Dawe take off after a dark shape, with swords drawn. Verran was outside the barn, trying to round up the goats and shoo them into the building. The fencing around their corral had been broken in one place, and Blaine saw a smear of fresh blood.

"What happened?" Blaine asked.

"What's going on?" Piran said at the same time.

Verran put his hands on his hips, staring at the milling goats. He looked scared and upset. "We heard a ruckus, and Kestel came out to check. Next thing she's shouting and yelling, so Dawe grabs his sword and comes running. You know Kestel; she always has a weapon on her." He ran a hand over his face and pushed back a flop of hair.

"This...thing had broken the fence and was chasing the goats around. I ran out of the house after Dawe, just in time to see the creature take off and them go flying after it." Verran shook his head. "Kestel yelled for me to see to the goats, so here I am. But we're short two. That damned monster took two of our goats!"

Blaine could see how upset the attack had made Verran. Since he didn't excel at construction, he had taken on more of the work of caring for their growing selection of livestock. Chickens, rabbits, goats, sheep, and a pig now lived in the pens and barn, and they were negotiating a share of a plow horse with other nearby homesteaders, so Verran handled their turn of care and feeding for it, too. They had all grown more attached to the animals than initially expected, especially Verran.

Verran had survived the brutal transportation to Edgeland and three years in Velant, and now he looked on the verge of tears over two goats. Blaine laid a hand on his shoulder. "I'm sorry. Piran and I will help rebuild the fence. Make it stronger this time. But do you know what took them? Was it a bear?" Blaine replayed the memory of the dark, lumbering shape that was already nearly out of sight as Kestel and Dawe raged after it.

"I don't know what it was," Verran said. "It was the right size to be a bear, but it moved wrong. And the head was an odd shape. They say there are strange creatures in the wilds here, ones we didn't have in Donderath." His eyes widened as if with the chaos and the effort to save the goats, it had just registered what Kestel and Dawe had done.

"Oh, gods! They went after it!"

Blaine scanned the horizon, hoping to see their friends returning, but saw no one. He and Piran exchanged a glance. "You think we should track them?" Piran asked.

Part of him wanted to agree and take off in search of their friends. But with no snow on the ground, tracking wouldn't be easy, and he trusted Kestel and Dawe not to engage the creature if they could avoid it.

"We don't know where they've gone," he said. "And we also don't know whether that thing had friends. We'd probably better see to the corral, and figure out how we can make it stronger. Now that one of them's found us, they'll be back."

Verran stayed in the barn, calming the frightened goats and arranging a temporary pen. Blaine and Piran gathered some wood, tools, and nails, and headed for the ruined corral.

"Looks like Dawe and Kestel got more of the roof finished

while we were gone," Piran said, eyeing the nearly completed barn.

"That's good. If we can get a little more done ourselves, having the work crew come out for the day they owe us might finish it off," Blaine agreed.

They stopped at the gate to the corral. "Shit," Piran said. "Whatever it was that did this is going to be a problem."

The corral had been made from stout logs as uprights and cross pieces, with wooden slats nailed between the horizontal supports to keep the goats from jumping through. One section had been smashed, leaving four deep claw marks in the wood. The weight and strength necessary to create that damage made it clear that the creature posed a significant threat.

"We were lucky," Blaine replied as he began picking up splintered pieces and tossing them outside the fence." It could have gotten more of the goats—or gone after Verran."

A candlemark later, Dawe and Kestel came trudging back, unbloodied and dejected.

"We lost it," Dawe informed them. "Hard to track it without snow, and the thing moved damned fast." He turned to Verran. "I'm really sorry."

Kestel swore a blue streak, letting them know how she felt about the failure to avenge the dead goats.

Blaine clapped a hand on Dawe's shoulder. "Glad you got back safely." Kestel stayed a distance away from the others, and Blaine knew when her temper was high, she didn't want to be touched, even in reassurance. Her murderous expression made no secret of her mood.

"I'm going to go split some wood," she muttered and strode toward the pile at the back of the house.

"Was it a bear? Big cat?" Piran asked.

Dawe shrugged. "We didn't get a good look at it. It was the size and shape of a bear, but it didn't run like one. It was quick like a cat, but the movements and profile were all wrong." He met Blaine's eyes. "I don't think it's something we've seen before."

"Shit." Blaine put his hands on his hips and turned to survey the horizon as if he might suddenly spot the creature. "I guess it's not a surprise. The bigger the colony gets, the farther out into the wilderness we push. Homesteads. Logging. Stands to reason that we'll run across whatever lived here first."

"The question is—how do we keep those things from coming back?" Verran asked. He had regained his composure, and now he just looked angry. "We don't need to kill it if it will just stay away."

"If we had someone with more than hedge witch magic, they could probably make a barrier. But they don't send mages to Velant." Piran remarked.

"No, but don't underestimate what a good hedge witch can do," Blaine said. "Let's get the fence fixed and reinforced, and tomorrow I'll go see the wise women about a warding of some kind."

"Be careful," Piran warned. "We don't need to attract notice —or call attention to the hedge witches we do have."

Blaine held up his hands, palm out, in appeasement. "I'll be careful. But we're not the only ones out here on the edge of the colony, and those creatures are likely to come back. Maybe the wise women already have something figured out that we haven't heard about. If not, we won't be the only ones who need a solution."

"I'm not telling you not to go," Piran said. "Just…be careful."

Blaine raised an eyebrow. "That's rich, coming from you."

"Yeah, well. I'm all about 'do as I say, not as I do,'" Piran tossed back with a grin.

The sound of an ax cracking through logs let them know

Kestel was working out her anger. "Come on," Blaine said. "Let's finish up the fence." He glanced up at the barn roof, taking stock of just how much progress his friends had made while he and Piran were in town.

"You got a lot done," Blaine said.

Verran managed a smile. "We didn't want to get too far behind and figured that you and Piran were doing your part in town, so we'd step up. I swear Dawe and Kestel didn't let me build anything too important."

Verran's skills weren't quite as bad as he suggested, although construction didn't come naturally to him. Nailing the stall dividers together and building shelves for storage suited his abilities quite well.

"It looks good," Blaine replied, relieved that they hadn't lost time. "And the people who were part of our shift to rebuild the shops owe us a day out here, just like Piran and I owe each of them a hand. With that much help, we might just have it finished sooner than we thought."

By the time they finished with the fence, the sun was low in the sky. Blaine had lost track of when he heard the woodcutting finally stop; the sound went on for a long time, a testimony to Kestel's foul mood. When Blaine, Piran, and Verran finally dragged themselves inside, Dawe had a kettle of cabbage and potato soup ready, along with fresh bread.

Kestel had washed away the sweat of the hunt and the hard labor of splitting wood. Windburn reddened her cheeks, and the look in her eyes now seemed more regretful than homicidal.

"I think until we see if the hedge witches can help us, one of ought to sleep out in the barn with the animals," Kestel said after Blaine and Piran had filled them in on everything that happened in Bay-town.

"Bad enough to lose more goats," Piran replied, "but worse to lose one of us."

"Nothing survives an ax and a sword," Kestel returned, giving Piran a level glare.

"Nothing that we know of," Blaine said. "Verran and Dawe said the thing you saw was much faster than normal. Fangs, teeth, and muscle are already advantages in a fight. Speed would be lethal."

"Then take a crossbow," Kestel muttered. "It won't outrun that."

"I think you're just in the mood to kill something," Piran joked. He was always the one most likely to poke the bear and survived because Kestel usually enjoyed his humor. Today, Blaine wasn't sure he'd have risked it, given her temper, but Piran—as usual—was undaunted.

"I am. And that might include you," Kestel replied, although her tone tempered her words. She shook her head. "I just don't like being a target. We've worked too damn hard to build what we have here for some mad bear-thing to set us back."

"I'll leave in the morning, first thing," Blaine promised. The White Nights made it more difficult to gauge time, and judging by intervals marked on wax candles was only approximate. To prevent utter chaos, the colonists did their best to maintain a schedule that mimicked the day and night cycle back in Donderath. Blaine had no intention of barging in on the wise women after they had already retired for the evening.

"All right," Kestel gave in grudgingly. "I hope they can help. But if they can, why aren't wardings already a matter of course? The colony isn't new."

"No, but for years, it didn't go this far out into the wilds," Piran said. "I doubt anyone bothered to map the wilderness or figure out what lived here. It's not like the people in charge care whether we live or die."

Blaine figured Piran was correct. No one from the colony ventured to the mountains visible in the distance on a clear day.

Judging distance across the empty wasteland tundra was difficult, and Blaine reckoned that the mountain range was much farther away than it looked. Hunters stuck close to the settled areas, not daring to travel far beyond the edge of civilization.

"When I go to see the wise women, I'll stop by Johan's farm and see what he's heard from the hunters. If the creature comes back, we should put a hunting party together," Blaine replied.

"If that happens, count me in," Kestel said. "That thing came on our land, broke our fences, and took our goats. It's personal." The fire in her eyes reminded Blaine that Kestel's crimes had included more than a few assassinations.

"We wouldn't have it any other way, sweet lady," Piran said, rising from his chair and giving an elaborate bow with the courtly sweep of his arm. He looked so completely out of place that they couldn't help laughing, even Kestel. Piran's grin made it clear he counted lightening the mood to be a success.

Blaine made good on his promise early the next day, hitching a ride with a wagon bound for Bay-town to get to Johan's homestead. The old hunter's cabin sat on the small square of ground that was the allotment given to an individual convict when he earned his Ticket. Every inch was put to good use, with a well, neat garden beds, a coop for chickens and an enclosure for goats. A scrappy dog barked at Blaine's approach, and he noticed sigils carved into the wooden gateposts that he did not recognize.

"Quiet, Henry," Johan hushed the dog, which returned to his side. "Hello, Mick. Didn't expect to see you here." He opened the gate, and Blaine noticed that the older man made an odd gesture over the latch before releasing it.

Johan motioned for Blaine to follow him into the cabin. The hunter walked with a pronounced limp, a reminder of a hunt gone wrong. He wore a knit cap pulled down over his bald pate, and a jacket over his homespun shirt and trousers.

Inside, the cabin had a practical comfort to it that appealed to

Blaine. Johan lived alone except for Henry the dog, and he was in his sixth decade—old for Edgeland. Despite his injury, Johan still hunted, and his exploits were legendary—even if they were, as Blaine suspected, somewhat embellished. Still, he had been hunting in Edgeland longer than most people. If anyone should know about the creatures that hid in the shadows of the mountain, it would be Johan.

"I don't get much company," Johan said, taking a kettle off the hearth. He filled his own cup and took down a second up from a shelf for Blaine. The *fet* was brewed strong and dark. "What brings you here, Mick? I don't imagine you came to hear my stories, since you've heard them all plenty of times down at the Crooked House."

Blaine chuckled. "Actually, I did. I need to hear your tales about the monsters out on the ice."

Johan sat back in his chair, cradling his cup in his hands, and considered his words for a moment before speaking. "Huh. Well. You've been out on hunts, Mick. We keep to the hunting grounds for a reason. There are things out there, in the wilderness, that are much worse than bears and wolves."

"One of those things raided our goat pen yesterday," Blaine replied. "If we had a truce with the monsters, I'm not sure they're honoring it anymore. Our homestead is one of the farthest out, but there are a few others—and when the next batch of prisoners get their Tickets, they'll push farther yet."

Johan nodded. "I saw the carcass of one of those creatures, some years back. It was the size of a boar, with a pushed-in face and squashed nose, with sharp teeth and tusks, and nasty claws. I don't know what killed it. Not sure I want to know. But the body was all torn up, chewed on, too. Looked like something had eaten its fill, and tried to drag it away. I think maybe we scared whatever-it-was off for a while, but I expect it came back. Don't waste food up here, man or beast."

The thought that a creature like that faced its own predators made Blaine shiver. "How do we keep things like that away from our farm? I didn't live through Velant just to get torn up by a monster."

"The wise women gave me some mixtures to put all around my land—smells like hog waste, only worse," he replied, wrinkling his nose. "Gave me some other charms, too, to bury in the ground. And one of them taught me to carve those marks in the fence posts. So far, that's all worked. Even the foxes and wolves keep clear."

"I'm heading to the wise women after this," Blaine replied. "I figured they'd know something. Can you teach me to make the witch marks?"

Johan drained his cup without even grimacing at the bitter mixture. "I can. You don't have to be a witch to make them work —the magic's in the intent, or so she said when she gave them to me." He peered at Blaine in challenge. "But you'd best hope the guards don't come sniffing around. If they notice them, they take a dim view of that sort of thing."

Blaine gave a harsh laugh. "I do my best to stay far away from the guards."

Johan shrugged. "Ain't you the one who lives with Piran Rowse and Kestel Falke? Trouble seems to follow them."

Blaine couldn't argue that, nor the fact that he'd ended up crosswise with the guards himself on too many occasions. Even in Velant, Prokief's dislike seemed oddly personal, though— thank the gods—the commandant had not bothered to cause problems for Blaine since his release.

"Lately, we've been too busy for that," Blaine told him. "We're trying to get set up before the Long Dark sets in."

Johan got up and limped toward the fireplace, then came back with a small chunk of smooth wood. He pulled a knife from the sheath on his belt and scratched the same symbols into the wood that Blaine had seen on the fencepost.

"This is rough magic," Johan said. "Hedge witch stuff. Still, it works. Drawing the marks like this don't mean a thing. They're just scratches. To make the magic work, you need to will it into the wood. Intention, like I said. Then you seal it with a drop of your blood, smeared across the markings. If you're doing a big fence, and you don't care to bleed that much, they told me I could piss on it, too. Didn't try that, but I imagine it would work."

"Can more than one person help set the wards?"

Johan shrugged. "I suspect so. Don't know why not. But mind, the warding only lasts until the person who sets it dies."

"All right," Blaine replied. "You said it kept away regular foxes and wolves. What about bad people?"

Johan burst out laughing. "You mean like convict-type people? Son, we're all bad people up here, thieves and liars and murderers. If the wardings kept out bad people, I wouldn't be able to get to my own house."

Blaine smiled ruefully. "Guess you're right on that," he allowed. "I didn't say it quite right. I meant people who intend to do harm."

"I don't rightly know," Johan replied. "I ain't never had anything stolen, but then again, folks know I'm quick with a knife. And there's nowhere for a thief to run up here, so unless he can eat what he steals, it won't do him much good—he'll be caught quick. But still…no one's broken in or bothered my things. So whether that's the marks or my reputation for being a tough son of a bitch, I couldn't tell you."

Blaine finished his cup of *fet* and spent a while trading news from Bay-town with Johan, who seemed to enjoy the company. Henry curled at Johan's feet, and the older man reached down to pet the dog's ears now and again. Finally, Blaine took his leave and promised to stop by with a loaf of bread in payment for the advice, then headed down the road.

It was a long walk to reach the compound where the wise women lived. They were the matriarchs of the colony, the elders who had survived a harsh life in Donderath, the horror of Velant, and the hardscrabble existence of Edgeland. Those who no longer pursued a trade in town had moved to a self-sufficient homestead, where people who needed their help or advice sought them out.

He waited nervously at the gate after ringing the iron bell. Inside the fence, a garden of herbs, vegetables, and healing plants sprawled in full summer glory. The squawk of chickens and the bleating of sheep sounded from close by. The main house was a functional rectangle, large enough to house quite a few residents. A black cat slipped in and out between the plants, while a large dog came racing toward the gate, barking an alarm.

"That's enough, Ivan." The speaker, a stout woman with short gray hair and a round face, appeared from somewhere amidst the flower beds, and the dog quieted immediately. She wiped her hands on the dirt-streaked gardening apron she wore over a tan homespun shift. Ivan kept a wary eye on Blaine, but he wagged when she came closer and patted him on the head.

"I'm Mick McFadden," Blaine hurried to introduce himself. "From the homestead down the road a piece. I'd like to speak with you. We've had an attack from a wild creature, and we were hoping there might be some kind of protections your folks might help with."

"My name is Mariel," the woman replied. She gave a hand signal to the dog, and he trotted off, back toward where the sounds of livestock rose. "I can't promise we can do anything, but I'd like to know more about these attacks."

Blaine followed Mariel to the small courtyard in front of the house, where benches near a patch of wildflowers afforded a place to enjoy Edgeland's rare moderate weather. Today was cool but not cold, and Blaine enjoyed the sunshine while it lasted, before the long night set in.

"Tell me," Mariel commanded. Though a foot shorter than Blaine, the woman had a sense of presence and carried herself like someone who expected people to listen when she spoke.

Blaine recounted what had happened with the goats, and the way the beast had easily outpaced Kestel and Dawe when they pursued it. Mariel's eyes narrowed, and she pursed her lips as she considered his story.

"That's not good at all," she replied. "We've heard reports from the hunters that they've seen creatures out on the ice that aren't anything they recognized from Donderath. A few hunting parties haven't returned, and the traces that were left didn't match the behavior of regular bears or wolves."

Edgeland had plenty of "normal" predators—bears, wolves, and big cats. Even the moose and elk prized by the hunters had dangerous antlers and could be fierce when cornered. Blaine had heard some of the old men down at the Crooked House tell tales of monsters that lived in the mountains, but he had chalked that up to tall tales. Now, after talking with Johan, he knew there was a seed of truth in those stories.

"Can you do anything to ward off those creatures?" Blaine asked. "We've built stronger fences and hung up all the scrap metal we could find, so it bangs together in the wind, thinking to scare them off. But we were hoping that maybe you had wardings of some kind, for protection?"

Mariel nodded. "We have some natural banes that we can make for you. They work well against regular predators. I can't guarantee they'll hold off these strange beasts. We've tried to gather everything that's known about them, and it's hard to tell facts from stories."

"Anything would be appreciated," Blaine replied. "I fear that the farther out the homesteads spread, the more of these problems we're likely to have."

"I agree. This latest group to earn their Tickets pushed the edge of the colony farther out than ever before," Mariel said. "It will only get worse, as more convicts become colonists, unless Donderath stops sending us their exiles."

If Edgeland stopped being useful as Donderath's dumping ground, the kingdom might forget they existed at all. Herring and minerals aside, the goods that Edgeland sent back to the homeland was of much less value than the prison itself. The dark humor of the colony being an oubliette no longer seemed funny. Oubliettes were places wretches were consigned until they starved to death. The comparison had never been flattering, but now Blaine found it chilling. If Donderath stopped sending supply ships, Edgeland would find survival even more difficult —maybe, impossible.

"Wait here," Mariel instructed. "I'll fetch you some of the mixture we've put together, and make a few adjustments. A bit of something special might help." Whether or not that extra boost came from magic, she did not say.

Alone in the garden, Blaine watched the cat slink beneath the leaves. Then he realized that there were several cats of various colors, all silently hunting whatever small vermin had the bad luck to trouble the plantings. Ivan, the dog, left the cats alone and didn't return. Before long, Mariel came back with a large jug. Even at a distance, its contents smelled foul.

"This isn't pleasant, but that's the point," she confessed, setting the heavy container on the ground. "The mixture is potent, but it seems to work. I've added in some extras, which will hopefully hold off the kind of creature you described. Best you do this right away, while you can still dig in the ground before it freezes. Make a hole about as deep as your four fingers together, and pour in five or ten drops in each hole. Make your holes about every six feet, all the way around your property. If you have any of the mixture left, save it to reinforce the wardings later."

"What does it do?" Blaine asked.

"It's a combination of scent marking and plant magic, with leaves and powders that carry a strong protective energy," Mariel replied.

"Thank you," Blaine said. "I'm very grateful."

Mariel nodded in acknowledgment. "You're welcome. And if you hurry to the road, there should be a wagon passing soon," she added with a smile.

Blaine suspected the woman's foresight informed her, but he was grateful for a ride to take him back to the homestead. He had no sooner reached the side of the road when a wagon master came into view. Blaine hailed him and arranged to be let off near the farm.

The jug was too heavy to carry at arm's length, but holding it in the crook of his arm made Blaine's eyes water long after his nose no longer registered the stink. He took the container straight to the barn, though he felt certain the odor lingered on his clothing even though he hadn't spilled a drop.

From the reaction of his friends, Blaine knew the smell clung to him, but despite their pinched noses and tearing eyes, they listened as he recounted what he had learned from Johan and Mariel.

"Still got plenty of daylight," Piran said when Blaine finished. "The sooner we finish, the sooner we can all sleep in the house instead of having to sit up on watch in the barn."

Verran and Kestel took the chunk of wood Johan had used to show the sigils, and set about making fence posts and gates with the protective runes. That left Blaine, Dawe, and Piran the task of digging holes, pouring in the hedge witches' mixture, and filling them back in again, all around the edge of their property.

"The plot didn't seem this big, before we had to dig a hole every six feet," Piran grumbled after they had been at their task for several candlemarks.

"I'm never going to be able to smell anything else, ever again," Dawe replied. "By the gods! That's awful stuff!"

Blaine shrugged. "I guess the creatures think so, too. Maybe they think something bigger and badder has already marked the territory. And I'm certain Mariel added a magical element. But no matter how bad it smells, it's worth it if the potion works."

When they finally finished, the day was far spent, and they trudged back to the house. Blaine's arms and back ached from the digging, and he blamed the nausea he felt on the rank odor of the mixture. But the perimeter had been warded, and if Mariel was correct, they were safe.

"I should be hungry, but thinking of food after that awful smell makes me want to retch," Piran confessed.

"I'm a little queasy, but not enough to pass up dinner," Dawe replied. His tall, lanky build always looked a little gaunt. "I'll eat yours if you don't want it," he teased.

"Forget that," Piran replied. "I'll eat. Probably can't smell a damn thing, but I'll eat."

They took pains to wash up before they came back to the house, although Blaine and the others had been careful to keep the noxious mixture from touching their skin. They took turns standing by the fireplace, hoping the smell of smoke would override the potion's smell.

Kestel and Verran wandered in just as Dawe put a cauldron onto the hearth full of potatoes, leeks, and onions. That, along with the loaf of bread that sat cooling on the table would be soothing and filling.

"By blood and piss, we should be warded," Verran announced. Kestel had a cloth wrapped around her left palm, making it clear who had contributed what to the undertaking. "Let's just hope it works."

They bantered over dinner, jokes and comments that were comfortable and familiar. Near the end of the meal, Blaine cleared his throat.

"The group from our rebuilding shift should be out in the next day or so, and that should finish off the barn roof. The fences are done, and the house is complete." His heart beat faster, since he knew what he was about to say. "With all that done, and the harvest coming up, we'll be in good shape for winter, all set up. So I was thinking about it, and...I've decided to marry Selane at Light's End."

3

LIGHT'S END

BY THE TIME THE WHITE NIGHTS ENDED AND THE LONG DARK loomed ahead, the colony was ready for the Light's End winter festival. Colonists worked in teams or individually on ice sculptures and snow statues in fanciful shapes. Candles inside the ice sculptures made them glow, a refusal to allow the darkness to win. Residents hoarded food and special ingredients to recreate feast day foods from back home. Some sported embroidered vests or aprons worn only for special occasions. Garlands made from straw flowers hung across the village green and adorned windows and doorways.

Here in Edgeland, the feast day was one of the most important times of the year, when the long days gradually gave way to night.

Edgeland made as merry as its limited resources allowed. Colonists hoarded candles to be able to splurge come feast day, while Ifrem and others brewed extra beer and distilled more whiskey, and bonfires lit the gloaming. Verran and the other musicians played for the colonists who sang and danced at the gatherings held throughout Bay-town, and for once, the guards kept their distance.

Tradition held that Light's End was also a time for endings and beginnings. Those who had lost friends or loved ones visited their graves, to say their name and recite a blessing. The wise women's magic could prevent conception, and meant few babies were born in Bay-town, but those that were, received a prayer to the gods for a good life. Livestock was also blessed, shops received a thorough sage smudging, and huge cauldrons of bean soup offered colonists a warm supper said to bring good luck in the new year.

The wise women presided over births and deaths, handfastings and housewarmings, and were the ones colonists called for help when illness struck people or animals, or blight-withered crops. They were the history keepers and the judges, and in the eyes of the colonists, far more credibly the lawgivers than Prokief would ever be.

Handfastings were popular at the festival, for the symbolism of ending the past and starting fresh. And so Blaine found himself standing inside a large circle of candles, palms sweating and mouth dry as he awaited his bride. Behind him, his housemates stood in as family. Mariel and several of the wise women led the procession that led Selane and her chosen family— Annalise and Mistress Dennison—to the circle.

Blaine tugged at his collar. Behind him, Piran chuckled at Blaine's nervousness. Dawe shushed Piran. Verran played a popular ballad on his penny whistle. Kestel stood to Blaine's right, watching the proceedings with an unreadable expression, scanning the small group of witnesses and well-wishers as if she expected an assassin to pop from their midst.

Selane looked pretty and happy, with her hair in an elaborate braid, woven through with straw flowers for good luck. A beautifully embroidered robe, borrowed for the occasion, covered her workday dress. Blaine had chosen his best shirt and pants, and with a haircut and a fresh shave, tried to make himself presentable. He met Selane's gaze and smiled as Mariel led her to the circle of candles.

Selane wore a crown of woven straw and carried a bundle of dried flowers and a small fir bough. She walked into the circle and stopped, facing Blaine, ready to begin the ceremony.

Up here at the end of the world, the exiles had shed many things from their homeland, but the festivals and rituals remained. As custom demanded, Blaine withdrew a hunting knife from the sheath on his belt and presented it across his open palms.

Selane accepted the knife-gift and passed it to Annalise. Mistress Dennison gave Selane a gift for her response—another knife, with two rings slipped onto its pommel. Blaine let her lay the blade on his outstretched hand and inclined his head in acceptance. Mistress stepped closer, taking the knife and removing the rings. Dawe had forged them from copper, using his expertise as the silversmith he was before his exile. Selane slipped the larger ring on Blaine's hand, and he did the same for her with the smaller ring. Then Mistress took their hands and lightly bound them together with a ceremonial cord, completing the handfasting.

The next moments passed in a blur. All Blaine saw was the light reflected in Selane's eyes and the promise of her smile. He had grown very fond of Selane, and if it wasn't quite the passion he had felt for Carensa, it was more than enough to fill the cold, lonely nights with a lover and companion.

Piran gave a loud whoop from behind them. Verran's song changed from a popular love ballad to a jaunty dance tune. Blaine led Selane out of the circle and out among their friends, who greeted Blaine with backslaps and Selane with hugs. The crowd had been making merry all day, so few people held back when Verran's music called them all to dance. Ifrem served drinks, and a table placed at the edge of the clearing held a variety of special breads and treats made specially for the feast day and for the wedding.

"You make me very happy," Blaine said, taking Selane in his arms and swaying to the music.

"You make me happy, too," Selane replied, meeting his gaze. He could read her affection and desire in her eyes.

Tonight, they would dance and see out the last of the feast day with their friends, then retire to a room upstairs at the Crooked House that Ifrem had reserved for them. Tomorrow, Blaine would bring his new wife to the homestead, where she would live for three days each week, then spend the other four days staying with Mistress Dennison and Annalise at the chandlery.

Most people in town knew Blaine, and many remembered Selane from the candle shop. Acquaintances cornered them in between songs to pass along congratulations and well-intentioned advice. Several candlemarks into the evening, Blaine paused as he sipped his drink and glanced around the still-crowded room. He spotted Verran taking a break with the other musicians. Piran and Dawe lounged in a corner with some of the men they all knew from the herring boats. But Kestel was nowhere to be seen.

"I'll be right back," Blaine said to Selane and wove through the crowd to reach Verran. "Where's Kestel?"

Verran looked up, pausing from the rowdy conversation among the other performers. "She caught a ride back to the homestead a few candlemarks ago. Said she was worried because one of the sheep was sick and wanted to keep an eye on the ewe."

Kestel was arguably the most sociable of all of them, aside from Verran. It wasn't like her to leave one of Edgeland's rare celebrations early. Then again, the responsibilities of the farm were new to them all, and for as cynical as Kestel was about people, she seemed exceptionally concerned about the livestock's wellbeing.

"Piran said he has a ride lined up for the three of us once things here break up," Verran added. "So she won't be alone long. We'll check on her and the sheep when we get back."

That lessened Blaine's worry, although he still felt unsettled. Then someone clapped him on the shoulder to offer best wishes, and he chalked his uneasiness up to wedding-day jitters.

The crowd drifted away around twelfth bells. Piran, Dawe, and Verran said their goodbyes, along with offering some ribald suggestions, and headed out to the wagon that would take them back to the homestead. Once Ifrem closed the bar, the rest of the wedding guests and onlookers cleared out, leaving Blaine and Selane to head back to the pub alone.

"It was a lovely evening, but I'm glad it's over," Selane confessed once they reached the privacy of their room.

Blaine drew her close for a kiss. "Agreed. But I'm glad it's just us now." She settled against him, and he wrapped his arms around her, taking in the warmth of her body and the smell of her hair. Truly happy moments were rare on Edgeland, and Blaine was intent on enjoying every second.

———

When Blaine and Selane reached the homestead the next day, he paused to consider how the farm might look to her. The house withstood its first winter in good stead, sturdy and warm. The barn and outbuildings had weathered storms and remained solid. A good first crop from their planting filled bins with cabbages and other vegetables that would winter over, and come spring, their chickens, rabbits, and goats were likely to multiply. Blaine felt a surge of pride that he and his friends had managed to create all this from their convicts' allowance, and a rush of warmth at the family they had built, which grew now by one new addition.

"It's very nice," Selane remarked, standing next to Blaine and slipping an arm around his waist. "You've all worked hard to make it happen." She looked up at him. "You know that I'll do my share, the days I'm here. I want to belong here, with your friends."

He bent to kiss her forehead. "You do belong. Always." He took her hand despite their heavy gloves, and they walked down the lane to the gate. Blaine made the gesture that released the wards to let them through, then reactivated the sigils.

"There's something I want to show you before we go inside." He led Selane to a small hill at the edge of the fenced area. "During the White Nights, you can see all the way to the harbor," he said, pointing. "It's peaceful up here. You can almost forget where we are." Blaine didn't point out that if he looked in the other direction, he'd see the hulking shadow of Velant Prison.

"It's beautiful," Selane said. "I'm looking forward to seeing it in the spring."

Blaine smiled. "There are some trees and bushes that bloom when things get green. I like to come up here when I need to think." He remembered something and dug a hand into his pocket.

"I made this for you. It's just something little, but I had some time on my hands, and…well. I thought you might like it." He handed over a small wooden carving of a bird he had whittled. Blaine had taken up whittling during the long evenings last winter and had been pleased when others could identify what he'd tried to carve.

"Thank you," Selane said, folding the carving between her hands. "It's lovely." She stretched up and kissed him on the cheek. "I know I'm going to like it here."

The smell of fresh bread and cooked sausages filled the house, enveloping them as they entered. Dawe was in the kitchen, and he smiled when they came in. "We wondered how long it would take for you to make it out here," he said, stepping away from the table where he was working the dough for another loaf. "There's hot bread and fresh butter, and plenty of sausage," he added, gesturing toward plates.

Blaine helped Selane with her coat, and they hung their hats and scarves on pegs near the door, leaving their wet boots near the entrance as well. Selane had only brought a few items with her, since she would be splitting her time between the homestead and the chandlery, so there was little to move into Blaine's room.

"Thank you. It smells wonderful," Selane said, stepping up to take a slice and spread it with butter. Blaine did the same, suddenly aware of just how hungry he was.

"Where is everyone?" he asked Dawe.

"Piran is sleeping off what he drank last night," Dawe replied with a look of exasperation. "Verran went out to feed the chickens, and then see if he could help Kestel in the barn."

Blaine frowned. "Did things go badly with the sheep she was worried about?"

Dawe shrugged and looked away. "I think the sheep was all right, in the end. But Kestel spent the night in the barn, just in case. After what happened in the fall, she doesn't like when we all leave at once, says it leaves the whole place vulnerable."

Selane went to pour both of them cups of *fet* from the kettle on the hearth, and Blaine wrapped a warm sausage in another slice of bread. "We set all the protections," he replied and remembered that he hadn't told Selane everything about seeking the wise women's help with the creature that had attacked the goats.

"You know Kestel," Dawe said. "She's wary—and usually

rightfully so. It can't be helped, sometimes, for us all to be gone, but I think it's a good idea to do it as seldom as possible."

That could be difficult during the weeks when Blaine and Piran went out with the herring fleet, and Verran had his regular nights to play at the Crooked House. Dawe worked when the blacksmith needed an extra hand, which was more and more often as more convicts became colonists. Once Dawe saved enough money to have his own forge at the homestead, he wouldn't need to leave, but that was a distant dream.

"I can't say that I'm happy about leaving Kestel here alone for long stretches, either," Blaine countered. "Doesn't seem fair."

"I can take care of myself." Kestel appeared in the doorway, looking a bit worse for wear from her night in the barn. Her cheeks and nose were red from cold, and bits of straw clung to her cloak. "There's just not much call for what I'm good at here in Edgeland, so I might as well be the one to tend the animals and keep the farm running while you all bring in the money we need to pay for things."

Of course, if the homestead really did well, they had talked about earning some additional coin selling off the portion of the harvest they couldn't eat or store themselves, extra wool, and surplus goats, rabbits, and sheep. Dawe and Kestel had even plotted to foray into making cheese and butter from the goats' milk. In time, that could leave Kestel presiding over a busy—and lucrative—farm market, and Blaine knew she would do very well.

"Welcome," she said to Selane as if realizing, belatedly, that she hadn't greeted them. "And congratulations." Her voice sounded unusually clipped.

"What's wrong?" he asked.

Kestel glanced at Selane as if unsure how much to say, then seemed to realize that the newcomer was now a member of the family. "I think someone—or something—is watching us."

"The beast that took the goats?" Dawe asked.

Kestel shrugged. "Not sure—but I'm going to find out. I was jumpy when the wagon dropped me off, and I've lived this long listening to my hunches. Once I got inside the gate, I was fine, but I'm sure there was something out there."

"Why would anyone watch the homestead?" Selane asked, looking alarmed at the thought. Blaine reached out to take her hand.

"It might be a creature and not a person," he replied, although that might not be exactly reassuring. "The protections we put around the property to keep out danger should work against both."

"Ah. You went to the witches." Selane smiled. "Mistress and I are sure the protections we got from the witches saved our building when the shops burned. We used magics like that all the time, back in Donderath."

"Has anyone seen the creature around?" Blaine asked. These last few weeks, he had been busy earning pay by helping the herring fleet repair the boats and mend the nets, as well as taking care of his chores around the homestead. A few ships had come from Donderath, more than a month late from when they were due, and Blaine had helped to unload them, to earn a bit more coin. He hadn't seen anything amiss, but his work in town meant he finished up at the farm at odd times, and he had been tired enough that he probably hadn't been alert enough to notice.

"Verran said he heard strange noises outside the fence when he went to fetch eggs in the morning, but it was dark enough he couldn't see anything," Dawe replied. "We can ask Piran for details when he sobers up, but he walked the fence—inside—with a lantern one of the nights you were in town because he thought he saw movement but didn't find anything."

"I don't understand," Selane said. "Why would anyone want to hurt you?"

"The beast we chased off might have gotten hungry enough to try again, or there might be more than one of them," Kestel replied, reaching for a slice of bread. "As for people—Piran always manages to annoy whoever's nearby. Maybe someone is holding a grudge."

"I don't owe anyone money, and I haven't done anything interesting enough to earn a grudge since gods know when," Piran said, wandering in from the common room. His hair was askew, and he looked sleep-rumpled, but otherwise in remarkably good shape considering how much he had to drink the night before.

"Good to know," Blaine said, unable to contain a chuckle at his friend's appearance. Selane was certainly seeing everyone without pretense.

"I didn't even get into a row with those drunk sailors, down at the pub," Piran added. "Gods, they were obnoxious! I think they're taking a worse level of riff-raff aboard ships now than when we were transported. I'm not sure how they tell the convicts from the crew, if that lot was anything to judge by."

The ships from Donderath came later and later now, and no one official said why. Unofficially, Blaine had heard plenty down at the Crooked House, and from the men who helped unload the cargo. People hoarded any supplies that couldn't be made or grown in the colony or went without if the prices rose. The few essentials and minor comforts that shipped from the kingdom not only made the harsh conditions a little easier but were a final bond to the place that had once been home. Now, even that tie seemed frayed and likely to sever.

As for why the ships were delayed, Blaine feared that the whispers were true. Donderath was at war with neighboring Meroven, which shifted priorities. Worse, a blockade or Meroven-funded pirates could wreak havoc on Donderath's trade, creating hardships for the kingdom and leaving the needs of a colony of ex-convicts entirely forgettable.

"Maybe they are," Kestel said, with the look in her eye Blaine had come to associate with the former assassin at her strategic best. "If the rumors are true about war, then better sailors might have joined the navy or been conscripted. That would leave the merchants with the dregs, or even what the press gangs could supply. If that's the case, then some of those sailors might be desperate enough to jump ship and try to stay in Edgeland, to save their own skins."

Dawe raised an eyebrow. "Someone might actually think it was better to be in Edgeland than in Donderath?"

Blaine expected a cheeky rejoinder from Piran, but instead, the former soldier looked thoughtful. "Yeah, they might. If things weren't going well. Or if they had someone after them. You'd have to bear a pretty hard grudge to follow someone all the way up here."

Kestel shifted her stance, but she looked away before Blaine could get a read on her expression. Perhaps the idea of war bothered her as much as did Blaine, though they owed no continued loyalty to the kingdom that sent them to the end of the world.

"Edgeland would be a hard place to blend in for someone who just managed to show up," Dawe mused, taking one of the now-cold sausages that remained on the plate. "The only strangers are the ship crews, and they come and go with the boats. We might not all know everyone, but between the time in Velant and needing to pitch in together in Bay-town, we've at least seen everyone who belongs here. An outsider would get noticed."

"It's not like we've got anything to steal," Piran added. "No one's got gold or gems stashed away." He paused and gave a pointed look in Kestel's direction. "Do they?"

She shook her head. "No. Wouldn't do much good up here, anyhow, even if I did—which I don't."

Blaine glanced at Selane, relieved that she seemed to be following the conversation intently. "There were some things that went missing last week, after the ships left," Selane volunteered. Everyone turned to look, surprised she had spoken up. Blaine knew that while Selane might seem quiet, she had a quick mind and a sharp sense of humor people sometimes overlooked.

"I heard Mistress talking to the potter and the blacksmith. The potter said someone had taken a shirt from where he'd left it out to dry, and he was angry because after the fire, he didn't have clothes to spare," she reported. "And the blacksmith said he was missing a blanket he keeps to put over horses when they come to be shod."

"Doesn't prove anyone jumped ship," Blaine pointed out. "Not when half the people up here got sent north for thieving."

"No, but those are the kind of things someone who had arrived unprepared would need," Piran mused. "Food and clothing."

"And a place to stay—don't forget that," Dawe said. "Where no one was likely to find them. Up here, it's not like they can just take off into the forest and live wild. Edgeland's not that forgiving."

Blaine had heard enough that what had started as wild speculation now seemed possible. "We don't know for certain about any of this, but our hunches have kept us all alive this long. So let's keep our ears open, and watch for anything strange, and maybe we'll figure it out."

Kestel excused herself to wash up after a night in the barn. Piran meandered toward the table, laying claim to the remaining food. Dawe went to tend his bread, which left Blaine and Selane to get settled in.

"I hope you like it," Blaine said as he showed her around the common areas of the house, and the room they would share.

Selane took his arm, nudging close. "It's very nice—and warm. I haven't been to any of the other homesteads, but I always thought they were more like a rough camp. You've made a proper home here."

Blaine nodded, unable to keep back a proud smile. His own home had been an estate, yet it lacked both safety and the kind of warmth provided by caring people. After his mother was killed, his Aunt Judith had tried to step in and provide care for Blaine and his brother, Carr and their sister, Mari, but Blaine's abusive father meant there could never be any real security. Ironic that he had found a true home only after being exiled for his father's death.

"Eventually, I hope all my mates bring home someone of their own," Blaine said. "Even Piran, gods help us," he added, but the fondness in his tone took the sting from his words. "One large, rowdy, and inappropriate family."

Loud barking woke Blaine in the middle of the night. Ed, the watchdog Verran had proudly acquired—along with two barn cats—was clearly unhappy about something, and trying his best to scare something off or summon help.

"What's going on?" Selane said in a sleepy voice, burrowed beneath the blankets.

"I don't know, but I'm going to find out. Stay here," Blaine said. He threw on his clothing, and came out to the hallway, finding the rest of his housemates also roused and heading for the door. Despite it being so late, they each gripped weapons. Kestel had a very illegal crossbow and a somewhat larger-than-legal knife, while the rest held knives or contraband swords. The vicious cold required that they stop for coats and boots, but then they headed out toward where Ed yapped and howled, with

Kestel and Dawe circling around from the back door, while the others went out the front.

"There. Do you see it?" Blaine pointed at a dark shape that lunged toward the fence, only to scramble backward when a silver glow lit up where it had touched the wardings.

"I see it, but what is it?" Piran echoed.

Like the monster Verran had described from the last attack, the creature had the bulk of a bear, with broad shoulders and thick legs, walking on all fours. But in the moonlight, Blaine could make out a face and head shaped all wrong, with laid-back ears and a lantern jaw.

The thud of a crossbow firing echoed in the night as a quarrel flew, hitting the creature just behind the shoulder. Verran threw a knife, and it lodged in the other shoulder. The monster reared up on its hind legs, revealing a body covered in black, matted hair. Blaine didn't know what the creature was, but it certainly wasn't a bear.

Another thud, another arrow, this one striking the beast in its chest while it stood upright. Even from a distance, Blaine could see that blood soaked the ground around the monster, but the repeated strikes only seemed to anger it, not deter it from breaking through the wardings.

"Can it get through?" Piran asked, picking up a sizable rock and throwing it hard. The rock struck the creature in the head, and it staggered, but then let out a loud bellow.

"I don't know," Blaine admitted. "Any fence can be scaled if someone wants to get in badly enough."

Their swords did no good without being closer, and going outside the fence to battle the monster would be suicidal. Blaine hoped that between Ed's barking and their assault, the creature would decide to pick an easier target. That worried Blaine, because the longer the fight went on, the more chance the beast had of finding a way around the wardings.

A blur of movement and a rush of wind, and the creature was suddenly gone, but its terrified howl echoed in the still night.

"What just happened?" Piran asked, staring at the spot where the beast had been seconds ago, a rock already gripped in his hand, ready to throw.

"There was a shadow, moving too fast to be anything normal," Kestel said, still holding her crossbow, alert for a trick.

Dawe nodded. "Yeah. I saw a form—couldn't make out the details, but it seemed solid—and it must have carried off the creature."

"From the noise the beast made, I don't think they were friends," Verran observed. "What in the name of the gods could scare that monster—let alone carry it off in the blink of an eye?"

"Nothing we ever want to meet," Blaine affirmed. His heart pounded, and he couldn't help wondering whether the wardings would have repelled the shadow figure, had it wanted to get through the fence. "Another good reason to stay out of the wilds."

Piran met his gaze. "Yeah, but when the White Nights come back, we hunt out there. I really don't want either of those things hunting us."

————

Blaine rode into Bay-town with Selane when she returned for her apprenticeship at the chandlery. She bid Blaine goodbye with a lingering kiss filled with promises for their next time together. He found himself whistling as he walked toward where the herring boats were dry-docked, something he hadn't felt like doing in a long time.

On the long passage from Donderath to Edgeland aboard the convict ship, Blaine had despaired of finding any reason to go on living. If Carensa hadn't been watching him board the ship from the dockside, he might have given in to his bleak mood and jumped into the harbor, letting his chains drag him to the bottom. In Velant's harsh conditions and on the receiving end of Prokief's casual cruelties, Blaine had thought, more than once, he would never make it out alive—and found that he didn't care.

Walking out of Velant with his Ticket of Leave meant he had a new start, to make the best life he could with his friends beside him. Falling in love with Selane meant daring to believe that he could have the companionship his heart yearned for, as part of the misfit family they had created. Back in Donderath, he had envisioned his future with Carensa including children of his own. Few in Edgeland chose to bear children; conditions were too harsh, and the future too uncertain. Blaine and Selane had decided against it, though he didn't know if a few years might change their minds. Still, his heart felt as light as it had ever been since his imprisonment, and while a cynical voice in the back of his mind warned such happiness couldn't last for long, Blaine intended to make the most of it.

"Marriage agrees with you—all three days of it!" One of the men in the large shipwright's building clapped Blaine on the shoulder with a broad paw of a hand. He was older than Blaine by at least a decade, with short-cropped hair starting to go silver. "I'm a married man myself—back home, and again up here," he added with a guffaw. The men sanding down the ships and repairing the sails joined in the laughter.

"Nothing wrong with finding someone you like to share the warmth," another man said, rolling his eyes at the first speaker's joke. "Makes the long nights easier, too."

A knowing chuckle spread through the group, and Blaine felt his cheeks color, though he had no cause for embarrassment. "We're here for the duration. Might as well settle in and make the best of it," he replied.

"Don't let those idiots bother you." Jed was one of the

captains, someone Blaine considered level-headed. "Edgeland's a harsh place to be alone. The work's always lighter with two." He winked. "Been a married man since I got my Ticket fifteen years ago, and my Bessie's the only good thing about this godsforsaken hunk of ice. If you found someone, good for you." He looked out across the group busily mending nets, sealing the sides of the boats, and sewing sails. "And for those of you who haven't met a partner—a bit of advice. Wash the herring stink off yourself, and see if that helps!"

Blaine joined in the laughter, knowing the ribbing was all good-natured. As hard as the work was aboard the ships, the crews bonded from adversity and danger. He'd never been happy about working the herring boats, but it was much better as a colonist than on the prison boats.

He fell into the rhythm of his work, getting lost in the repetition of sanding areas that needed fresh sealant, primer, and paint. A bit of conversation caught his attention, pulling him out of his thoughts.

"...worse than the usual lot," one of the men said, gossiping with the others as they repaired the nets. "Heard them down at the pub, going on about how the ships can't hardly find enough men to sail them, what with the war."

"It's true then? Meroven and Donderath are still at war?" One of the other men asked. Everyone seemed to hear that comment, because work stopped, and they all turned to listen to the reply.

"The only news I've got is what I heard from the sailors who came in with this last cargo ship," the first man replied. "Wouldn't exactly say they were reliable, since they were drunk off their asses. Didn't look like the kind to hear anything firsthand from anyone important. But that's what they think, or they've been told—that the war is getting worse, and it's causing problems."

388 · GAIL Z. MARTIN

"Did they say what's gone wrong?" One of the sail riggers asked.

"Same stuff that usually does it, probably. One side wants something the other side has. Just like two dogs with a bone," the net mender replied. "I wouldn't expect the likes of them to know. Whatever they would hear probably wouldn't be the truth, anyhow."

The group spent the next candlemark debating the news, but Blaine didn't join in the conversation. He felt a curious mix of sadness and worry, for the impact the war would have on the friends and family they had all left behind. But it came with an odd detachment, as if he'd heard the gossip about some distant land, not a place he'd once called home. Edgeland was where he belonged now, and Blaine had resigned himself to the idea that he would never see Donderath again. But a long, drawn-out war could cause problems for the colony, in ways they might not be able to easily work around. He was glad, once more, that the homestead could be so self-sufficient. If the war worsened, they would need every advantage to survive.

After a while, the men tired of that topic, and the conversation ranged from the awful cold to the price of ale, to the luck— or lack thereof—of some of their personal lives. Blaine let his attention wander, although he enjoyed the camaraderie. He had learned long ago that in the absence of any real news, the minutia of people's daily lives and relationships quickly filled the gap.

The time went by quickly, and when they stopped for the day, the bells in the tower let Blaine know he could stop by to pick Selane up from the chandlery for dinner at the Crooked House. It might not always work to align their schedules of when work demanded they be in Bay-town, but Blaine figured it mattered more to them as newlyweds than it might later on.

"How was it, being back at the shop, a married woman?"

Blaine teased as Mistress Dennison waved to him when he came to the back door. Selane would come back to stay with her and Annalise at the shop, and Blaine would share one of Ifrem's rooms with Piran and Verran while they were in town to work.

"Nice," Selane replied, taking his arm. "How about you?"

"Got some ribbing from the rest of the crew, but compared to what Piran dishes out on a daily basis, hardly anything annoying at all."

"We got a bit of news, from the customers who came in," Selane went on. "Anderson's sheep are sick—thinks they got into a bad patch of weeds. Esbet's goat bit her, and George's hens seem to be laying poorly." She chuckled. "Not exactly exciting stuff."

"Probably better that way. Exciting things tend to mean trouble."

Selane frowned. "Wait, there was something else. Dav, the blacksmith, came in to buy candles and asked if we'd had anything stolen. Seems there were more reports of things going missing—including two hunting knives from his forge."

Many weapons were forbidden, another way to keep Prokief's iron grip over the colonists. But the reality of life on Edgeland required knives for hunting and filleting the herring catch, as well as for protection against wild creatures and use in everyday work. Once again, Blaine wondered whether the thefts were random, or if someone from outside meant to cause trouble.

"No idea who took them?"

She shook her head. "Not from what Dav knew. If someone did jump ship, we wouldn't hear about it. Sailors go to the brothel or the pub. They don't come to Bay-town to buy candles!"

The cold air smelled of fish, sea water, and woodsmoke. Most of the shops were closed, but many of the tradesfolk who ran them worked well into the evening to make the wares they would sell the next day. Selane, Annalise, and Mistress Dennison were likely to go back to pouring and dipping candles as soon as their supper break was over. Blaine might spend his evening at the Crooked House, but he and Piran would both be up very early to go back to working on the boats, while Verran would play for the pub's patrons nearly until dawn on a busy night.

So many people were packed into the pub when they got there that Blaine and Selane had to slip sideways through the crowd to get to the bar. More to the point, Blaine didn't recognize about half the customers, which meant they were sailors from the *Wind Witch*, the long-overdue cargo ship.

The sailors were well into their cups, laughing and poking fun at each other, a loud and rowdy bunch. Despite the crowding, enough regulars stayed around the edges and near the bar that Blaine suspected they were on hand should the mood turn surly. He found Piran and managed to put Selane between them, though he saw her palm a small knife, just in case.

"A bit loud in here," he called to Piran, who also looked as if he'd already made a good start on his ale.

"Our new friends are having a good time," Piran replied, and though his voice was neutral, his narrowed gaze scanned the crowd for potential trouble.

"They're paying coin, so they can be loud as they please," Ifrem remarked as he filled tankards for Blaine and Selane.

Blaine glanced at Piran. "Heard anything interesting?"

"All depends on what you think is interesting," Piran said. "They compared the brothels here in Bay-town to the ones in other ports. That was plenty interesting for me."

"Doesn't matter, does it? You aren't going to get to those ports." Blaine pointed out.

Piran gave an exaggerated eye roll. "You're no fun, Mick. A man needs goals."

"Hey! Hands off my drink!" One of the sailors gave the red-haired man next to him a shove which sent him reeling, nearly knocking down two bystanders.

"Gods above and below, have you lost your mind? Why would I want your drink when I have my own?"

"Dunno. Why did you want the belt you stole from me?"

"You're drunk—or stupid. I didn't steal your belt. I didn't steal anything!"

"Yeah? Then where did it go?"

"How in the name of the gods should I know where your belt is?" the red-haired man protested. "You're daft. Addled."

"I'll addle you!" The sailor launched himself at the red-haired man, throwing the first punch. His opponent got in a fist to the gut before their crew members pulled them apart.

"Both of you, back to the ship," a tall man ordered. "If you're so worried about your things, go guard them. Maybe you'll catch the real thief."

The two men glared at each other but didn't try to argue. Blaine wondered if they would make it to the ship without a brawl, and figured that as long as it happened outside of the Crooked House, it didn't matter.

"Been a bit of thieving going around, seems like," Ifrem said when he refilled Piran's ale, dropping his voice so only the three of them could hear him above the din. "Someone tried to get in through the kitchen door last night. Probably figured they'd steal some food and ale. Wardings kept them out, but it's been a long while since we've had a problem like that. Glad as I am to see the ship come, I'll be happy to see it go. They're a bad lot, this bunch."

Blaine hadn't been impressed by the crew of the convict ship that transported him to Edgeland, but they were a notch or two above the likes of the sailors crowded into the pub tonight. These men had the look of pirates, unkempt and wild, and he considered what it meant for them to stand out like that among ex-convicts.

Much as Blaine wanted to savor the evening with Selane, he feared this crowd would quickly turn violent again, and wanted her well away from the pub if that happened. "Come on," he said, wrapping an arm around her shoulders. Ifrem handed them both food wrapped to carry with them, gave a nod of his head toward the kitchen, letting them slip out unnoticed. The kitchen staff barely spared them a glance, and when they went through the back door, he saw deep scratches where someone had tried to break the lock.

"I'm sorry—"

Selane stood on her toes to kiss his cheek. "Nothing to be sorry about. Not your fault they're asses." She smiled. "I made it through Velant, too. Remember? So I'm tougher than I look."

"I was hoping that we'd put all that behind us, once we got out."

Selane slipped her arm through his. "That would be nice, but it won't happen. We changed, in there. Can't go back to who we were, before. And we can't forget, not with it sitting there on the cliff, watching us," she added with a shiver. Velant was positioned like a fortress, on a bluff overlooking the sea, in view from most of the colony as if it were a reminder that their freedom, once granted, could also be taken away.

"I know," he said, pulling her tightly against him for warmth as they walked. He felt a pang of guilt that he had not told Selane or any of his housemates his full story, or his real name. But he'd sworn on the transport ship that if his past was taken from him, then he would make his own future, and he'd done everything possible to keep that vow.

"Maybe things will quiet down, once the ship leaves," Selane said. They walked quickly back toward the chandlery because of the winter cold, though Blaine felt sad their time together had been so brief tonight.

"Perhaps. And if someone was stealing on the ship, then maybe the thief will go with them. I guess we'll know, one way or the other."

He bid Selane goodnight at the chandler's back door and waited until he heard the latch click behind her and saw the lantern in her window flicker before he headed back to the pub. A rowdy group of men passed him on their way back to the ship, joking and singing off key, barely sober enough to walk. Blaine stayed out of their way and didn't relax until they were well past him.

By the time he got back to the Crooked House, the sailors were gone, and only the regulars remained. Verran's music had shifted from sea shanties to ballads and popular tunes from before their exile, and the mood in the room had grown much more relaxed without the rough newcomers.

"Verran could be down here for another couple of candle-marks, but I'm tired," Blaine said when he finished another ale.

"I'll go up, too." Piran drained his glass and put coins to pay his tab on the bar. "We have to be working on the boats at the ass end of dawn."

Unlike the sailors, Piran showed little indication of how much ale he had consumed, though Blaine reckoned it was quite a bit. He glanced down toward the end of the hallway, to the room where Ifrem's long-term mystery guest had taken up residence.

"He never comes out," Piran said of the secretive renter as they went into the room they shared with Verran. "I've heard all kinds of theories. Bastard prince, compromised spy, even that's he's King Merrill's disgraced brother, exiled from court."

Blaine snorted. "I suspect that if he were any of those, Kestel would know—and she'd have told us."

Piran shrugged. "Maybe, maybe not. Still, I'm curious. How does he manage to stay here without earning his keep? Or maybe he's related to Ifrem, and Ifrem is letting him stay out of some kind of family debt?"

Blaine shook his head. "I doubt it. There's probably a very boring explanation."

"Where's the fun in that?"

Blaine looked out the window as Piran plumped the straw mattresses to get out the worst of the lumps. The waning moon shone over the waves, casting the cargo ship in silhouette. Most of the town was dark, but a few lanterns glowed in windows. In the distance, on the cliffs, he could make out the dark shape that was Velant, and despite the distance and his hard-earned Ticket, he shivered.

———

Two days after Blaine returned to the homestead, Ed the dog woke them again in the middle of the night with furious barking. This time, Selane insisted on going with him, leaving a warm bed for the bitter winter night. She grabbed a long knife, ready if there was trouble.

"What now?" Dawe asked as they closed in on the place where the wardings glowed silver. "It doesn't look big enough to be one of those beasts again."

"Whatever it is, it doesn't belong here, and it shouldn't be trying to get over our fence," Kestel replied, with her crossbow drawn and an arrow already nocked.

They closed the distance, approaching with caution. Piran led the group and stopped abruptly. "It's not a beast. It looks like a man."

"Why in the name of the gods would anyone come all the way out here at this time?" Verran demanded. "There are plenty of homesteads closer to town if they meant to steal eggs or grab a chicken."

Ed stopped barking once they got closer as if he'd decided that he was off duty now that they were present. He stayed close to Blaine, ready to attack if the stranger moved.

"You think he's dead?" Dawe asked. "He seems to be trapped in the warding."

"I could poke him with a stick," Piran volunteered.

"We don't know how the warding would react to that," Kestel warned. "For all we know, it killed him."

"It didn't kill that creature," Piran argued.

"It was a lot bigger than a man," Blaine reminded him. "But Kestel's right—no need to find out the hard way." He moved toward the nearest gate.

"What are you doing?" Kestel followed, keeping her crossbow trained on the intruder.

"We can't just leave him there," Blaine replied. "If he's dead, he'll stink."

"If he's dead, he'll freeze. We won't smell a thing until spring," she replied.

He gave Kestel a look. "I really don't want Ed barking his fool head off for a few more months. And we need to stop the warding from flashing. Someone will notice."

Kestel didn't look convinced, but she and Piran followed Blaine to the gate. Blaine made the gesture to release the sigil protection on the fence, and the silver glow blinked out.

"Help me get him inside," Blaine said. Kestel kept the weapon trained on the stranger, while Blaine and Piran dragged him into the compound. Blaine reactivated the protections, and Piran rolled the man over to get a look at his face.

"Huh. Doesn't look familiar," Piran mused. "How about you?"

Kestel and Blaine both shook their heads. "Never seen him before," Kestel said. "And I pay attention to faces. I'd know."

"I don't think he's supposed to be on Edgeland," Blaine said, searching beneath the man's cloak for weapons. He found five knives of differing size, including two which he recognized as the work of the Bay-town blacksmith.

"At the least, we know who robbed Dav," he said. "Let's get him into the barn and tie him up, and then we can see why he decided to pay us a visit."

"He's a bit too well-armed for my taste," Piran remarked as they hauled the man to the barn. Selane and the others followed, curious and worried.

"Makes me think he wasn't just after some eggs," Kestel replied. "You sure you don't owe him money, Piran?"

"Settled my gambling debts and my bar bill when I got my pay," Piran answered. "So the answer would be 'no.'"

"You sure you haven't seen him?" Blaine asked Kestel, who studied the man's features once they had him tied hand and foot and lit a lantern.

She shook her head. "No. But those hands…he's not a sailor. Not calloused enough. Doesn't have the look for it, either."

The unconscious man didn't have the face or build to stand out in a crowd. He looked to be about Verran's height and build, but given how many weapons he was carrying, Blaine suspected that the man could handle himself in a fight.

An ugly suspicion prickled at the back of his mind. "Ifrem said someone tried to get into the back of the Crooked House, and his wardings kept them out. Now, this. What if he wanted something to do with Ifrem's mystery boarder? Or you?" he said, looking right at Kestel.

He waited for Kestel to poke a hole in his theory. "It's possible," she replied. "Unlikely, but possible. I mean, at least for me. We don't know anything about Ifrem's boarder."

"One way to find out," Piran said. He brought a box over and placed it next to one of the unused stall fences, and tied the unconscious man in a seated position. Then he went out to the horse trough, chipped away the ice on top, and came back with a partial bucket. He sloshed the freezing cold water into the man's face.

The stranger came around with a gasp and shook the water out of his hair. He looked at them, wild-eyed. "What happened?"

Kestel held a long knife in front of her and stood close enough to the prisoner to use it. "You came out here to trespass, maybe steal, maybe hurt us. Our dog saw you, and you fainted."

Piran smirked at the simplified story but did not correct her. "You're a long way from anywhere, buddy. How come you're out here in the middle of the night?"

"I don't have to tell you anything. Take me to the guards."

Kestel shook her head. "Nah. We'll handle this ourselves. Piran's got a nasty temper. Mick was sent away for murder. And I was an assassin." She gave a predatory smile. "The guards don't know you're here. No one is coming to rescue you. No one on Edgeland will notice if you disappear. So talk."

"Let me go, and I'll tell you everything."

Piran's punch snapped the man's head to one side. "Wrong answer."

"Why should I tell you anything? You're just going to kill me."

Kestel shrugged. "True. But we can do it slow, or fast. Up to you."

The thief swallowed hard. "You don't have to kill me."

"Yeah, we do. But I can make it painless," Kestel replied. "What'll it be? It's all the same to me."

The thief glanced from one of his captors to another, but if he was seeking mercy, he found none. He shivered from the soaking, and he licked his lips nervously. "I owed money, gambling debts, and I couldn't pay. He told me that if I'd do a job for him, he'd clear my debt."

"Who?" Piran pressed.

"The man who ran the card games. He's connected somehow to Lord Nestor. Said he'd not only wipe my debt but give me some silver as well. All I had to do was solve a problem." He slumped. "Didn't say I had to sail to bloody Edgeland to do it. But by the time I found that out, I knew too much to back out."

"What was the problem, and how were you supposed to solve it?" Blaine asked, suspecting he already knew the answer.

"I was supposed to kill the spy, and the man hiding at the pub. Didn't tell me who he was, just that he was 'dangerous' and needed to be dealt with." The captive glared at Kestel. "I guess she knew things he didn't want anyone to find out."

"Oh, you have no idea," Kestel replied. "I know why I'm a threat, although Nestor must be addled to be worried about it with me up here. But I'm curious about the man at the inn. Why did Nestor care?"

"All I know is that I was warned he might be a witch, and they gave me a medallion to keep him from putting me under a spell."

Piran walked over and pulled out a charm that hung from a leather strap around the man's neck. "Either this is worthless, or the protections on the inn—and on our fence—are stronger than your little trinket. Looks like they weren't real worried about your safety."

"You stowed aboard one of the ships?" Kestel asked.

The prisoner nodded. "Yeah. Damn miserable, it was. A whole month, getting by stealing food and water."

"Try it in chains," Verran snapped.

"How were you supposed to get back after you killed us? And did you realize that if you had been able to break in, you'd have faced six of us, not just me?" Kestel asked.

"Figured I'd get you all in your sleep. I've done a bit of knife work before." He licked his lips again. "As for getting home, I had a token I was supposed to give to Commander Prokief. They said he'd protect me and get me a way back."

Blaine and the others exchanged glances. "Did Prokief know you were coming?" he asked.

"Tell the truth," Kestel warned. "Even if he did, it doesn't change what happens to you. People go missing up here all the time. Lots of wild animals. Awfully hard to recognize a body once the wolves have been at it."

The prisoner swallowed hard. "No. I don't think so. If Nestor sent word to him, it wasn't through me."

"Are you the only one Nestor sent?" Piran ran a hand over the bruised knuckles of his fist as if he were considering taking another punch.

"There weren't any other stowaways, not on the boat I was on, anyhow."

"How did Nestor even know that I'd survived Velant and that Ifrem's guest was here?" Kestel asked.

The stranger shook his head. "I don't know. I was going to go to debtor's prison, and they said they'd fix it for me."

Kestel motioned for the others to join her a few feet away, close enough that she could still keep an eye on the prisoner.

"We have to kill him," Piran said. "If we don't, he'll go to Prokief—and find a way back to Nestor."

"And Prokief will come looking for us, and Ifrem's secret boarder," Blaine added.

"He's been played for a fool, but I don't see another option," Dawe said. "And he was willing to do murder for money."

Kestel shrugged. "That, alone, doesn't make him a bad person." She met Dawe's gaze, challenging him to say otherwise.

"Of course not," he backtracked. "But you had reasons."

Kestel didn't say much about her past, but Blaine knew that

she had killed the noble who ruined her mother's life. After that, women seeking to be rid of their abusive husbands sought out her help—as a spy or assassin—and she became the last-resort protector. "Yeah. I did."

"If he doesn't kill us, and he tries to go back to Donderath, he'll go to debtor's prison. If he stays in the colony, and Ifrem finds out he tried to break into the pub, he'll take care of the problem himself," Verran said. "And if he goes to Prokief, there'll be the dark gods to pay for all of us."

"Nestor isn't going to want a witness who might blackmail him," Selane said. "If he's sent a note to Prokief, I suspect it's with orders to have the man killed."

Blaine nodded. "Agreed. And if there was a note to Prokief in advance, he can hardly send his guards around to see if anyone's seen his benefactor's pet assassin. As you said, people who wander around in the dark get lost—or eaten."

"All right," Kestel said. "Piran and I will handle this. You can all go back inside." She glanced at Selane. "She doesn't need to see this."

Selane raised her head. "You think I didn't see worse in Velant?"

"If murder's going to be done on our behalf, then we can have the balls to bear witness," Blaine said. Verran and Dawe nodded.

"Don't blame me if you throw up," Kestel said with a shrug.

The condemned man must have known his fate was sealed. Or he was just too stubborn to beg. He met Kestel's gaze as she strode forward, but he said nothing.

"You answered our questions. We'll make it quick. Close your eyes."

The swish of a knife across the man's throat did the deed, leaving Kestel and the sawdust of the barn floor sprayed with blood. Blaine trusted Kestel to know how to kill swiftly. He doubted they could have expected the same mercy from the stranger if he had succeeded in his mission.

"How are you going to get rid of the body? The ground's too hard to bury him," Dawe asked, always practical. Beside him, Verran's jaw was clamped tight, probably fighting the urge to retch. Selane's grip on Blaine's arm would probably leave marks, even through his coat, but she remained standing, paler than usual, expression impassive.

"If we leave now, we can take him down the road to Sawyer's farm, and heave him into the pen with the pigs. Might be gone in the morning, if they're hungry enough," Piran replied.

Verran raised an eyebrow. "I'm fascinated, and also disturbed that you already had that thought out. Have you done this before?"

"Not here," Kestel answered.

"And if Sawyer comes out tomorrow and finds a partially eaten body?" Dawe asked.

"If we clean up the blood in here, there's nothing to tie him to us," Piran said. "And I think we all just agree, if we hear about it later, that it's a shame some drunk got lost and fell into the pig sty."

Kestel and Piran insisted on being the ones to get rid of the body, leaving Blaine and the others to shovel up the bloody sawdust and mix it in with the compost. If there was any cause for question, Verran suggested they say they butchered a sheep and it went badly.

They washed up in the icy water of the horse trough. Blaine knew none of them would be going back to sleep, so he put a log on the fire and set a kettle to boil. None of them felt like eating.

"Are you all right?" he asked Selane as she stood by the fire, trying to get warm.

"Not really," she replied. "I think we did what we had to do. And I believe he would have killed us all like he intended. But watching someone die isn't easy. It shouldn't be. It's not the first time I've seen it—but all those other times show up in my nightmares."

Blaine had witnessed brutal deaths in Velant. They haunted his dreams, as did his memory of killing his abusive father. "If they do, I'll be here for you," he promised, drawing her into his arms.

Privately, he worried about Kestel and Piran. Piran's time as a soldier had left him mind-scarred, and he woke many nights reliving the worst of battle. Blaine's time in Velant had made his dreams dark as well, so he understood. Blaine knew Kestel well enough to realize that she wasn't nearly as cold as she wanted others to think. Verran and Dawe would probably handle the ugly situation best. Dawe would spend time hammering out his feelings in the forge, while Verran would lose himself in his music.

"Do you think Lord Nestor will send another killer?" Selane asked, her voice muffled within the circle of his embrace.

"If he does, we'll be ready. I promised I'd protect you. We'll all protect each other—keep each other safe," Blaine promised. He hoped with all his heart that he could make good on that promise.

FEVER AND FIRE | SIX MONTHS LATER

"THAT'S ENOUGH DRINK FOR YOU," IFREM ADVISED THE VERY drunk sailor. "Go back to the ship and sleep it off."

"If I can find the ship, I'm not drunk enough by half!" the sailor slurred, but when he raised his tankard, he stumbled backward and would have fallen if his friends hadn't steadied him.

"Bloody ship," one of his mates grumbled. "I hope they conscript the lot of you for this godsforsaken route, and let us sail in decent waters again."

The pub's rowdy hubbub suddenly stilled.

"Say again?" Ifrem asked in a deceptively neutral voice. "What's this about conscripts?" Blaine and Piran, standing at one side of the bar, exchanged a glance.

The drunk sailor's friend elbowed the man in the ribs. "What'd you open your mouth for, Fred?"

Ifrem poured another drink and held it out toward Fred, then pulled back when the sailor reached for it. "What about conscripts?"

"Captain told us, what with the war and all, we were needed for more important routes," Fred bragged. "Said they might just conscript some of the colonists to ferry prisoners up here. Not like you've got anything else to do."

The poor sot was too far gone to feel the mood of the pub shift. Ifrem's smile went from welcoming to wolfish. "Is that so?" he asked. "Maybe the king needs able-bodied men for the front lines of the war," he added with a smile that bared his teeth. "Or crews for warships."

Fred paled. He turned to his friend and grabbed frantically at the man's shirt. "Oh gods, Ben! Do you think that's it? They're going to send us off to war!"

Piran left his spot near Blaine and sauntered toward the men. Ifrem and Blaine exchanged a glance. Piran was always a wild card, and he could make a situation worse just as easily as he could diffuse it.

He pulled the more sober friend, Ben, out of Fred's desperate grip and pushed him against the bar. The sailors took a step toward him, but the sound of chairs scraping against the floor and men getting to their feet made them freeze.

"Now about that war," Piran said pleasantly, with a grip on the sailor's arm that kept him in place. "Tell us everything you know."

Ben and Fred looked around at the pub regulars, who outnumbered the group of sailors. Even Fred seemed to sober up quickly. "Most of the fighting's up on the border, with Meroven," Ben replied. "Been going on for a while now. We all thought it'd be over, but it's not."

"They keep wanting more soldiers, and the ones that marched off haven't come home," a third man, on the other side of Fred, added. "Then lately, there've been pirates outside the harbor, attacking the ships coming or going. Hard to get shipments in from elsewhere, and bloody awful trying to sail past them to get out."

"Pirates—or a Meroven blockade?" Piran asked.

"Didn't stop to ask," Ben replied. "But we almost didn't outrun them on the way here. I've got no desire to see them again on the way in."

"That's why the ships are getting later and later?" Ifrem questioned.

"Been enough merchant ships that can't come into the port or don't want to risk facing the pirates that there isn't enough of what they used to bring in to go around," Ben said. "Prices are up. The shopkeepers are on the wharves arguing with the ship captains about not getting their cargo. Seen some nasty fights."

Blaine raised an eyebrow. If the sailor's account was true, things had gotten much worse back in Donderath.

"They already emptied the jails, sent all those fellows up to the war," Fred added, then hiccupped.

Blaine and Piran had remarked months ago that the sailors on the cargo ships coming into Bay-town seemed to be a rougher sort than in their early days in the colony. If Fred's news was correct, he and his friends might be pulled off to fight, and getting any shipments at all could become even more difficult.

"What does Meroven want?" Ifrem asked.

"Land," Fred said. "And all our cows and women." His eyes grew wide, and his voice dropped as if he were sharing a terrible truth.

"Shit, you've got it wrong," Ben argued. "They don't want cows and women, you dumbass. They want the ore mines."

"I heard that their leader is a dark witch, and he wants our souls," the third man said. "It's those damn, bloodsucking *talishte*. They're the ones who caused this."

Ifrem handed over the promised drink to Fred, who downed it in one move. "Get out of here. Sober up. And take your friend over there with you. He doesn't look too good." One of the sailors sat alone at a table, flushed and sweating. "Don't come back until you sleep it off—if you're still in port."

Fred and Ben stumbled out, leaning on each other to remain upright. The third man went to fetch the other sailor, who had a coughing fit that doubled him over when he tried to stand. None of the regulars spoke until the newcomers were out of the room.

"Do you really think they'll make us work the ships?"

"Doesn't Meroven have its own cows?"

"What if Meroven sails its ships up here?"

"Why would the biters want to start a war?"

The questions came so thick and fast that Ifrem gave an ear-piercing whistle and held up his hands for silence.

"One at a time!" he thundered.

"You think Prokief would let them put us on a ship that goes anywhere near Donderath?" the blacksmith countered. "He wants us where he can control us. I can't imagine Prokief going along with that."

"If it were just about cows, it wouldn't be a full-out war," the potter mused. "Just a border skirmish. Can't imagine that Meroven doesn't have plenty of women, either. Maybe that's just what they told the men to get them to sign up."

"Meroven might blockade the harbors in Donderath, but they've got no cause to sail all the way up here, unless they're hungry for herring!" Mistress Dennison remarked, which got a laugh. Selane stood next to Blaine, and leaned against him, slipping an arm around his waist, and he drew her closer.

"As for the *talishte*," Ifrem said, "I can't imagine vampires starting a war. But the bit about the Meroven general being a dark witch...that could be true. Hope it's not. Wouldn't be a good thing. But it's possible."

At this hour, most of the pub's regulars were usually on their last drink before going home. But tonight, the sailors' news gave everyone a second wind, and they crowded around the bar, ordering another round as they debated the possibilities. Some spun out wild theories while others considered the more practical aspects of war's impact on their homeland.

"If Meroven won, or something happened to King Merrill, what would happen to Prokief?" Piran wondered aloud. "Would a new king put his own man in place? Or just forget about the prison and the colony?"

That drew worried looks as the patrons who were still left at the bar considered the possibilities. "Don't think either would be good for us," a man ventured. "Prokief's bad, but at least we know what to expect from him. We wouldn't know how to work around a new man."

"Prokief doesn't get much oversight from the king, but the threat of it keeps him from being worse than he is," Blaine replied. "If he wasn't worried about reports going back to Merrill, if he thought the king was too busy to notice what went on here…it certainly wouldn't go well."

That was quite an understatement, Blaine thought with a sick feeling in the pit of his stomach. Prokief was a vicious, brutal tyrant who enjoyed the life-or-death power he held over his inmates and the colonists, even with the possibility of tales being carried back to the king. With no oversight at all, Prokief's abuse would grow worse. Blaine feared that if that day came, the prisoners and the colonists might rise up, pushed too far, and they would have a riot—or a coup. The result might be too bloody and costly for either side to claim a win.

"There's naught to do about it from up here," Ifrem sighed. "Go home, all of you. I'm tired, and I'm almost out of ale. Not going to tap a new barrel at this time of night."

The others headed for the door in twos and threes, still talking in low tones or speculating how things might play out. Piran bumped Blaine's shoulder. "I'm going up. Verran went to bed a while ago."

Blaine nodded. "I need to walk Selane and Mistress

Dennison back to the shop, and then I'll be up. Don't take all the blankets."

Piran grinned. "No promises. Don't worry, I'll leave the moth-eaten one for you."

The endless summer days had given way to the Long Dark again, and the weather turned colder. Blaine flipped his collar up against the wind, gripping Selane's hand in his, inside a pocket as they walked back to the chandlery. Half a year had passed since Blaine and Selane made their vows, and the arrangement of splitting time between work in Bay-town and chores at the homestead still worked well. This trip had two more days remaining before they went home, and Blaine found himself restless and edgy, eager to be away from town.

"I'm grateful for all the sheep and pigs that are being raised out on the farms," Mistress remarked. "Gives us tallow for wax and wool yarn for wicks, if we can't get materials from Donderath. At least we won't be in the dark!"

Selane burrowed close to Blaine, and he doubted it was just because of the wind. The most comfortable life on Edgeland was harsh compared to what most people enjoyed in Donderath, both from the weather and the lack of commonly used goods. The colony had focused on self-sufficiency as the supply ships' arrival grew more erratic. At this point, with all of the established homestead farms and the tradespeople in town, the colony might survive if it were completely cut off, but surviving would grow even more difficult.

And while Blaine doubted that Meroven would think of raiding Edgeland if it were to win the war, sooner or later someone was bound to remember the "lost" colony and come to investigate, if not for the herring then for the gems and ore from the mines. He doubted that encounter would go well.

"We have our hands full with another winter," Blaine urged. "Let's not borrow trouble."

"Do you think the wolves came back to the farm while we've been gone?" Selane asked, with a strained smile that told Blaine she was trying to force bigger worries aside.

"If they did, I imagine Kestel and Dawe sent them running," Blaine assured her. "Dawe's been practicing with a slingshot and Kestel is…Kestel. I'm not worried about the wolves."

That wasn't entirely true. Wolf attacks had grown more frequent of late, to the point where the wagon masters who drove produce from the homesteads into the town market had taken to riding in pairs, so that one could drive off wolves by hurling rocks. So far, neither the drivers nor their horses had been killed, but Blaine had heard of a few encounters that had been too close for comfort.

Their wardings and the protections the wise women gave them for the perimeter of their land had been strengthened, and they hadn't seen the black beast again since the mysterious shadow carried it off. But Blaine found himself wondering whether the wolves were harrying the farms now because bigger predators had forced them out of the game lands where they usually hunted.

They arrived at the chandlery, which broke Blaine out of his thoughts. Mistress Dennison bid them goodnight, allowing for a private farewell at the door.

"I'm looking forward to going home," Selene murmured, turning to face Blaine. "I'm happy with Mistress, but I love the time we're at the homestead."

"So do I, and we'll be back soon," Blaine replied. He bent to kiss her, a lingering touch that promised much more when they returned to the privacy of their room at the farm. "Splitting our time makes it all the better when we can be together. Keeps us from taking it for granted."

She laughed. "Are you afraid I'll get bored with you?"

Selane shook her head. "Have no fear. I feel like I'm always learning something new about you."

Blaine hid the wince he felt, knowing how much he still held back from Selane and his friends about his past. It shouldn't matter now, and perhaps, if they knew, it wouldn't. All of them had secrets and scars, and their sins had earned them transport to the prison. Yet Blaine couldn't help fearing that his crime—no matter how justified—might make the others view him differently, and he didn't want that, especially not with Selane.

"I like finding out new things about you, too," he replied, forcing his fears aside. "I want to spend the rest of my life doing that."

"Hm," she murmured. "I like the sound of that." The wind gusted, and she shivered. "I'd best go in. It's freezing out here, and you have to walk back to the pub."

Blaine gave her another peck and drew back. "I'll be fine. Make sure you're warm enough tonight. You don't want to catch a chill."

She disappeared inside, and Blaine saw when her candle lit the window of her room above the shop. He jammed his hands in his pockets and hunched his shoulders against the cold, keeping his head down and picking up his pace, thoughts full of war and wolves.

———

The gossip from the sailors was all anyone wanted to talk about the next day when Blaine and Piran went to help patch the herring ships and mend sails and nets. Blaine guessed it was at least a break from discussing all the possible ways to trap wolves, which had been the previous topic that had the town chattering. No matter where Blaine caught a snippet of conversation, it always came back to the war.

"—swore I'd never set foot on a ship again, and I won't do it now just to get shipped back and killed in a war."

"—ship us back, how're they going to keep us from deserting as soon as we set foot on land? Can't keep us chained up if they want us to fight, and as soon as I'm free, I'm gone."

"—empty out the prison, that won't hurt the colony. But if they take colonists, who's going to run the homesteads and the trades?"

The debate went round and round, but lacking better information from back in Donderath, all of it was guessing and outrage. The discussion grew loud and impassioned, and Blaine guessed it was probably the most any of the boat crews had talked about their homeland in a long time.

Pounding on the door led to sudden silence. Blaine grabbed a scraper, and Piran picked up an awl. All around the room, people armed themselves with tools that could be used as weapons, not knowing who was on the other side of the door.

Piran threw the door open. Blaine didn't recognize the man who stood outside, but his eyes were wide and his expression desperate. The man smelled of sweat and sickness. His skin was sallow, his face gaunt. The shirt and pants he wore hung off him like a scarecrow.

"Please, we need healers to come to the ship. There are sick men, very ill."

Blaine remembered the sailor in the pub the night before who looked unwell. Cold dread settled in his stomach. "What kind of sickness?"

The man shook his head. "We don't know. Everyone seemed all right when we left port, except the ones who drank too much the night before. By the time we were several days into the voyage, some were ill. Then more. Some recovered. Most didn't. It got worse while we were at sea. We barely had enough crew to make it here."

"And you're telling me that you came into port, let sailors leave the ship and come into the town, when you knew people were sick?" Piran looked ready to throw a punch.

"No one was supposed to leave the ship," the man replied. "If there were any of our men in town, they left against orders."

"Bloody lot of good that does us now!" Piran snapped. "They went to the pub. Gods, no wonder they were so quick to get drunk. Dead men walking, weren't they? And now they've probably spread it to everyone who was there, and those people carried it back to their shops and farms—"

Piran was red in the face with anger. Blaine laid a hand on his arm in warning, but Piran shook him off, although he didn't take a swing. "And now you want to send our healers into a plague ship? What if they die, and the sickness spreads here? Who's going to heal us?"

"The captain was going to come ashore and find healers, but he's sick now, too. I'm the first mate."

"Your ship came in last night. I thought it was going to wait until a reasonable time in the morning to unload the cargo, but you can't, can you?" Blaine asked.

The man shook his head. "No. We can't unload, and we can't sail home."

"Don't you have a ship's healer or a mage on board?" Piran demanded. "Why can't they deal with the sickness?"

The man hung his head. "We had both. They did all they could, but it only saved a few."

"Shit," Piran swore. "How many of you are left?"

"Perhaps a hundred still able to go about their duties, who didn't get sick or got better. Maybe that many who can't leave their beds. And the rest…"

"Are you saying that a third of your crew is dead?" Blaine asked.

"About that many, yes."

KING'S EXILES • 413

The men working on the herring boats had gone quiet. They kept their distance, which was probably wise, Blaine thought. After all, he and Piran had been in the pub with the sailors, so if their ill humors spread, perhaps it was already too late for them —and perhaps for the men they had worked with all day.

Selane was with me. And Mistress. His heart raced. *Oh, gods no. Please, no.*

"Get back on the damn boat," Blaine said. "If the healers are willing, they'll go. If not—"

He let the consequences of the healers' rejection go unsaid. The man nodded and trudged back to the ship like he was headed for the gallows.

"We could ask the guards to check into it," one of the fishermen suggested hopefully. "If there's going to be plague here, at least it could kill off the guards and do us a favor."

Blaine shook his head. "Plague doesn't choose. If it comes, no one is safe."

"A third didn't sicken or recovered," Piran repeated. "A third died. And we don't know how many of the ones who are sick now will either die or get better. Gods above! We thought it would be bad if Prokief conscripted us to sail the ships. But if the sickness claims as many here as it did onboard, we'll be hard-pressed to keep the colony going."

One of the men looked up from the net he was mending. "Why should we send them our healers? They're not colonists. If they die, they die. If they don't, then they won't need a healer, will they?" The other fishermen nodded in agreement.

It set wrong with Blaine not to help, but he was torn, recognizing that survival for the colony might very well depend on containing the plague and leaving the crew to their fate.

"We're not the ones to make that decision," Blaine said. "That's something for healers to figure out for themselves. I'll go see Ifrem. He can put out the word."

"What will happen to the sailors who don't die, if there aren't enough to sail the ship home?" another man asked.

Blaine shook his head. "They'd have to stay until another ship came."

"And what do we do with a ship full of dead men in the harbor?" The question came from Tom, who was stitching sails.

"Burn it to the waterline," Piran replied.

"Prokief's going to love that," the sail-mender retorted.

"Let's worry about that when the time comes," Blaine said. "If anything is to be done to save them, it needs to be soon. Keep working. I'll be back."

Piran insisted on accompanying Blaine, looking more serious than Blaine had ever seen him. Even in the worst of Velant, Piran's dark humor had always defied the fates. "We can't go back to the homestead until this is over," Piran said, his tone grave.

Blaine's breath caught as he realized the truth in Piran's comment. "No. Verran, too. He was in the pub last night as well."

"Half of the people in town were at the Crooked House," Blaine added. "And plenty of them went back to their farms or spent the day in their shops seeing more people. We don't know how the sickness spreads."

"I remember, when I was in the army, we were out in our camp, and every last man got the shits. It was awful, like someone turned you inside-out and lit your guts on fire. We wanted to die. First one man, then his tent-mate, then their friends, on and on."

Blaine nodded. "Back in Donderath, there was a plague in the city. A whole street, struck down. The constables bricked up the entrance and let them die."

"Well, that's pleasant," Piran said. "Can't exactly brick up Bay-town."

It would be even worse, Blaine knew, if the sickness spread to Velant. In the close quarters of the prison, aided by hunger, cold, and overwork, the prisoners would die in droves. Once, when he was among them, he might have considered that a kindness, compared to the nightmarish conditions of the jail. But now that he realized he could make a decent life for himself, a home, a family, Blaine knew that the convicts still had a reason to survive.

"What do you think the healers will say?" Piran asked, nudging Blaine from his thoughts.

Blaine shook his head. "I don't know. Can't blame them if they don't want to risk themselves, but the sailors deserve better. It might not matter whether they go or not. If it's a plague that spreads easy, it's already among us. Might take a few days to show who's sick, but once it starts, it'll moves fast."

They reached the Crooked House and found only the locals. Verran played an upbeat tune, while the regulars talked in low tones, and a few played cards or dice. Piran went to talk to him as soon as his song was finished. Blaine headed to the bar, where Ifrem was busy pouring drinks. He waited until the patrons had their orders, and Ifrem turned to him.

"Quiet afternoon. I'm surprised the sailors aren't back."

Blaine drew a deep breath. "About that…one of them came to the dry dock where we've been fixing the boats. Said they need a healer. There's sickness onboard, bad enough that they've lost about a third of their crew, and half of the ones who are still alive are ill."

Ifrem's eyes widened. "By Torven's horns! Did they unload their cargo?"

Blaine shook his head. "No. And the men who came here last night weren't supposed to be off the ship. But they were, and one of them didn't look healthy. So it's up to the healers whether they go or not."

Ifrem's silence meant he was thinking, Blaine knew. "Prokief is going to want that cargo," the tavern master said finally. "So either the sailors bring it off, or they send us to get them. If they carry the sickness, it'll come to the town either way."

Blaine nodded. "I figured. But the healers—"

"The healers will do as they please," Ifrem said. "No matter what Prokief decrees. As for the sickness, there's nothing the guards can do. Bay-town isn't like Castle Reach. There aren't alleys to close off or brick up. So if the plague or pox or fever comes, it'll sweep through like a fire, and there's no good way to stop it."

"If we could let the homesteads know, limit the number of people that go back and forth—"

Ifrem grimaced. "Maybe. But if all the farmers stop coming into town, we starve. And people came and went last night and all day today. I fear that choice has been made for us."

"All right," Blaine replied. "But I need to send a note to Kestel, letting her know that Verran and Piran and I are staying in town until this runs its course. Do you have paper and a pen?"

Ifrem inclined his head toward the back of the pub, where he had his office in a room off the kitchen. Blaine went to find what he needed and paused as he thought about the wording.

Kestel and Dawe—

A ship brought a sickness with it that killed many of the crew. We're afraid it will spread to town. P, V, S and I won't be home until this runs its course. We don't want to spread it to you. Please stay at the farm until this is over. Wish us well.

—Mick

He folded the note and dripped a bit of candle wax to seal it, then wrote Kestel's name on the front. Some of the colonists could read and write, at least a little. He and Kestel were among the few with much formal education, though many of the long-time colonists had taught themselves and learned from others. Even if the wagon master he hailed to deliver the message couldn't read, he could follow Blaine's instructions. He left the pub, hoping he could find someone heading out to the home-steads and flag them down.

"Hey, Mick. You need a ride out to your place?" Ted, the wagon driver, asked when Blaine stopped him.

"Nah, got work to do here," Blaine hedged. "But I need to send a message to Kestel. Can you take this to her?" He handed off the sealed paper.

Ted glanced at it. "Fancy, ain't ya? Sure. I can do that. Heading that way now. Something going on?"

Blaine hesitated, unsure what to say. If they were lucky, the illness might not ravage the colony like it had the ship. He'd given up believing in good luck or the gods' intervention when they'd clapped the manacles on him for transport to Velant.

"Just some things I want her to send in on the next load," he said, glancing away. "Nothing important."

Ted tucked the paper into his coat. "I'll probably come back in late tomorrow, or early the next day, so I can bring what you want. I'll just tell her to flag me down. I'm usually on the road about the same time each day."

Blaine thanked him and added a few coins for his bother, which Ted happily accepted. He watched the wagon roll into the night, recognizing the fear that knotted his gut. If the sickness spread, many of the people he knew could be dead in days. So might he. Blaine had faced that knowledge many times in Velant, but despite the colony's hardships, he had stopped facing each day as if it might be his last. Now, that icy realization settled over him, and his shiver had nothing to do with the temperature.

Raised voices drew his attention as Blaine walked back toward the Crooked House. His heart sank when he saw four

418 · GAIL Z. MARTIN

guards outside the pub. The bell in the tower began to ring off-schedule, calling the townspeople to the square.

Men and women gradually assembled, coming from their shops and trades, glancing around warily to figure out the reason for the gathering.

"There's a problem getting the cargo off the ship that came in last night, and I need twenty-five men to get it unloaded, and another twenty to see that it gets split right between the warehouses on the docks and the wagons for the prison," the captain shouted. "And I need a healer. There're sick men on board." When no one moved immediately, his scowl deepened. "Do I need to pick volunteers at sword's point?"

Piran had left the pub at some point and joined Blaine. They exchanged a glance and moved forward to join the rest of the reluctant "volunteers." Going aboard the ship might be as good as a death sentence, if their exposure to the sick sailors in the Crooked House hadn't already been enough to seal their fate. But Blaine knew that the captain would have his workers, no matter what it took, and that any reluctance would only make things worse.

The men around them talked in low tones as they followed the guards down toward the waterfront, wondering about the unusual request. The ship's crew always unloaded cargo. It didn't take long for them to connect the absent sailors and the request for a healer.

"—there's something wrong. Else why aren't the sailors here?"

"—some kind of sickness, if they need a healer. Oh gods, what if it spreads?"

"—don't like the look of this, not one bit."

Someone must have sent word, because Aisha, one of the healers, joined them before they reached the dock. She spotted

Blaine and Piran and made her way over. "Do you know what's going on?"

Blaine explained in low tones, although the others would learn the truth soon enough.

"Do the guards know?" she asked.

Blaine shrugged. "Probably not, or at least, not the extent. All they care about is the cargo. The ship and the crew aren't any of their concern once they get what they paid for."

From the look on Aisha's face, Blaine figured the healer had an idea of the nightmare waiting for them. "I'll do what I can," she said. "But this could be bad—"

Piran nodded. "We know. But there's no stopping now."

At the dockside, the guards split the men into two groups, sending some to prepare the warehouse and fetch wagons. The torches by the dock and the moon were enough to light their way to the wharf, but wouldn't help them navigate onto the ship.

The captain turned to the guard on his right. "I don't see anyone on deck, and no lights down below. Go on board, find out why, and get the door to the damn hold open. And while you're there, kick their lazy asses. The more men, the faster we're done."

The guard headed off, up the gangplank. Blaine watched, feeling his dread deepen. Everything about the situation was wrong. Plenty of cargo boats came into Skalgerston Bay during the Long Dark, but none ever sat, dark and silent, like a ghost ship. Usually, lanterns lit the deck as the crew took care of chores and repairs, and the portholes on the sides glowed with candlelight. The *Sea Wench* looked lifeless and abandoned. Blaine wondered if the remaining sailors had succumbed, or they were busy somewhere in the interior, caring for their sick shipmates.

The wait dragged on, and behind them, the big doors to one of the nearest warehouses rumbled open. Moments later, more light lifted the gloom on the dock as lanterns lit up the inside of the storage building. Hoofbeats and the clatter of wagon wheels announced the arrival of the other conscripted helpers.

"Where in Raka are they?" the captain fumed at the delay. Finally, the door to the cargo bay opened, and the ramp slid forward, landing one edge on the wharf with a thump. Lanterns illuminated the dark hold, silhouetting the guard and two strangers.

"What are you waiting for?" the captain snapped at the townsmen. "Start unloading the boat!"

Blaine and the other men headed up the wide ramp, into the dimly lit hold. Even before they reached the entranceway, the stench of death and the sour smell of sickness nearly made him gag.

"Gods above and below, it's true! This is a plague ship!" one of the men behind Blaine wailed.

The guards closed in behind the group, crowding them forward. "Get to work!" the captain yelled, although he and three of his guards kept their distance. The healer took a lantern of her own and headed up the gangplank, going on deck to search for the crew.

When Blaine and Piran reached the hold, Blaine got a look at the crewmen the guard had mustered to help. They looked as bad as the man who had come to find a healer, pale and hollow-cheeked, as if they had escaped Death's clutches by a hair's breadth.

The men from town spread out, hurrying to unload and leave the death ship behind as soon as possible. Blaine recognized the first mate. "We brought a healer," Blaine told him. "How's your sick crew?"

The first mate shook his head. "Bad. We seem to be losing more in this group, and no one knows why. The captain's dead."

"I'm sorry," Blaine replied, getting into position so he and

Piran could lift one of the crates. He glanced toward the guard, who was looking in the other direction. "Go find the healer. She'll need someone to show her where to go." The man nodded gratefully and slipped away. Blaine felt certain the guard hadn't studied any of the crew's faces enough to tell them apart, and he wouldn't miss one man in the hubbub of unloading the ship.

For the next several candlemarks, Blaine and Piran carried the heavy wooden crates down to the wharf, where the other shift of townsmen divided them between their destinations. The crewmen helped move the crates from the back of the hold to the front, but even that appeared to tax their strength. Most of the men looked as if they were barely staying on their feet.

Finally, when almost all the cargo had been unloaded, Aisha came down from the upper decks and crossed to where the guard stood.

"There are seventy-five sailors who are too ill to walk, and more than one hundred rotting corpses," she told the guard. "I can't take care of all the sick myself. I need you to send for more healers."

"Don't the ships have healers of their own?"

"They're dead," Aisha snapped. "So unless you want the boat in port permanently, filled with dead bodies, I need more healers."

The guard glared at her, but Blaine could see that the healer's raw assessment scared the man. Grudgingly, he beckoned for one of the townsmen who was coming back up for another load. "Go fetch all the healers you can bring. If they don't come, we'll make them come. And hurry up about it. There are more boxes to carry."

The man took off running. Blaine wondered if he would come back. After a couple of candlemarks, his nose lost the ability to the smell the decay quite as strongly, but he could see that their fellow workers were obviously rattled by the condition of the crew, and they could easily guess the source of the foul odors.

Aisha walked with Blaine and Piran as they headed for their next crate. "What is it?" Blaine asked. "Pox? Plague?"

She shook her head. "Fever. Starts with a cough, then aches and tiredness. Fever sets in, and stomach problems. Gets hard to breathe. Then the fever spikes. If it doesn't come down quickly…" Aisha didn't have to finish for them to get the gist.

Aisha slipped away, going back to do what she could for the dying men. Blaine and Piran exchanged a look as they balanced their load. "Shit. That's even worse than I expected," Blaine said.

"Now what?" Piran asked as they grunted and huffed, shuffling their way toward the ramp.

"We see what Aisha and the other healers say when they come back. At least now, we know what to look for. Not that there's much we can do about it," Blaine replied.

They finished around supper time, and despite the cold, Blaine found himself wishing for a bath to wash away the sweat from the heavy labor, and take the stink of the cursed ship out of his hair and clothing. When the guards finally released their unwilling helpers, the somber group made their way back toward the Crooked House in near silence.

They reached the pub, and Blaine hesitated, not wanting to expose even more people to the ill humors from the ship. Piran sighed.

"Mick, it's too late. Half the men who were out and about in Bay-town this morning have been on that boat or close enough. And most of the people in the pub were there when the sailors came in. Face it, we're done for."

"Then I guess we'd better get a drink while we still can," Blaine replied.

He had originally planned to go see Selene this evening, but he wanted to clear his head from the awful situation aboard the

Sea Wench. If Ifrem had a bundle of sage, Blaine thought he might light it and let the smoke do its best to purify him, or at least remove the smell.

When they walked into the Crooked House, the first thing Blaine noticed was the quiet.

"Where's Verran?" Piran asked, looking around. Their friend took occasional breaks from playing music, but he was usually somewhere in the common room, drinking with friends, playing a friendly game of cards.

"Maybe he went out back for a smoke," Blaine suggested, but despite his tone, he was worried. "You know he likes that pipe of his."

They headed to the bar. Ifrem looked up when they approached. "If you're looking for Verran, he went up a while ago. Said he wasn't feeling well. Didn't look too good, either. I sent the kitchen girl up with a bowl of broth and some bread, and a slug of whiskey. That's usually good for whatever ails you."

"I'll go check on him," Blaine volunteered. "But I've got to eat something first. We worked all day with no lunch." In truth, the smell had killed all thoughts of food, but now they that were away from the ship, he felt his stomach growl.

Ifrem sniffed, then took a step back and eyed them both, as well as the others who had filtered in from the work detail. "Sweet Torven and Esthrane! You stink."

"I was hoping you had some sage we could burn," Blaine said. "The situation on the ship—it was even worse than we thought."

"Did you see anything?" Ifrem asked. He reached beneath the counter and pulled out a bundle of dried leaves that he kept for times when a drunk puked in the common room. Blaine held it to a candle and lit the end, holding in close enough that the smoke bathed him, and then handed it Piran, who did the same.

424 • GAIL Z. MARTIN

"We didn't, but Aisha did," Blaine replied. "And what we didn't see, we could smell."

Ifrem set out a plowman's meal for both of them, which they wolfed down and followed with shots of whiskey. When he finished, Blaine turned to Piran.

"I'll go see how Verran's doing. Why don't you make your way around the room, and see what's being said? Just...try not to start a riot. I'm not in the mood for it tonight."

Piran grinned. "There's never a bad time for a riot," he answered, but his smile looked strained.

Blaine headed upstairs with a heavy heart. He consoled himself with the thought that Verran had survived a harsh life on the streets in Castle Reach as well as the dangerous sea voyage and three years in Velant. Surely after all that, Blaine hoped, a fever wouldn't be what took him.

Maybe a sane man would leave town and hope the fever passed him by. But Verran was a mate from Velant, one of his "family," and a friend. Blaine knew he stood every chance of catching the sickness if he stayed to nurse Verran, and no guarantee it would keep the musician from dying. But he was certain Piran and Verran both would stay, if the situation was reversed.

He paused in the hallway as he caught a whiff of the same sickbed smell from the ship, but thankfully, without the stench of death. When he knocked at the door, the only reply was a groan. Blaine stepped into the room and caught his breath at what he saw.

Verran lay in the bed, nearly as pale as the sheets. He had seemed fine the morning before, healthy and in good spirits. Now, he was flushed with fever and sweat beaded on his forehead, soaking his nightshirt so that it clung to his wiry frame.

"Go 'way," Verran croaked. "You'll get sick." His rough voice sounded so different from the smooth tones of his singing, as if it hurt to make any noise at all.

"Too late for that," Blaine said with a bitter chuckle. "I've been on the plague ship. If Torven intends to take me, he'll do as he pleases."

Verran's response was part moan, part cough, accompanied by an awful sound of tightness in his chest. From the way he sprawled across the bed, it looked as if he had fallen onto the mattress and not moved since then.

"Ifrem sent up food. Did you eat?"

"Uh-uh," Verran managed. He pointed to a bucket, and Blaine could figure out the meaning from the smell.

"You're throwing up and sweating out too much water," Blaine said, trying to remember how his Aunt Judith back home had dealt with sickness. "You've got to drink, just a bit at a time. It will help."

Verran made a noise in protest. Blaine scooted a chair to the bedside and pulled the tray of food closer. Broth, bread, water, and whiskey were a sickbed meal, and perhaps exactly what the patient needed.

"The broth's gone cold, but that might be easier on your throat," Blaine said. "It's in a tankard, so it's easy to drink. I'll prop you up and steady your hands."

Verran might have wanted to argue, but he clearly lacked the strength to do so. Blaine arranged the pillow and Verran's cloak to sit him up enough to help him drink. He took the tankard of broth and lifted it to Verran's dry lips. "Here. Just a mouthful. We'll take it slow."

Blaine vaguely remembered having a bad fever as a child. Judith had nursed him, keeping him amused with stories from the myths as well as tales from her younger days in the king's court. He recalled little except how desperate his parched body was for any liquid, and the soothing tether of his aunt's voice, giving his mind something to hang onto while his body fought to survive.

426 • GAIL Z. MARTIN

"That's good. Very good," Blaine said as Verran swallowed. He imagined his friend wanted to roll his eyes in annoyance but figured his own eyes hurt too much to bother.

"When I was a boy, I caught the fever. My aunt sang to me. I won't inflict that on you, since I can't sing," Blaine said, giving his best effort at keeping his tone light despite his worry. "But I have a few stories you might not have heard."

They passed the next few candlemarks like that, with Blaine stopping his tales every so often to help Verran swallow a bit more liquid. He began by telling Verran about unloading the ship, leaving out the horrific death toll, or the condition of the crew. Instead, he focused on the heavy crates, Piran's obscene remarks over being pressed into service, and the bits of gossip he overheard from the other men in the cargo hold. Then he searched his memories to remember every tale he could remember from books he had read or stories his aunt had told him.

Verran dozed off from time to time, and Blaine let him sleep, keeping watch to assure his breathing didn't falter. He didn't know how many of the town's healers had been sent to the ship, but he hoped at least one would return soon enough to help Verran recover.

Blaine felt the hard work catch up to him in every aching muscle, and he fell asleep in the chair, rousing only from a knock at the door.

"Mick?" Piran opened the door and walked in. "Gods," he murmured, taking one look at Verran. "How is he?"

Blaine shook his head. "He's feverish, but not raving, so that's something. I'm trying to help him drink, but it's slow going. What's happening downstairs?"

Piran jerked his head, a signal for Blaine to step out into the hallway. Blaine glanced at Verran, but the other man was sleeping and wouldn't notice his absence. He followed Piran out and closed the door quietly behind him.

"I don't want to leave him alone for long," Blaine confided in a near-whisper. "I'm worried."

"Yeah. Me, too," Piran replied. "I'm worried about all of us. People are getting sick all over Bay-town. And it's all since the sailors came ashore."

Blaine swore under his breath. "Well, there's no changing it now. I sent the note to Kestel, and hopefully, she and Dawe will sit things out."

"Ifrem's asked that any healers who come back from the ship come by the pub. People are queuing up to ask for help. I'm afraid that there won't be enough to go around."

"If the wise women are willing, perhaps they can provide poultices and elixirs, even if they aren't healers. What about Annalise, the other apprentice to the chandler? She was learning potions, wasn't she? Maybe there's something she can mix up that will at least let the poor bastards sleep, or breathe easier."

Piran nodded. "I'll ask. Ifrem sent me up with some whiskey for you, and wanted to know if you need anything else for Verran."

Blaine shook his head. "It'll probably take him all night to drink the broth and water, and I don't know if I can get the whiskey into him, though it would help with sleep and pain." He paused. "Wait—can you bring up a pitcher of water, a bowl, and some clean rags? If I can get his fever down, it might make a difference."

"A good slug of whiskey is some of the best medicine there is," Piran agreed. "Think of how it makes you feel warm but ends up letting you freeze, if you're out in the cold? A bit of that might do the trick, getting the heat out of him."

"Have you heard anything more about the *Sea Wench*?"

428 • GAIL Z. MARTIN

"Aisha sent word, as well as asking for whiskey and water. It's like something out of the Unseen Realms onboard, from what she says. Bodies stacked and rotting because there were too many to throw overboard in the harbor, and nowhere to put them. And this last bunch to get sick seem to be having the hardest time of it."

"Maybe the first ones to be sick were still strong, but as the conditions got worse, it wore down the others. We saw that enough times in Velant."

Piran shrugged. "Could be. But everyone downstairs is worried. Even the guards are keeping their distance. I think the first group to get sick were all in the pub when the sailors came in. But now? After unloading the ship, and all the people nursing the sick?"

Blaine understood. He'd had a cold feeling of dread in his belly since they'd learned of the sickness, and now his worst fears were playing out.

"Naught to do but try to come out the other side, like we did at the prison," he replied. "I'd better get back to Verran. What are you going to do?"

"I'll come up to take a turn and let you sleep," Piran said. "Maybe if I whistle Verran's favorite songs, he'll wake up to prove he's better at it than I am."

"Your whistling isn't too bad. But please don't sing. We don't want to send him running to the Valley of the Gods!"

Bleak humor had gotten them through the worst of their convict days, and Blaine saw in Piran's eyes an understanding of how dire their situation was. "I can't promise," Piran replied. "Maybe he'll wake up just to make me stop."

An odd thump in the next room made both Piran and Blaine exchange worried glances. The noise came from the room where Ifrem's mystery guest lived.

"He can't be sick. He never comes out of his room," Piran said.

"Someone brings up his food. Probably Ifrem. And Ifrem's been around the sickness."

Piran nodded. "All right. I'll go tell Ifrem, and I'll be back with water and whiskey for you. Tell Verran to hold on. Dawe and you aren't nearly as much fun to annoy, and Kestel kicks my ass."

Blaine let himself back into their room and replaced the bedside candle, which had burned to a stub. He walked to the window and looked out across Bay-town. Despite the cold, people were usually abroad at this time, but the streets were nearly empty. Lights flickered in most of the windows, and Blaine wondered how many of those people were barricaded into their homes or shops, hoping to avoid the sickness, and how many others nursed a friend or loved one or sat vigil by the dying.

He couldn't imagine the horror of being stuck aboard the *Sea Wench*, out on the ocean, with more and more of the crew members falling ill or dying day by day. Even at Velant's worst, they had been able to bury or burn the bodies, or make a cairn in the most severe weather, but there were no such options for sailors who died since the ship made port. He figured that those who died on the voyage were thrown overboard. It had been like that on the convict ship that brought him and Verran to Velant. Many of their fellow passengers had not reached Edgeland.

"Come on," Blaine urged. "You've got to come through this, Verran. Dammit! You don't get to leave us like this. Not after everything we've been through. You do not get to die, do you hear me?"

Piran brought up the materials Blaine requested. "How can I help?" he asked.

Verran had grown even warmer in the last candlemark, tossing and turning in dreams. He moaned or grunted in his sleep, but didn't respond when Blaine tried to wake him. Instead, he would jolt at odd intervals, eyes going wide but unseeing, as if terrified from his nightmares but not able to break through to the waking world.

"We've got to cool him off."

"I could open the window. It's plenty cold outside."

Blaine shook his head. "That might be too much of a shock. But you've got the right idea." Blaine soaked two of the rags in the water basin, then wrung them out. "Put these on the outside sill for a few minutes, and help me get Verran undressed."

Piran did as he was told, and came back as Blaine attempted to wrestle their friend out of his nightshirt. "What are you doing?"

"Remember how, when someone almost freezes to death, the trappers taught us to warm stones and wrap them in towels and put them in the armpits and behind the knees to get the blood warm?"

"Aye. And elsewhere as well. But I don't think he's going to want a freezing cold cloth near his plums!"

Blaine pulled the sweat-soaked shirt free. Verran flopped in his arms, unconscious, his skin hot to the touch. "I wasn't going to put them there—unless we get desperate. Better frozen plums than dead."

"If I get sick, do your best, but don't ice my privates!"

"No guarantees," Blaine retorted, not looking up as he settled Verran back in bed. He wanted to get his friend to sip water but feared he would choke. Piran brought him the two cloths, and Blaine sent him back to the window with three more.

Verran gasped when the cold cloths touched his burning hot skin, but even the extreme temperature change did not rouse him. It didn't take long for his fever to warm the wet towels, but the cold wind outside chilled them again just as quickly. Blaine and Piran passed the next few candlemarks swapping out the cloths and wiping down Verran's body, slipping bits of ice from the ledge outside the window between his lips to get water into his parched throat and cool him from the inside out.

"We're either going to kill him, or you're a bloody genius," Piran grumbled. He and Blaine were both exhausted, catching catnaps in the time between changing the rags. But finally, in the early hours of the morning, Blaine realized that Verran's skin had begun to cool.

"I think we did it," he said, giddy from worry and lack of sleep. Verran's breathing was regular and his pulse steady. While Blaine was in no hurry to wake his friend, figuring that rest was the best elixir, he was relieved when Verran's sleep was peaceful.

"The healers never came back," Piran observed. "And we didn't hear back from Annalise, either."

Blaine stretched out on the floor beside the bed and wrapped himself in his cloak, barely able to keep his eyes open. "Probably busy with other things. Whole town's sick. But...I think he's going to be all right." If Piran responded, Blaine didn't hear, because he fell asleep as soon as the words passed his lips.

When Blaine woke, he thought it odd to see the sunrise, with orange light outside their window lighting up the darkness. He blinked and rose to his elbows, staring at the strange light. *It can't be a sunrise like that. It's the end of the Long Dark. So what in Raka—"*

Fire. Oh, gods. Is the town burning again?

Blaine struggled to his feet, feeling the night spent on hard wooden floors in every joint and sinew. He staggered to the window, trying to loosen his stiff limbs, still bleary-eyed from the previous day's exhaustion.

Bonfires dotted the main street and lit up the square. Blaine stared, uncomprehending, as the flames leaped high against the dark sky. The realization of what he was seeing made him stumble, and he barely caught himself against the doorframe.

Pyres. Those are all pyres for the dead.

"Piran." Blaine's voice was a dry croak. "Piran!"

Piran startled awake and came up to a crouch, ready to fight. It took a few seconds for him to realize he wasn't under attack, and he gave Blaine a confused look. "What? Why did you wake me up?"

"Look."

Cursing under his breath, Piran hobbled to the window to join him, moving like a man twice his age. "I've gotten too damn old to sleep on the floor," he grumbled. "What in the name of the gods is so damn important—"

His voice drifted off as he looked out at the bonfires. "By Torven! Are those…"

"Pyres. And it looks like people are carrying bodies out to them, so there's not just one corpse per fire," Blaine replied.

"Sweet merciful Esthrane. How many?"

Piran Rowse rarely let his emotions show. Their hard years in Velant had afforded Blaine more glimpses of Piran's true feelings than anyone other than their housemates had seen. Now, Piran looked completely bereft, and at a loss for words.

"I don't know."

Piran blinked as if to assure himself that his vision had not failed him. "Mick, what's that?" he asked, pointing toward the horizon.

Blaine stared at the sight of a ship at full sail, leaving the harbor, aflame. The fire covered its deck and licked at the masts and rigging, teasing at the billowing canvas. "It's the *Sea Wench*," he whispered. "My gods, did they light themselves on fire?"

Both of them stood at the window, watching the flaming ship sail into the distance. "Do you think Prokief did it?"

"Do you think the survivors were onboard?" Blaine countered, aghast at the possibility.

A knock sounded, and Ifrem opened the door. He glanced to where Verran slept, and visibly relaxed when he noted that the musician was still breathing.

"You saw?" Ifrem asked, nodding toward the window.

"The pyres, yes. But what's going on with the ship?" Blaine asked.

Ifrem set a tray down on the bedside table. It held three bowls of porridge, a pitcher of water, and a half bottle of whiskey. "Apparently, the surviving crew members set the sails, lashed the wheel, and set fire to the thing, before jumping ship. They're hiding in the warehouse with their cargo, but I don't imagine it'll be long before Prokief hears and sends the guards to figure it out."

"So they intend to stay on Edgeland?" Piran questioned. "I guess they didn't have enough men to sail back, even if they burned the corpses here."

"I haven't seen them," Ifrem said. "Got my information third-hand, with plenty of witnesses backing it up. Wasn't sure quite how many stayed, but less than a hundred was the guess. I imagine they'll try to go back with the next ship to come into port, assuming there's room. Until then, we'll need to feed them, I suppose."

"The sailors can help with chores, since so many people are sick," Blaine replied. "They can't hide for long. We'll be short-handed, between the sick and the dead. Let them earn their keep."

Ifrem shrugged. "It's not my call, but that makes sense. I'll suggest it. 'Course, it all depends on how Prokief takes the news."

"He's not going to want more mouths to feed at the prison, and even he might pause a bit over clapping the crew of a merchant ship in irons," Blaine said. "The men who own the North Sea Trading Company wouldn't take kindly to treating their crew like that, and if they're rich enough to own a fleet of cargo ships, they probably have King Merrill's ear."

"Wouldn't know about such things," Ifrem answered. "But I still don't imagine Prokief will take the news well." He glanced down at Verran. "How is he?"

Blaine wiped a hand over his face, pushing back the hair that fell into his eyes. "His fever broke. He's been sleeping, and I figured that's what's best for him. Once he wakes up, we'll get some food into him, but I'm hoping that since he's made it this far, he'll be all right."

"How's your mystery boarder?" Piran asked. "We heard some noises over there."

Ifrem sighed. "We did our best, but he died during the night. I'm thinking that he must have felt sick for a while without letting on. Either that, or it hit him hard and fast."

"Who was he? If he's dead, surely it's not secret anymore," Blaine said.

Ifrem hesitated, then nodded. "His name was Tomas. He had been the lover of Lord Nestor's wife. When the lord suspected, she sent Tomas away, thinking Nestor meant to have him killed. Tomas bought passage on a ship under another name and had enough gold with him to buy one of my rooms and all his meals for as long as he wanted."

"So a while back, when you thought someone tried to break into the pub, you figured they might have wanted more than your ale."

"Maybe. Then again, the thief didn't come back, so we'll never know."

Blaine carefully avoided looking at Piran, since they knew exactly what had happened to the assassin. "Is Nestor still alive?" he asked.

"I imagine so. Although he wasn't a popular fellow. A few years back, I remember hearing about an attempt on his life. Would have been around the time your ship came to Velant."

That confirmed the link in Blaine's mind, and answered why Kestel had been so convinced that the would-be killer had to vanish. "Sounds like he got to live a longer life up here than he would have had in Donderath."

"Not much of a life, stuck in his room. He said that Prokief might recognize him, and so he didn't dare go out. Tomas did some whittling, like you," Ifrem added with a nod toward Blaine, "to pass the time. Brought a few books with him. From what I saw of his room and the things he had me buy, some needlework, too. I guess it was better than staring at the walls."

"Have you burned the body?" Piran asked.

Ifrem nodded. "On one of the first fires. I did my best by Tomas when he was alive, but I couldn't let him stink the place up. And if Nestor ever cared, it's over now."

Blaine thought of the assassin and his bloody end, and the ignominious send-off he received. "It certainly is," he replied.

Footsteps on the stairs made them all look up. Annalise hurried down the hallway, lifting her skirts to help her run. "Is Mick here? Mick McFadden?"

Blaine felt his heart skip a beat. *Surely not. Please, no.* "I'm here. Been sitting up with a sick friend."

"Come with me," Annalise said. "Mistress and Selane, they're ill. Hurry."

Piran clapped a hand on Blaine's shoulder. "Go. I'll stay with Verran. And—for what it's worth, I hope the gods favor you."

Blaine followed Annalise down the stairs and out the back door. The smell of burning flesh rose with the smoke from the pyres, and he fought the urge to gag.

"How bad?" he asked as they walked quickly across the road, skirting the crowds of mourners and onlookers gathered around the pyres. For once, the guards were nowhere to be seen, and Blaine wondered if they had left the town on its own to avoid contagion, or if they were down on the wharf, dealing with Edgeland's newest, temporary, colonists.

"They were both well yesterday morning," Annalise replied. "We've been so busy, everyone coming for candles or asking me for protection spells or potions. Ifrem sent word that your friend was sick, so Selane wouldn't worry about you. Then during the day, Mistress's head hurt, and later, her stomach. She nearly fell, and we got her up to bed."

Annalise looked near tears. "I hoped it was just overwork. I thought I could help with my potions and spells. And they did help, I think—for a while." She shook her head. "Then, later, her fever spiked. Selane and I took turns staying with her. She got so hot, I thought it would burn me to touch her. Her fever came down some, but she won't wake. And now, Selane's sick as well. She's asking for you."

Blaine felt a stab of fear in his chest. He told Annalise what they had done to help Verran, and she promised to fetch rags and water. "What about the healers? Do you know where they are?"

Annalise looked like she was at wit's end. "I've put out word, but almost everyone in town is sick. I don't know if they'll come in time. I've done what I can with what I know, but I'm just good with herbs and a bit of magic, not a real healer."

"Can the wise women help?" Panic had begun to drive out exhaustion, making Blaine feel jumpy and scattering his thoughts.

"Like the healers, they're stretched thin. I heard that the sickness has reached some of the homesteads. They might have gone out to help."

The cold wind blew through Blaine's hair and touched his neck like icy fingers. Bay-town's healers sufficed for normal problems, helping when people were hurt on a hunt or in a fight.

Colonists were a hardy lot, by virtue of having survived so much to reach this place. Serious illnesses were rare.

But sickness on such a massive scale had not struck Baytown since Blaine had been there, or for many years before that. There just weren't enough healers or wise women to help everyone, so those who received aid first were more likely to survive than those left waiting their turn.

"We'll do right by Selane and Mistress," he assured, promising both Annalise and himself.

The only lights in the chandler's shop were in the upstairs living quarters. Blaine had never been to those rooms, since Selane shared them with Mistress and Annalise. He had expected sparely decorated rooms like those above the Crooked House and was surprised to see that the space looked comfortable and cozy.

Three beds lined up against one wall. A table with three stools sat on one side of the fireplace, and shelves held pots and other items for cooking. On the other side of the hearth was a bench and a high-backed chair, and Blaine supposed that was where Mistress and her apprentices passed what little free time they had.

Selane's groan sent Blaine hurrying to kneel beside her bed. A glance at the next bed revealed Mistress Dennison in her night-dress and sleeping cap, lying pale and far too still. Blaine took comfort from the flush in Selane's cheeks and the redness of her lips that she was not yet too far gone. He reached out to take her hand, hot to the touch.

"Mick." Selane's words were barely a whisper.

"I'm here, love. I'm not going to leave you, so don't you dare leave me. You stay with me. Do you hear me, Selane? We're going to help you get better."

Annalise brought the water and rags as Blaine asked, then

refilled a pitcher of drinking water. It sat on the table next to a bottle of whiskey.

"Do you have soup? Broth?"

"I went to the butcher yesterday and bought a chicken. Then they got sick, and I put it in the snow beside the shop, to keep. I ate some bread and cheese yesterday, trying to take care of Mistress."

Blaine nodded. "Help me get the wet cloths cold outside on the window sill, and then I'll place the rags while you make a pot of soup. Doesn't need much in it; bone broth is best, although you and I could do with a bit of meat and vegetables, I supposed. Can you do that?"

She nodded. Blaine hated to ask when it was clear Annalise was so tired she was barely standing, but he knew they would all weaken faster without some nourishment, and soup would be easy to spoon into Selane's mouth.

Annalise went down to get the chicken, and Blaine arranged the freezing cold rags as he had for Verran, taking advantage of the few moments of privacy. He stroked the sweat-soaked hair back from Selane's forehead and pressed a kiss to her brow, figuring that whatever ill humors carried the disease already had their chance to cling to him. Selane stirred at his touch.

"Mick." Once more, barely a whisper. She did not open her eyes, and Blaine wondered whether she had heard his response. It broke his heart to realize she might not know he was with her.

Blaine rarely prayed, since so many of his prayers in Velant had gone unanswered. Kestel kept the shrine for all of them, and he overheard her asking the gods for favor, to help a sheep struggling to birth a lamb, or for good weather for the crops. More often than not, she asked for protection, especially when they went out to a hunt or to the herring boats.

He wasn't sure Charrot cared about the likes of him, but for Selane, he would gladly beg the mercy of the High God.

"Merciful Charrot, Highest of the High, and your faithful consorts, Esthrane and Torvin, I ask you to heal Selane and her Mistress. Please, m'lords and m'lady, see fit to save their lives. If you sent this plague because we've angered you somehow, then take me. I've earned your wrath. But please, please, spare them."

He came to an awkward close, trying to remember what Kestel did when she made her sacrifices. Aunt Judith hadn't kept an altar when Blaine was growing up, perhaps because she felt that the gods had already deserted them. He silently promised to make an offering when he got back to the homestead, hoping that would suffice.

Blaine found himself waiting for a response and sighed. He didn't really expect a flash of light or a sudden recovery. Those were the stuff of myth, stories told around campfires and embellished with the telling. But he would be grateful and more than satisfied if Selane's fever would break as it had for Verran, and if Mistress would wake up.

Annalise worked at the table to ready the soup, leaving Blaine to rinse and chill the rags himself. Each blast from the open window made him shiver, and he did the best he could to keep the full brunt of the wind from striking either of the sick women. The fire chased the worst of chill out of the room, though given the winter cold outside, Blaine guessed that it was still cool enough in the room to keep their patients from sweltering.

In between cooling and repositioning the rags, Blaine sat beside Selane's bed and talked to her of anything light-hearted he could think of, tidbits of gossip or funny things he had observed. When he exhausted those topics, he told her stories, and out of desperation, sang the songs he remembered from the pub, making up the words when his memory failed him.

"She was worried about you," Annalise said when Blaine finally paused to drink some whiskey and water. "Ifrem's note

440 • GAIL Z. MARTIN

helped. Selane talks about you all the time. She tells me stories about your housemates and the animals at the homestead. You've made her very happy."

Blaine managed a smile. "She's made me happy, too. She's like a patch of sunlight when everything is so dark."

Annalise pushed a strand of hair behind her ear and set the cauldron on the fire to cook. "Perhaps by the time the soup is finished cooking, she'll be able to have some." After checking on Mistress to no avail, Annalise sat down at one of the stools by the table.

"She liked working with you and Mistress," Blaine said, figuring that since he had exhausted everything he could think of to tell Selane, it might serve the same purpose for her to overhear the conversation with Annalise. "She says you make her laugh."

Annalise blushed and looked down. "She's being kind. I seem to have a knack for noticing things that are odd, or not quite the way they should be, and it amuses her when I point them out." She picked at the seam of her apron, and Blaine guessed that she felt nervous around him, since they weren't well acquainted.

"Sometimes, we make up rhymes to occupy us while we work with the wax. Dipping candles takes a long time. Pouring is faster, but it's easier to get burned." Small pink spots on her hands testified to having learned that lesson painfully.

"Or some days, we play guessing games," Annalise went on. "Even Mistress joins in, if she's having a good day." She dropped her voice, though it seemed unlikely that her employer would overhear. "Mistress hasn't been well, even before the fever struck," she confided. "Her joints ache, and I think she has some trouble with her heart. That's why she was keen to take on both Selane and me, to help with the work. It was getting to be too much for her."

The harsh conditions on Edgeland and the privations of

Velant went hard on a person, making it difficult to judge their age. Even more so if their life before transport had been a struggle. Blaine had guessed Mistress Dennison to be in her late fourth decade, or perhaps a bit older. That wasn't particularly old back in Donderath, for those who came from a noble house or a prosperous merchant family.

But from what Selane had told him, Mistress had been a colonist for almost twenty years, after having been sent away for stealing food in Castle Reach. Blaine did not doubt that the hardships of life here took a toll. He glanced at Mistress and thought that her skin had a new, grayish cast, and that she breathed more shallowly.

"Perhaps it would cheer Mistress if you reminded her of some of those happy times," Blaine said. He didn't want to frighten Annalise, but he felt certain that the older woman was slipping away.

Annalise's expression told him that she understood. She knelt next to Mistress's bed and took her hand between both of her own.

"Do you remember the first day you let me dip the candles, and I got as much wax in my hair as on the wick?" Annalise asked, blinking back tears. "Or when I mixed the berries wrong and turned that whole batch of wax black? How about the first time you let me make the scent for the wax, and I used the wrong plants?" She shook her head.

"You never screamed at me, or hit me, even though I know my mistakes cost you money. You trusted me, and you took me in, gave me a home, looked out for me. Taught me a trade." Tears started down her cheeks.

"I can't repay you," she added, as her voice broke. "I had nothing. Was nobody. And you became my mother, and gave me a sister," Annalise added, glancing toward Selane. "I always tried to do my best, to not let you down. But maybe," she said, looking up at the ceiling and swallowing hard as she tried to keep from sobbing, "I can make sure that what you built carries on."

If Blaine hadn't been sure that Annalise knew Mistress was dying, her tears left no doubt.

"I will never be what you are, but I will try every day of my life, and keep you in my heart." Annalise held the dying woman's hand. She looked up at Blaine. "I'm not going to let go, until she's gone."

Blaine nodded, not trusting himself to speak. He busied himself changing out the wet rags, and while they chilled outside the window, he brought back a cool cloth to wipe Selane's face, and a bit of ice to press between her lips.

"There. That's better, isn't it?" he asked as he gently cleaned away the sweat from her forehead, stroking her cheek, watching the throbbing of the pulse at her throat.

He forced himself to smile, believing that even if Selane couldn't open her eyes to see him, she would hear it in his voice.

"Can you smell the soup? Fresh chicken. A little onion. And some tea, when you feel like it." His voice broke, and he squeezed his eyes shut, turning his head and grimacing to stop the tears from coming.

Not now. She's still with me. I won't cry while she's here with me.

In the next bed, Mistress's breath caught and ended with a dull rattle. Annalise buried her head in her arm and wept, shoulders shaking, still clutching Mistress's hand.

"When the White Nights start, we'll go back up to our hill, and look out over the colony," Blaine murmured. "And there will be new rabbits, and lambs, and goats at the farm. Ed will be so happy to see you—he always wags his tail so hard when you come home." The dog had chosen Selane as a favorite, much to Verran's pretended annoyance and Dawe's amusement.

"I just want you to come home with me, Selane. Please, I need you."

Eventually, when her tears were spent, Annalise rose and placed Mistress's hands on her chest in a final good-bye. She rose and went to stir the soup, but Blaine could still see her shoulders shaking and hear the hitch in her breathing as she sobbed.

"The soup is ready," she said finally, fussing over setting out bowls on the table. Blaine remembered how, in times of crisis, Aunt Judith had focused on details as a way of getting through the situation, minute by minute.

"I don't think we dare give her any, unless she wakes up," Blaine replied. "She could choke." He knew he should eat, but had no appetite. Annalise pressed him to take a bowl, and he swallowed mechanically, tasting nothing.

Blaine had not slept soundly the previous night, and his body ached for sleep. But he feared that his time with Selane was rapidly coming to an end, and he didn't want to miss a moment. He went back to singing songs and telling tales, repeating some when he ran out of new ideas. Annalise listened in but said nothing. At times she stared out the window or sat quietly at the table, but Blaine doubted she actually saw what she was looking at, lost in her own thoughts.

Not long after the midnight bells, Selane's eyes opened wide. Her body stiffened, and for a few seconds, Blaine hoped the fever had broken. But she collapsed onto the bed, staring sightlessly, breath and pulse gone.

Blaine gathered her into his arms, rocking her against his chest, far past caring whether the fever took him, too. For as hard as he had fought to survive against his father's abuse and the conditions in Velant, he no longer cared if he went on.

I'd only just found her. And loving her made everything else

444 • GAIL Z. MARTIN

so much easier to bear. Knowing what he had, and lost, would make the absence all the lonelier.

Finally, when he could weep no more, Blaine laid Selane carefully on the bed and wiped his face dry. The last few days had taken their toll. His head throbbed, and his throat felt like he had swallowed ground glass. Exhaustion threatened to drop him in his tracks, and the soup he had eaten rebelled in his stomach.

"I'll carry them down to the pyres," he said. "Help me wrap Mistress in her bedclothes; we can give her that dignity, at least." Together, they made a shroud of her sheets, and Blaine hefted her body into his arms. Her thin body seemed to weight almost nothing, and he thought again about Annalise's comment that the older woman had not been well. *I hope she's at peace. None of us left behind are, that's certain.*

Annalise followed him and his grim burden, approaching two pyres until they found one that could accommodate a new corpse. Blaine's feet dragged on the walk back, knowing what must come next.

He kissed Selane's forehead before he and Annalise repeated what they had done for Mistress. Selane's body felt leaden in his arms, and he struggled to put one foot in front of the other. The distance to the pyre seemed longer than the whole of Edgeland, and the flames, as he consigned her body to the fire, seared his lungs and scorched his skin.

Blaine saw the shroud catch, quickly engulfing the body beneath. Then his knees gave way, and he dropped to the cobblestones, as the world went dark.

———

"Welcome back." The voice belonged to Verran, and it sounded just like it always did, which for some reason Blaine couldn't quite remember, should have been odd.

"What happened?" Blaine opened his eyes and found himself upstairs at the Crooked House. He thought that wasn't quite right, but his memory seemed hazy.

"We nearly lost you and Piran both," Verran said. "Damn fools."

Blaine heard Verran's words but could make no sense of them. His confusion must have been apparent on his face.

"You've been out of your head with fever for two days, and slept through the third one after you had the good sense not to die," Verran snapped.

Selane. Oh, gods. She's gone.

Memories filtered back, of the small upstairs room, a shrouded body, and a funeral pyre.

"You both gave us all a scare," Verran said. "Kestel has been sending notes with every wagon driver coming into town, and expecting updates with every wagon going out."

"Selane—" His voice sounded like a dry croak, even to his own ears.

Verran's expression softened. "I'm sorry, Mick. You don't remember?"

Blaine nodded, squeezing his eyes closed. "I just...wanted to be able to bury her ashes."

Verran was quiet for a moment. "Ifrem must have guessed. He brought a box with some of the ash from that pyre. There's no way to know for sure..."

Verran didn't have to finish the sentence. With so many bodies burned to stop the contagion from spreading, it was impossible to be certain that the ashes were actually hers. Still, it was something to take back to the homestead, to anchor her memory on the windswept hill they liked to visit. Blaine was resigned to taking what he could get.

"Piran?" he rasped.

"Came around a bit earlier. Still looks like he's been to Raka and back. You both do." Verran bit his lip as emotion overcame him. "Idiots. Should have just left me."

"Not on my watch."

Blaine drifted in and out of sleep. When he woke, Verran plied him with soup, whiskey, and water. Sometimes, he swore he heard Verran's pennywhistle in his dreams.

Finally, Blaine woke and decided it was time to try to get up. As soon as he moved, Verran ran across the room, steadying him as he rose on wobbly legs, and catching him before he fell.

"Let's take this slowly," Verran said sternly. "After everything we did to keep you from dying, I'd rather not have you hit your head and bash in your skull."

"I need to take a piss."

"I'll bring you a bucket."

Blaine didn't have the energy to argue, and the close quarters of the prison and the homestead made the desire for privacy moot. He fell back into bed, surprised how quickly his energy was spent.

"A couple of days made a big difference for me," Verran assured him. "You'll start feeling more like your old self by tomorrow, especially if you drink and eat. Don't worry about sleeping—you're not missing anything exciting."

"Oh?"

Verran chuckled. "Not much, anyhow. Everyone's either sick, recovering, or trying to hold the place together while so many other people are out. I heard the guards tried to give the sailors that jumped ship a hard time, but it was just like you said— Prokief couldn't touch them." His eyes narrowed, as if he wondered how Blaine's guess had been so correct.

"The pub's been slow. A lot of work didn't get done because people were too sick, and now everyone's trying to catch up. Ifrem managed not to catch the fever, amazingly enough. The only good part about all this is that the guards have kept their distance the entire time." He grimaced. "Maybe they've died and we don't know it."

"They'd just send more."

"Yeah, I imagine so." Verran held out a glass of water and helped Blaine sit up enough to sip from it. Just for good measure, he followed that with a glass of whiskey. The liquid felt like fire going down, and Blaine knew there wouldn't be enough of it on Edgeland to ease his grief once his mind cleared enough to process his loss.

Verran must have guessed his thoughts, because he laid a hand on Blaine's shoulder. "Why don't you rest a bit, and then if you want to sit up when Ifrem brings up dinner, I can help." He made a show of sniffing the air. "And we'll get a bath drawn. You stink. Piran threw me in a tub as soon as I could walk. I have to admit, it felt good."

Blaine nodded, already half-way asleep. When he woke again, he smelled food, and his stomach rumbled.

"We've got hot tea and some stewed chicken," Verran said. From the other bed, Blaine heard Piran groan, proof that he was also alive and on the mend.

"Kestel and Dawe—" Blaine began.

"Have been holding up tolerably well, so they say," Verran replied. "Between the two of them, they've taken care of the animals and seen to the chores that couldn't be put off. I imagine they'll be glad to see us again to help with the work, if for no other reason."

Except that Selane wouldn't be going home, Blaine thought, feeling the loss in his chest. Having the ashes to bury was something, at least, to preserve her memory. But this was far from the future he had dared hope for.

Since the gods had apparently determined that it was not his time to die, Blaine figured he had better do what was necessary to get out of bed and back to the homestead. He pushed himself up on his elbows, and let Verran help him sit up enough to eat. Verran rewarded him with a tired smile and drew the small table up close enough for Blaine to reach the bowl of stew.

"Eat all you can. I'll talk to Ifrem about that bath."

———

Three days later, Blaine, Piran, and Verran were finally in the back of a wagon headed for the homestead. Despite his heavy coat, hat, and scarf, Blaine felt the cold wind like a knife, much more than usual. He figured that was due to the fever, and wondered how long it would be before he regained his strength.

He didn't have to question how long it would take to feel back to normal. Without Selane, that would never happen.

"Are you going to be all right?" Piran asked, raising an eyebrow. They knew each other too well to keep secrets, at least, not this kind of falsehood.

"I made it this far, I'll get through it," Blaine replied, looking at the horizon. "Not exactly all right but…here."

"It's a start," Piran said with a shrug. "Sometimes, that's all you can do."

They had only been gone for two weeks, but it seemed like forever since Blaine had laid eyes on the farm. It didn't seem possible that the homestead could look unchanged, when Blaine's world had turned inside-out. Verran paid the wagon master while Piran and Blaine climbed down from the back.

Ed's furious barking greeted them, as the dog ran back and forth inside the fence, crazed with excitement. Verran let them through the warding and closed the protections behind them, as Blaine bent to pet the dog, barely able to keep the animal from leaping into the air with joy at their return.

"You're back!" Kestel came running, and Dawe loped behind

her. Kestel threw her arms around all three of the men, managing to pull them into a hug that still nearly crushed his ribs.

"Good to see you," Dawe said, grinning broadly and clapping them on the shoulders.

Kestel released them and looked up at Blaine. "I'm so sorry," she said, meeting his gaze. "Ifrem sent a note."

Blaine nodded, afraid that if he tried to speak, he might not find his voice. Piran covered for him by jumping into the conversation. "Do I smell smoked pig? Were you planning to throw us a welcome home feast, or planning to eat all the good stuff before we got back?"

Mercifully, the others let him trail behind them as they headed into the house. Blaine veered off, grabbing a shovel from the barn, then walked up to the hill, with Ed following on his heels.

He chose a spot where the thin soil ran deep enough for a proper hole to protect against wild animals and the harsh weather. Then Blaine withdrew the box with Selane's ashes from beneath his coat and laid it in the hole. After a moment, he covered it over and then sat down on a large rock nearby. When the White Nights returned, the rock would give him a view of both the mounded dirt and in the distance, the cold gray sea.

"I hope you're somewhere warm and safe, where you never have to be frightened or hungry again," Blaine said, wondering if Selane could hear him. He'd never seen a ghost and hoped Selane's spirit wasn't trapped on Edgeland, but speaking aloud soothed the ache in his soul.

"I'll visit you here, and tell you all about what's going on. Not much interesting, I don't imagine, but still." He squeezed his eyes closed. "I know you'd want me to keep going, but I'm not sure how. I'm going to miss you so damn bad."

He let tears fall until he could breathe again. "Anyhow. I

thought you might like it on our hill. I will never forget you. Rest easy, Selane."

Blaine heard the crunch of a twig snapping. Ed bounded up, wagging as he recognized the intruder. Blaine turned around and saw Kestel on the path. She could move with the silence of a cat if she wanted to, so he knew she had intentionally made the noise to announce her presence.

"I came to see if you needed anything," she said, not trying to close the distance, as if she understood his need for space. "And to let you know that we're all very glad to have you back. We'll help you get through this. That's what family does."

Blaine nodded, still looking at the horizon. After a few moments, he heard Kestel head back down the trail toward the house. He sat a while longer, watching the sea, feeling the rustle of the wind. Donderath would never be home again, and Selane was lost to him. Grief still cut sharply and deep. But he had a home, and friends, and a place where he belonged, here on Edgeland.

It was enough to make a new beginning.

BONUS

A Kestel Falke Origins Short Story

1

RECONCILING MEMORY

"SLEEP NOW." KESTEL FALKE PATTED THE SHOULDER OF THE man who lay next to her tangled in the sumptuous satin sheets. He had paid well for her company, presenting her with a diamond bracelet for a weekend's pleasure.

Her companion did not stir. Kestel smiled, assured the potion she drugged him with had taken effect. He might have slept soundly without the drugs, after demonstrating more amorous vigor than Kestel expected of a man his age. Still, she dared not take a chance that he might wake and find her gone from his bed.

Duke Leon Hastings lay on his side, with his right arm crooked beneath him. The lantern's glow revealed the tattoo of a falcon in flight, the mark of his noble house. The sight of it goaded Kestel, to remember the purpose that brought her to Hastings's bed. He wanted to believe that he hadn't paid for her services, and she allowed him to believe the lie. More powerful men than Hastings had bribed her with exotic and costly gifts far surpassing the gems in the bracelet, all for a few hours of her company.

Kestel slipped the sharp silver knife from where she

concealed it in her discarded skirts, along with a small glass vial. She turned over the sleeping man's right hand and made a tiny cut on the skin of his wrist, just deep enough for blood to bead. She gathered a few droplets in the vial, then used Hastings's kerchief to staunch the flow and wipe the cut clean. Moving silently, Kestel replaced the vial in a hidden pocket of her skirts and withdrew a silk pouch.

Kestel smiled as she rose from the bed, gathered a satin robe around her and slipped the knife into a pocket. Let Hastings believe he pursued her; the falsehood suited her purposes. Her seduction of him had nothing to do with sex except as the lure best suited to draw in her prey. For months she had made certain to be within sight of Hastings but always out of reach, on the arm of one patron or another she knew he envied. Men like Hastings were easy to read, even easier to manipulate. Seeing her with those men made Kestel a coveted possession to be pursued and won at any cost, just as she planned.

She glanced back at the unconscious, naked man. Sleeping with him had been a distasteful means to an end, but she had done far worse things to achieve her goals. After the first rough encounter that took her innocence, Kestel learned to step away inside her mind to a safe distance as her body went through the motions. She had better things to think about, like vengeance.

Kestel stopped to glance in the large mirror that hung on the wall across from the bed. Leon Hastings liked to watch his conquests, voyeur and victimizer wrapped up in one. Kestel moved so that she blocked the sight of him with her body and ran a hand through her dark red hair, assuring the curls fell just so. She bit her bottom lip, making it plump and reddened, then smoothed her hands over the satin that clung to her curves. If she encountered anyone in the hallway, they would see nothing but a courtesan, one more of the elder Hastings's conquests. Men would pay no attention to anything except the rise of her breasts and the slant of her hips, and women would not bother to give her a second glance, merely happy that Hastings found an outlet for his debauchery that did not include them. They would see what they wanted to see, and Kestel herself—the woman who was more than the sum of her beauty and body—would be invisible, as she liked it.

Moving silently, Kestel slipped out of the bedroom. Getting inside the manor house had been the whole purpose of the tryst. She found Hastings no more repulsive than any of her other clients, bored and lecherous rich men who needed to prove to themselves that their youth had not fled. Yet Hastings offered Kestel something far more valuable than the diamond trinket she would break apart and sell for weapons, potions, and spells. He was one of the final pieces in a puzzle Kestel had been working on for nearly a decade, and now that he had granted her safe passage inside the house, Kestel intended to put the opportunity to good use.

The old lech had been more helpful than he knew, vainly showing off his manor as he attempted to impress the courtesan whose affections he had pursued for months. Fate had given Kestel a beautiful face, a sumptuous body, and a mind as sharp as the blade hidden beneath her robe. She'd taken those assets and clawed her way into the Donderath court as the most sought-after courtesan in the kingdom, including King Merrill himself among her many lovers. The secrets she learned, she parlayed into influence or on occasion sold as a spy. One rich man's bed at a time, she gained the information to exact her revenge.

Plied by brandy and Kestel's flattery, Duke Hastings regaled Kestel with stories of his ancestors' glorious exploits, as well as his own long-faded military honors. Her rapt attention and a hand on his arm had been all it took to loosen the duke's tongue, making it easy for her to turn the conversation to his son, Damian.

Kestel's lip curled as she remembered the duke's obvious pride as he spoke about Damian. She'd hung on the duke's every word as he spilled the details she had gone to his bed to discover. He'd even pointed out the door that led to Damian's rooms, though he was quick to add that his son was in Castle Reach right now, possibly at the Quillarth Castle itself, busy with important tasks. Papa's pride and joy.

Kestel found her way back to Damian's rooms without incident and picked the lock easily. She let herself inside, closing the door behind her, and waited for her eyes to adjust to the darkness. Here in his private rooms, she could pick up his scent, a mixture of sweat, cloves, and brandy. It sickened her. Kestel lit a lantern and shuttered all but one pane to allow her to see without attracting attention.

An oil portrait hung over the mantel, and Kestel stopped to get a better look at her quarry. Damian Hastings was now a man in his forties, but the portrait showed him much younger, just in his early twenties. *That's what he looked like, when it happened.*

The figure in the portrait looked down on the room with patrician entitlement, a scion of wealth and privilege. Strong jaw, high cheekbones, wheat-blond hair, and grey, cold eyes made him handsome, but no compassion tempered his demeanor. Age and dissolution made it difficult to see the resemblance to his father. The older man's profile was lost in jowls and bags beneath his eyes from overindulgence, and the last time Kestel had spotted Damian, he looked well on his way to the same fate.

Not that he'll live that long.

She tore herself away from the portrait of her quarry and moved farther into the room, seeking the objects she needed. A comb on Damian's dressing table provided a few strands of hair, which she tucked into a silk pouch. She cut a small corner from the hem of a well-worn shirt and plucked a few bristles from his shaving brush. Together with his father's blood, the items would be all she needed to draw the younger Hastings to his death. Kestel smiled, the first time she felt truly happy in a long time. Soon, very soon, she would have what she desired for so long.

Kestel blew out the lantern's candle, replaced it where she found it, and let herself out of Damian's room. As she rounded the corner into the next hallway, a servant looked up, startled to encounter anyone at this time of night.

"Can I be of service?" he asked. Kestel noticed what he omitted. "M'lady" would not be forthcoming for the lord's paid companion, not even from one of the servants. Kestel ignored the slight, smiling in the secret knowledge of what was to come.

"I didn't want to wake Lord Hastings," she replied, making damn sure her tone reminded the man that paid or not, she had the ear of his master and shared his bed. "I can't fall asleep. I'd like a brandy."

If the servant thought to question, he thought better of it. She did not have to answer to him.

"Of course," he replied. "Shall I bring it to m'lord's rooms?"

Kestel nodded. "I'll wait just inside the door. Knock softly. He's sleeping well, and I don't want to disturb him." If the witch who sold her the potion told the truth, Hastings would sleep through cannon fire for a few more candlemarks, but the lie made a convenient excuse.

"As you wish."

Kestel watched the servant disappear, then made her way back to Hasting's rooms. She replaced her knife in its sheath and hid the silken pouch in the hidden pocket of her skirt, patting it once in satisfaction. *So close. After all this time, so close.*

When a soft rap came at the door, Kestel was waiting. "Do you require anything else?" the servant asked, extending the silver tray on which waited a goblet of brandy.

Kestel took the goblet with an enigmatic smile. "No. I have everything I need."

———

"Are you certain this will work?" Kestel eyed the witch appraisingly. For her part, the witch had the good sense to flinch.

"Yes, m'lady. I've warded the room he always takes at the Rooster and Pig when he comes into Castle Reach to drink and gamble." She held up a hand to forestall argument. "No one saw me. I know what I'm doing," she added with a dour look.

"Once he's within the warding, the spell will activate on his blood," the witch went on. "It won't trigger to anyone else. You'll be able to enter, but he won't be able to leave. No one will hear what goes on inside until his death breaks the spell."

A slow smile touched Kestel's lips. "You do good work."

"And you keep me alive to do more of it," Surana replied. "We work well together."

With any other witch—and Castle Reach had many—the chance of betrayal would have forced Kestel to cover her tracks. She and Surana had history, old bonds that traced from when neither of them yet wielded the influence they would later acquire. Two young girls, hungry and alone, trying to keep body and soul together in the city's rough neighborhoods. Their shared sins long ago became too numerous and too entangled for either to attempt to leverage that knowledge against the other. And in the years that passed, both Kestel and Surana had gained the skills and hard edge that enabled them to use the talents they possessed to make their mark in the world.

"You're certain he's the one?" The tone in Surana's voice made it clear that she understood the gravity of the situation.

Kestel nodded. "He has the mark. It's him."

Surana withdrew a cloth-wrapped parcel from her bag. She handed the item to Kestel balanced across her palms. "I bathed the blade in spelled water that held the items of his you brought me," she said as Kestel took the knife from her and reverently peeled back the coverings. "Don't make a habit of it: dark magic like this is going to take me a while to recover from."

Kestel's brow quirked up and she looked at Surana, worried. Surana shook her head. "You've been after this son of a bitch for a long time. It was worth it. My gift to you—like I promised all those years ago."

I'd give you his head on a pike, if I could. A pledge of undying friendship from one young girl to another, on a night they'd huddled in a cold deserted building too hungry to move and too frightened to venture out.

I'll slit her throat for you, someday. Kestel had already made good on her part of the bargain long ago, ridding the world of Surana's drunken, abusive mother. She had been Kestel's first kill.

Surana's sad smile suggested that she knew the turn Kestel's thoughts had taken. "Worth it," she repeated. "Just make it count." A cold glint came into her eyes. "And enjoy it."

Kestel embraced Surana and watched her friend walk away. The farther she was from the Rooster and Pig tonight, the better. Kestel had every intention of surviving the night's work, but no illusions about the likelihood of the events transpiring without a hitch. Killing a nobleman's son would earn her the noose if she were caught. *Then I just better not get caught.*

Kestel's paid her informants well for their tips and their silence. She'd gained a dangerous reputation even in the city's roughest sections. Damian Hastings was a slave to his habits, and tonight he would come into the city to oversee his father's business dealings during the day, then bet and drink all night. Kestel would be waiting.

She paced the small room. Engraham, the owner of the Rooster and Pig, kept a large room for regular lodgers, and a few other discreet rooms for the wastrel nobles who came to gamble in the secret, hidden room beneath the tavern where fortunes were gained and lost. Most people knew the Rooster and Pig for its excellent bitterbeer, but in the upper circles of society, the tavern was most popular for its illicit games of chance and clap-free whores. Damian Hastings was an ardent patron, though luck was against him as often as not.

Tonight, though he did not know it yet, Hastings's luck had turned.

Kestel's heartbeat quickened as she thought about what she meant to do. *So many years, leading up to this. And if I succeed, when it's done, and he's dead, what then? What purpose do I have, once vengeance is satisfied?*

She had no answer for that question. Serving as a courtesan to the rich and powerful meant she no longer went hungry or cold. Her patrons kept her comfortably ensconced in a private apartment not far from Quillarth Castle, and their money assured she dressed and ate every bit as well as her noble clientele. The trifles and gifts they bestowed paid for protection, or were carefully hidden away should an emergency strike. Being a wealthy man's companion paid well, a means to an end. Kestel regretted nothing.

When Damian entered the room and closed the door behind him, Kestel was waiting, just outside the reach of the lantern's light.

"Who's there? Show yourself!" Damian must have sensed her presence and remained sober enough to realize it could mean nothing good. But when he turned to open the door and shout for help, the knob remained stubbornly immobile.

"You can't leave," Kestel said, sashaying out of the shadows.

Damian began to pound on the door, shouting for assistance.

"They can't hear you." She waited for him to spend himself, crying out until his voice grew rough, slamming his fist against the door.

When Damian turned to face her, his rum-bleary eyes held fear and uncertainty. "Who are you? Why are you here?"

"Show me your wrist," she demanded, letting her knife glint in the lamplight.

Damian raised his arm and turned it so that the falcon tattoo showed clearly. "My father's a duke. You can rob me, but you'll pay for it." He gathered his wits and drew himself up, as if reminding himself not to show weakness to an inferior. Drink gave him courage; privilege made him belligerent.

"I'm here to kill you," Kestel replied. Now that the moment she'd been waiting for was finally here, Kestel felt nothing. No elation, no sense of triumph, just a deep, aching cold.

"I'm worth more alive," Damian countered. "My father would pay a ransom."

"You're worth more to me dead." Kestel stopped beyond Hastings' reach, knowing that even weak animals became dangerous when cornered. "Don't you want to know why?"

Damian's eyes narrowed. "Did I bed you and then move on?" His expression grew patronizing. "Darlin', I'm sorry if you expected more, but you really should have known better."

Once, his comments would have made fire surge through Kestel's blood. Now, all that remained was ice. "Fifteen years ago. You raped a woman in the alley behind this tavern, a serving girl. Bring anything to mind?"

Damian licked his lips nervously. "Not really. There've been so many—"

"She bit you, and cut you with a piece of glass."

A nasty glint came into Damian's eyes. "That little wildcat? Oh yes, I remember her. Left me with a scar," he said, moving his right wrist to reveal the faint remainder of a bite mark. "Taught her a lesson real good." He looked Kestel over, his expression torn between appraisal and a leer. "She was your mama? You look like her. Bet you're a wildcat, too."

"She didn't want your attention. She wasn't yours to take. And she never recovered from the beating you gave her."

Damian shrugged. "She was no one of consequence. Just another slattern. Like mother, like daughter."

Kestel knew Damian intended to bait her into making a rash move. He outweighed her, and his fondness for rough company had no doubt taught him how to fight dirty. Kestel smiled, confident in Surana's magic.

"She was of consequence to me." Kestel lunged forward, slicing down across Damian's chest with the spelled knife, scoring a cut deep enough to slash through his clothing and open a bloody furrow across his ribs.

"You bloody whore!" Damian roared and started toward her, only to freeze, eyes widening and hands clutching his chest.

"Do you feel it?" Kestel stepped back, well out of his reach, as Damian fell to his knees. His breath hitched, and his face paled as the magic coursed through his veins.

"What did you do to me?"

"I wanted you to feel what my mother felt that night." Kestel's calm, quiet voice held the promise of violence. "Fear. Helplessness. Impotent rage."

Damian's body shook as the spell's grip tightened. His breaths came in short, hard pants, and sweat glistened on his forehead. "You choked her. Held her down and kept your hand on her throat while you forced her. Hit her when she fought you. Cut her. Took what you wanted and strangled her with your own hands, then pulled up your pants and walked away like you'd just taken a piss. I saw you. I saw it all, but I was too young to do anything about it—then."

"You filthy bitch, I'll kill you for this!"

"No, you won't. The spell is fatal. No one can hear us, no one will come to help. Just like no one came to help my mother." Watching Damian suffer fulfilled a long-held goal, but

Kestel knew it could never restore what had been taken that night.

"You're going to kill me over a serving wench?" The incredulity in Damian's eyes might have been laughable if the reasoning behind it had not cut so deeply.

"No, I'm putting down a rabid dog who killed the most important person in my world."

The tremors that shook Damian's body grew more violent as the poison progressed. Blood leaked sluggishly from the chest wound, staining his silk shirt and dripping down onto the carpet. His skin was flushed and clammy, and the faint blue tinge to his lips told Kestel vengeance would not be far off.

"We could have struck a bargain. I could have made you rich."

"I didn't want a bargain. Or your money. I saw you kill her. And all I've ever wanted since that night is to see you dead by my hand."

Damian fell forward onto his hands and knees, retching up bile. He fell face down into his vomit, eyes rolling back as the tremors grew worse until convulsions racked his body, arching his back and drawing the muscles of his face into a rictus grin.

Kestel watched, disappointed at the cold emptiness of her victory. She harbored no illusions that her mother would be proud, either of the murder or of who and what Kestel had become to achieve her goal. But as she watched Damian struggle for his last breaths, saw the fear in his eyes as the light in them faded, the small girl who watched her mother's death from the shadows of a stinking alley finally stopped being afraid. Kestel wrapped her arms around herself, reassuring what remained of that young child, promising that she would keep her safe forever. Vengeance wouldn't bring her mother back, but it did mean one fewer monster lived to repeat the crime.

When she was certain Damian was truly dead, Kestel wiped

her knife on his pants, sheathed the blade, and broke the warding, slipping out the back door and into the night. She did not see
the cloaked figure, watching from the shadows.

———

Kestel paced in her apartment, restless and on edge. Killing
Damian marked the pinnacle of her life's work, the realization of
the dream that had spurred her on night after cold and terrifying
night. Wanting him dead, needing revenge, had given her life
purpose, and absolved her in her mind's eye of the sacrifices and
sins necessary to achieve her goal.

Now that purpose had been fulfilled, and there was nothing
to take its place.

Her status as one of the most sought-after courtesans in the
court had its perquisites. This apartment, paid for by her patrons,
easily supplied the comforts due a lesser noble. Her wardrobe,
food, and jewelry, all came from the largesse of her patrons past
and present. Kestel knew that few courtesans retained their
charms and patrons for long. She made provision for the time
when she left the business, by choice or not. Yet she never
expected this emptiness. No thrill of victory, no satisfaction of
completion. Just a dark void that sapped her energy and turned
her thoughts in circles.

A soft rap at the door startled Kestel from her thoughts. She
tensed, drawing her knife and keeping the blade behind her back
as she moved. Kestel expected no visitors, and could think of no
one who would be welcome right then.

A lone woman in a cloak stood in the doorway. "Please, let
me in. I mean you no harm."

Wary, Kestel took a few steps back to allow the newcomer
to enter. *If I have to kill her, fewer people will see if I do it
inside.*

"I know what you did at the Rooster and Pig," the woman said quietly.

Kestel kept her face unreadable. "I have no idea what you're talking about."

The stranger lowered the cowl that kept her features in shadow. Kestel recognized her from court, the wife of a minor lord, or maybe it was a duke. Someone of enough importance to be in the outer circles of prominence, yet not sufficiently influential to bother remembering.

"I know you killed Damian Hastings."

"If you believe that, and you came here to tell me, you're not very smart." Kestel kept her voice low and quiet. She had already considered half a dozen ways the woman could die without anyone being the wiser.

"I'm not going to turn you in."

"You're going to try to blackmail me?" Kestel's smile was cold. "I don't play that game." She made sure her blade glinted in the candlelight, a warning.

"I want to hire you."

That brought Kestel up short. "Hire me? Look, you're very pretty, and I won't say that I've never taken a woman patron, but it's not really my…"

"I want to hire you to kill someone, like you killed Hastings."

Kestel stared at the woman. "I'm not an assassin."

"You could be."

Kestel gave an incredulous chuckle. "You're crazy."

"Hear me out." The stranger looked utterly serious. "I went to the Rooster and Pig tonight to beg Hastings for his help. One of his guards took advantage of my daughter. Because of him, she hanged herself. I meant to offer Hastings any payment he wanted to punish the man who hurt my baby. I didn't care what it cost me." She paused and took a breath to steady herself.

"Then I saw you go in, and I waited. I thought—well, that doesn't matter now," she said, ducking her head. Kestel knew exactly what her unexpected guest thought, that Kestel and Hastings were meeting for a tryst.

"When you came out, I went in and found him. And then I knew what happened, what you did, and I realized you could help me."

"I'm really not—"

"Please," the woman cut her off. "Do you know how many wronged women would pay handsomely for you to kill the men who hurt them? How many came to the beds of men they didn't love because of arranged marriages, sold off like trollops by their fathers or older brothers? Men who beat them, rape them, abuse their children, threaten their sons and daughters if the women dare complain?" Tears pooled in the stranger's eyes.

"You are privy to secrets. You have access to the wealthiest and most powerful men in the kingdom. These women would pay you well, and you'd have no fear of them revealing your secret. Exposing you would expose them. They would lose everything."

Kestel opened her mouth to say, *I'm not an assassin*, and then shut it again. *I sleep with men for money. I betray secrets for money. I've spent a lifetime plotting to murder someone. I've got precious little virtue left to squander, and at least this way, I do some good for women like mama. Women who might not have to die.*

Purpose. The realization hit Kestel hard enough to make her take a sharp breath. This stranger offered her something more than money, more than vengeance. A chance to do something that mattered, to redeem herself. A reason to live.

Kestel lowered her knife. "Your proposal intrigues me," she said and gave a genuine smile. "Come in. Let's talk."

ALSO BY GAIL Z. MARTIN

Darkhurst

Scourge

Vengeance

Reckoning - *Coming in 2019*

Ascendant Kingdoms

Ice Forged

Reign of Ash

War of Shadows

Shadow and Flame

Convicts and Exiles (Prequel)

Chronicles of the Necromancer / Fallen Kings Cycle

The Summoner

The Blood King

Dark Haven

Dark Lady's Chosen

The Sworn

The Dread

The Shadowed Path

The Dark Road

Legacy of the Necromancer

Coming in 2020

Deadly Curiosities

Deadly Curiosities

Vendetta

Tangled Web

Inheritance - *Coming Soon*

Trifles and Folly

Trifles and Folly 2

Assassins of Landria

Assassin's Honor

Sellsword's Oath - *Coming in 2019*

Night Vigil

Sons of Darkness

C.H.A.R.O.N. - *Coming Soon*

Other books by Gail Z. Martin and Larry N. Martin

Jake Desmet Adventures

Iron & Blood

Spark of Destiny - *Coming in 2019*

Storm & Fury

Joe Mack Chronicles

Cauldron - *Coming Soon*

Spells, Salt, & Steel: New Templars

Spells, Salt, & Steel: Season One (Collection)

Night Moves - *Coming Soon*

Wasteland Marshals

Wasteland Marshals - *Coming Soon*

Other books by Larry N. Martin

Salvage Rat

The Splintered Crown

ABOUT THE AUTHOR

Gail Z. Martin is the author of *Vengeance*, the sequel to *Scourge* in the Darkhurst epic fantasy series, and *Assassin's Honor* in the new Assassins of Landria series. *Tangled Web* is the newest novel in the series that includes both *Deadly Curiosities* and *Vendetta* and two collections, *Trifles and Folly* and *Trifles and Folly 2*, the latest in her urban fantasy series set in Charleston, SC. *Shadow and Flame* is the fourth book in the Ascendant Kingdoms Saga and *The Shadowed Path* and *The Dark Road* are in the Jonmarc Vahanian Adventures series. Co-authored with Larry N. Martin are *Iron and Blood*, the first novel in the Jake Desmet Adventures series, the *Storm and Fury* collection, and the *Spells, Salt, & Steel: New Templar Knights series (Mark Wojcik, monster hunter)*. Under her urban fantasy MM paranormal romance pen name of Morgan Brice, Gail writes the *Witchbane*, *Badlands*, and *Treasure Trail* series.

She is also the author of *Ice Forged, Reign of Ash*, and *War of Shadows* in The Ascendant Kingdoms Saga, The Chronicles of The Necromancer series (*The Summoner, The Blood King, Dark Haven, Dark Lady's Chosen*) and The Fallen Kings Cycle (*The Sworn, The Dread*).

Gail's work has appeared in over 40 US/UK anthologies. Anthologies include: *Tales from the Old Black Ambulance, Across the Universe, Release the Virgins, The Big Bad 2, Athena's Daughters, The Weird Wild West, Alien Artifacts, Cinched: Imagination Unbound, Gaslight and Grimm, Baker*

Street Irregulars, Journeys, Hath no Fury, and *Afterpunk: Steampunk Tales of the Afterlife.*

Where to find me, and how to stay in touch

Find out more at www.GailZMartin.com, at DisquietingVisions.com, on Goodreads https://www.goodreads.com/GailZMartin, on www.Pinterest.com/Gzmartin and on Bookbub https://www.bookbub.com/profile/gail-z-martin. Gail is also the organizer of the #HoldOnToTheLight campaign www.HoldOnToTheLight.com Never miss out on the news and new releases—newsletter signup link http://eepurl.com/dd5XLj. Join her free Facebook fan group, the Shadow Alliance https://www.facebook.com/groups/435812789942761

Support Indie Authors

When you support independent authors, you help influence what kind of books you'll see more of and what types of stories will be available, because the authors themselves decide which books to write, not a big publishing conglomerate. Independent authors are local creators, supporting their families with the books they produce. Thank you for supporting independent authors and small press fiction!